ALSO BY MELISSA GOOD

Dar and Kerry Series
Tropical Storm
Hurricane Watch
Eye of the Storm
Red Sky At Morning
Thicker Than Water

Terrors of the High Seas

Melissa Good

Yellow Rose Books

Nederland, Texas

ISBN 1-932300-45-7

First Printing 2005

9 8 7 6 5 4 3 2 1

Cover design by Donna Pawlowski

Published by:

Yellow Rose Books
PMB 210, 8691 9th Avenue
Port Arthur, Texas 77642-8025

Find us on the World Wide Web at
http://www.regalcrest.biz

Printed in the United States of America

Chapter
One

THE GOLF CART snaked its way down the sidewalk, startling several peacocks on its way to the docks. It pulled to a halt next to the water, alongside a 54-foot Bertram bobbing in the light chop of the waves.

It was sunny but cool, a gorgeous crisp day, and the occupant of the cart paused to admire that fact as she got out and stretched. Appropriate to the weather, she wore sturdy cotton shorts and a light tank top over a one-piece bathing suit. Her medium length, blonde hair was pulled back in a ponytail, currently poked through the rear of a bright blue baseball cap with a small, embroidered Dogbert on the front.

"Wow," Kerry Stuart stated with a grin. "Perfect weather."

She turned and hoisted a crate of supplies from the back seat of the cart, hugging it to her as she made her way up the gangway propped against the side of the Bertram. The boat rocked under her as she stepped off onto the deck, and she found herself rolling with the motion.

"Yo ho, yo ho, a pirate's life for me," Kerry warbled softly, nudging open the door to the cabin and stepping down inside. She crossed over to the small galley and put down the supplies, then busied herself tucking the fresh foods into the little refrigerator.

There was milk, cream for coffee, butter, and a nice piece of Swiss cheese along with honey ham for sandwiches. Peach and tangerine yogurt for snacks, and a dozen eggs for breakfast joined the store, followed by a loaf of cinnamon raisin bread and a box of frosted strawberry Pop Tarts. Kerry regarded the Pop Tarts bemusedly, and then tossed a package of miniature carrots in next to them. It was the last of the things they had to load before they set off, and she hummed as she worked, hardly believing it was finally the day they were leaving.

She'd tried to take off a few days before they went on this trip, but one thing after another kept happening at work, and finally it'd just been easier for her to go in and take care of stuff rather than let it sit and fester, or worse.

But starting today, her office had strict orders that any call to her cell phone had to be in the event of a complete catastrophe; she was expecting her staff to handle everything else without her input.

It was, after all, the holidays, near the end of the year, and if there was any time she could just disappear for a week, this was it.

Kerry straightened and opened the cabinet above the refrigerator, stocking some essential groceries in it. "Can't sail without these." She shook the box of Frosted Flakes gently. "Or those." Cans of soup followed, for quick snacks after night dives. She tended to come up chilled, and the cold fruit Dar was partial to didn't quite fill the bill for her.

The pop open cans of pineapple and oranges went up next to the soup, along with a couple of jars of jam and one large one of peanut butter.

Finished, she rested her elbows on the counter and gazed around the boat in appreciation. To one side there was a small eating area, a table with sea green and navy fabric seats semi-circling it. On the other side of the cabin was a working/living section with a television and VCR, and built in storage for their hobby gear. Her book bag was already nestled in one of the chairs — Kerry had decided to work on some longhand poetry on the trip — and Dar had stashed a painfully intricate ship model in a drawer to occupy her idle moments.

The boat rocked gently as a set of footsteps sounded on deck, soft and muffled as though the newcomer was barefoot. Which, of course, she was.

Kerry glanced up as Dar entered the cabin, ducking her head to clear the low entrance and giving her a rakish grin as she tossed a duffel bag onto the table on the other side of the galley. Her partner was dressed in a pair of denim cutoffs that were just barely legal — there were more threads and rips than fabric — with a ribbed, white tank top tucked into them.

"Hey there, gorgeous," Kerry greeted Dar. "That the last of it?"

"Lock, stock, barrel and body wash," Dar confirmed. "We're ready to take off outta here."

"Ooo..." Kerry did a little happy dance. "I am so ready for this."

Dar walked around the edge of the couch and encircled Kerry in her arms, then pulled her into a close hug. "Me too," she agreed. "Mom and Dad are waiting for us to pull out. They're going to pull into our slip while we're gone."

"Cool." Kerry was busy sucking in lungfuls of delightful coconutty smelling Dar. "I'm glad they're staying with Chino. She loves Dad."

"Mm," Dar murmured. "I think he's trying to sucker my mother into getting them one."

Kerry's brow crinkled. "I thought she was allergic to dogs?"

Dar released her, but slid an arm over her shoulder as they walked toward the cabin door. "She claims to have grown out of it." They emerged onto the deck.

"I'll leave the cart there for them, then," Kerry commented. "Ready for me to cast off the lines?"

Dar trotted up the stairs to the bridge and perched on the leather-covered seat. "Let me get the engines spooled up, then yeah, let 'er loose."

Kerry went to work with a will, drawing up the gangway and lashing it into place, then hopping off onto the dock as the low thrum of the twin diesels rumbled to life. She went to the stern line and released it, then did the same with the bow, tossing the ropes onto the deck before she leaped after them.

We're free. Kerry felt like bouncing up and down and letting out a yell, but it was early yet and there were people who slept on board their boats docked in the Island's marina, so she regretfully stifled the impulse. Instead, she dutifully walked around the perimeter of the deck, checking over the side for debris or errant lines from other boats. "Clear!" she called up to Dar.

Dar nodded, her pale blue eyes alert as she carefully backed the large boat out of its slip. "Radio the dockmaster, would you?"

"Aye, aye, cap'n," Kerry chortled, before ducking inside the cabin to grab the radio mic. "Dockmaster, dockmaster."

A soft crackling sound came from the speaker, then, "Island dockmaster, go ahead."

"This is *Dixieland Yankee*, leaving the dock." Kerry had to grin at the name of the newly re-christened boat, the most dignified of the possible choices they'd come up with. Dar's aunt, from whom she'd inherited the craft, had declined to name the motor yacht, merely referring to it by its registration number when needed. "We have a float plan filed for the American Virgin Islands."

The radio digested the transmission for a moment. "Roger that, *Dixieland Yankee*. Have a good trip."

Kerry clipped the mic onto its holder and slipped back outside and watched the concrete and wood dock recede as Dar skillfully handled the big boat. They backed into the relatively narrow throughway, then Dar nudged the throttles from reverse to forward and swung the bow toward the dock entrance, keeping the speed just above idle.

Once they were clear of the pylons, Kerry climbed up the ladder to the flying bridge and joined Dar. The boat was moving slowly, but there already was a nice breeze, and it was mussing Dar's dark hair and getting it into her eyes. Kerry tugged at a lock. "Want me to braid this?"

"Sure." Dar set her bare feet on the console bars and leaned back. She felt Kerry's fingers slide across her scalp and that, combined with the gorgeous weather and the fact that they were headed out for a solid week of vacation together, made it just about a perfect moment.

A week. No cell phones, no laptops, no PDA's, no pagers. Just a week of sun, sea, diving, and the two of us. Dar flexed her hands on the throttles, feeling the smooth stainless steel under her fingertips.

"What's that grin for?" Kerry asked, finishing her task and resting her chin on Dar's shoulder.

Dar wiggled her toes. "I'm trying to figure out what to do first," she admitted. "We could stop for a quick dive on the way down to the cabin, or pull into Largo for lunch or—"

"Both," Kerry broke in. "We can stop at Pennekamp and do a little reef diving, then go to that little dockside crab shack that always looks like it was built for a horror movie."

"Sounds like a plan," Dar agreed, notching the throttles ahead just a bit as they cleared the dock complex. They warily pulled out into the main channel, watching for speedboat traffic. As they turned into the cut, the wind picked up and their speed increased, the sea's soft chop rustling against the bow of the boat.

Kerry was content to lean against her, one arm draped over her shoulders and her chin still resting on Dar's shoulder as they passed a couple of small sailing boats. "Dar, is that woman naked?"

Dar's eyes shifted. "Yeah, and boy, is that gonna be a painful sunburn." She shook her head. "Some people just have no sense."

"Ow." Kerry clucked her tongue. "I'm going to go put away the last of our stuff, see if we need to pick anything up in Largo." She gave Dar a kiss on the cheek then climbed down the ladder and disappeared into the cabin.

Dar plucked the water bottle out of its swinging holder and drank from it, then put it back. She opened the small cabinet under the bridge console and selected a CD, waiting while the player sucked it in, then adjusting the volume as the music started. As the land receded behind them, she felt the tensions and pressures of their life doing the same.

The wind blew against her skin, feeling cool and wonderful. She cleared the inner buoy and opened up the engines a little, sending the bow up as she hummed along to the music.

Diving; rustic but romantic dinner; an overnight stay at the new cabin; then the long trip out to the islands. Dar exhaled in utter satisfaction. *Life just doesn't get any better than this.*

Kerry walked past the portholes, tucking back the drapes to let the sun into the cabin. She unlocked the catches and propped the small, round windows open, enjoying the nice breeze the motion of the boat was creating. With a satisfied nod, she retrieved Dar's duffel and carried it into the cabin's compact bedroom, setting it on the bed before she unzipped it. She took a moment to open the hatch down there as well, grinning as a tiny bit of spray hit her.

The bedroom had drawers built into the bulkheads and under the bed to save space — every square inch of room was thriftily used for something. Kerry patted the bed. It wasn't as comfortable as the waterbed in their condo, but she suspected that after a long day of diving, swimming, and other activities, she'd be able to sleep on the deck itself.

"And I have," Kerry reminded herself. She removed Dar's extra shirts and bathing suits, folded them neatly and put them in one of the drawers. "Hey, wonder if I can talk Dar into getting a hammock for the deck. We can sleep out there one night."

Kerry gathered their bathroom sundries and carried them into the tiny head, then found spots for the various bottles and jars. They would, she realized, be seriously bumping into each other in there — both were used to the much larger confines of the condo where they each had their own bathroom.

Kerry cast an assessing eye at the bitty shower and wondered if they could both fit into it. An eyebrow quirked. *Might be interesting to try.*

There had been two more small bedrooms past the master suite. One, they'd left with its double decker bunk, but the other, up in the very bow of the boat, they'd stripped the beds out of and kitted out as storage for their diving gear and Kerry's underwater photography equipment. She stuck her head inside and gave the BCs and regulators a quick once over, then out of habit checked the valves on the strapped down tanks to make sure they were closed tight.

The boat was also outfitted with a desalinator, which would take in seawater and produce water both for drinking and for cleaning. Kerry felt reassured by that; running out of water on the ocean wasn't funny. Since the wind was almost as constant as the sun, it was very easy to become dehydrated out there.

In addition, on the outside deck, Dar had installed a small air compressor so they could refill their own air tanks while they were out on the water, and a rinse sink to toss their gear into. It made the boat a very comfortable place to be, and Kerry suspected that even the extended length of time they'd spend on it this trip wouldn't be too much of a hardship.

She took the duffel bag and folded it, then tucked it away in a drawer under the bed. Wandering back up the short flight of steps into the main cabin, she snagged a bottle of water and made her way back out onto the deck. The city was falling away behind them — buildings crisply defined in the clear air. She could see the huge cranes of Port of Miami loading freighters, and in the distance, the outline of a moving cruise ship made its stately way through Government Cut.

It was a pretty view, but Kerry knew where a prettier one was, and she hauled herself back up the ladder and took possession of the second chair in back of the engine console. Now all she could see was sun, water, and Dar. She wriggled into a comfortable position and relaxed, content to let the salt air wash over her as they headed out to sea. Dar had a Jimmy Buffett CD playing, and Kerry rocked her head back and forth to the upbeat tune. "Hey."

Dar shifted in her seat and looked over. One dark eyebrow lifted in inquiry.

"You ready for a totally rocking week?"

Dar propped a bare foot up against the console and leaned forward against her knee, surveying the almost endless horizon in front of them. "Oh, yeah." A grin split her face. "I sure am. Hope the company is up to doing without the both of us at the same time."

Kerry grunted in acknowledgment. "I'm sure they'll manage to muddle through for a week, Dar. What could happen in seven measly days?"

"Yeah," Dar agreed. "I'm sure they'll be fine."

They both listened to the music for a few moments, contemplating the clear blue sky and rich, green sea before them. Then two heads turned and they regarded each other.

"Let's not think about it." Kerry grinned. "We'll just jinx them."

Dar merely waggled her eyebrows in answer, and gave the engines a little more gas.

Chapter
Two

IT WAS ALMOST dusk by the time Dar shifted the diesels into reverse and idled them into the much smaller dock outside their cabin. She maneuvered the Bertram carefully, sliding into place and holding it there until Kerry could leap off onto the wood and secure the lines to the cleats onshore.

When Dar had first come into her Aunt May's estate, she'd been a little wary of driving the large yacht. After all, other than some clandestine ventures on government-issue vessels, most of her piloting had been done on much smaller boats. However, she'd been working on the water since she was four, and it hadn't taken her long to master the big boat's powerful engines and imposing size, and after that she'd sort of enjoyed taking the vessel out. Pulling up to some out-of-the-way shrimp shack in the thing and sauntering off to get a Coke in front of a legion of goggling guys tickled her sometimes dark sense of humor.

Now she handled the throttles with a master's touch as she held her ground while they were tied. The boat bumped gently against the pylons, buffered by the large rubber bumpers Kerry had tossed over the edge of the dock, and Dar shut down the engines, flexing her hands as she removed them from the throttles.

As the sound died, the peacefulness of the place surrounded her, and Dar spent a moment just gazing at their little piece of paradise before she took her sunburned self down the stairs. It wasn't a large lot, just big enough for the cabin, the sandy ground that led down to the dock on one side and to a small beach on the other, and on the far side of the cabin—a driveway winding up to the road.

It was shaded though, with a thick stand of trees, and surrounded by patches of foliage on either side, so the effect was of snug isolation on this little point of the Key. It was calm, almost sleepy, and Dar liked it. *Equally important*, she thought, *Kerry really likes it too.*

And so far, it had been a great day. The quick dive stop had turned into a deep wreck excursion, followed by lunch inside a tiki hut, followed by a very nice reef dive in the late afternoon. They hadn't been doing that much diving lately, and Dar felt pleasantly tired and a little embarrassed that she'd forgotten to put on enough sunscreen and had mildly toasted herself.

Ah well. She stretched, hopped up onto the edge of the boat, and stepped off onto the dock. Kerry was returning from opening up the cabin, a splash of pink making her fair lashes stand out vividly. "Everything okay?"

"Looks like it."

Kerry waited for Dar on the end of the dock, then fell into step beside her as they walked up the short path. Having started out as a ramshackle old barn for a larger house that had once stood nearby, the cabin had evolved beyond recognition since they'd first purchased it. They'd ripped down most of the original building and rebuilt, using native stone for the foundation.

In the rear, facing the water, there was a small porch. They climbed the two broad steps up to it and crossed to the door, the new planks squeaking a bit under their weight. Someday, Dar wanted a padded bench or maybe one of the swing chairs like they had at the condo out there, but at the moment the porch was just an empty space.

Kerry pushed the door open and they entered; the strong scent of fresh wood and varnish washed over them. Inside, they'd chosen to keep the wood walls and stone floors natural, and the large room in front would eventually have comfortable chairs where they could sit and look at the wonderful view out the big picture windows.

Behind that room, a small kitchen was tucked into one corner, and in the other, a hallway led back to the master bedroom. Two more doors extended past that, an office for each of them — complete with high-speed network access, printers, and everything else they'd ever need to run work operations from the cabin if they wanted to. Dar was particularly proud of the gigabit Ethernet hub and cabling she'd spent one weekend installing.

Aren't too many rustic cabins, Kerry acknowledged, *that can claim their own Fractional T1 and Cisco router.*

They were still missing the living area furniture, some of the smaller kitchen appliances, and a lot of other trimmings like rugs and stuff for the walls, but already the place was taking on a certain personality of its own — a reflection of both of theirs. "Looking good in here," Kerry remarked as she closed the door behind them. The air was cool and dry, evidence of the newly installed air conditioning unit.

"Definitely." Dar grinned. The ceiling arched up to a skylight that let even more sun into the living room and lent a sense of lightness to the rich wood interior. "I really like it."

Kerry glanced up at her. "Me too," she admitted. "It's..." She turned around and surveyed their little castle. "Don't get me wrong, Dar. Only an idiot would complain about where we live, but this place is kinda special."

Dar nodded. "It's ours," she replied simply. "We designed it. We made it. Hell, we helped build it." A not-quite-stifled yawn interrupted her speech. "Whoa."

"Teach you to chase flounder." Kerry chuckled, slipping an arm around Dar's waist. "I got some great pictures of you doing that, you know."

"Oh great, more fodder for the bathroom wall," Dar replied drolly.

"Hmm..." Kerry mused in mock speculation. "Yeah, that would work with the silver and blue fixtures in there." She glanced into their bedroom, starkly empty save for a neatly folded inflatable bed in the center. It was a large room, with two polarized floor-to-ceiling dormer windows on either side of where the bed was. A door in the rear led to a bathroom that had a stall shower and a large, thoroughly decadent spa tub. Around the top of the room ran a wooden ledge, common throughout the cabin, and Dar had already threatened to install a train set that would make its way around the place on top of the rail.

They were like a couple of kids, Kerry had to admit privately, furnishing their first tree house. She half expected to come out one day and find a tire hanging from one of the banyans outside. Of course it would be a high-technological tire, with three hanging points and a custom-molded interior ring. What was it that Dar had once referred to their place as? Microsoft Rustic.

True. Kerry smiled. But they both liked their comforts, were used to the gadgets, and they could afford them. So, why not? "How about something cold for dinner, and a pot of coffee?" she suggested.

Dar considered. "Tell you what—you start the coffee, and I'll walk down to the corner and get the something cold." She nibbled Kerry's nose. "We need sugar anyway."

"Mm." Kerry leaned into the kiss, her fingers trailing over Dar's bare arm. "Boy, you're warm."

Dar chuckled softly under her breath. "Gimme a minute and I'll be even warmer." She cupped Kerry's chin and kissed her again, catching lingering traces of the tangerine yogurt they'd shared not long before. "You got a little burned, too."

"Oh," Kerry murmured. "Is that why I have chills?" She felt Dar's arms fold around her. "Funny, they're getting worse. Maybe you should hold me tighter."

Dar chuckled. "Hedonist."

"Mmhm." Kerry let her hands slide over Dar's back as she continued exploring with her lips. Then she exhaled, and nuzzled

Dar's neck, reveling in the peace, the quiet, and the fact that it was just the two of them.

"Think you'd better blow up the bed," Dar whispered in her ear.

"Oh yeah?"

"Yeah," Dar replied. "'Cause I need to take care of those chills. Don't want you catching cold."

Kerry rested a hand on Dar's hip. "Sweetie, you're the one causing the chills." She ducked her head and nipped at Dar's breast.

"And because it's the only furniture in the place," Dar teased. "I figure we can inaugurate that spa tub, then have dinner in bed."

"Or dinner *and* bed," Kerry replied, her eyes twinkling. "Sounds great to me either way." She kissed Dar again, then nudged her belly. "You go, I'll blow."

Both of Dar's eyebrows hiked up.

"Careful, they'll stick like that." Kerry reached up and yanked an eyebrow down. "Wouldn't you look silly?"

Dar stuck out her tongue. "You're in a mood," she remarked. "I like it." She gave Kerry a tickle across her ribs, then headed down the hallway to what they thought of as the back door to the cabin.

It was, of course, the front door, but since they tended to arrive by boat, they didn't often enter that way. Dar passed the small utility room with its unused connections for the washer and dryer that hadn't been delivered yet, and entered the plain open space near the outer door to the cabin. She turned the lock and let herself out, then closed the door behind her.

They had put a porch in front too, but smaller than the one that faced the water. It was surrounded by a sturdy wooden flower box that was hip high on Dar, and there was a gate flanked by two wrought iron, coach-type lights. Dar opened the gate and walked through, heading along the neat, rock-defined path up to the road.

The yard was more sand and scrub than grass, typical of the Keys, and was bordered by a Chinese cherry hedge. Dar broke into a jog as she passed it, then ran lightly down the road towards the small, what Kerry called "charmingly rustic" market just at the next crossroads.

She made the trip without bumping into another soul until she pushed open the door to the market and walked inside. The shop had well-stocked shelves, a respectable collection of fresh fruits and vegetables, and best of all, a very fresh seafood counter in the back. Dar headed for it, then examined the choices laid out on ice in the cold case.

"Well, hello there, young lady."

The cheerful voice almost made her jump. Dar looked up to see the owner standing behind the fish case, wiping his hands on a towel. "Evening."

"Got some great looking crabs today."

Dar's eyes twinkled. "Not today, thanks. Gimme a pound of the shrimp and two of the tails." She watched contentedly as the man wrapped up the chilled, already cooked seafood. "Thanks." She accepted the package and went toward the dairy case, not really paying attention when the market door opened.

"Hey, mister."

Aware that the salutation didn't include her, Dar studied her choices in milk, cocking half an ear behind her mostly because the rough voice that had spoken had set off her trouble sonar.

"What can I do for you?" the market owner replied.

"Got any shotgun shells?"

After a moment's pause, the owner chuckled. "Son, this is a grocery, not a Sportsman's Paradise," he said. "We don't sell no guns here."

"Aw, man, you mean I gotta go up to the Wal-Mart? That sucks! Why don't you get them stuff here? You got all kinds of other crap!"

"Well, you gotta get a license, for one thing — "

"So? Go get one!" The voice was getting belligerent. "You're supposed to get what people need, right?"

Dar set her package down and replaced the sugar she'd been considering; then she circled the row of canned goods and examined the noisy newcomer. It was, as she'd suspected, a boy in his late teens, dressed in an NRA T-shirt and jeans with patches consisting of Confederate flags. "Oh, look," Dar muttered under her breath. "Walking stereotype. Wonder where his pickup's parked."

"So get off yer ass and get us some service here!" the boy demanded.

"Now, look, son — "

"Don't you call me that, you old jackass!"

Dar walked over. "Excuse me."

The boy turned, irritation switching to lechery in the blink of a hormone as his eyes took in Dar's suntanned, mostly exposed body. "Hey, baby! What c'n I do for ya?"

Detecting fermented malt, Dar's nose twitched. "Stop breathing."

He blinked. "Huh?"

Dar abandoned that tack. "You go to the hardware store for bread?"

"Naw."

"So why come here for gun supplies?"

The boy didn't seem to mind the questions, his eyes busy taking in Dar's athletic form. "'Cause it's closer'n hauling my ass up the road to the Wal-Mart." He grinned suddenly. "You wanna ride in my truck?"

"No," Dar replied. "What are you shooting?"

"Huh?"

"You're buying shotgun shells."

"Yeah?"

"What are you going to shoot them at?"

"Signs," the boy replied amiably. "Or them little deers, or whatever."

Dar frowned. "For what?"

"Fer fun," the boy said. "You wanna come? I got me a box of shells. Just wanted some more in case I find me some 'gators or something. You up fer some fun, baby?"

Dar stared at him for a moment, then felt the wash of adrenaline and anger sweep through her. "Sure." She grinned. "I love fun." She moved in a blur, drawing her right hand back and cocking it, then letting loose and cracking the now really smirking boy across the chops. He spun away from her and fell over a stack of beer cases, slamming his head against the doorpost.

"That was fun." Dar stalked after him intently. "C'mere, you brainless little punk." She grabbed him and yanked him to his feet, shoving him against the wall. "You think hurting animals is funny? I think this is funny." She nailed him in the groin with her knee, then tossed him against the door.

"Hey! Hey!" The boy scrambled to his feet. "Ow! Son of a bitch! Ow!" He bolted for the door, a trail of blood from his nose left behind him, and got through it an instant before Dar could latch onto him. He raced for the pickup parked outside and jumped in, started the engine, and roared off while Dar glared at him from the doorway.

She waited for the taillights to disappear around the first bend, then stepped back inside the store and dusted off her hands, shaking her head in disgust. "Another fine example of why stupid humans shouldn't breed."

The grocer was laughing as Dar walked back over. "Ma'am, I think you made an impression on that kid."

Dar retrieved her package and her sugar, then added a few other things before she plunked it all down on the counter and dug out her wallet. "You get much of that here?"

"Not a lot." The owner rang up her purchases. "You new in the area…" He glanced at the credit card Dar handed him. "Ms. Roberts? Thought I'd seen you around once or twice."

Dar leaned against the counter. "Not exactly," she allowed. "I grew up on the Navy base, but I've been living up in Miami for a while. Bought the old Potter place last year."

He looked up at her, honestly surprised. "You did?" His

interest was kindled. "Now, I was hearing some big-shot computer executive bought that place."

Dar tipped her sunglasses down and cool blue eyes regarded him with some amusement. "That would be me."

The man gaped a moment, then burst into laughter. "Well, kick mah ass," he managed to get out. "You sure don't look like a Bill Gates, now do you?"

Lucky me. Dar grinned in wry acknowledgment. *Lucky Kerry, too.*

"Been talking about all the work going on up there. You pretty much just built the whole thing all over again, didn't cha?"

"Pretty much," Dar agreed, signing the slip for her groceries. "Just getting the last stuff done."

"Well, then," the man took the slip and tucked it into the drawer, then held out a hand, "welcome to the neighborhood, Ms. Roberts. Hope to see more of ya."

Dar returned the clasp. "Careful what you ask for," she drawled, giving him a wry wink before she picked up her bag and sauntered out, content with her brief entrance on the sleepy town's unsuspecting stage.

AFTER DAR LEFT, Kerry spent a few moments wandering around the cabin. She walked over to the wall and laid her hands flat on its surface, basking in a sense of ownership she found almost intoxicating.

Ours.

Kerry turned and leaned against the wall, letting her eyes roam around the room. When she had put her name on the title next to Dar's, this cabin had become the very first real thing she could call her own, and she felt very differently about it than she did about the condo.

She turned and peeked into the kitchen, at the sleek, well-fitted appliances she'd picked herself, and the pretty marble countertop that provided a place to sit and have breakfast. It was cute and cozy.

Kerry smiled as she walked over to the bedroom, rubbing her fingers against the wooden doorjamb as she entered. It was her favorite room in the cabin, and not just because of the obvious. She knelt and started the small motor that would inflate the Aerobed, then walked over and inspected the bathroom, approving the neat work around the sunken spa tub. One corner of the space was a glassed-in shower, the other was the tub, and between lay a large vanity flanked by not one, but two toilets.

Kerry liked that. She and Dar had pondered over the notion for quite a while before they'd decided to have it done. The vanity had a three-quarter mirror around it, providing just enough privacy. She opened the cabinet, idly looking at the few supplies they'd left there.

This would be only the third night they'd spent at the cabin, and she found herself looking forward to the time when all the furniture would be there, and the place gained a sense of...home.

She left the bed to inflate and walked back to their dual offices, now just empty spaces waiting for the delivery of the custom-made desks they'd ordered. Both rooms had big windows and skylights. Once the furniture was in, they could plug into the company network as easily as if they were at the condo. Or at the office. She was looking forward to spending more time there.

The pump cut off and she returned to the bedroom, picked up the sheet set, and shook it out over the queen-size, double-height air mattress. She tucked in the fabric, then unfolded the comforter she'd brought with her from Michigan and settled it over the bed, tossing their pillows up to the head of the bed when she finished.

Kerry walked back into the living room and retrieved the overnight bag they'd brought in from the boat. She zipped it open, smiling as familiar scents were released from the clothing and other sundries inside. Two towels were on top. She removed them and put them in the bathroom, then took out the shirts they both liked to wear before bed.

It had taken her a little while to get used to sleeping in the nude, but once she had, she'd become almost addicted to the primal comfort of snuggling under the covers with Dar, and she found she slept like an absolute rock once she'd tucked herself around her partner's body.

Her ears perked up as she heard the back door to the cabin open, and Dar's rhythmic footsteps approached.

"Ker?"

"In here," Kerry replied, turning as a dark head poked into the bedroom. "Just getting stuff out."

Dar held up a brown paper wrapped package invitingly. "Dinner?"

Kerry held up her shirt. "Shower first?"

One of Dar's eyebrows quirked. "I'll stick this in the fridge," she remarked with a knowing smirk before disappearing in the direction of the kitchen.

Kerry chuckled softly to herself. "Heh." She dropped the shirts onto the bed and eased her light cotton blouse off her shoulders, wincing slightly at the sting of a mild sunburn. "Ouch."

"Uh huh." Dar had returned, bearing a small blue jar. "Figured we both could use this." She held up the cold cream. "With aloe."

"You rock." Kerry held out a hand and led Dar to the bathroom, opened the shower door, and reached in to start the water running. The first time they'd stayed in the cabin, the electricity hadn't even been on, and after bravely bearing the oppressive heat inside the half-finished building, they finally admitted defeat and curled up together out on the beach, hoping against hope they'd escape both crabs and foul weather.

They had, but Kerry had found tiny, suspicious red marks on her neck that had worried her a lot until Dar rather sheepishly admitted to having made them with some overenthusiastic nibbling.

Ah, love. Kerry turned to see Dar with her disintegrating shorts unbuttoned and her tank top half over her head. She reached over and tickled her belly button, watching Dar's abdominals contract as she chuckled in reaction. Blue eyes emerged a moment later as Dar got her shirt off, and shook a finger at Kerry in mock remonstrance.

Kerry relented as she pulled off her own shirt, feeling a light tickle as Dar unhooked her bra. They finished getting undressed and squeezed into the shower together. "Ooo," Kerry hissed as her sunburned skin protested the pressure of the hot water. A moment later, the pressure ceased as Dar stepped between her and the spray.

"Hang on." Dar adjusted the water to a little cooler temperature and less force. "There." She dropped her arms around Kerry and pulled her closer, rubbing her back gently. "Better?"

"Much." Kerry nuzzled between Dar's breasts. "That wreck today was awesome. The visibility was incredible."

"Yeah." Dar squeezed out some coconut body wash and started rubbing it over Kerry's skin. "Did you get a shot of that sand shark?"

"The one that was fascinated by your flippers? You bet." Kerry lathered up a handful of soap and started washing Dar. "For a minute there, I thought it was going to start munching on you."

Dar squirted some shampoo on her partner's damp head and worked it in with her fingers, massaging Kerry's scalp as she got the salt water and sand out of it. "I did too," she confessed. "Did you see me grab my knife?"

Kerry was busy scrubbing Dar's thigh. "Yep. That was the best picture. That wreck in the background, all that white sand in front of it, and you and the shark facing off. Perfect."

"Uh oh. I sense more bathroom art." Dar gave a mock sigh. "If you put it up in the office, every ten minutes you'll have to answer 'which one's the shark?'"

Kerry snickered, her shoulders shaking as she patted Dar's side. She caught Dar's right hand and rubbed her thumb over the top of it affectionately, then stopped and examined the skin more closely. The knuckles were slightly swollen, and a scrape marred the second one. Her eyes lifted in question to meet Dar's.

Dar continued rinsing Kerry's hair with her free hand. "I ran into a brain-cell-deficient organism at the market." She grinned rakishly. "Some punk who thought bullying old men and shooting animals was a good time."

"Ah." Kerry brought the knuckle up and kissed it. "I love it when your Robin Hood streak comes out. Did you really hurt him?"

"Nah. I hit him in the head and the nuts." Dar turned and got them both under the spray, rinsing off the coconut body wash. She started to lather shampoo in her hair, but felt Kerry tugging her down, and gracefully lowered herself to her knees, giving her shorter partner access to her head.

Dar slid her hands up Kerry's strong thighs and playfully nibbled her navel as Kerry washed her hair. She felt the surface under her lips move a little more strongly as Kerry inhaled sharply. Slowly, she worked her way up, past the curving arch of Kerry's ribs to her breasts, feeling the fingers tangled in her hair move with a suddenly insistent rhythm.

Teasing, she nipped at the underside of one breast then, even over the pattering of the water, heard Kerry's ragged intake as she went a little higher. With a smile, she released Kerry's nipple and eased to her feet, planting kisses up the center of her partner's breastbone until she reached the lips waiting for her.

Kerry's body slid against Dar's, and Dar felt Kerry's hand slide up the inside of her thigh. The water washed the shampoo from her hair down both of them as they kissed and exchanged more intimate touches. Dar fumbled behind her and shut off the faucet, then booted the door open as they eased out of the shower and reached for towels.

The slightly rough surface of the terry cloth was like an explosion of sensation against her already tingling skin, and Dar found her own breathing growing short as Kerry dried her off and she returned the favor. They managed to find their way through the still-unfamiliar confines of the cabin's bath and the short distance to the bed, falling onto it and rolling as the air mattress bucked with unexpected motion.

"Used to the waterbed." Kerry chuckled softly, as she recaptured Dar's lower lip in her teeth.

"Ungh." Dar stretched out, then wrapped her body around Kerry's, claiming possession of every inch of her. She slid a leg between Kerry's and felt her partner's body lean against hers, a rush of warmth after the cool air of the room. Kerry's hand cupped her breast and an almost primal growl emerged from her.

Before rational thought became impossible, Dar did briefly hope they wouldn't forget this bed had no retaining bumpers. Damn floor didn't have any padding and neither of them really bounced well.

"Rrr," Kerry burred, as their lips once again tasted each other.

Dar stroked her delicately and the sound deepened to a groan. She stopped worrying about the floor.

KERRY PULLED TO a stop at the corner and waited, allowing a car to pass before she eased up on the throttle a little and turned onto the main and only street that went through the town. She settled her weight on the motorcycle and enjoyed the breeze as it blew against her, gaining guilty pleasure from the fact that she'd shucked the long-sleeved leather jacket tucked into the strap at the back of the bike for her short trip up the road. It was early, the sun just easing over the trees, and the weather was crisp and cool; she'd taken a calculated risk that her growing mastery of the relatively sedate motorcycle wouldn't make her regret it. She was, after all, wearing her jeans and boots and helmet, so leaving her upper body unprotected was hopefully just a limited exposure. So to speak.

Dar was getting the boat ready for the next leg of their vacation, so Kerry had volunteered to make the short run up to the nearest Wal-Mart for a few things they'd realized they'd forgotten. Dar had laughed and accused her of just making an excuse to take the bike out, but since she liked to ride it as much as Kerry did, the accusation was specious at best.

"Vroom, vroom." Kerry glanced down at the Honda Shadow Spirit, then quickly focused her eyes back on the road.

Since there wasn't much traffic down there, they'd decided to purchase the bike for local errands, especially since they usually arrived by water. It had taken a few weeks' practice, but Kerry was really enjoying the bike. There was a sense of wildness attached to it that she found appealing, and she always felt a little rebellious when she took the motorcycle out.

Kerry passed through the quiet, empty stretch of scrub and trees, completely alone on the road. The peacefulness appealed to her, reminding her just a little of some of the areas near where she'd been born, where one could drive for an hour or so and not see any habitation around them.

She idly imagined driving the cycle down her street and pulling into her parents' driveway, then had to stop when she almost lost control of the darn thing while laughing. "And they thought a Mustang was bad."

After another few minutes, she was entering civilization again, a cluster of buildings and crossroads that were fairly new in appearance. She pulled into a left-turn lane, then swept through the green light into the parking lot of the twenty-four-hour Wal-Mart.

There were several cars there already, but Kerry pulled up to the very front and smoothly stopped, nudging the kickstand down and securing the bike as she dismounted. She pulled off her helmet and ran her fingers through her hair, then strapped the helmet to the back seat. A brief glance at her reflection in the front store windows made her grin. "Kerrison Stuart, biker chick." She shook her head. "No one in my family would believe *this*."

An advertisement posted on the window caught her eye. The blonde brow reflected over it quirked. Squaring her shoulders, she confronted the door and pushed her way through it.

DAR WALKED AROUND the boat, making a last minute inspection before they cast off. She was wearing her swimsuit, with a pair of cotton surfer shorts and a bright blue T-shirt over it. She tucked her hair up under a baseball cap and poked her head inside the diesel chamber, checking the engines with a knowledgeable eye. Satisfied, she pulled herself slowly up the ladder to the bridge, favoring the shoulder she'd hurt not long before.

It annoyed her that the shoulder still bothered her, but not enough for her to break down and go back to the therapist. She was slowly getting back her normal range of motion, and she figured maybe the long week of swimming and relaxing might do the trick so she could finally put the injury behind her.

Dar checked the global positioning system and the radio, then spent a moment with her eyes closed going over the safety equipment she had on board. She wasn't paranoid, but this was the first time she was taking the boat across wide-open water and if anyone knew how much respect the sea was due, this sailor's kid surely did.

Satisfied with her preparations, Dar nodded. *Okay.* She climbed back down the ladder and dusted off her hands, then spotted motion near the cabin and walked to the side of the boat, peering around the pylon. A tall, husky man in a police uniform was walking toward her, and for a chilling moment she thought about Kerry heading out on the bike. Watching his face intently as the man came closer, she leapt ashore.

"Help you with something?" she asked as he came to a halt.

He had sandy hair and a moderately good-looking face. "Well, maybe." He glanced at a small notepad. "Would you be a Ms. Roberts?"

"Yes." Dar heard her own voice come out clipped and no-nonsense.

It didn't seem to faze him. He nodded and tucked the notepad away. "Old Bill Vickerson told me I might find you here. Had a little dust-up by his place last night, didn'cha?"

Dar relaxed, confident at least that whatever this was, it didn't involve Kerry. "Something like that." She didn't see much point in denying it and wondered briefly if her temper had gotten her into something very inconveniently sticky this time. "What's this all about, Officer...Brewer?"

The police officer studied her. "Fella you whumped up on was my little brother."

Oh boy. Dar put years of boardroom practice into effect, and merely raised an eyebrow. "And?"

For a minute, Officer Brewer chewed the toothpick he had in his mouth, then he chuckled. "You're a cool one, aren't you?" he commented. "City lady like you, here by yourself in the boonies, faced with a cop with a family reason to slap cuffs on ya."

Dar snorted, chuckling dryly.

Now his eyebrows lifted. "No dice, huh?" He waited a moment, then chuckled as well. "Cool customer, that's for sure." Unexpectedly, he held out a hand. "Ms. Roberts, you done me a good deed, and I wanted to say thanks."

Knocked a little off balance, Dar nevertheless took the hand and returned the strong grip with one of her own. "I'm not really sure I understand," she admitted, "but it beats handcuffs."

The police officer gave her a wry grin. "My brother's a jackass," he said straightforwardly. "D'you know what kind of a pain in my butt it is to have to arrest family? I done it six times now. Kid never learns."

"Ah." Dar nodded slightly.

"Bunch of his deadbeat friends went looking for trouble up near Big Pine last night, racing and shooting at each other. They ran their asses off the road and wrapped themselves 'round a tree," the policeman said. "We took four body bags full of burnt parts to the morgue."

Dar winced.

"Woulda been five," Officer Brewer said. "But because my jackass brother was nursing a sore jaw and a lump on his nuts, his sorry ass lived to get me in yet more trouble." The man sighed. "So, thanks, Ms. City Slicker Computer Big Shot. I owe you one."

It took a moment to sort out the various sentiments, but Dar eventually decided things had turned out well. "Don't mention it."

A rumble caught their attention, and the policeman turned as a motorcycle and rider came right up the side path and practically onto the dock before it rolled to a halt and the rider jumped off. The cycle came to rest on its kickstand as Kerry pulled off her helmet and strode towards them, her boots sounding loud on the wooden planks.

"Well now," Officer Brewer studied the oncoming woman, "what do we got here? You travel with one of them radical, liberal, revolutionary types?"

"What?" Kerry stopped, took off her sunglasses, and regarded him. "I'm a Republican, thank you very much." She snorted and turned her attention to Dar. "What's going on?"

Dar gazed fondly at her. "Officer Brewer just stopped by to welcome us to the neighborhood."

"Oh." Kerry relaxed and gave the officer one of her more charming smiles. "That's really nice of you. Thanks."

Brewster chuckled. "Well, I won't keep you ladies. Have yourself a nice trip, y'hear?" He turned and walked off the dock, circled the motorcycle, and paused to admire it. Then he kept going down the path and out of sight.

Kerry watched him go, then turned. "Welcome Wagon at seven a.m.?"

Dar put an arm around her shoulders. "Let's get loaded up and get out of here before the town mothers show up with cookies." She walked Kerry over to the bike. "I'll tell you the rest when we get out of the dock."

"Uh oh." Kerry lifted her packages off the vehicle and hefted them. "I'll get this on board if you want to stash the bike, then we're outta here."

Dar poked her finger at a bag. "Are those what I think they are?"

"Guess you'll have to wait and find out." Kerry shooed her. "C'mon. I hear stingrays calling my name." She made her way down the dock to the boat, hopped on board, and disappeared.

Dar reviewed the start of her day and decided it augured well for a far more peaceful end to it. *Good thing*, she chuckled to herself, as she pushed the motorcycle into the small garage and securely locked it. Her plans for the evening definitely would not tolerate any interruption.

She checked the doors to the cabin one last time, then set the alarm and walked back to the boat. She released the front line, then the rear one, and tossed them onboard, jumping on as the boat started to drift slightly in the outgoing tide.

The breeze was rising as Dar started up the engines and slowly reversed them away from the harbor, making sure she was well out before she nudged the throttles into forward and swung the bow around, pointing it out toward the endless blue horizon. She settled her bare feet against the console and gave the engines gas, feeling the surge of power as they headed outbound.

Chapter
Three

KERRY LET HERSELF drift on the slight underwater current, watching the slanting rays of the sun filter down and touch the reef over which she was swimming. A small school of bright blue and yellow fish went sweeping by, wheeling and pausing for some unknown fish reason but giving her an excellent photo opportunity, which she took immediate advantage of.

The pale sand and darker coral outlined the colorful fish as they swirled around her, leaving her behind as they found another patch of ground to explore. Kerry watched them swim off, then rolled over onto her back and relaxed in the light green sea as she examined the reef for more wildlife.

One thing that had always surprised her was how noisy it was underwater. In a pool or in the lakes of her birthplace, the sounds were absent or muted. But here in the ocean, nearly everything made a racket. Lobsters and other crustaceans clicked against the coral, shells tumbled in the underwater current, rattling along, even the sand made a swishing sound as it was moved.

Their regulators were the loudest, though. The bubbles created a low rumbling sound, and each intake of breath brought to mind the rasping of Darth Vader.

Kerry exchanged her regulator mouthpiece for the smaller one clipped to her vest and took a sip of water, rinsing it around her mouth before she swallowed, then replaced her regulator and took a breath. A clown fish approached her warily, inspecting the edge of her fin before it darted off. Then a tiny cuttlefish, almost transparent, floated in front of her mask, its fins almost brushing her nose. Her eyes focused on it, a structure so intricate it seemed like the finest blown glass.

The perfection of the universe brought its own awe, Kerry had found, and its own peace.

A soft knocking caught her attention and she looked around, spotting Dar hovering over a coral outcropping nearby, gesturing her over. She flipped lazily to horizontal and flexed her thighs, waggling her fins to propel herself through the water. Dar reached out and snagged a strap on Kerry's buoyancy compensator vest as she neared.

Kerry drifted, looking where her partner was pointing. "Oomfp." The sound of surprise came out around a burst of bubbles. A large sea turtle was huddled behind the rock, watching them warily. A piece of seaweed hung out of its mouth and swayed in the current, and Kerry quickly brought up her camera and focused it. Just as she opened the shutter, the animal released the seaweed, poking its tongue out at Kerry as it was captured on film.

She heard the faint sound of Dar laughing as she drifted back, and they watched the turtle return to its feeding. Then Dar checked her dive computer and pointed at the time on it.

Kerry nodded in understanding. It was a shallow dive; if she looked up, the boat would only be twenty feet or so above her head. But it was their second dive of the day, and she knew Dar preferred to stay on the cautious side when it came to bottom time. She covered the lens on her camera and clipped it to its holders on her vest, then followed Dar toward the anchor line of the boat.

Out of long habit, they paused at ten feet, where the wave action overhead started to make itself felt. The seas were fairly calm, but there was enough of a chop to keep the boat at a steady rock, and Kerry could see the dive ladder moving up and down at the back of the stern.

Like flying a plane, where the takeoffs and landings were the trickiest, in diving it was getting in and out of the water that usually presented the most difficulty. Once you were in and down, things were usually a breeze. Kerry watched Dar release her grip on the anchor line and head for the ladder, her hands reaching down to remove her fins as she approached it. She waited for her partner to grab the moving ladder and toss the fins up out of the water with her other hand before she let go of the line herself and followed.

Dar waited for the stern to dip down so she could get her feet on the bottom step of the ladder, then she reached up to the upper rung and hung on, letting the wave action pick her right up out of the water and into the late afternoon sunlight. She stepped up into the boat and shucked her tank and vest, clipping them to holders before she turned around and reached down to grab the back of Kerry's air tank as she emerged from the sea.

Kerry was no weakling, but pulling one's self and forty pounds of equipment out of the water onto a pitching boat after a long day's diving was a lot to ask, and Dar saw the quick look of appreciation she got as she pulled her partner on board. "Here, give me that." She reached over and unsnapped the catches that held the vest across Kerry's chest and loosened the inner waist strap as she removed the tank.

"Ugh. Thanks." Kerry pulled off her mask and scrubbed her

hand over her face. She could taste salt and the rubber from her regulator on her tongue, and what she really wanted was... *Ah.* "I love you." Her hand closed around the plastic bottle of Gatorade as she loosened her weight belt and let it drop to the deck.

Dar chuckled. "You're welcome." She dunked Kerry's camera in the fresh water bucket next to the ladder, and tossed in their masks and snorkels as well. "Can you grab me some oranges?"

"You got it." Kerry patted her face dry with a towel, then ran it quickly over her body before she went down the stairs into the cabin. She sucked on the Gatorade as she opened the refrigerator and removed a pop-top can of mandarin oranges. She took it, a spoon, and a packet of crackers and peanut butter and returned to the deck.

Dar had unhooked the tanks and put them into the cradles next to the compressor, and hosed down the BCs that were already hanging there. She was rinsing Kerry's regulator with careful hands when Kerry eased up next to her and bumped her lightly with one hip. With a quick grin, Dar put the regulator down next to hers on the counter and took the can of fruit.

They sat down in the comfortable camp chairs on the back deck and relaxed, putting their feet up in the attached footrests as the boat rocked gently in the waves. "That was nice," Dar commented, removing the top from her can. "Not much current down there, either."

"Nmpf." Kerry shook her head, her mouth full of cracker and peanut butter. "Gorf. Sorry." She swallowed down the mouthful and chased it with some Gatorade. "Yeah, it felt so great just to be down there." Her eyes swept the horizon, then she got up and looked around to the front of the boat. "Especially out here, where it's just us, the sky, and the water."

Dar nodded. "We're still in the straits; we could just stay anchored here for tonight."

Kerry faced into the wind, listening to the rhythm of the waves. "Or?"

"Or we could head south."

"Is there a prettier place down south?"

Dar sucked on an orange. "Not that I know of."

"Here sounds perfect to me, then." Kerry wandered back over and sat down. "How about we have a snack up front and watch the sun set?"

"Sounds perfect to me," Dar echoed with a grin. Then her head cocked, and she glanced off into the distance. "Looks like we have company." Her ears identified the sound of engines. They grew louder and louder, until a speck resolved itself into a massive yacht, half again as large as theirs, cleaving the water at top speed as it headed south.

"Well." Kerry took in the solid black hull with red and silver piping. "How's that for posh?" The ship was flying several colorful pennants, and its brass fittings shone brightly in the sun. "Who do you think it is, Dar? Some really rich Northern type?"

"With no taste?" Dar grinned wryly. "Foreigner, maybe."

The boat roared past, its wake making the *Dixieland Yankee* rock vigorously back and forth for several moments. The newcomer headed toward the horizon, several figures visible on its stern deck.

"They'd better watch that draft; we're in shallows." Dar frowned, got up, and reached for the radio. She keyed it. "Black and red Giarenno headed south through the straits, do you copy?"

She released the mic, and heard only static. Her brow contracted. "Black and red Giarenno headed through the straits southbound, do you copy?"

There was more answering static, then a sharp crackling. "This is *Cordon's Empire*. Are you calling this vessel?" The voice was abrupt and impatient.

Dar keyed the mic. "Roger that, *Cordon's Empire*. This is *Dixieland Yankee*. You just passed on my port side. Be advised you have less than ten to fifteen feet to bottom in the area."

There was a moment of silence before the clipped reply. "We do not need the advice. Please do not contact this vessel again."

The sound of the transmission terminating was the auditory equivalent of an arrogant slap, and Dar expended a few outraged breaths just glaring at the radio before she turned and delivered a murderous look at the retreating yacht. "You're welcome and kiss my ass, *Cordon's Empire*," she replied. She hung up the mic and returned to her comfortable chair with a snort of disgust. "Jackass."

"Mm." Kerry licked a bit of peanut butter off her thumb. "Bet he didn't know who he was talking to."

Dar bit an orange slice in half and snapped it up, doing her best wild animal snarl. "I'd say I hope he bottoms, but the satisfaction wouldn't be worth the damage to the reef."

Kerry finished her cracker. "You're right," she agreed. "Tell you what—if you get the deck pad, I'll bring a bottle of something cold and we can let Mother Nature do her thing."

Dar dismissed the rude boater and willingly turned her mind to more pleasant things. She got up and rinsed out her can, squashed it in her hands, and put it into the recycling container. Then she opened the storage bench and pulled out the large double pad they liked to sit on up front and slung it over her shoulder while Kerry ducked back into the cabin.

There were layers of light clouds on the horizon, and Dar imagined it would be a gorgeous sunset. She mused happily on that as she made her way around to the front of the boat, settling the pad down and going to the very front of the bow.

Kerry took out a bottle of chilled Riesling and inspected two glasses, setting them down while she put together a bowl of finger foods — cubes of cheese and pieces of fruit — and tossed in a handful of chocolate kisses and a few carrots just for color and balance. Whistling softly, she picked up everything and carried it up the stairs, bumping the button on the sound system just before she went out on deck.

Soft strains of music emerged as she balanced along the edge of the boat, climbing up on the bow as Dar turned and spotted her. A smile appeared on Kerry's face as she took in the sight of her lover burnished in golden sunlight, and it only broadened as Dar came to her side, took the bowl from her, and dropped down on the pad.

While Dar stretched out to full length, resting on one elbow and crossing her long legs at the ankles, Kerry settled down cross-legged to open the bottle. A soft pop rewarded her efforts, and she put down the cork with its puller and poured Dar a glass of wine with a casually expert motion. She handed the glass over and poured her own, then accepted Dar's invitation and sat in the circle of her arm as Dar rolled over onto her back and they leaned against the slope of the boat's bow.

The sun began to slip behind the clouds, sending spears of russet through them, and Kerry found herself content to just watch, lulled by the gentle motion of the waves and a feeling of comfortable tiredness from their diving. She sipped her wine, rolling the sweet richness in her mouth, and nibbled on some cheese. She was starting to feel an emotional weight lift off her shoulders. The stress of the past month seemed to lose its grip on her, and she let her head rest against Dar as she soaked in the peace like a bit of sea sponge.

"My mother once painted a sky like this," Dar said. "I remember it... from when I was still in grade school. She had it hanging over the couch in the living room."

"Mm." Kerry tilted her head, amazed at the vividness of the color. "It's so rich. Why is that, Dar?"

"Angle of inclination." Dar exhaled. "And the moisture in the air."

Kerry took a sip of her wine as she gazed at the sky. "Or maybe God's just in a great mood," she murmured. "I know I sure am." Her eyes drifted from the sunset for a moment. "Thank you for having this incredible idea."

Dar lifted her glass and touched its rim against Kerry's. "Here's to us." She took a mouthful and waited for Kerry to do the same, then she gracefully inclined her head and they kissed, exchanging a little wine and a lot of affection.

The breeze lifted a little and tangled their hair together as they settled down to watch the day's ending.

DAR WAITED UNTIL the sky was completely dark and the canopy of stars fit over them from horizon to horizon. It was an amazing sensation—hearing the rustle of the waves and seeing nothing but flat blackness that extended to a sparkling blanket seemingly rising out of nothing.

Kerry was curled up next to her, fast asleep. After their long day of diving and sun, that wasn't surprising, really, but Dar was glad to see her partner getting some much needed rest. Her father's death and the stress of the previous month had taken a lot out of her, and Dar intended their little trip to be as relaxing as possible. She lifted her hand and combed her fingers through Kerry's hair, brushing it back from her face.

Kerry's eyelids trembled just a little, and she stirred, snuggling closer to Dar and sliding an arm over her stomach. Then she relaxed again, a puff of exhaled breath warming Dar's skin.

"Atta girl," Dar murmured, watching the slow rise and fall of her lover's ribcage. "You just take it easy. No getting sick." Kerry had an appointment with their family doctor scheduled upon their return, to repeat tests that not long ago had shown a dangerous rise in her blood pressure, among other things. *To hell with the company.*

Both of them leaving at once was throwing ILS into chaos, but Dar couldn't care less. Given her own behavior to the contrary, Dar readily acknowledged the hypocritical nature of her wanting Kerry to put herself before work, but it was what she wanted nonetheless and she refused to apologize for it. She idly twirled a bit of Kerry's pale hair around her finger, admiring its softness. Already two days in the sun seemed to have lightened it, or maybe Kerry's deepening tan just provided a greater contrast. *Whatever.*

Dar watched Kerry's jaw muscles move a little, then her eyes fluttered open and the tip of her pink tongue appeared. "Hey, sleepy." She ran the tips of her fingers over Kerry's back as the smaller woman stretched.

"Mmmm..." Kerry rolled over and gazed up at the night sky. "Oh, that's gorgeous," she murmured. "Look at those stars. There must be a zillion of them."

"Mmhm." Dar eased onto her side and wrapped her arms around Kerry, gazing at Kerry's profile. "Beautiful."

Kerry felt the attention and turned to meet Dar's eyes. She still felt sleepy, and a little bemused at having dozed off over their little snack, but she had no real desire to do much about it other than snuggle back up against Dar's warm body and return to her dreams. She lifted a hand and stifled a yawn. "Think I overdid it today."

Me, too, Dar concurred in wry, silent agreement. "How about a shower and an early bedtime," she suggested.

"Ooo." Kerry found the idea very appealing. "Yeah, I like that." She laced her fingers with Dar's. "We could have some hot chocolate. It's a little chilly out here."

With a smile, Dar lifted herself to her feet and offered Kerry a hand up. They walked together single file around the side of the cabin and down into the stern. Dar turned on the outside lights and reviewed their gear. "I'm going to pull in the buoy. Meet you inside."

Kerry unexpectedly circled her with both arms and gave her a big hug. "Me and some hot chocolate'll be waiting." She released Dar and gave her a pat on the side, then eased through the cabin door.

Dar chuckled softly to herself as she walked to the side of the boat and pulled in the buoy line, then secured the orange buoy to the side of the boat and removed the upright, flexible pole that held their divers flag. The flag indicated to anyone passing by that there were divers under the water, possibly near the surface, and theoretically the boaters would give the spot a wide berth.

However, as in coastal areas where manatees lived and signs to that effect were posted, adherence to the rules varied from ship captain to ship captain, and if you were in an area used by numerous pleasure boaters, you took a risk. Dar herself had a small scar on her back from when she was younger and a miscast shark hook had snagged her and almost pulled her air hose from her first stage.

Out here, there wasn't much chance of that kind of problem. Dar fastened the flag into its catches and cast an eye around the stern, checking to make sure everything was in its place. She nodded in satisfaction and entered the cabin, closing the door behind her. Kerry was in the small galley, busy with the cocoa tin, her dark purple swimsuit outlining her body nicely. They had the hatches open, so the night breeze was blowing through, cooling the place off without them having to actually run the small air conditioning unit with which the boat was equipped.

"Everything shipshape, cap'n?" Kerry asked, looking up at her with a mischievous grin.

"Argh." Dar made a quasi-pirate noise. "I'll duck into the shower first."

Kerry continued her task. "We could try getting in there together."

Dar snorted, shaking her head. "Not even if we were Barbie dolls." She entered the head and flipped on the light, stripped out of her suit and hung it on one of the hooks on the back of the door. They had gotten tubes of body soap, conveniently able to also hang on hooks, and she squeezed out a generous amount of apricot scented wash as she turned on the water and stepped under it.

It felt very good to scrub the salt spray off her skin. Swimming in the sea was interesting, and often refreshing, but the minerals in the water made a shower afterwards something she always looked forward to. It also helped prevent sea lice. Dar loved marine life in all its forms, but she drew the line at providing a home for it on her person.

Dar rinsed her hair, then stepped out from under the shower and toweled herself off. She opened the tiny medicine cabinet and removed a glass bottle, unscrewed the top, and pulled out the dropper and filled it. She tilted her head and let several drops fall into her right ear, then did the same with her left. Ear infections weren't something she much liked, either, and the drops would dry out her ear canals and help prevent infection.

She tucked the towel around her body and sauntered back out into the cabin. "Next." She traded places with Kerry, who slipped past with a grin. Dar relaxed against the counter as she waited for the water to boil, reaching up and turning on the marine radio to listen to the weather reports.

Funny, how the crackling of the radio and the sound of the shower are so similar.

The water kettle hissed. Dar turned and picked it up, then poured water over the cocoa mix in the cups on the counter. The scent of chocolate enveloped her and she grinned, stirring the foamy liquid with a spoon to make sure it all dissolved. She retrieved the milk from the refrigerator and put a little in each cup. She was just adding an artistic dollop of whipped cream when Kerry emerged and wandered over, the fresh scent of apricot rising from her skin.

They dressed in T-shirts and sat down together on the couch in the living area, putting their feet up on the bolted down table. Kerry sipped her chocolate as they listened to the waves for a bit, then she turned to Dar. "You know, I was just thinking—it's really funny."

Dar eyed her. "Yeah?" She waited for the punchline.

"We never really talk to each other." Kerry watched the expressive face across from her. When Dar blinked and put down her cup, her eyebrows contracting, Kerry nodded. "See?"

"Huh?" Both eyebrows went up and Dar gave her an unfeigned look of bewilderment. "Are you saying we have trouble communicating?"

Kerry shook her head. "No. We communicate perfectly; we just never talk." She suppressed a grin. "What I mean is, like when I just said that: you didn't have to say anything to me, I knew what you were thinking."

Dar relaxed. "You did?"

"Sure." Kerry pitched her voice a little lower in mimicry of Dar's. "'What the hell is she talking about?' I can tell by your face, by how you move, almost, what you're feeling."

Dar considered that thoughtfully. "Well, we do spend a lot of time with each other," she allowed.

"True. And it's hard to have good, vigorous debates with someone you agree with most of the time," Kerry said. "We haven't had a fight in a long time."

A dark eyebrow crawled up Dar's forehead. "You want to have a fight?"

"Actually, I was listening to a radio program the other day on the way to the Kendall office. This guy was saying how it is a sign of a healthy relationship when you have fights, because you aren't repressing anything."

Dar's other eyebrow joined its mate. "Are you repressing something?"

Kerry pointed at herself. "Me?"

"Yeah."

"No. Are you?"

Dar frowned. "Not that I know of." She suddenly became aware of the humor in the situation. "If you really want to test the theory, we could invent something to repress, then have a fight about it."

"We could do that. Or we could just do this." Kerry leaned over and kissed Dar. "Which is a heck of a lot more fun."

Dar chuckled, and cupped Kerry's cheek as she removed the chocolate from her lips. Then she rested her forehead against Kerry's, and her face grew thoughtful. "I think people start fighting when they stop communicating," she said. "Or if they never could to begin with."

"Is that what happened to you before?" Kerry asked.

Dar nodded silently.

"I was thinking about that when I was listening to that guy." Kerry took a sip of her cocoa and offered her cup to Dar. "He said it's easy to fall in love with someone, but it's a lot harder to learn to like and live with them." She reached over and brushed a lock of hair out of Dar's face.

Dar licked her lips. "I like you." She smiled. "I think I said that the first time we had dinner together."

Kerry smiled back. "Yes, you did, and so did I." She studied Dar's face. "I really liked you, and I wanted to be friends with you long before I figured out I was head over heels in love."

They looked into each other's eyes for a long moment. Finally, Dar took a breath. "Kerry?"

"Yes?"

A pucker appeared between Dar's eyebrows. "Why are we having this conversation?"

"Well," Kerry squiggled closer, "I didn't want to save it for a dusty hospital stairwell, and it's late, and I'm wasted, and it beats me reciting my brother's latest attempt at poetry." She kissed Dar gently. "We have to have these angsty, soulful, heart to heart talks sometimes, Dar, else we'll get cootie points in Love Court or something."

Dar grinned. "Wanna hear a secret?"

"Sure."

"I have been repressing something."

Green eyes opened wider. "Really?"

"Yeah." Dar took the mostly empty cup from Kerry and set it down. "The desire to take you off to bed. C'mon." She held out her hands and when the blonde took them, pulled Kerry to her feet and into her arms. "Ker?"

"Mm?" Kerry murmured.

"If you ever think we're not communicating," Dar looked at her seriously, "talk to me."

Kerry blinked, then nodded. "Ditto," she replied.

Dar carried the cups to the sink and ran water into them, then accompanied Kerry to the bedroom. Kerry pulled back the down comforter and they crawled into bed, snuggling together as Dar put out the bedside lamp. With the hatches open, they could hear the sea, and a nice breeze puffed around the cabin, reducing the feeling of being enclosed.

The boat creaked a little, and the rocking motion soothed her. *The sounds are different from the ones at home, or even in the cabin,* Kerry thought. She felt her eyes closing and let the wave of sleepiness in, already looking forward to the morning. Stifling a yawn, she drew in a breath of warm, Dar scented air, and dropped off to sleep.

Chapter
Four

IT WAS MID-AFTERNOON already, and they'd been making good time. After an early morning romp in the sea, Dar fired up the boat's engines and headed southeast, crossing the ruffled blue-green Caribbean as the sun tracked steadily overhead.

Dar pored over the chart clipped to the console in front of her, marking out a route on the plastic sheet with a big purple marker. She checked the GPS against the chart and grunted, satisfied with their progress and with her navigating skills. She nudged the throttles forward a little and rested her elbows on either side of them, gazing out at the horizon with a slight grin.

Hands-on had always been something she'd enjoyed, right from the very start of her career. It was one thing to sit in some boardroom with a pad of paper and argue about how to do things, but a very different thing to be able to put your hands on the technology and actually do it yourself. It's what had set her apart from the rest of the management at ILS. Dar had worked very hard to keep her skills current, and she was very, very proud of the fact that she could go into their state-of-the-art ops center and run every piece of technology inside it. It wasn't always easy. Her position kept her very busy and the tech changed every day, it seemed. But Dar had decided she never wanted to be in a place where her staff knew more about what they were doing than she did, so she put in the long nights, bought the new manuals, and occasionally even took things home so she could take them apart and play with them.

Being able to captain her ship across the sea had been just another challenge, and again she'd put in the time to brush up on her charting and diesel skills. Her peripheral vision caught a change in the depth meter and she studied it, then altered their course just a little, steering the *Dixieland Yankee* into a deeper channel.

With no other immediate piloting needs to see to, Dar picked up the pencil next to the notepad and started idly sketching. At first she doodled in the horizon and the boat's bow, but that got boring, so she started looking around for something else to draw. She leaned back and looked down, then grinned. *Ah.* Her pencil moved against the paper as she focused on her new inspiration.

KERRY PUT HER pen down for the nth time and let her head rest against the chair. She was ostensibly working on poetry, but the sun, the mild drone of the engines, and the sweet sea air were combining to subvert her creative intentions in favor of some lazy daydreaming.

She wiggled her bare toes contentedly. Dar had promised a twilight dive when they neared the Virgin Islands, then dinner at a small place she'd last visited just before they'd met. "Fresh conch chowder." Kerry licked her lips thoughtfully. "Sounds great, just so long as you don't think too much about what a conch actually looks like."

"You say something?" Dar called down from the bridge.

"No, sweetie," Kerry replied. "Just mumbling to myself." She worried a grape off its stem from the bowl next to her and popped it into her mouth. "Whatcha doing?"

"Driving the boat."

"That all?" Kerry asked, tipping her head back and looking up, one hand shading her eyes.

"Doodling."

"Yeah? What this time?"

"Nothing you'd wanna see," Dar remarked with an easy grin. "How's the writing coming?"

Intrigued, Kerry tucked her book into the side pocket of the deck chair and put down her fruit bowl. "It's not," she admitted, getting up and walking to the ladder, stretching out her body as she did. "Sad to say, I'm too lazy to even write today." She climbed up onto the bridge and put her arms around Dar, gazing down at the pad in front of her. Then she blinked. "Yikes."

Dar snickered. "Toldja."

"That's me."

"Sort of, yeah," Dar agreed.

Kerry eyed the sketch, which showed a reasonable rendering of the boat's stern, with her sprawled in the chair. "You're getting pretty good at this, you know that?"

"Depends on what I'm drawing," Dar said with a shrug.

Kerry gave her a kiss on the top of her head. "I'll take that as a compliment," she told Dar, as a memory floated into her mind's eye.

Another day, another meeting. Kerry carried her notes into the big conference room and paused; most of the table was already full up. That left the end seat, which was always Dar's, and an empty one on either side of it. Hm. *Kerry walked around to the left hand side and sat down in the chair beside Dar's.* I should come late more often. *Then she had an excuse to sit next to her boss and not have anyone think it was strange.*

Dar *entered, and as she circled the table, she raised her eyebrow just a trifle at Kerry's choice of seats, but her lips quirked into a tiny grin at the same time, making Kerry's insides warm as their eyes met.*

Kerry felt herself blush and she studied her notes, trying not to show the unsteady confusion pulsing through her body, reacting to Dar's very near presence as the woman sat down and their forearms brushed.

Dar leaned back in her chair and balanced her pad on her denim clad knee as she asked for the weekly report.

They were in casual wear, and Kerry found herself wanting to reach over and touch the soft cotton Dar was wearing. She folded her hands together and sternly told her body to behave, hardly believing how out of control she felt around her new lover. Especially since the more experienced Dar was seemingly quite unaffected by it all, breezing through their workday as though nothing at all had changed between them.

Kerry, on the other hand, felt like she had "I'm with her" tattooed on her forehead. She sighed and picked up her water glass, taking a long sip as the operations staff started their recitations. The water didn't help much. She was almost hyper sensitively aware of Dar's every motion, every sound—from the faint shifts of her clothing on the leather chair when she moved, to the light scrape of the pencil lead with which she was doodling.

Lucky Dar. *Kerry snuck a look at her boss, who looked relaxed as she glanced up from her doodling as each staff member spoke. Dar seemed almost bored, or a least borderline inattentive, giving the speakers a brief nod as she accepted their reports.*

"Next." *Dar kept her eyes on her pad.* "Did you get those servers?"

Mark had to report in the negative. "Not yet, boss. Two more days."

Kerry looked at him, seeing the wince as he waited for Dar's reaction, along with the rest of the staff.

"Okay." *Dar nodded.* "What else?"

Everyone around the table looked at one another in surprise.

"Um." *Mark wasn't one to look a gift horse in the mouth.* "We've...uh...got some problems in Canada two big pipes down and they're complaining."

"And?" *Dar continued her sketching, cocking her head to one side.* "Can we fix them?"

"Not without digging up some fiber."

"Guess they'll have to wait then," *Dar replied.* "Tell our fiber contractor up there to call me with an estimate when he gets a chance."

Another round of puzzled looks circled the table.

"Uh...okay," *Mark said.* "That's all for me."

"Anyone else?" *Dar's gaze sharpened and she scoured the group with*

*ice blue eyes. "No? Good." She stood up, casually ripped off the top sheet
of her pad, and tossed it over to Kerry before she picked up her coffee cup
and headed for the door. "Budgets are due next week. Don't be late."*

*The door closed behind her, and everyone relaxed. "Whoo." Mark
wiped his brow in exaggerated relief. "Got off lucky this week!"*

*"Yeah. I thought she was going to roast your butt. How'd you do
that, Mark?"*

"Right time, right place. Caught her in a good mood."

*"The one time this year. Go figure." Charlene rolled her eyes. "What
caused that, I wonder? She get to fire someone this week?"*

*Kerry didn't hear any of it. Her eyes were on the casually tossed
sheet in her hands as she stared at the neatly shaded sketch in the center
of it. Her own image looked back at her, a very creditable rendering
outlined in a roughly shaped heart, with Dar's initials on the bottom.*

*"Maybe it was because she got to cancel that planning contract.
She's always hated that guy's guts."*

"Nah. I bet she denied that Sales request again."

Kerry very carefully opened her folder and put the loose sheet inside.

"Hey, Kerry."

Kerry looked up. "Yes?"

*"What's the deal? You know what's got big D in such a mellow
mood?"*

*"Yes. Matter of fact, I do." Kerry exhaled, biting off a grin as she
stood up and pushed in her chair. "See you guys tomorrow." She walked
out with a jaunty step, closing the door behind her.*

Kerry ruffled Dar's hair. "All this pretty scenery, and you have
to draw me?"

"All those pretty fish, and you have to take *my* picture?" Dar
countered drolly, wrapping one arm around Kerry's leg. "We'll be
at the dive site in an hour. You up for that, or do you want to give it
a miss and just go to dinner?"

Kerry leaned against the captain's chair and let her head rest on
Dar's shoulder. "Does my utter laziness show that badly?" she
complained. "I fell asleep twice down there in the chair. I don't
know what's wrong with me."

"We're on vacation. You're supposed to be lazy," Dar stated,
her eyes scanning the horizon again. "We can go straight in."

Kerry chewed her lower lip, then shook her head. "No. I'm
going to go make some coffee. I really want to see that old wreck,
Dar. You made it sound really cool." She straightened up and put
her hands on Dar's shoulders, massaging them lightly. "Let's go for
it."

Dar relaxed, enjoying the strong kneading. "You sure?"

"Positive." Kerry gave her a kiss on the back of the neck. "Take
me to the galleon, Cap'n Dar."

"Aye, aye, matey," Dar replied promptly. "Who knows? Maybe we'll find us some pieces of eight."

Kerry chuckled, resuming her position draped over Dar's shoulders. "With our luck, all we'll find is jellyfish or a cranky moray eel."

"Or a pile of tin cans."

They both laughed, a sound muffled by the spray of the boat's wake to either side of them.

KERRY ADJUSTED HER mask, holding her hand over it and her regulator as she stepped to the back of the boat and paused, then took a big step off and plunged into the water.

It was always a bit of a shock — going from the light and breezy air into the dense, blue water. She sucked in her first breath off her tank, feeling her body adjust as the familiar above-water weight of herself and her equipment moderated in the water's buoyancy.

While she waited for Dar, Kerry held on to the anchor rope with one hand and tightened the straps on her BC with the other. Her ears popped, and she gently pinched her nose closed and blew out a little, equalizing the pressure in her middle ears. Just then, the water was disrupted by Dar's entrance, her tall figure in a whirl of bubbles that cleared as she made her way over to where Kerry was waiting.

Dar's eyes flicked over her, Kerry noticed, checking her gear out of endearing habit. She endured the scrutiny, and in return she snugged Dar's tank a little tighter and pulled her hair out from under her BC. Dar winked at her and pointed down, and Kerry nodded.

They started down the anchor rope, descending slowly through the water toward the ocean floor sixty feet below. Diving deep was different than reef diving, Kerry had discovered. You encountered a lot of sensations you didn't get in the shallows, like thermoclines — layers of colder water that crept up and enveloped you unexpectedly as you descended, and the awareness of the sea pressure slowly growing against you. Breathing was just a little tougher, and the sense of being a part of the ocean was greater down there since you tended to look down more than up, and the surface was much further away.

They reached the bottom, a patch of soft, creamy white sand that had a few sparse stalks of seaweed poking up through it. Dar checked her dive computer, then motioned Kerry to follow her and started off.

Kerry obliged, staying to one side, out of the draft of Dar's fins. Her partner's leg kicks were a little slower than her own, but more powerful, and Kerry put some effort into keeping up against the light current. They approached a rock escarpment, and as they did, Dar half turned and made a motion near her mask, as though she were snapping a picture. Understanding that a photo op was about to be encountered, Kerry unclipped her camera and adjusted it, then swam after Dar as they crested the escarpment and could look over it.

Wow. Kerry's eyes widened and she quickly focused on the scene. Forty feet below them was a valley of white sand, and half buried in the sand were the reef-encrusted remains of an old wooden ship. The visibility was incredible, even at this distance, and she kept snapping as they descended toward it.

Schools of fish darted amongst what was left of half broken spars, and one entire side of the front of the ship was gone, leaving a huge hole big enough to admit the largest of the fish swimming around it. Kerry clipped her camera to her vest and just enjoyed the moment, stretching out her arms and releasing some of her buoyancy. She fell through the water in a glide very much like slow motion flying, twisting her body to change angles as she approached the wreck.

Bits of the ship were strewn across the bottom, where they'd scattered when she went down or in the storms afterward. Kerry spotted lumps of metal and she swam over to investigate, reaching out with a gloved hand to touch metal links half the length of her arm. *Anchor chain*, she realized.

She left the chain and headed toward the tilted, coral-encrusted deck, surprising a school of grouper that scattered when she drifted over them. A grumpy looking barracuda remained, however, glaring at her from between a hatch and a piece of collapsed spar. Kerry slowly lifted her camera and drifted down to eye level with the denizen of the deep, focusing on the fish's intimidating jaw. She snapped the shutter, then moved away, watching the 'cuda watch her as she entered a school of angel fish.

They poured over her and she rotated onto her back, looking up at them outlined against the surface like a far off mirror above her. Then she inhaled in surprise as a small squid jetted by, almost within her grasp, its tentacles trailing behind it and brushing her arm.

This sensation of floating in an alien world was still so amazing to her, even after a year. She twisted and looked around, finding Dar floating nearby, her hands clasped on her stomach and her fins crossed as she watched. Kerry grinned and gave her a thumbs up. Dar grinned back, then pointed toward the hole in the side of the ship and raised her eyebrows in question, visible even over her mask.

Ah! A new adventure. Kerry nodded, following readily as Dar, her underwater lamp clasped in one hand, led the way toward the interior of the boat. As they reached it, Dar turned on the light and edged inside, carefully examining the space before she proceeded, motioning Kerry after her.

Before she followed Dar inside the ship, Kerry did a quick check of her BC to make sure all her hoses were tucked into their holders and nothing was dangling. She pulled out her own light and turned it on, illuminating a ghostly world of algae-incrusted wood. The structure inside was heavily damaged, but her imagination was able to fill in the missing pieces.

She could envision the sailors who'd lived there, and the cargo they carried across the warm basin of the Caribbean. Long ago, this ship had held dreams. Now all that remained were ghosts, and the flash of odd eyes as her flashlight skimmed over the interior. For a fleeting moment, the thought occurred to her that the eyes belonged to those lost souls who went down with the ship, still there after all these years. Then a lobster scuttled by her, waving its claws menacingly, and Kerry jumped, almost cracking her head against the wood above her. *Okay*, she told her imagination sternly, *save it for topside*. With a shake of her head, she drifted down toward the bottom of the hold. Tiny fish swirled around her curiously and as her light reflected off something unidentifiable, she peered closer.

Dar approached, lifting her dive computer and displaying the time they had remaining. Kerry nodded, then pointed with her light, catching the flash again. They both swam closer, peering under the collapsed ribs and time deteriorated cases piled on the bottom, resting against what had once been the side of the ship.

Dar tried to edge closer on one side, but her bulk kept her from getting any nearer. Frowning, she motioned Kerry over, but even Kerry's smaller form was too wide to fit through with her tank on. Dar considered a moment, then she turned Kerry around and unclasped her tank from her BC, holding it in one hand and moving it to one side.

Kerry grasped the spar and pulled herself down, now just able to get between the wood and the side of the ship. She could see the shining something, and as she squiggled closer and her motion brushed a collection of algae off it, it resolved itself into a flat surface. She felt Dar's hand on her hip in a reassuring pat, and she edged a little further, now able to put her hand on whatever it was.

She just about panicked when an eel suddenly erupted from around the object, squirming right past her neck toward Dar and giving her a lash with its tail on the way out. A muffled burst of noise came from Kerry's throat, sending a stream of bubbles upward, but after a jerk behind her as Dar got out of the eel's way, the comforting pat returned.

Jesus. Kerry flexed her hand and reached a little further, getting her fingers around the surface and tugging. It resisted her pull but she persisted, and with the faintest crackling as she freed it from the growing coral, it came loose and she brought it closer to her mask.

It was a box. The shine had been the hammered metal insignia which covered it, though corrosion had mostly obscured the design. Kerry started backwards, glad for the grip on her belt that was guiding her out of the tight spot.   Dar peered over her shoulder as she reattached Kerry's tank, and they both gazed curiously at her find.

A buried treasure. Kerry blinked delightedly. Even if it was, as it appeared to be, just an old box, still—the box held history, and it fascinated her. She clutched it tightly as they made their way out of the hold and into the open sea, which seemed brilliantly lit by sunlight now that they were out of the darkness of the ship.

Dar gave her a big thumbs up and Kerry returned it, grinning around her regulator. They leisurely made their way back to the anchor line, carried now by the drift current going in the opposite direction. Kerry tucked her treasure away in her BC pocket as she gripped the line, ready to just watch the show around her as they slowly made their way out of one world, and back to their own.

"WHOO." KERRY RUFFLED her hair dry with a towel and padded across the deck. "Dar, that was awesome."

Dar looked up from the basin, at the bottom of which rested their little prize. She studied Kerry's face, a smile on her own responding to the honest delight she saw there. "Yeah, it was, wasn't it?"

Kerry applied the towel to her lover's body, drying the droplets of seawater off it. "That eel scared the poo out of me, though. Did it hit you on its way out?"

"Right in the mask, yeah." Dar chuckled. "Bounced off me and just kept going. He was a big one." She glanced up as the sound of far off engines disturbed the otherwise peaceful air, and watched as a small tender approached, slowing when they came even, very obviously giving them the once over.

Kerry peered over Dar's shoulder. "What's that all about?" she queried. "We've got the dive flag out. Is there a problem with that here?"

"Nah." Dar frowned. "There's a thousand old wrecks like this around these islands. That's just an old island freighter. Some of the historic wrecks have no-dive zones, but not this area."

"So what's their problem?" The small boat circled them lazily, then after a moment, roared off.

Dar watched the small boat retreat into the distance. "Beats me." She shrugged. "Maybe they're not used to people using a 56 foot Bertram as a dive platform." She finished covering the seawater-filled water well that held the box they'd brought up. "Let's leave that in there until I figure out how to take it out of the water and not have it fall to bits on us."

"Rats." Kerry's arms circled from behind and gave Dar a squeeze. "I wanted to open it up and see inside." She inspected the basin. "I know it's nothing much, just an old cigar box or something, but—"

Dar turned around and returned the hug, giving Kerry's neck a friendly scratch. "I think we might need some oil first...to keep the wood from drying out. Tomorrow, okay?"

"Mm." Kerry licked a few remaining drops of water off Dar's throat. "Okay." She released her lover, but took her hand and led her over to the cooler. "Share an iced tea with me?"

"Sure." Dar waited while Kerry opened the bottle and took a swig, then accepted it and sucked down a mouthful herself. She swished the tea around before she swallowed it, clearing the last taste of saltwater and rubber from the dive. "All right, how about we pull up anchor and go get us some conch?"

Kerry stifled her mild amusement over the casual speech, wondering if Dar knew how much she sounded like her father sometimes. In the office, it almost never showed. There, Dar's vocalizations—when they weren't wall-rattling yells—were crisp and sharply professional. Only when they were alone and her lover was relaxed did her Southern upbringing tend to slip in. "Sounds great to me, Dixiecup," Kerry teased. "I'll go pull in the buoy."

Dar captured her with one long arm and pinned her up against the bulkhead. "You making fun of my accent, you little Yankee?"

"Nope." Kerry ran her hands over Dar's still damp body. "I love your accent. I wish you'd let it out more often."

One of Dar's eyebrows lifted expressively.

"I so want to hear you tell Jose to 'get yer damn ass outta mah office.'" Kerry giggled. "Yah damn little pansy assed pissant."

Dar burst into laughter. "He'd piss in his pants."

Kerry nodded cheerfully. "Exactly!"

Dar's chuckles wound down, and she quieted. "It's funny...you liking my redneck side."

"Why?"

She shrugged. "It just is. To me, anyway. I worked so hard to cover all that up," Dar said. "I remember sitting in a management meeting once, after I'd made regional director, and listening to three of the other people there trash one of the Southern project managers." She exhaled. "Called him a hick and a lowlife redneck."

Kerry sighed. "They make fun of everyone, Dar."

Dar nodded. "I know. But this was different, because it might as well have been me they were talking about, only the other guy wasn't bothering to pretend." She gazed thoughtfully over Kerry's shoulder.

"Mm." Kerry was slowly rubbing Dar's back, easing the tension she felt there. "What did you do?" she asked softly.

"Called them jackasses and told them to go find some class before the company had to buy it for them," Dar admitted.

"That's my Dar." Kerry leaned her head against Dar's collarbone, soft chuckles emerging from her throat.

"Yeah, well." Dar had to smile herself. "After that, they never did say anything about rednecks in any meeting *I* was in."

No. Kerry hugged her frequently curmudgeonly boss. "I bet they didn't." *Just like no one says anything about you... in any meeting I'm in. Damn right.*

Chapter
Five

THE SMALL ISLAND they pulled into was definitely laid back. As they approached, Kerry peered over the railing with interest, noting the gorgeous white beach and the cluster of small, sun bleached buildings behind the spare, patched together docks. "Now, Kerrison," she murmured to herself, "we're not doing the Waldorf here."

Of course, she wasn't dressed for the Waldorf, anyhow. Kerry glanced down at her stonewashed, white short overalls and sandals, her lips twitching as she imagined her family's reaction to the worn fabric and the cutoff, sleeveless gray sweatshirt she wore under it. "I'm just a proper marine vagabond, I am."

Dar skillfully navigated the Bertram into a slot at the end of the dock. Kerry tossed the bow rope to the young boy who ran up to greet them, then took the stern rope and jumped onto the wooden surface, pulled the line taut around the rusted cleat, and tied it off. "Thanks." She smiled at the boy, who shyly smiled back at her. He had dark skin, and brown shaggy hair and eyes, and he was dressed in a pair of denim shorts and nothing else.

His eyes went past her and widened a little. Kerry turned her head to see Dar leaping off the boat, a broad grin on her face. "Hey, Rufus," she said, pausing and sticking her hands into her pockets. "What do you think?"

"Wow!" the boy replied. "Killer boat, Dar!" His eyes roved over the vessel. "C'n I ride it?"

Dar chuckled. "Later, yeah." She put a hand on Kerry's shoulder. "This is my friend Kerry. Kerry, this is Rufus."

Rufus studied Kerry warily. "Hi."

Kerry held a hand out. "Hi, Rufus. Nice to meet you." She waited for the boy's hesitant handclasp, and then returned it gently.

Rufus backed off a step. "I'll go tell dada you're here, Dar," he said, and then he turned and ran off, bare feet almost soundless on the wood.

Dar exhaled as she watched him go. "I'm looking forward to

seeing his father," she said, guiding Kerry up the dock. "He was in the service with Dad."

"Ah!" Kerry smiled. "His friends are always interesting people."

"Mm," Dar agreed. "He doesn't know." Her eyes flicked to Kerry's face. "About my father being alive. There're no phones out here. I think he keeps it that way on purpose. Dad was going to make a run out here, but I told him we were stopping, and that I'd pass the news."

Kerry read several levels of meaning in her lover's words. "Hm." She studied the small cluster of weatherworn buildings. "I'm looking forward to meeting him, then. He lives here?"

"He runs the joint we're having dinner at," Dar said. "After he got discharged on a medical, he came out here and set up this place. He and his partner—they do all the cooking and brew their own beer."

Kerry's ears perked up. "Partner?" she queried. "Partner, like you and me partner?"

Dar nodded.

"Hmm."

"They adopted Rufus. He showed up one day on a little raft and just refused to leave."

Kerry absorbed all that as they walked off the dock and onto a shell-strewn path. As they approached the buildings, a figure came out onto the porch of the largest one, placed hands on the porch railing and leaned on it.

"Look at what that damn wind blew in, wouldja?"

The man behind the railing was tall and had a chunky build, but that's not what Kerry noticed. He was also missing a leg. Below his right knee, swathed in an overlarge pair of dark green khaki shorts, extended a metal frame. On the end of the frame was a well-worn shoe. He had thick, silvered brown, curly hair and a bushy beard, and his skin was criss-crossed with thin but noticeable scars.

Dar lifted a hand. "Howdy, Charlie."

The man limped down the wide, wooden steps and came to meet them, pulling Dar into an enthusiastic hug. "Damn, it's been over a year, Dar. Where've ya been?"

Dar released him. "Here and there," she replied. "Charlie, this is Kerrison Stuart." Her arm draped over Kerry's shoulders. "My chosen one."

The man turned to study Kerry, who was hard pressed to hide her bemused surprise at Dar's new term for her. "Ahhh, so that's where you been, huh?" He held out a hand. "Ms. Stuart, it's an honor and a pleasure."

"Mine too." Kerry rose to the occasion, clasping his hand firmly. "I hear you make some mean conch chowder."

Charlie laughed, clapping Dar on the shoulder and gesturing toward the larger building. "C'mon. Let's go siddown and let me prove out my reputation. We got some catching up to do." He limped ahead of them, obviously used to his disability to the point where it didn't appreciably hamper him.

Kerry and Dar followed after him, Dar with her arm still draped over Kerry's neck.

"Chosen one?" Kerry inquired softly, giving her lover a curious look.

Dar's jaw bunched, and she glanced down at the ground before she snuck a look at Kerry's face. "I'll explain later," she murmured as they reached the steps. "It's a compliment."

"Duh." Kerry bumped Dar's hip with her own as they walked up the stairs. "Looks like we'll have lots of interesting things to talk about tonight."

"Hm." Dar held the door open and they went inside.

KERRY GLANCED AROUND curiously at the inside of the little shack. They were seated at one of six tables, all made of hand worked driftwood. The room wasn't much bigger than her bedroom at the condo, though at the rear, swinging doors led into the kitchen. Though the large, square windows on three sides of the room let in the glow of sunset and a cool breeze, the place was lighted by oil lamps hanging on the walls and sitting on the tables.

Two other tables were occupied, one by two scruffy-looking men in beachcomber outfits, and the other by a handsome islander and his female companion, who — to all appearances — were on their honeymoon.

"Smells great in here," Kerry commented, sniffing appreciatively at the spicy, delicious scents coming from the kitchen.

A quirky grin twisted Dar's lips. "Not too rustic for you?"

"Dar," Kerry frowned, glancing down at herself, "did I forget to rip the alligator off my shirt pocket or something today?"

Dar fingered the woven rope salt and pepper holder. "Just kidding."

"No, that's the second time you brought this up." Kerry shook her head. "Are you really that sensitive about dragging a Midwestern WASP around with you?" She turned her head and regarded Dar seriously, finding soft, round blue eyes gazing back at her. "Honey?" She put a hand on Dar's in pure reflex.

After a moment, Dar cleared her throat with a touch of sheepishness, and propped her chin on her fist. "Yeah, I really am that sensitive," she admitted quietly. "Sorry."

Kerry relaxed a little, stroking Dar's fingers with her own. "I'll just have to work on that, then." She glanced up as Charlie limped over, almost jumping up to help him as he navigated a tray toward them.

"Naw, just siddown, there, little lady." Charlie managed to get the tray on the table without spilling a thing. "Go figure. Bud's over on the big island, right when I need 'im." He set a large bowl of steaming, spicy scented, almost stew-like soup in front of each of them. "There ya go."

"Wow." Kerry blinked at the mass of rich broth and seafood. "This looks great."

Charlie grinned at her. "Ya got good taste, but I knew that— seeing as you picked old Dar here. Get you anything else for now?"

Kerry looked up at him. "The biggest mug of beer you have. I think I'll need it."

An even bigger grin split his face. "You got it. Dar, same for you?"

Dar nodded vigorously.

"All right. I'll get these here folks taken care of, then we can sit down and catch up... how's that?" Charlie picked up his tray.

"Sounds great," Dar replied. "Thanks, Charlie."

He winked at them, then limped back toward the kitchen, disappearing behind the two swinging doors.

Kerry waited a few moments, watching Dar out of the corner of her eye. The dark haired woman was fiddling with her spoon, a pucker visible above her eyebrows. "Dar?"

"Hm?"

A tumble of words suddenly filled Kerry's mouth and she let them out, almost without thinking. "You want to talk about it?"

Dar cocked her head, gazing at Kerry curiously for several heartbeats, then she put her spoon into her chowder and stirred it. "It's...um..." She hesitated as Charlie returned and put two huge tankards with nice, foamy heads down in front of them. "Thanks."

Kerry grinned in appreciation. "Ditto."

Charlie chuckled, and then headed off toward the next customers.

Kerry took a sip of her beer. It was rich, with a nutty taste— smooth, and very, very potent. "Ooh." She licked her lips. "This could be dangerous."

"It is." Dar took a sip of her own brew, then a second, longer one before she set the mug down. "The last time I was here, I got in trouble with it." She studied the tankard. "Charlie and my father were good friends."

Kerry accepted the sudden change of subject with grace. She made an encouraging noise. "Mmhm."

"But Dad and Bud never got along," Dar continued with a sigh. "Bud hated him, and it took me a long time to figure out why." She glanced at Kerry. "The last time I was here, he told me that he was glad Dad was gone."

Kerry stopped dead in mid-motion. She put her mug down and looked around the place. "What the hell are we doing here, then?" she asked with a sputter. "That guy's lucky he's not around. I'd kick his ass. For that matter, why didn't you?"

Dar grinned wryly. "He was drunk, I was halfway there, and he ended up apologizing for being a jackass," she said. "He told me then that he'd always been convinced that Dad was after Charlie."

"Wait." Kerry covered her eyes. "Wait...wait...wait. He thought your father..." She peeked between her fingers. "Your father, Andrew Roberts, the sailor man, the most hetero male I think I've ever known, was chasing his partner?"

Dar nodded. "Yeah."

A clue waddled inside the door and pecked Kerry on the foot. "So you're nervous about telling them he's alive."

Dar nodded again. "Yeah." She exhaled, scrubbing her face with one hand. "Isn't that pathetic? I can tell the president of Exxon to tap-dance on his boardroom table, but I get nerves doing this."

"Relax." Kerry felt a sense of relief at unknotting Dar's mood. "We'll get through it... after we get through this really great smelling soup and this awesome beer." She patted Dar's knee under the table. "I'm sure it'll be okay."

"Yeah." Dar visibly unwound, taking a spoonful of the chowder. She chewed it, swallowed, then reached over and brushed her knuckles against Kerry's cheek. "Thanks. I know I'm acting a little off tonight."

"You're never off," Kerry reassured her, then sampled some of the chowder. "Oh, wow! This is awesome." Spicy, it was full of seafood, from shrimp to scallops to its namesake conch. "You better eat yours, before I do."

Dar stifled a grin, resting her chin against her fist as she consumed her soup.

IT WAS FULL dark out before Charlie finished taking care of the five other groups of patrons who came in. He dusted his hands on his shirt and limped over to their table, settling down in a chair across from Dar. "Well, Dar, how've you been?" he asked.

"All right," Dar drawled softly. "You?"

The grizzled man nodded. "Life's been good," he said. "Quiet out here, but the place has a good rep; we make out all right." His eyes flicked around the room. "Bud's doin' okay. He's putting on some weight, but he's finally chilled out and decided he likes the life out here."

"Glad to hear that." Dar could feel a light buzz from the beer, and the meal—a large plate of fresh fish after the chowder with a whole loaf of fragrant herb bread—was making her sleepy.

Kerry was finishing off her tankard, the light from the oil lamp casting her light green eyes in shades of amber. She was watching them quietly, her weight shifting slightly to bring her knee into contact with Dar's as she listened to the conversation.

"What about you?" Charlie asked. "Aside from the obvious." He turned a grin on Kerry. "Tell me about your chosen one here."

"What would you like to know?" Kerry asked with a charming smile. "I work in the same business as Dar does...I'm from Michigan...I love your cooking and your beer..."

Charlie chuckled delightedly. "Can't ask for better than that," he said. "So you do that computer stuff, huh? That where you two met?"

"More or less, yes," Kerry agreed. "We've been together over a year."

"I knew you'd find a good one." He turned his eyes to Dar. "I said you would, didn't I?"

"You did," Dar admitted. "Though," she waggled her hand, "I'm not sure which one of us found the other." She took a deep breath and decided to just get it over with. It was late, and she was tired. "A lot of things changed for me this last year."

"Yeah?" Charlie leaned on his elbows, watching her.

Dar nodded, then lifted her head and met his gaze squarely. "My father's alive," she stated softly. "He came home." She felt warmth close around her knee as Kerry's fingers tightened comfortingly.

Charlie simply stared blankly at them for the longest time, then he slowly let out a breath and looked away. "Well, damn," he whispered. "Ain't that something." His hands were shaking visibly as he picked up the glass he'd brought with him.

"It was," Dar agreed. "He...just contacted me one day...and, um..." She shook her head. "He'd been hurt pretty badly, but they patched him up, and there he was."

Charlie nodded faintly. "He okay?"

Kerry's ears picked up.

"Yeah." Dar smiled. "He retired from the service. He and my mother got a boat, if you can believe that, and they're living on it. Having the time of their lives." She sipped at the remainder of her beer. "He was planning a trip out here in a couple months, but I told him I was swinging by, so I'd let you know."

Charlie absorbed all that, a shuffle of emotions flickering across his face. "Damn, Dar," he finally said, "what a kickass thing to happen. That's great." A smile appeared, trembling only at the edges. "You must have been some kind of stoked."

Dar's face relaxed into a rare, broad grin. "Stoked." She

laughed softly. "Yeah."

"Wow." Charlie collected himself. "I hardly know what to say." His eyes went to Kerry. "Dar's dad is a heck of a guy."

Kerry draped an arm over Dar's shoulders. "I know. He adopted me," she said. "I love both of my parents-in-law very much."

The kitchen doors creaked open. Charlie turned as Rufus poked his head shyly inside. "Hey, Rufie, c'mon over here."

The boy obeyed, coming over and resting his hands on the table. Charlie put his arm around him. "We adopted Rufie here," he said. "He's learning how to run the kitchen, right, Rufie?"

"Yep." Rufus grinned. "Dar's gonna gimme a ride on her boat, dada."

"Is she now?" Charlie asked. "Think she'd give me one, too?" He glanced at Dar. "You in a rush out of here?"

"Nah," Dar replied easily. "We're just planning on bumming around, doing some diving. Kerry and I needed some time off."

"Great." Charlie seemed to have recovered his spirits completely. "Bud's due back tomorrow; I know he'd love to see you," he said. "You need a bunk for the night?"

Dar shook her head. "We're fine on the boat. You'll have to let me know what dock power costs. No BS, Charlie. I can afford it."

He chuckled. "So you said the last time." He stood up. "Great. We'll see ya tomorrow, then. I gotta get this place cleaned up, and get this little pup to bed."

"Bye." Rufus waved at Kerry. "Nice t'meet you."

"Nice to meet you too, Rufus," Kerry replied. "See you tomorrow."

"Bye, Dar."

"Night, Rufus," Dar said, watching as the two disappeared into the kitchen, leaving her and Kerry alone in the room. With a sigh, Dar leaned her head against Kerry's. "I'm trashed."

"Me too," Kerry murmured. She decided to put off discussing the odd evening until after a good night's sleep. "You interested in a nice, soft bed?"

"That means I have to get up and walk, huh?"

"I could try carrying you."

Dar stood and pulled Kerry up with her. They left the tiny restaurant and walked down the path, now lit only by the moonlight that poured up from the beach. It was incredibly quiet, only the surf sounds breaking the night, and the faint whispers of the leaves around them rustling in the breeze.

Kerry put her arm around Dar's waist and leaned her head against her shoulder as they walked. She tried to think about what she'd heard, but the two tankards of very good beer thwarted her best efforts, and she finally had to be content to simply concentrate on getting back to the boat. "Urmph." She stifled a yawn as they stepped off the dock and onto their deck.

Dar opened the door to the cabin and they went inside. Kerry was already shucking her overalls as she trudged into the bedroom. She pulled off her cutoff sweatshirt and stood for a moment, swaying gently. Dar took her by the shoulders, guided her to the bed, and pulled down the light blankets. Kerry crawled gratefully into its soft confines and waited until Dar slid in behind her, the warmth of her bare skin brushing against Kerry's in a very pleasant way.

Thoughts buzzed like bees through her mind, but she shooed them away as she tangled her arms and legs with Dar's and snuggled close to her, leaving the problems for another day.

Chapter
Six

DAR LET HER eyes drift open as the sunlight poked its way inside the hatch, dusting the bed with a square of buttery warmth. She remained still for a while, watching Kerry sleep curled up against her, the blonde woman's arm wrapped around Dar's waist.

Kerry has always been that way, Dar reflected idly. Even when they'd barely known each other, she'd noticed Kerry's almost unconscious instinct for close contact—a hand on the back or the shoulder, making a connection with her that seemed as natural to her as breathing.

Dar had at first been bemused at that. She never could stand anyone putting their paws on her. Then she'd suddenly realized one day, after Kerry had put both hands on her shoulders as she'd stepped around behind her in a meeting, that far from objecting to it, her body was craving the touch.

Dar gazed wryly at the roof of the cabin. *Shoulda been your first clue, bucket head.*

Kerry shifted, rolling onto her other side and releasing Dar for the moment. Since she was awake anyway, Dar decided to get up and shake out the cobwebs, and maybe surprise her lover with breakfast. She carefully slid out of bed and tucked the covers in around the blonde's sleeping body, then ambled into the corridor and down to the head.

A quick scrub of her face with cold water and an experiment with Kerry's new sparkly toothpaste later, Dar emerged from the bathroom in her swimsuit, pulling her hair back and fastening it with a bit of elastic as she walked.

The boat was moving gently and she rocked with it, making her way out onto the back deck and into the sun. It was very quiet on the dock, and they were still the only boat there. The beach was empty of everything except for a few gulls, and the water around her was still, with only a few ripples and pops to indicate the presence of the marine life below the surface.

Beautiful morning. Dar hitched herself up on the stern railing and hooked her feet under the bottom rung. She leaned back and stretched her body out over the water, holding the position until she felt her spine pop gently into place. Then she extended her arms out and did a few slow rotations, giving her entire body a good warm up.

Satisfied, she pulled herself upright, then just for fun did a couple of sets of sit ups before she unhooked her legs and hopped off the railing. Cautiously, she extended her arms and checked her range of motion, pleased when her injured shoulder responded with only a mild grumpiness, allowing her to swing her arm in almost a complete circle.

Ah. Dar chuckled happily to herself. The diving and relaxing seemed to be doing the trick. With a contented grunt, she checked the boat's lines and rigging, then went back inside and made her way to the galley. She filled the water pot and put it on the burner, then examined her choices for breakfast. *Ah.* She plucked a box from the cabinet and set it down, then turned to get a bowl.

Halfway around, she stopped, feeling a sudden prickle up her spine. A hoarse cry sent her bolting for the bedroom. She shouldered the door open to find Kerry thrashing, apparently caught in a nightmare, her hands clenching into fists in the sheets.

"Ker!" Dar quickly caught hold of her and shook her gently. "Kerry!"

"N...no! *No! No!*" Kerry woke up abruptly with a gasp, her eyes snapping open wide. She looked around wildly, stopping when her eyes met Dar's. "Oh," she exhaled, still breathing hard. "Dar."

Dar rubbed her shoulder. "Easy."

Kerry lifted a shaking hand to her head. "Shit."

"You okay?" Dar asked quietly.

"Yeah. I'm fine," Kerry replied, trying to collect herself. "I'm okay."

Kerry was, Dar had long ago decided, really good at a lot of things. Lying wasn't one of them. She slid under the covers and folded Kerry into her arms, pulling her close in an attempt to comfort her. For a moment, she thought the effort was going to fail, then Kerry's body relaxed and slumped against hers as Kerry buried her face in Dar's shoulder. "Shh." Dar stroked her disordered hair. "It's okay. I've got you."

"I hate nightmares," Kerry whispered.

"I don't think anyone likes them, sweetheart," Dar said. "I know I don't." She rocked Kerry a little, unsettled by the spate of bad dreams her partner had suffered from ever since they'd gotten back from Michigan. The worst of the recurrent nightmares was of Kerry watching her father die in the hospital, and Dar found herself wondering how long it would take for that horror to fade. "Was it the same dream?"

"Yeah." Kerry lifted her head and rested her cheek against

Dar's arm. "Bah." Her voice had lost its hoarseness, though, and seemed more normal in tone. "What a way to wake up."

Dar stroked her cheek. She could see the sparkling remains of tears caught in Kerry's lashes, but her expression had relaxed and she appeared much calmer. "And here I thought I'd let you get a little extra sleep. Shoulda woke you up and made you go do calisthenics with me."

"Mm. Yeah," Kerry agreed with a wry smile. "Or at least let me watch." She poked Dar in the belly, a reassuringly playful action. "I don't wake up like this when we wake up together."

No, Dar realized. *That's true.* "I'll keep it in mind next time." She gave Kerry a hug. "Interest you in some breakfast?"

A green eyeball peeked up at her. "You cooking?"

"Yep," Dar said. "Unless you think that might seem like too much of another nightmare."

Kerry smiled wanly. "As long as it comes with some aspirin. I've got a headache that would knock down an AS400 at a hundred paces."

Dar slid her hands up to clasp the back of Kerry's neck, kneading it gently. Kerry slumped against her again and her eyes closed as Dar carefully probed the tense muscles she found under her fingertips. "Hang on." She eased a knot at the base of her lover's skull and felt her vertebra shift. "Hm."

"What's the verdict, Dr. Dar?" Kerry asked.

Dar kissed her on the head. "Dr. Dar says you get to spend the entire day lazing around with me and relaxing."

"Ooh." Kerry exhaled. "That sounds like great medicine."

Dar gave her a last rub and then got up from the bed. "I've got some water on. C'mon."

Kerry willingly scrambled out from under the covers and followed her like a puppy, one finger hooked in the back of Dar's swimsuit. She released her partner as they came even with the bathroom. "Let me just put something on, and wash the sleep out of my eyes."

Dar kept going, ducking behind the counter and reaching for the rattling water pot. "Hush." She scowled at it as she picked it up and poured the boiling water into the cups she had ready. She left the grounds to steep while she got out two bowls, then filled one from the box she'd gotten down earlier. She then removed some strawberries from the small refrigerator and set to work cutting them into slices, which she let fall on top of the cereal. She had finished several when Kerry appeared, her hair damp and her body clad in a T-shirt.

Kerry went over and leaned on the counter, resting her cheek against Dar's upper arm. "Thank you for cooking my Wheaties, honey."

Dar laughed silently.

"You made them just the way I like them." Kerry plucked a flake from the bowl and put it into her mouth, chewing it. "Just right."

"You're welcome," Dar drawled. "Want to go outside?"

"Sure." Kerry turned and opened the refrigerator, removing a yogurt and adding it to the tray Dar had sitting on the counter. She put the two cups of coffee and some milk on it as well, then stepped back as Dar finished pouring her own breakfast into a bowl and picked up the tray.

She followed Dar onto the back deck, smiling a bit as the cool sea air blew against her. She waited for Dar to put the tray down on the little table, then she took her usual left hand seat and reached for her coffee. A few sips of the brew seemed to ease her headache, and she leaned back, propping one bare foot up against the footrest and gazing off toward the horizon.

The nightmare had shaken her. Kerry put down her cup and picked up her bowl, pouring some milk over the flakes and patting them down with her spoon. She took a mouthful and chewed, one ear cocked to catch the louder crunching as Dar munched on her favorite Frosted Flakes.

Watching her father die had been bad enough. But in her dream, after she relived that again, and again, and again, her father's stiffened figure would be replaced with Dar's, and the feeling of utter helplessness and the shock of loss drove her to wake screaming every time.

Kerry forced herself to swallow past the sudden lump in her throat.

"Ker?"

How does she know? Kerry glanced to her right. "Hm?"

Dar was watching her with an expression of concern. "You okay?"

C'mon, Kerrison, get yourself together and let it go. It's just a damn dream. "Yeah." She smiled at Dar, trying to convey her gratitude without saying it.

Apparently receiving the message, Dar's face relaxed and her eyes gentled.

"So." Kerry firmly shifted her focus. "Tell me more about Charlie and Bud." She dug into her cereal again. "And Dad."

"Mmph." Dar swallowed a mouthful of flakes. "Long story."

"My favorite kind," Kerry said.

"They were in a special training class together," Dar said between bites. "Dad says from the very start, Bud was always confronting him, challenging him, while Charlie was just the opposite."

"Uh huh."

"So, after they graduated, the three of them plus about six other guys were assigned to a special ops unit, and they shipped out for six months," Dar went on. "Dad said Charlie was a great guy, real friendly, all right to hang out with, but Bud was your typical antisocial, military hardass."

"I see."

"They were...somewhere...and ended up under fire," Dar said. "I don't really know what happened, and I'm not sure I want to ask Dad, but they walked into a mine, I guess. They lost two guys and Dad ended up carrying Charlie out."

"Oh."

"After that, Charlie got discharged, and a month later, Bud didn't re-up. They hung out around the guys at the base, though, and it came out that they were lovers."

"Ah." Kerry finished her cereal and started on her yogurt.

"So then, Bud accused my Dad of chasing after his partner. He somehow was convinced that the only reason Dad got Charlie out of that firefight was because he wanted to impress him and get between the two of them." She shook her head. "Bud's a couple chips short of a motherboard, if you ask me."

"No." Kerry disagreed mildly. "He's just not facing the real picture." She swallowed a mouthful of the plain dairy and pointed the spoon at her partner. "He doesn't want to think about the fact that the guy he's in love with is head over heels in love with your father."

Dar stopped eating, the spoon still in her mouth. She turned round, almost comical eyes on her partner.

"Don't tell me you didn't know that," Kerry spluttered. "C'mon, Dar!"

Dar removed the spoon. "Kerry, it took a medical exam for me to figure out I had a crush on you. Gimme a break, okay?"

Suppressing a smile, Kerry went back to her cereal as she watched Dar process out of the corner of her eye.

"Son of a biscuit."

"You realize what a can of worms we just opened, right?"

"Son of a biscuit."

KERRY SIPPED FROM the straw in her glass of iced tea, her eyes scanning over the book in her lap. She and Dar had just finished lunch, and true to her word, Dar was sprawled in the chair next to her, doing nothing more than beautifully taking up space, her body splashed with sunlight.

Her mystery novel was interesting, but from time to time Kerry found herself sneaking looks at her companion. Dar's bathing suit clung to her body and outlined its sculpted lines, which held a hint of dynamic motion despite the light doze Dar was in.

She was glad to see the bruising had faded around Dar's shoulder, leaving only a faint discoloration that was hardly visible against her tan. Kerry had also noticed that despite her stubborn refusal to go to her prescribed therapy sessions, Dar had mostly stopped favoring the injured arm. *Lucky thing.*

Her own dislocated shoulder had taken weeks of physical therapy to ease, and she was still being careful of it when she attacked the climbing wall at the gym. Kerry shook her head in wry bemusement and returned her attention to her medieval mystery. She stretched out her bare legs and crossed them at the ankles, then looked up from her book as the sound of a boat engine broke the peaceful silence.

A small tender was coming around the corner of the island. Kerry tipped her sunglasses down and squinted, wondering if it was the same boat that had passed them by the day before. It was about the same size, but as yet it was too far away for her to tell for certain. It was coming closer, though, and by its arc Kerry suspected its destination was the dock. She set her book down and reached over to close her fingers around Dar's wrist.

"Hm?" Dar stirred, turning her head towards Kerry. "What's up?"

Kerry pointed. "Company."

Dar pulled off her sunglasses, revealing sharp blue eyes that scanned the newcomer intently, all trace of sleep gone. "Ah," she murmured. "Our curious friends."

"It *is* them? You can tell?"

Dar nodded. "Same ID numbers on the bow."

Kerry squinted, then turned and looked at Dar in amazement. "You can read those?"

Her partner gave another nod and a shrug. "Yeah. It's..." Dar made a vague motion near her face, "close up stuff I have a problem with." She paused. "Sometimes."

Kerry wasn't sure if she should be more shocked by the boat, or by Dar's frank admission of her vision problems. She finally decided to deal with the boat first. "They're coming here."

"Looks like it."

"It could just be coincidence," Kerry reasoned. "Maybe they heard about the food."

"Could be," Dar agreed, settling her glasses back onto her nose and resuming her relaxed posture. "Guess we'll find out."

Kerry felt a prickle of apprehension, unsure of what they might be getting into. She watched the boat come nearer and nearer, then slow as it prepared to dock several slips away from them. It occurred to her that both she and Dar were far out of their usual world, and if real trouble found them, it might not be as easy to deal with as their usual day-to-day crises were. Dar, however, seemed to be completely at ease, so Kerry leaned back in her chair and opened her book, found her spot and continued to read.

The small boat docked and four people got off, three men and a woman. Two of the men continued up the docks toward the buildings, but the third man and the woman headed toward the *Dixieland Yankee.* Kerry kept her head down, but watched them from behind her sunglasses as they approached, evaluating them.

They were dressed in sharply pressed shirts and Docker shorts, with conspicuous gold at their throats and wrists, and Kerry got an immediate impression of sophistication and money. The woman had blonde hair a few shades darker than her own, pulled back in a neat tail that exposed an elegantly made up face with high cheekbones. Carrying herself with a sense of aggressive self-possession, she was the one who was leading the way toward the boat.

The man behind her was tall, dark haired, and skinny to the point of emaciation. He had a high forehead, and he was carrying an over-the-shoulder briefcase with a satellite cell phone clipped to it.

Maybe they just want to say hello, Kerry reasoned. *Maybe they just like the boat. Maybe —*

"Ahoy, there," the woman addressed them. "Excuse me."

Sounds about as friendly as an auditor with hemorrhoids. Kerry closed her book and looked over, aware of Dar's watchful alertness next to her. "Hi," she replied. "Something we can do for you?"

The woman put her hands on her slim hips and regarded Kerry. "We're looking for some information. Maybe you could help us?"

Hm. "Sure, if we can. Would you like to come aboard?" Kerry politely replied.

They stepped onto the railing, then down onto the deck and approached the two of them. Kerry watched their eyes flick to Dar, who was to all appearances blissfully asleep. The woman returned her attention to Kerry.

"My name is Christen Mayberry," the woman stated. "This is my associate, Juan Carlos." She paused, giving Kerry an inquiring look.

"Kerry." A sudden impulse toward reticence took hold. "Roberts." Her ears heard the faint snort of surprise from Dar, and she smiled. "Nice to meet you."

Christen cleared her throat. "I represent a salvage consortium. We've contracted to do some research and location work in this area. We saw you out by the straits yesterday, and I was wondering what your interest here is."

Kerry sorted through that and felt a sense of relief. "Nothing, actually." She gave the woman a reassuring smile. "We're just on vacation."

"And you picked that spot at random?" the man interjected.

"No." Dar's low voice broke in. "I picked the spot because it's got a great view and nice fish." She lifted a hand and tipped her glasses down, exposing her eyes, which studied their visitors.

"No offense." Juan Carlos smiled at her. "See anything good?"

"Moray eel as tall as I am," Dar drawled softly. "And a lot of clowns."

"Well, that's great then." Christen's attitude suddenly shifted. "You going to be around long? Maybe we can do dinner. We're new around here and we don't know many people." She leaned against the back railing. "The locals are pretty tough nuts to crack."

Kerry and Dar exchanged quick glances. "We'll be around for a few days, yes," Kerry replied. "I'm sure we can get together."

"Great." Christen smiled. "Nice to meet you, Kerry." Her eyes shifted to Dar questioningly.

"This is my partner, Dar," Kerry supplied. "Nice to meet you, too."

"We will be seeing you around, I'm sure," Juan said. "This is a lovely boat you have."

"Thanks," Dar replied. "What's your consortium salvaging? I didn't think there was anything around here worth going after."

Juan looked at Christen. "It's a private commission," Christen said. "We can't really discuss it." She took Juan's elbow. "We'll drop by later to set a date for dinner. Let's go, Juan." Christen and Juan turned and jumped off the boat, then strolled down the dock together.

Dar and Kerry watched them go, and then looked at each other. "What the heck was that all about?" Kerry asked.

"I don't know." Dar sat up and rested her elbows on her knees, studying Kerry. She gave a half grin. "What was that name change all about?"

Kerry nibbled her lower lip.

"I'm not objecting," Dar said. "Just a little surprised."

Kerry crossed one ankle over her knee and rubbed a bit of sand off her skin. "You know," she finally said, "I'm not really sure why I did that." Her head tilted to one side, and she peered at Dar with sheepish honesty. "Let me think about it for a while."

"Sure." Dar nodded. "As for our visitors... I don't know what their game is, but now I'm wishing we'd brought the laptops with us."

"To find out who they are?"

"Yeah."

Kerry drummed her fingers on arm of the chair. "Well, I guess we'll just have to ferret that out the old fashioned way," she said. "You don't think they're going to be a problem, do you?"

"Nah." Dar shook her head. "Just some gold diggers. We might not hear from them again, now that they know we're not after whatever they're looking for." Dar put her glasses back on and resumed her comfortable position.

"That's true." Kerry tucked her knees up under her chin and wrapped her arms around them, gazing out at the sea thoughtfully. "They were a little weird, though."

"Mm."

"Preppy," Kerry added. "I don't know, Dar. They just didn't seem like sea types. You know what I mean."

Dar opened one eye. "Maybe they're the business end," she suggested. "The money people."

Kerry pursed her lips. "I just didn't like them."

"Well," Dar captured her hand and squeezed it, "I've always trusted your people judgment," she said. "Why don't we —"

"Hey, Dar!"

Dar sat up as they heard footsteps approaching rapidly. Rufus was running down the docks toward them. "Hey," Dar greeted.

He stopped short of the boat. "C'n I come on board?"

Dar waved him over. "Sure."

The boy grinned and scrambled onto the boat, looking around wide-eyed as he walked across the stern deck. "Wow."

"Nice, huh?" Dar stood up. "Want to see inside?"

"Sure!" Rufus followed her eagerly as she opened the door, looking up at her in awe as he walked under her arm. "Boy, Dar, you got a lot of muscles!"

Kerry muffled a giggle as she caught the look of bemused consternation on her partner's face.

"Yeah, I sure do," Dar replied. "That's kinda weird for a girl, huh?"

"Yeah." Rufus nodded solemnly. "But it's really cool. Can you wrassle a gator?"

Dar chuckled. "C'mon."

They disappeared inside, leaving Kerry to resume her quiet pondering. She leaned back in her chair and exhaled. "What the hell is going on with you, Kerrison?" She rested her head against her fist and looked inside herself for an answer.

Finally, she lifted her eyes and exhaled, nodding a few times. Had her family had so enraged and disgusted her, Kerry mused, that a part of her wanted to just leave them behind? Maybe that same part thought that using Dar's last name instead of her own would rid her of the nightmares.

Is that good or bad? Kerry wasn't sure. It hadn't seemed to bother Dar, though. In fact, Kerry suspected Dar kinda liked the theft of her surname. With a thoughtful frown, she picked up the strong golden chain on her neck and regarded the ring through which it was threaded. She and Dar both wore their commitment rings the same way, and now she studied the inscription on hers carefully.

Forever.

Kerry smiled and pushed herself to her feet, shaking her head as she walked toward the cabin. A motion caught her eye and she turned to watch a much smaller boat, just a motored skiff, pull up to the dock and tie on.

The motor died, and a tall, grizzle-haired man with a husky build got out. He was dressed in faded, patched fatigues and a black tank top, and he adjusted a blue cap as he paused on the dock. His eyes fell on their boat, and he turned and examined it carefully from bow to stern. Then he pivoted on his heel and headed up toward the buildings, walking with a determined, powerful stride.

"You know," Kerry leaned on the edge of the cabin door, "if I were the gambling type, I'd bet that guy's name is Bud." She watched as the man passed Christen and Juan coming back the other way, brushing by them without a word. The two continued back to their boat, but not without a look in Kerry's direction. "This is starting to look squicky."

"Did you say something, Ker?" Dar appeared at her elbow. "I'm just going to kick the engines on and give Rufus the ride I promised him."

"Sounds like a great idea." Kerry patted her on the side. "I'll untie us." She jumped onto the dock and set them free, aware of being watched from across the way.

Something is definitely going on. Kerry suspected that sooner or later they'd be finding out what it was.

Chapter
Seven

IT WAS SUNSET when they pulled back into the dock, having enjoyed their late afternoon ride. Perched on the bow of the Bertram as Dar navigated in, the first thing Kerry noticed was that the small tender was gone.

Rufus was a cute kid. Kerry found his enthusiasm over anything nautical adorable, and watching Dar explain the working of the large diesels was a precious moment she wished she had on camera. Rufus obviously adored her partner, and even now he was glued to Dar's side as she edged the big boat into dock.

Kerry made a mental note to get Dar to let her bring the craft in sometime, though this tiny dock probably wasn't the best one to start with. Dar had to shift the diesels into reverse twice and then into idle, before they drifted into place. As they gently hit the bumpers, Kerry stepped off and secured the lines. The setting sun was turning the white beach sand a deep gold and painting the wooden buildings into a tropical watercolor scene. She leaned against a pylon and stuck her hands into her pockets, simply enjoying the view.

"Hey, Ker." Dar jumped off the boat and onto the dock. "See that?"

Kerry obligingly peered down Dar's arm. Her eyes widened. "Whoa...what *is* that?"

A young woman was racing around the waves on what looked like a surfboard, but this surfboard had a handle and, apparently, an engine. As Kerry watched, the girl zoomed around in a big figure eight, effortlessly racing over the surface of the water. Kerry clutched Dar's shoulder. "Ooo," she crooned. "I want." She craned her neck to see better. "That rocks!"

Dar smirked. "I thought you'd say that." She turned and watched Rufus jump off the boat. "Okay, Rufus, tell your friend he's got a customer."

"Cool!" Rufus grinned at both of them. "I'm gonna go tell 'im. Go see papa Bud, too." He pattered off down the dock, only to turn and race back, throw his arms around Dar and give her a hug.

"Thanks for th' ride!"

"No problem." Dar seemed a little embarrassed, but she returned the hug before she sent him on his way again. "Nice kid."

"Mmhm," Kerry agreed. "He's got great taste in heroes to worship."

Dar rolled her eyes. "Don't you start that, Kerrison."

Kerry snickered. "But it's so cute," she teased, reaching up to tweak Dar's cheek. "C'mon. How about a shower before we go to dinner?"

They had turned to go back onto the boat when heavy footsteps made them look around. Charlie was limping down the dock toward them, giving them a friendly wave. "Ho, Dar!"

Dar lifted a hand in greeting. "Evening, Charlie."

The big ex-serviceman halted as he reached them. "Evening, you two. Listen, got a favor to ask."

"Sure," Dar replied easily.

"Damn fuel delivery's being held up 'cause of weather down south. We gotta shut down tonight. Mind if I bring over a potluck on your pretty boat here?"

"Not at all," Dar said. "We've got a table inside. How about we go out and do it under the stars?"

Charlie beamed. "Sounds great. Bud'll love that. It'll take 'bout forty five to an hour; see you then?"

"Sure."

Charlie turned and limped up the dock, waving his hand in farewell.

"Well," Kerry mused, "that's interesting. I guess they use a generator for power, right?"

"Yep." Dar stepped onto the boat and offered Kerry her hand. "So we get to be hosts for the evening. That work for you?"

"Definitely." Kerry allowed herself to be pulled on board. Quite unreasonably, she'd developed a wary dislike for Bud, whom she hadn't even met yet, and she was glad their first encounter would occur in their home territory.

It isn't really fair to the guy, she acknowledged. Kerry reasoned it was mostly her gut level reaction to someone who professed a dislike for someone she dearly loved and admired, and she was willing to give the unknown Bud a chance when she met him, especially since Dar seemed to be at least willing to sit down to dinner with him.

But still... Kerry entered the cabin after Dar and cast her eye around it. "Go grab a shower first, I'll straighten up in here."

Dar looked around and then gave her a wry look. "Oh, right. It's trashed. Thanks, Ker," she teased, referring to the customarily neat appearance of their joint living space. But she ambled towards the head anyway, filching a towel on the way.

Kerry drummed her fingers on the galley counter, thinking hard.

DAR BROUGHT THE pot of coffee to the table and resumed her seat. They'd finished dinner, and the conversation had gotten more casual as the night had gone on. Bud was behaving, and he'd discovered Kerry was a camera fan after his own heart. Dar suspected the evening was going well and she relaxed, sneaking a glance outside at the dark, restless sea.

She'd anchored them near their dive from the prior day, and the moon had cooperated, lighting up the area with a ghostly silver glow. The ocean was picking up a bit, rocking the Bertram lightly but not enough to really bother anyone.

"So, Dar." Charlie's voice caught her attention. "You got any plans for your vacation?"

"Not really," Dar replied. "We've just been picking spots and diving, taking it easy," she said. "It's been a busy year."

"S'what I heard," Bud said. He had a very deep voice that was typically emotionless. It matched his dark, somewhat hooded eyes, and the watchful gaze he habitually wore. "Scuttlebutt said you folks got to take over all the armed service gigs."

"That's right," Kerry responded with a smile. "Starting in January, we'll be taking over a lot of infrastructure. Should be quite a project."

Bud eyed her. "Careful they don't mess you up. You know the Navy, Dar. If they can point a finger, it's in your eye."

"They're not that different from any other company," Kerry told him. "Trust me, when you're the outsourcer, if they can blame you for anything, they will. We have to deal with that all the time."

There was a momentary silence, then Bud cleared his throat and looked at Dar. "Heard about your dad," he rumbled. "That's good stuff, Dar."

Kerry neatly retracted her mental claws and took a sip of beer.

"It was..." Dar studied her glass, "one of the most amazing things in my life." She shook her head. "But then, this last year's just been full of things like that for me." Twinkling eyes shifted to Kerry.

"He living down near the old place?" Charlie asked.

Kerry chuckled. "Right now, he and Mom are puppy sitting for us," she replied. "They usually live on their boat, though."

Bud snorted. "Boats? Puppies? That ain't the same people I remember."

Dar shrugged. "Things change. People change. They went through a lot."

Bud snorted again and Kerry's claws emerged, just a bit. "I like their boat. I think it was a great choice for them to live on," she replied.

"Yeah, well, if you say so," Bud said. "Musta changed a lot if Ceci Roberts'll park her butt on some fishing dingy."

"Oh, I doubt she'd do that," Kerry said. "But..."

Kerry paused as the sound of engines came through the half open windows. She looked out, as did the rest of the table, and saw a large, well-lighted craft cruising slowly past them. "Hm."

Dar leaned on the back of the banquette and studied it. "That's a big one."

Bud got up and positioned himself behind her, crouching down and resting his elbows on the sill. He squinted, studying the ship's line. "Huh." He pointed. "Got a search light on it. Just hit us."

Charlie was also now peering out the window. "Hey, you know, I think I saw that boat two days ago off the lee side of our island," he said. "Big, ugly, black thing."

Kerry rested her chin on Dar's head. "Dar, that can't be that obnoxious boat that passed us in the straits, can it?"

"Hard to say," Dar murmured. "Let's go check it out."

They got to the door, but as Dar opened it, a loudspeaker suddenly cut the night.

"*Dixieland Yankee*, do not pull anchor. Stay where you are and prepared to be boarded."

Dar blinked, and then abruptly her brain kicked into gear. "Boarded? Who in the hell is that?"

Charlie watched over her shoulder as the boat started coming in at them. "Some very big shot with a ton of money, tell ya that."

Dar headed for the bridge. "Kerry, go watch the anchor, will ya?" she shouted down as she scaled the ladder. "You guys, hang on!"

Bud turned and poked Charlie in the chest. "That means you, muskrat. I'm going up top." He turned and followed Dar up to the bridge. Charlie remained in the doorway, holding on and watching the big ship approach.

Dar swung behind the console and hit the switches to retract the boat's anchor, her eyes darting out toward the oncoming ship. "Feels like I'm trapped in a cheap movie of the week," she muttered, glancing up as Bud appeared next to her. "This happen a lot out here?"

Bud didn't answer.

Kerry's voice rose up from the bow. "Anchor's in!"

"Get off the topside!" Dar yelled back, as she punched the starter buttons for the diesels. The engines caught at once and rumbled into life.

"*Dixieland Yankee*, I repeat: stay where you are. You are trespassing in restricted waters."

"Are we?" Dar asked.

"My ass," Bud muttered. "This thing got legs?"

"Kerry!" Dar bellowed.

"I'm down!"

"Hang on." Dar shoved both throttles forward and heeled the boat over, watching the bow rise as the dual diesels dug into the water. The bigger boat was moving to intercept them and a searchlight hit her in the eyes. Dar cursed and kept the wheel turned, just clearing the other boat's bow before she whipped the wheel straight and gave the engines full throttle.

Their conjoined wakes rocked the Bertram, then the boat leveled out and Dar turned her eyes toward the depth meter, checking their draft. Behind them, the bigger boat had turned to follow, and she heard the roar as their engines were let loose in the chase.

"What in the hell is this?" Dar snarled.

Bud chuckled dryly, the first time he'd laughed that night. "Welcome to the Caribbean, Paladar. There still be pirates here, y'know."

"Pirates in seventy-freaking-foot, mansion cruisers?" Dar asked, glancing behind them. "Jesus!" The searchlight pinned them, and she could hear the engines getting louder. "Kerry! Strap everything down!"

"Already there!" Kerry yelled back. 'What the hell is going on?"

"*Dixieland Yankee*. If you don't reduce speed and go to idle, we will halt you by force. Please obey."

"Kiss my ass." Dar flicked two switches on the console and nudged the throttles a little further.

Bud was wedged between the seats and the console as their speed increased and the wind slammed against them. "You ain't much of a rule follower, are you?" he commented.

"I *make* the rules," Dar replied. "Hang on." She set two final switches, glanced behind them at the boat rapidly gaining on them, and shoved the throttles all the way forward. With a throaty roar, the engine superchargers cut in and the bow planed up out of the water as their speed doubled.

Bud clutched at the railing. "Shit."

Dar looked back, and felt her heart rate slow a little as the other boat stopped gaining as quickly. She looked again, swallowing a nervous lump as she frantically tried to figure out what to do next. The compass showed them going south, and the depth finder showed good depth under their keel. The only question was: where the hell was she going, and what was she going to do when she got there?

KERRY EXHALED IN relief as she saw the big vessel drop a little further behind them. "Excuse me." She gently eased past Charlie, who was still in the doorway to the cabin. "This is getting very icky."

"No shit." Charlie eyed the big boat. "What the heck did you girls get yourselves into?"

"I wish I knew." Kerry strode into the cabin and went to the storage chest, flipped the seat up and pulled out a long, black case. She set it on the table and undid the catches, lifted the lid and laid it back. Inside rested a powerful, blued black shotgun, giving off the very distinct scent of gun oil.

"Ah." Charlie was at her shoulder. "Shoulda figured Dar'd have one of these."

Kerry pulled the gun out and opened the stock. "It's not Dar's," she murmured, flipping open a door in the case and removing shotgun shells. "It's mine." She glanced up at the surprised man. "I've been shooting since I was eight." She closed the shotgun and pocketed a handful of extra shells, then headed for the door.

She'd never really liked guns. Handguns, in fact, scared the daylights out of her, as she'd realized when they'd been faced with one in Chicago. But Kerry had realized that she hated the feeling of being helpless even more, so she'd gone out and gotten herself a gun she at least had experience with.

Kerry was pretty sure her father had never intended his forced familial skeet lessons to have this particular result. She had always found it ironic that of all her cousins and siblings, she was the only one who could hit anything smaller than a Volkswagen Microbus with any regularity. She still remembered those frosty fall days with reporters in full attendance, watching as adolescents barely able to lift the damn rifles gamely plugged away at skittish, fleeting, clay plugs.

She stood next to the door and peered out, holding the shotgun close to her body. If she squinted, she could just see figures moving out onto the bow of the larger vessel, one manning the annoying searchlight and two others approaching the railing.

Charlie limped up behind her and shut off the light in the cabin, affording them a better view. "No sense putting up a target," he commented. "Wonder what they're after?"

"I have no idea." Kerry inhaled sharply as she realized the bigger boat was gaining on them again. She made a grab for the doorframe as the Bertram heeled over, then accelerated again in a new direction. "Jesus, Dar."

Being in international waters, there wasn't anyone, really, they could call. They could, Kerry realized, get into very real trouble out there and it would be weeks before anyone knew about it. "Dar?"

"I know!"

Kerry exhaled.

"Ker?"

"Yeah?"

"This could get nasty!"

Kerry stepped out onto the stern and worked the shotgun mechanism. "I'm armed."

"Great." Dar felt more than a little frazzled. "Here I am playing Captain Kidd, and I've got Wyatt Earp on the stern."

Bud leaned over the edge of the console and regarded Kerry's wind buffeted form. "She know how to use that thing?"

Dar grunted, focusing on her route. Ahead of her, the sky no longer held stars, and as she stared ahead, lightning fluttered, outlining huge thunderheads. She pointed. "That the storm you were telling me about?"

"It's a storm," Bud stated. "You figgering to head into it?"

"Not exactly." Dar looked behind her. The big boat was definitely gaining on them now. "But it could get a little rough." She plotted a course and then settled herself, wrapping her legs around the captain's chair. "Kerry, stow it! I'm gonna be moving!"

She heard the cabin door slam. "All right, asshole. Let's see if you can stick with me." Dar headed between two tiny, uninhabited islands. The Bertram raced over the waves, which were now perceptibly choppier. The searchlight zapped over their heads. Dar felt its glare on her neck and she pulled the boat into a gentle arc, first one way and then the other.

A popping sound brought her head up and around. Both she and Bud ducked as a flare seared past their starboard side. Dar spent an unfruitful moment wishing like hell her father was beside her, and then directed her full attention to threading the boat through the narrow channel.

"Getting shallow," Bud offered.

"I know." Dar kept one eye on the depth meter, and the other on the blinking buoys the marked the route. A roll of thunder rumbled overhead, almost obscuring the sound of the engines. Another flare screeched by, this time on the port side. "Next one's coming right up our backs, I'm guessing."

"Inta the engine cowling," the laconic ex-sailor stated. "Fastest way to stop you."

"Thanks." Dar's eyes narrowed and she inched her route slightly to her left. Then without warning, she spun the wheel, sending the boat into a rapid curve. She straightened out and then went right again, daring their pursuer to follow them.

She heard their engines rev as they accepted her challenge, and with that sound, Dar smiled. "Gotcha," she whispered, ramming the throttles home and skimming down a specific line in the sea with a light, precise touch on the controls.

Bud was gripping the console, his eyes wide. "Dar, you're gonna bottom."

Dar watched the depth meter. "C'mon...c'mon." It sounded a warning, and she kept her fingertips on the wheel, mentally crossing other body parts and just wishing. The Bertram threaded a tiny line down the center of the meter, the klaxon blaring louder and louder as the sounds of their pursuers also got louder.

"Jesus Christ!" Bud yelled. "You have all lost your damn minds!"

"Nah." The boat flashed over a section of water, then the klaxon cut off, just as they heard a horrific crunching sound behind them. Dar chanced a quick look behind her and saw the big boat heeling off to one side, its engines dying and panic on the bow. She faced forward again, into the rain now hitting the shield around the console. "I just play a mean game of chicken."

Every nerve in her was alive. Dar could see her own grin reflected in the glass, and she just barely kept herself from letting out a wild yell of triumph. "All right," she was proud of the even tone in her voice, "now let's get outta here."

Bud unglued his hands from the rail. "Whoinhell taught you to drive?" he growled.

Glinting blue eyes reflected back in the windshield. "My dad," Dar replied, savoring the moment. Then she keyed the mic for internal communications. "Kerry?"

"Here." Kerry's voice sounded a little out of breath. "Holy shit, Dar!"

"Yeah." Dar trimmed the engines, which now labored against the rising seas. "Out of the frying pan... I'm gonna circle back around and see if I can get past this storm and come back into the island from the other side."

"Anything I can do?"

"Monitor the radio. See if you can pick up those bastards calling for help. I want to know who they are."

"Right."

Dar clicked the mic off, and clipped it. "Board me, will you?" she muttered. "I don't *think* so."

KERRY PUT THE mic down, but left her hand on it for a long moment as her nerves steadied. "Okay," she finally said, gathering her composure and pushing away from the wall. "Glad that's over."

"Me, too," Charlie agreed. He was seated securely in one of the chairs bolted to the deck. "Now, whatinthehell was it?" He got up and peered out the window. "Sumbitches bottomed, huh?"

"Yeah." Kerry walked over to the galley and removed a bottle of Gatorade, popped the top and sucked down several mouthfuls.

She set the bottle down. "Now all we have to worry about is the weather." She walked back over to the radio, set it to fast scan, and turned the volume up. The shotgun was already tucked back into its case under the seat, and now that the immediate danger was over, Kerry felt her entire body shaking in reaction.

Adrenaline rush, the hard way. With a sigh, Kerry sat down in the other bucket chair and let her hands rest on her thighs.

"Ain't' your cuppa brew, is it?" Charlie asked.

Kerry gave him a wry look. "I'm a Midwestern Republican with a degree in Information Technology. What do you think?"

The big man chuckled. "You done pretty good, though," he said. "Where in the Midwest you from?"

"Michigan," Kerry replied. "Saugatuck."

"Been up there a time or two," Charlie said. "Got to do some dry suit work in the lake once upon a time."

Kerry was glad of the distraction. "Is there anything to see down there?" she asked curiously. "I always wondered. Other than downed freighters, I mean."

Charlie shrugged. "We weren't sightseeing," he explained with an apologetic look. "You could ask Big Andy, though. He did two tours up there." He paused. "Strange, talking about him real time now."

"I can imagine." Kerry leaned back, folding her hands over her belly. "I'll ask him, though." She smiled. "I remember the first time we went diving with him. He's like a fish." She waggled one hand in mid air.

"Always was," Charlie acknowledged. "A real natural. Used to watch him swim and wonder if he was hiding gills."

Kerry nodded. "I know. Dar's the same way."

"Ah." Charlie looked up as the door opened and Bud came in. He addressed his partner. "Didn't 'spect you'd get a wild hare ride with dinner, didja?"

Bud shook his head and snorted. "Crazy assed bastards," he said. "Near as crazy as the nut drivin' this thing."

One of Kerry's eyebrows rose. "I think Dar did pretty good," she stated. "They're on the rocks; we're not."

"Luck."

"With Dar? Never." Kerry got up and paced over to the galley, retrieving her bottle of Gatorade. "She always knows what she's doing." She sucked a mouthful of the drink. "Now we just have to find out who and why."

"Well, you could go back and ask," Charlie joked wanly.

"Lemme know if that's what you're gonna do. I'll swim back and tow..." Bud indicated his partner with a thumb, "this thing. I don't want no part of them people."

Kerry leaned on the counter. "Is this something that happens often? I know we were reading something in the Miami papers about modern day piracy, but I never imagined the pirates drove luxury yachts."

Bud and Charlie looked at each other but didn't answer.

Kerry's other eyebrow rose.

"They weren't pirates," Bud finally muttered. "Not the kind we have around here, anyhow."

Ah. Kerry noticed neither of them would meet her eyes. "So it does happen."

"Oh, well, you hear things," Charlie interjected. "You know."

Uh huh. "No, actually I don't," Kerry answered. "But then, what were these guys after?"

Bud shrugged. "Maybe they just didn't like Dar's attitude," he suggested. "Inherited trait."

Kerry was quite surprised to hear herself produce an almost audible growl. "Excuse me," she said abruptly. "Keep an ear on the radio. I'm going topside."

DAR UNCLIPPED THE plastic water bottle from under the console and gulped its contents, satisfied with her new course at last. They were headed into a little weather, the winds had picked up to about twenty knots and the seas were up, but the Bertram rode the surf solidly, and she knew she could make the eastward turn around the far side of the island in about ten minutes.

She turned around in her seat and looked behind her, shading her eyes against the rain. She could just see the other boat's running lights far back, bobbing up and down in the surf but coming no closer. The depth would have been shallow enough to rake the bigger boat's hull and maybe even puncture it, depending on how they hit, and though it was a wide sea and bad weather, Dar had absolutely no compunction about leaving them to their fate.

Dar swiveled around and thought about that for a minute. "Okay." She addressed the controls. "What would Dad do?" The dials and gauges peered mutely back at her. *Dad would...* Dar chuckled dryly. Her dad might have stayed and challenged the other boat, but if he'd done what she had, he might have at least called the Coasties for them; her mother wouldn't have. *To hell with them.*

Dar still felt pumped, almost giddy at her successful escape. She'd hoped the high speed run up the center of two parallel reefs, keeping her keel right down the space between them, would work, but she'd also known she was counting on luck and her own piloting skills a lot more than she should have.

But... Dar wiggled her fingers, looking at her strong hands. She'd done it. She chortled privately, clearing her throat and resuming a serious expression as she heard someone coming up the ladder behind her. A peek over her shoulder brought her grin back. "Hey."

"Hey, yourself." Kerry had on her rain slicker and was carrying Dar's. She took the seat next to Dar and handed her the slicker. "I've finished pooping in my pants now. How about you?"

Dar laughed as she leaned back and pulled on her bright red rain jacket. "That was something, I gotta tell you. What the hell was up with those people?"

Kerry leaned on the console. "I don't know, but we'd better find out, Dar. This is not funny."

"No kidding." Dar finished fastening her hood, then glanced at Kerry. "You okay?"

Green eyes blinked at her in the misty rain. "That was really scary."

Dar laced her fingers through Kerry's damp hair. "I know."

"Your old friends are making my nape hairs rigid."

"Sorry." Dar scratched her neck. "Bud's pretty abrasive," she admitted. "I've kept in touch mostly because of Charlie. He's a good guy."

Kerry sighed, aggravated. "He's married to a jerk."

Dar eyed her. "There're a lot of people who'd say the same about you," she joked. "That you're married to a jerk, I mean," she added. "Not that you *are* one."

"Pah." Kerry started laughing. "Okay, I'm cranky, I hate being scared, and mysterious black boats who do great pirate imitations really tick me off." She looked up as thunder rolled overhead. "Gee, thanks. That so helps."

Dar reached out and pulled Kerry over into her lap. She hugged her close as she made a slight adjustment in the boat's course and started her turn to the east. "We'll be out of the rain soon. We'll drop these guys off, then we'll head out to St. Johns. Once we're there, I'll call in and have that damned boat checked out. Sound like a plan?"

Kerry found that not even rain and two layers of plastic could ruin a good Dar hug, and she grunted softly as she returned it. "I like it," she agreed. "Do we have reservations on St. Johns?"

"Uh huh, at Caneel Bay," Dar replied.

"Is that the one with the seven beaches?" Kerry was intrigued. "And DSL in the rooms?"

Dar nodded. "With rental laptops. Got all the essentials covered."

Kerry briefly considered telling Dar that she had stashed one of their laptops, but decided it wasn't the time. "Be still, my technobeating heart."

The mic crackled. "Hey, Dar." Bud's voice came through. "Got a distress call casting down here. 117.9"

"Thanks. I'll tune it in," Dar answered. "We're coming in around the eastern side of your island."

"Yeap." The mic clicked off.

Dar frowned, then shook her head and tuned in the marine radio. For a few moments, there wasn't any sound, and she thought she'd gotten the wrong channel. Then a shrill feedback sound erupted and a voice came through.

"Mayday! Mayday! Help!"

"Oh, that's professional," Kerry sniped.

"This is *Siren of the Sea*...in bad weather... sinking..."

The words cut off. Dar peered at the radio, then looked behind them. "I don't think that's them."

"Help! This is *Siren of the Sea*... Thirty foot sailboat in bad weather. I lost my engine and snapped the mast lines. Taking on water."

"Oh, that's bad." Kerry sat up. "He needs help." She looked at Dar. "I've crewed a thirty footer, Dar. It doesn't stand a chance with no sail control."

Dar keyed the mic. "*Siren of the Sea*, this is *Dixieland Yankee*. Do you know your location? Over." She released the mic and waited. There was no response. "*Siren of the Sea*, do you copy?"

There was still no answer. Finally they heard, "Hello? This is *Siren of the Sea* to whoever's calling. I think I'm off St. Johns...off the western coast!" A break filled with static sounded before they made out, "...raining like hell! I think the swells are twenty feet!"

Kerry got up. "I'll tell our passengers and get out the safety gear." She kissed Dar. "Think we can find him?"

Dar flipped on the radar scope, which showed not much of anything. Given that she was not familiar with the waters and had no idea what she was really looking at, she didn't want to give Kerry false hopes. "Do my best," she replied.

"Done deal, then," Kerry answered blithely before she turned and made her way to the ladder.

Dar shook her head then plotted a new course, this one curving back toward the sound of thunder and the rising wind.

Chapter
Eight

DAR BLEW THE wet hair out of her eyes and leaned forward, peering with a scowl through the rain lashed darkness. The weather had worsened severely, and the boat was now being tossed by fifteen-foot seas. Dar had turned on the big searchlight on the bow, but it really did very little to penetrate the darkness. The light reflected off the huge raindrops and almost made it seem like she was plowing into a silver curtain.

The Bertram rolled in a swell and Dar turned into the wave, watching both her radar and sonar with careful eyes. She was concentrating so hard, she didn't hear Kerry come up the ladder and almost jumped right through the console topper when her partner plopped down in the seat next to her. "Yeeeah!"

Kerry sniffled and pulled her jacket closer. "Sorry." She patted Dar's back. "Didn't mean to scare you."

"Mmph." Dar collected her composure. She glanced at Kerry, watching her slit her eyes against the rain. "Y'know, there's no reason for you to suffer up here in this mess."

"Yes, there is," Kerry disagreed. She carefully put her elbows on the console. "I can either sit up here and brave the best Mother Nature can offer, or I can stay downstairs and chuck my cookies."

"Ah." Dar peered more closely at her. "Yeah, you look a little..."

"Just call me Kermit," Kerry admitted, swallowing. "Didn't think I got seasick."

"I think you can blame the weather this time," Dar comforted.

Kerry grimaced, and then managed a wan smile as the Bertram rolled in the waves again.

"Watch the horizon," Dar advised, reaching over and circling Kerry's wrist with two long fingers.

"Honey, I love you," Kerry leaned against Dar's shoulder, "but you don't have to hold my hand, really."

Dar chuckled softly as she pressed down on Kerry's wrist with her fingertips. "Try calling him again," she suggested, more to distract Kerry than because she believed the man in distress would answer. There had been no response to their last two hails, and Dar was afraid their unlucky friend had run into potentially fatal trouble.

Kerry took a few deep breaths, and then picked up the mic. "*Siren of the Sea, Siren of the Sea,* this is *Dixieland Yankee.* Do you copy? Over." She paused and listened to the crackling, closing her eyes as the boat hit a trough and pitched down.

Dar shifted her grip slightly and then pressed again, watching Kerry's face carefully. After a moment, her eyelashes flickered open and a look of mild surprise appeared. "Better?" Dar asked hopefully.

"Eyah," Kerry murmured. "Did you do that?"

Dar smirked.

"Ooh. I love you," Kerry said. "Hang on. *Siren of the Sea, Siren of the Sea,* do you copy?"

A harsh buzz suddenly cut the static, then a second. A bolt of lightning lit up the sky, and they both ducked in reflex. Dar grabbed Kerry and shielded her as she felt every hair on her body stand up. For that brief instant, the imperiled boat was forgotten; the storm was forgotten. Dar heard a loud crack, and then the glare vanished, leaving a wild blast of thunder in its wake.

"Holy shit." Dar looked up, searching the topmast anxiously, then her eyes went to their instruments, hoping like hell they hadn't lost the GPS or the sonar. She relaxed when the iridescent glow of the apparatus remained steady. "Wow."

"Dar?" Kerry's voice was muffled. "I think you can let me up now."

"Oh. Sorry." Dar straightened, but kept one arm around Kerry's shoulders.

"You all right up there?" Charlie's voice suddenly erupted in the radio. "That sucker hit the water just off the stern."

"We're fine," Kerry answered. "Everything's all right."

Dar glanced up at the sky. "This isn't gonna work. I'm going to turn and get out of here," she decided. "We'll report the mayday when we get into dock." She reset their course and checked the depth. "I'm not risking you or the boat."

"Dar."

Dar turned and looked her in the eye. "Yes?"

Kerry knew that look. She knew Dar didn't like to be challenged, especially when she was off balance and scared. Kerry could see the jangled nerves in her lover's eyes, and by the short, restless motions of her hands on the controls she knew that Dar's temper was very much on edge. "We're all he's got," she said very gently. "Can we try for a few more minutes?"

Dar very much wanted to say no, Kerry could read it. "Let me call him one more time and see if he can at least give us a click. If not," she watched the rain plaster Dar's hair to her forehead, half obscuring her eyes, "at least we tried."

A deep breath preceded her capitulation. "Okay," Dar said briefly. "Then, please, Kerry, go below."

"Okay," Kerry agreed, flexing her hand around the mic. She hesitated, set it down, then reached out and caught Dar's hand, squeezing it. "Thanks."

"Grumph." Dar adjusted the throttles and started the boat on a long, shallow curve to cut across the swells. She didn't want to turn too sharply and get caught inside them, since the waves were cresting up to around twenty feet.

"*Siren of the Sea...Siren of the Sea...*if you can hear this, please key in twice." Kerry requested, speaking clearly. She listened intently to the hiss. "*Siren of the Sea*, please key in twice if you receive this. We are trying to locate you."

The hiss broke, returned, and then broke again. Kerry grinned, then looked up at Dar.

"Could be coincidence."

"*Siren of the Sea*, please key in twice again."

Two clicks answered her again, and then a voice crackled through. "I'm here! Help!"

Dar sighed and shook her head. "We still don't have a chance of finding him," she said. "All I've seen on radar for the last half hour is..." Dar stopped, leaned closer to the small scope. "Wait." She increased the magnitude of the pulse and studied the screen, unsure. It might be a tiny blip, but then it might not. "Could just be wave return." But she was already swinging the wheel around and gunning the engines. "Either way, if that's not him we're going back."

"Right." Kerry put the mic down and stood. "I'm going to go up on the bow."

Dar's eyes widened. "Not without a safety belt," she stated flatly. "I don't want you launched overboard."

"Aye, Aye, cap'n." Kerry patted Dar, then made her way to the stairs, carefully climbed down them and stepped onto the pitching deck. Charlie and Bud were standing in the cabin doorway. "We think we see him," she said.

"'Bout time." Bud picked up the rope and floatation gear and slung it over his broad shoulder. "Seems like a lotta trouble for some jackass who didn't have the sense to get out of the rain." He got up onto the railing and walked around to the bow.

Kerry counted to ten under her breath as she got a double clipped safety rope and hooked one end onto the rail, then followed him. The wind hit her as she went around to the front of the boat, driving rain right into her eyes. Kerry gamely struggled forward, careful to keep her footing as she edged around the large cruiser cabin and emerged onto the sloping bow of the boat. It was pitching up and down, and seawater was crashing over the rails, chilling her even through her jacket.

She got to the very front of the boat and knelt, peering into the darkness. The swells rose and fell, making it hard to see anything at all. All Kerry could see was ruffling waves and rain.

"There." Bud was standing next to her. "To starboard."

Kerry strained her eyes. "I don't see anything... Oh. Wait!" In a break in the waves, she spotted a flash of white, then it disappeared. Her mind tried to resolve it as part of a sailboat, and failed. "Wh..."

Dar, apparently, had also seen it. The Bertram altered course to starboard, and the engine speed diminished.

Kerry leaned forward. Then the waves broke again, and she got another look. "He's capsized!" she yelled, recognizing the white flash as an overturned hull.

"Yeap." Bud didn't seem surprised. "Jerk probably didn't bring the sail in."

Kerry stood up, biting her tongue to keep back the sharp words. Their boat worked itself closer, and she could see the up-ended boat more clearly. "He's on the back!" She pointed at a dark, forlorn-looking figure clinging to the hull.

Then her eyes almost came out of her head as the sea in front of her dropped, and they were looking downslope at the shipwreck from twenty feet up. Kerry's stomach almost came out of her nostrils as the wave crested, then she hung on as the Bertram rode the wave down, its forward motion slowed.

The wave picked up the sailing boat and lifted it, then a cross wave unexpectedly tossed it to one side. As Kerry watched in horror, the small figure on the back flew off into the water and disappeared. Without really thinking once, much less twice, she unclipped her safety rope and jumped to the top of the railing, then leaped out into the darkness.

Hitting the water was a total shock. It was cold, and it grabbed her mercilessly and whirled her around. Kerry fought her way to the surface and realized she'd probably just made a really big mistake. A wave nearly swamped her, but she rode through it, then felt something hit her on the shoulder. She whirled to find the floatation ring next to her and grabbed it.

The storm was too loud for her to hear any shouting, but she knew it was there. A dagger of hot fear hit her in the gut, and she got an arm around the ring, glad for its buoyancy. Trying not to swallow the seawater constantly washing over her head, she turned and started for the last place she'd seen the hapless boater.

At first, it was hard to make any headway. Then Kerry discovered if she found the right waves, they'd take her where she wanted to go. She waited for one, then swam into it and let it carry her down and across the bow of the capsized boat.

The searchlight suddenly penetrated the rain, blazing across the choppy water. It tracked over Kerry, pausing a moment before it reluctantly moved on. Kerry's eyes followed it, then she lunged forward as she caught just a glimpse of a hand near the back end of the boat. She struggled toward it, hearing the rumbling roar of the big diesels behind her as the Bertram fought to hold its position in the water.

Kerry got her head above water and yelled. "Hey!" She flailed with her arms through the wave, feeling under the surface near the edge of the capsized hull. Three times and nothing, then suddenly her hand touched something that wasn't water and wasn't boat.

Her fingers closed, with a brief, heartfelt prayer to God that it was a person and not a shark she was grabbing onto. She felt cloth and pulled hard, heaving backwards with all the strength she could muster. It was like pulling at a wet, sand filled sack. "C'mon!" Kerry gave another tug. An arm broke the surface, then a dark, wet head.

For a moment, Kerry wasn't sure she'd been in time. Then the head lifted and the other arm flailed out, smacking against the boat. The man coughed, spitting up a mouthful of water.

"Here!" Kerry got his hands around the life preserver. "Hang on!" It wasn't easy, but she wrapped the device around him, then turned her head, searching for the boat on the other end of the line. Her strength was draining out of her, and the chill water was starting to make her shiver. Warm though the seas were this far south, at night, in a rainstorm, they were no bathtub.

"Kerry!"

Dar's voice through a loudspeaker was the last thing she'd expected. She blinked through the rain, hanging on to the rope.

"Clip on to the rope! We'll pull you in!"

Oh. Kerry fumbled at her waist, finding the belt, then the big metal clip that hung from it. She clipped it onto the rescue rope and wrapped her arm around her rescuee, feeling the powerful tug as she began to be towed back to the *Dixieland Yankee.*

The waves swamped over them. Kerry felt her body aching from the strain of remaining upright, and she reached up and clasped her hand over a knot in the rope to get a better grip. They got closer and closer to the boat, and as they did, she realized how high the bow was over their head. She was used to coming aboard from the stern, and now she wondered how they were going to manage.

The Bertram lunged forward and Kerry crashed into the hull, slamming her shoulder into the fiberglass. It knocked the wind out of her, and she dazedly pushed off before the belt tightened around her waist and she realized she was being pulled right up out of the water. "Hold on! Hold on!" she yelled, scrambling to make sure the straps on the preserver were tight. The man inside it seemed dazed, and he clutched at the rope with uncertain fingers.

Kerry felt her body clear the water, and she sucked in a breath against the painful grip of the single belt that supported her weight. She kept one hand on the hull and tried hard not to kick out, her other hand tangled in the man's sodden shirt as they were fished up out of the sea.

When they were about halfway up, lightning crackled and the boat rolled, pitching down so far her feet hit the water again. Kerry gasped as the wave rolled back the other way, slamming her against the bow with stunning force. In reflex, she reached a hand up, feeling for the railing and hoping like hell that didn't happen again.

Her back thumped against the hull and she felt a tingling start below where the belt was wrapped around her, the edges digging into her ribcage and almost cutting off her ability to breathe. She tried to pull up with her arms, but it didn't help, and she was on the verge of panic when suddenly hands were grabbing her arms and shirt.

The belt was released and Kerry was lifted over the railing, arms closing around her body and supporting her with a powerful strength she immediately recognized. She turned her head and buried her face against Dar's shirt, knowing now she was safe and everything would be fine.

"Got 'im!" Bud's voice broke through the rain. "Charlie! Get the hell outta here!"

Kerry felt the boat begin to move. The rain was still pelting her. Now that it was over, the adrenaline rushed out of her and she felt too weak to move. It was easier to just sit on the deck, wrapped in Dar's arms and half in her lap, limp as a dishrag. She could hear the man she'd rescued coughing, gagging up the seawater he'd swallowed. Her own mouth felt like she'd been sucking on caviar, and her throat was raw from yelling. "Buh."

Dar's arms tightened around her. "Let's get inside. I think my little hero here needs some hot tea."

Hero. Kerry blinked. "What?"

"He-ro," Dar whispered into her ear. "That's someone who does something stupidly brave and gets away with it."

Kerry frowned as she thought about what she'd done. *Good grief. I just saved someone's life, didn't I?* A tiny, incredulous smile crossed her face at the totally new sensation.

Wow.

HAVING RESUMED THE con, Dar shut down the engines, reaching up and pushing the rain hood off her head before she stood up. They'd outrun the storm, and now its fury was nothing but a heavy rumbling and flashes of light on the horizon. Dar exhaled, leaning against the console and trying to summon up the strength to go down the stairs. She was exhausted. Moreso, she suspected, from the intense, emotional stress than from the physical activity. Her hands were shaking, she noticed, and she had a headache that started at the nape of her neck and worked upward from there.

It was well after midnight, and heading for St. Johns tonight was out of the question. Even if the weather wasn't chancy, she didn't trust herself to pilot the boat, and so further investigation into their mysterious pirate encounter would have to wait for the morning.

Ah well. Dar shook herself. *Buck up, Paladar, and git yer ass moving.* She walked to the ladder and slowly made her way down it, stepped onto the deck and pushed open the cabin door. Dar entered and closed the door behind her.

Inside the cabin, Kerry was curled up on the couch in her robe. Bud and Charlie were sitting at the table, and their rescued sailboat owner was across from Kerry, swathed in a big towel.

Dar put a heavy clamp down on her immediate instincts, which were urging her to throw everyone off the boat so she could concentrate on her somewhat pale, and definitely ragged looking partner. Instead, she went to the galley and put on some water, fiddling restlessly with a spoon while she waited for it to heat.

"I was trying to get back into port," the rescued man was saying. "I don't know what happened. One minute, I was pulling in the mainsail, the next thing I knew, my engine dropped out and everything started going nuts."

"That can be scary, Bob," Kerry murmured. "I capsized in Lake Michigan once. Not fun."

"You can sure say that again!" Bob shook his head. He addressed Bud and Charlie. "You folks got a phone?"

"Nope," Bud answered. "Marine radio." He got up and walked out.

Bob blinked. "Something I said?" he asked hesitantly.

"Naw," Charlie reassured him. "Just been a long day." He cleared his throat. "Well, Mr. Gallareaux, I'm sure glad it all turned out all right. We got a spare bunk up top, if you like. You can get a run over to St. Johns tomorrow."

Bob looked pathetically grateful. "You all have been so nice." He glanced over at Dar, then looked at Kerry. "How can I repay you? You saved my life." He had kind, hazel eyes and a nice face, slightly rounded with high cheekbones.

A visible blush colored Kerry's skin. "I'm glad we could help." She smiled at him.

Now it was his turn to blush to the roots of his red, curly hair. "I feel like an idiot," he admitted. "I've been sailing since I was a kid. It's not like I'm a neo, but that storm caught me flat."

"Weather's like that down here," Charlie said placidly. "Well, let's let these ladies get some rest. It's been a busy night for 'em." He got to his feet and limped awkwardly toward the door. "We can kick the generator back on since it's late watch."

Bob stood, removing the towel from around him. "I appreciate the offer. I'm about tapped."

"We're heading to St. Johns ourselves tomorrow," Kerry said. "If you want a ride over, we can take you." Out of habit, her eyes flicked over to the Dar, who watched silently. "Right?"

Dar nodded. "Sure."

"Thanks," he replied simply. "Maybe I can start salvaging what I've got left there." Bob folded the towel and put it on the table, then followed Charlie. At the door, he turned and looked at them. "I owe you." His eyes met Kerry's, then he slipped out the door and closed it behind him.

After a moment of silence, Kerry rolled her head toward Dar and let out a half groan, half sigh. "Got any Advil to go with that incredibly wonderful smelling coffee over there?"

Dar blinked. "Headache?" she asked.

"Everything-ache." Kerry was glad everyone was gone. "I feel like I was run over by a truck." She cautiously straightened, wincing as her body protested. "Ow."

Dar gladly chucked her emotional turmoil in favor of this new issue to focus on. She brought over two cups of coffee and a bottle of Advil, set them down, then took a seat next to Kerry on the couch. "Where does it hurt?"

Kerry put a hand on her belly. "That belt nearly killed me," she joked wanly.

Dar untied her robe and opened it. "Jesus." Her eyes widened at the lurid bruise circling Kerry's waist. "I bet that hurts." She touched the bruise, then gently turned Kerry over. "All across your back, too."

Kerry found herself nestled against Dar's chest. It was nice, even though she was still damp. "Honey, you need to change. You're wet," she murmured. "You'll catch cold."

Dar examined another bruise crossing Kerry's spine. She probed carefully. "Does this hurt?"

"A little," Kerry replied. "More like an ache," she added. "I don't think anything's seriously damaged."

"Thank you for your opinion, Dr. Stuart," Dar remarked dryly. "Did you hit your head anywhere?" She slid her fingers up into

Kerry's thick, blonde hair and felt for any telltale bumps.

"No, I don't think so," Kerry said. "I'm just sore — that water was brutal."

Dar stroked the back of her neck and gave her a pat. "Well, that's what you get for being a hero," she told her partner. "You scared the sense out of me, you know that, right?"

Kerry rolled over and stretched out her body, putting her head in Dar's lap and looking up at her. "I scared the sense out of me, too," she replied. "I realized in mid air just what an incredibly stupid thing I was doing."

Dar's smile was fleeting.

Kerry studied Dar's face, seeing the residual tension in it. Her eyes were bloodshot and there was a deep furrow between her brows. She lifted her hand and touched Dar's cheek. "Do heroic things always seem so dumb?" Kerry asked. "I mean, when you think about what you did?"

Dar let her hand rest on Kerry's stomach, her thumb rubbing gently against the soft skin above her belly button. "Um." She exhaled, letting some of the tension dissipate. "It's a lot like pitching new technology."

Kerry blinked. "Huh?"

"If it works, you're a visionary genius; if it doesn't, you're a whacko," Dar explained. "You saved that guy's life — and it took a ton of guts to do it. You took a chance, and it worked."

"Hm."

"Just like I took a chance going through those reefs, and it worked," Dar added quietly. "If it hadn't, we'd be in real trouble right now, and if the waves hadn't broken right, you could have been in real trouble when you jumped." Dar cleared her throat, then leaned over and picked up the coffee, took a sip of it.

"Catching cold already?" Kerry teased, hearing the hoarse note in Dar's usually mellow tone.

"No." Dar put the cup down. "I was screaming your name so loud I lost my voice for a while." She sighed, her shoulders unlocking and slumping a little. She lifted a hand and rubbed her temples. "I think I'll have some of those Advil, too."

"Tell you what." Kerry heaved herself up off the couch. She tied her robe closed again, then took her cup of coffee and gulped down a mouthful. "Instead of drugs, how about we get you out of those wet clothes, and get us both into that nice, dry, soft bed."

"Yeah," Dar agreed. "That sounds great." She stood up and stretched, wincing at the pops as her back and shoulders released their wound up tension. "Hope that storm bypasses us."

"God, me too." Kerry stifled a yawn. "I want a nice, peaceful night's cuddle with you before we have to figure out what the heck is going on around here."

"Cuddle," Dar mused. "Yeah. I think I need a cuddle," she admitted. "I feel sandblasted."

Kerry captured Dar's hand and led her toward the bedroom. Inside, she turned and unbuckled the belt holding up Dar's shorts, unbuttoned them, and let them drop to the cabin floor. The dim light in the room threw Dar's face into shadows, but Kerry could hear her still-tense exhalation as she stripped off her short-sleeved denim shirt and tossed it onto the dresser.

Kerry removed her robe as Dar slipped out of her swimsuit. She set the robe down as Dar sat down on the bed and moved over to give Kerry space to climb in next to her.

It was dark with the hatches shut, and very quiet. The boat was rocking gently, its violent pitching just a fading memory as Kerry carefully lowered herself onto the soft surface. She reached for Dar, and found open arms waiting as they slid together into a tangled embrace. They both sighed, then chuckled.

"What a day," Dar said with a yawn.

"Mm." With her ear pressed against Dar's chest, Kerry could hear her heart beat. As she listened, one hand idly stroking Dar's side, the beats slowed and the tense body beside her relaxed, as did her own. "Hey, Dar?" she asked after a little while.

"Hm?" Dar's low murmur answered.

"Do you think those guys were just looking for a quick score?" Kerry asked, her mind still churning despite her exhaustion. "The pirates? Maybe they just saw an expensive boat, out at night, all alone."

Dar was quiet for a bit, apparently thinking. "Maybe," she replied eventually. "Boat this size, out this far...could be."

Kerry yawned again, her eyes closing against her will. "But you don't think so, do ya?"

"Given that their yacht could financially eat this one for breakfast?" Dar snorted softly. "Let you know tomorrow once I get a database run on 'em," she replied, rubbing Kerry's back lightly.

It was quiet again for a while. Kerry kept her eyes closed, but sleep was kept at bay by recent memories of the night. "Dar?" she whispered.

"Yes?" Dar seemed wide-awake.

"I didn't jump into the water to be a hero or anything stupid like that."

"I know." Dar stroked Kerry's cheek. "I didn't think you did," she replied. "Something had to be done, you were there, and you did it."

"Yeah." A pause. "Is that how it is with you, when you do stuff like this?"

"Stuff like what?"

"Heroic stuff. Like that time you stopped those carjackers and saved me; that kind of stuff." Kerry said. "Or what you told me you did for that lady in that bar when you were younger."

"Ah..." Dar cleared her throat. "Yeah." She sounded vaguely sheepish. "Yeah, I guess it is."

"Mmph." Kerry drew in a breath, then released it with a contented grunt.

The boat rocked. Thunder rumbled softly in the distance. Peace draped at last over two sorely tested souls.

Chapter
Nine

LESSON ONE. KERRY regarded her reflection in the mirror with critical eyes. *Heroism hurts.* She put her hands on her hips and shook her head at the truly spectacular purple, green and red mark right across her stomach. "Glad I never went for the bikini look," she remarked after a moment, chuckling and scrubbing her hands through her hair before she smoothed it down into some semblance of order. Breathing too deeply was painful and her back was stiff, but she suspected she'd survive — with a couple of painkillers and a dose of relaxing on the deck.

It was sunny and breezy outside, and a good night's sleep had restored most of her good humor. She brushed her teeth and slipped into an emerald green, one-piece swimsuit. "There." She took a cautious breath, then released it. "That sure looks better." Her eyes flicked over her body, now so used to her heavier, more muscular form that it was hard really to remember what she used to look like before she met Dar.

She gave herself a nod of approval, then emerged into the boat's main cabin. Dar was curled up on the couch — a tray of coffee, biscuits, and cut up fruit next to her on the table, and a magazine folded in her hand. "Hey, sweetie."

"Howdy." Dar laid the magazine down and shifted, nudging the tray toward her partner.

Kerry took a croissant, neatly split it, applied butter and jam to its surfaces, and retired to the couch herself, snuggling up in back of Dar and draping herself over her partner's lower body. "Mm." She nibbled her breakfast. "Whatcha reading?"

Dar held up the Unix systems administration periodical.

"Nerd." Kerry chortled softly, shaking her head. "Feeling better this morning?"

Dar stifled a yawn. "Yeah, a little sleepy, though," she said, reaching over to tug a bit of Kerry's hair. "What about you?"

"Well," Kerry swallowed a mouthful, "it hurts, I won't deny that." She licked a flake from her lips. "But in kind of a weird way, it feels good, because I know it was for a good cause."

"Huh." Dar flexed her hand absently, a faint smile crossing her lips. "I never thought of it like that, but yeah. I remember the morning after you got carjacked, when I couldn't even close my fist." She gazed at her fingers.

Kerry obligingly captured Dar's hand and pulled it closer, kissing it. "You were amazing."

"Ahem." Dar cleared her throat. She put down her magazine and pulled the tray closer, dumped cream and sugar into a cup, then topped it with a little coffee. "I'll be glad to get to St. Johns." She took a sip. "The place we're going to has great food, and better views."

"Ooh." Kerry accepted the subject change gracefully, giving Dar a fondly knowing look.

"And I really want to get a line on those bastards."

Kerry grinned. "Thought there was an ulterior motive there." She neatly took the cup from Dar's fingers, took a sip, and then put it back. "But that's okay, because I want to know more about them too." She rested her chin on Dar's hip, grinning happily.

"You're in a good mood," Dar observed.

"Yeah, I guess I am," Kerry agreed. "Storm and terror-filled nights do that to me, I guess." She paused, her brow creasing. "Once they're behind me."

"Uh huh." Dar regarded her drolly. "I'll have to remember that."

"Of course," Kerry drew a fingertip slowly down Dar's thigh, "hedonistic nights full of love and snuggling put me in an even better mood." She batted her blonde lashes at her partner. "Make sure you put that down, too."

Dar chuckled. "I knew that already," she drawled, running her fingers through Kerry's hair and watching green eyes close in pleasure. "Shall we get this tub ready to go?"

Kerry wriggled closer, squeezing in behind Dar until they were wrapped around each other. She rested her chin on Dar's shoulder and blew lightly into her ear. "How about we just take it easy for a while?" she whispered, watching the pale blue eyes inches from her blink and close slightly. "You in a rush?"

Dar eased over onto her back, then turned toward Kerry and slid her body up against her partner's. She pulled Kerry closer and kissed her gently, letting one hand slide down to rest at her waist. "No rush," she answered, rubbing noses with Kerry playfully. "But I just want to remind you that all the windows are open, and the gangway's down."

"Eerrwwooough." Kerry growled deep in her throat. "What a dilemma." She gave an exaggerated sigh. "Indulge my libido, or retain my upright Midwestern reputation." Outside, the deck creaked and Kerry's eyes widened as she started.

Dar snickered. "You can take the girl out of the corn..."

"I'll corn you." Kerry leaned forward and kissed her passionately, feeling Dar's body react as she pulled Kerry into a tight hug. Her ribs protested gently but she ignored them, preferring to concentrate on the jolt of sensual reaction that rapidly warmed her. Her hands eagerly explored Dar's body, her fingers sliding up under Dar's tank top to trace her breasts. The soft surface pressed up against her as Dar inhaled, and she found herself short of breath, as well, as she felt Dar's touch high up on the inside of her thigh.

Oh, to hell with my reputation. Kerry felt her swimsuit straps slide off her shoulders as she pulled Dar's shirt up, feeling the heat as their skin met and her weight pressed down against Dar's body.

"Hey!" A voice outside erupted suddenly. "Anyone home?"

Kerry found herself nose to nose with a lethally frustrated Dar, whose darkened blue eyes and definite snarl perfectly captured how Kerry herself was feeling. "Arggghh." She released the groan softly as she let her head drop to rest against Dar's collarbone.

"That about covers it," Dar sighed. "Oh boy." She cleared her throat and swallowed, attempting to collect her composure. She raised her voice. "Be right there." Then she added in a quiet but heartfelt tone, "You godforsaken son of a bitch."

Kerry started laughing. "Bookmark this," she advised her partner. "For later." With another groan, she reluctantly untangled herself from Dar's body and stood up, eased her straps back into place, and rubbed her face to clear the flush she knew was coloring it. "Jesus."

Dar stretched out on the couch and yawned, then curled up like a large, half- naked cat. She picked up her forgotten coffee cup and sipped at it, watching Kerry over the rim with a seductive look.

"You're not helping." Kerry ran her hands through her hair. "I take it you want me to go greet our guest."

"You invited him," Dar drawled.

"Yeah, what was that all about?" Kerry slapped herself on the side of the head, and continued to do so as she walked towards the cabin door. "Curse my parents for raising me with manners."

With a chuckle, Dar leaned back against the pillow on the couch and enjoyed Kerry's sexy little swagger as she ducked through the entrance and went out onto the stern deck. She heard Kerry greet their rescued mariner and she sighed as she rested her head on the soft fabric. "Curse you, Stuart."

"MORNING." KERRY LIFTED a hand to wave at the man standing on the dock. Bob was dressed in khaki shorts a little too big for him, and the polo shirt he'd been wearing the night before. In the daylight, his slightly round, cheerful face and curly hair presented a picture of a reasonably good-looking man about Kerry's age. "C'mon aboard."

Bob took her up on her invitation and crossed the gangplank. "Thanks. Good morning to you," he replied, as his eyes took in her swim-suited body. Politely, he glanced away. "Weather cleared up at least, huh?"

Kerry turned and surveyed the clear horizon. "Sure did." She smiled. "We're not really ready to get underway yet. Want to come in and grab some coffee?"

"That'd be great. Thanks." He returned her smile warmly. "Listen...I...um..." He glanced around, then back at her. "I really want to thank you again, for what you did last night."

Kerry felt a curious mixture of pleasure and embarrassment. "I was glad to help," she said. "I'm really happy everything turned out all right."

"Me, too," Bob replied easily. "But it wouldn't have, if it hadn't been for you." He courteously held the door for her. "I won't forget that."

"Well, you're very welcome." Kerry entered the cabin, her eyes automatically tracking until she found Dar's tall figure behind the galley. "Got some extra coffee there, Dar?"

Dar's eyes flicked past her and a wry grin appeared. "Sure."

"Morning," Bob greeted Dar.

"Hi," Dar replied. "I'm going to get us ready to take off," she told Kerry. "I want to run up and talk to Charlie for a minute before we go."

"Okay." Kerry traded places with her, reaching for the coffee. "Tell them I said hi, okay?" She really didn't have any desire to face the troublesome Bud.

"Uh huh." Dar patted her back, then slipped past her and headed for the door.

Kerry smiled to herself and shook her head as she got down another cup from the cupboard. "How do you take it?" She looked up, a little surprised to find Bob leaning against the counter.

"Black," he replied, accepting the cup she offered. "Thanks." He took a cautious sip. "So, Kerry, we didn't get to talk much last night. Where are you from?"

Kerry poured herself a cup and added cream and sugar to it, then eased out of the galley and took a seat at the small table. Bob settled next to her, patiently waiting for her to answer.

"Michigan," Kerry said. "What about you?"

"Thought I recognized the accent. I'm from Detroit," he said with a grin. "My family owns some property just outside the city." He paused, sipping his coffee. "You go to Michigan University?"

Kerry nodded. "Matter of fact, I did."

"I went out of state to college," he related. "Boston." A

thoughtful look crossed his face. "My father's family is from there. Old seafaring men, you know."

"Mm."

"That's where I learned to sail," he added. "When I was a kid, and then again when I got older. It sounded as if you'd sailed a lot." He neatly turned the subject back to her. "That one of your hobbies?"

Kerry looked up and found him watching her face with a faint, shy, half smile. "No, not now." She propped her head on one hand. "Underwater photography, and keeping up with work." She came to the vague realization that Bob was showing some definite interest in her, and couldn't decide if she was amused or embarrassed. "How about helping me get the boat ready? Dar should be back soon."

"Sure," he agreed amiably. "You name it, I'm yours."

Yikes. Kerry slid out from behind the table. She hoped the trip to St. Johns was a short one.

"You know, I think we've really got a lot in common," Bob added.

Not nearly as much as you think. Kerry gave him a brief smile and held the door open. 'Well, we've got some of the same interests," she allowed. "But I like brunettes."

"Huh?"

DAR STUCK HER hands in her pockets as she walked up the sandy path. Bob's arrival had definitely put a knot in her shorts, and she'd considered violating the common rules of hospitality when she'd almost succumbed to the urge to toss his preppy butt right off the boat.

Ah, Dar, she chuckled wryly at herself. *Your background's showing. He's not a bad kid.* She kicked a pinecone ahead of her and glanced up the empty path. *You'll drop him off in St. Johns, and that'll be that.*

She climbed up the steps to Bud and Charlie's restaurant, and paused with her hand on the door when she heard loud voices inside.

"Thought you could duck out on me last night, huh?" A snarl preceded, "Where's the money?"

"Look, I told you we don't have the cash." Charlie's tone sounded uncharacteristically tense. "You can't get blood from a damn rock."

"Yeah?" the strange voice answered. "Well, either you cough up that ten grand, or there'll be plenty of blood on the floor of this dump, got me?"

"We can work somethin' out," Bud interjected. "You gotta give us time. You know we're good for it."

"I don't know shit." The stranger laughed. "'Cept I know I'll be back here day after t'morra, and either you give me what you owe, or I'll take what I can get out of your skin."

Heavy footsteps headed toward her, and Dar only just stepped back in time to avoid being smashed in the face as the door slammed open. A tall, burly man in a tank top and jeans that were far too tight shoved past her, giving her a cursory glance as he went by.

Dar stared at his back before she turned and entered the restaurant. Her appearance startled Bud and Charlie, and they broke apart a little, before they recognized her and relaxed. "What's going on?" she asked without preamble.

"Morning, Dar." Charlie couldn't quite summon his usual friendly smile. "Get a good night's sleep?"

Bud studied the floor.

"Fine," Dar replied briefly. "What's going on?" she asked again.

"Not your business," Bud answered gruffly.

"Bud." Charlie frowned at his partner's intentional rudeness. "Just a little business stuff, Dar. Nothing major."

Dar put her hands on her hips and gave them both the kind of look she usually reserved for newly hatched sales managers questioning her decisions. "I deal with business 'stuff' all the time, and I never get threatened with bodily harm, though most of the people I deal with probably consider it," she remarked. "Can the crap. What's Cheapside Guido's problem?"

"It's *none* of your business!" Bud snapped before he turned and thrust his way into the kitchen. The hinged door flapped wildly behind him, then stopped with a sodden thunk.

Charlie sighed and rubbed his forehead. "Damn it."

Dar waited with moderate patience. "C'mon, Charlie. You really want me to just forget it and leave, I will," she offered. "But if you need help, I'm listening."

Charlie glanced toward the kitchen door, then shrugged. "We can handle it," he finally said. "It's just the loan we took out to start up this place." He plucked at the pocket on his shorts. "Taking a little longer to pay back than we'd planned, but we'll work it out."

Dar studied her father's friend. "He wasn't from Bank of America."

Charlie snorted softly. "Hell no. Two beat-up Navy scrubs — you think they'd give us a loan?" he asked. "We just went to the co-op. But anyway..." He determinedly regained his good humor. "Everything settle down from last night? We chit chatted with Bob for a while. He's quite a talker."

"Charlie." Dar leaned against the wall. She plucked a pencil from Charlie's pocket and picked up a piece of torn envelope that was sitting on the counter next to them. "Here." She wrote down a phone number, then handed the envelope and the pencil back to him. "If that shark starts biting your ass, call me."

Reluctantly, he took the paper. "Dar, I appreciate it, but we can handle this. Bud'd sooner cut off his arm than ask for help." He hesitated. "'Specially yours." His face was apologetic.

"Too bad," Dar told him bluntly. "Tell him to grow up and get over it."

Charlie winced.

"I have to ask people I can't stand for things every day."

"It's not that he doesn't like you, Dar," Charlie protested hastily. "He does. We both do. He just can't forget stuff in the past with your dad, and..."

"*I* am not my dad," Dar broke in, leaning forward. "In case you hadn't noticed."

"No, I know that." Charlie sighed. "I know that, Dar." He ventured a smile. "Though you did grow up to look a whole lot like him, y'know," he insisted stubbornly.

Dar sighed inwardly, then gave up the effort, deciding on a different tack. "Yeah, that's what people tell me," she admitted. "Listen, we're heading out. Anything you guys need out there we can drop off on the way back?"

Now that the conversational topic had changed, Charlie relaxed. "WD40," he joked, tapping his artificial knee. "Always running out of the damn stuff." He cleared his throat. "Listen, Dar, you guys were asking about pirates last night."

"Hm?" Dar crossed her arms.

The big ex-serviceman glanced around. "They ain't always what they seem," he said.

"What do you mean?" Dar asked.

"Chuck!" Bud's voice interrupted. "Fish man's here!"

Charlie glanced at the kitchen. "Them jerks last night, they ain't the kinda pirates we know about," he said quickly. "That's all I'm saying. Good luck, good trip." He put a hand on the door, then took a last look at Dar. "Tell your dad I said hey."

Dar watched him disappear, then released a sigh, letting her glance travel around the inside of the tattered and somewhat threadbare restaurant. With a silent shake of her head, she turned and left the room, emerging back into the sunlight. The island's emptiness surrounded her, and as she walked back toward the dock, her mind turned over the puzzle pieces that, though scattered, were beginning to nudge at her with their curious nature.

She spotted the loan shark as she walked onto the dock. He was standing next to a small, racy looking runabout with another man, half his size. They were both looking at the *Dixieland Yankee*, and they turned to watch Dar as she approached the boat.

"Hey, baby," the bigger man yelled over. "That your boat?"

Dar paused and looked at him over the top of her sunglasses. "Yeah," she replied briefly, as she paused to unloop the bow line.

"Want a good man to drive her?"

Dar tossed the line onboard then walked to the stern, released the boat, and leaped onto the back deck. "No thanks." She dropped the line and dusted off her hands, turned her back on the two of them, and ignored their ribald laughter.

Kerry emerged from the cabin, an almost fierce grin crossing her face as she spotted Dar. "Thought I heard you," she greeted her lover. "We outta here?"

"Oh yeah." Dar made her way up to the flying bridge. "Let's go find some better scenery." She took her seat and started up the engines, adjusted the throttles, and eased the boat out of the dock. At low tide, maneuvering in the cramped space was even more difficult, and she had to really concentrate to avoid taking out part of the dock on her way out.

She cleared the last pylon and turned into the channel, feeling the wind pick up as she increased speed and headed out across the green-blue water.

KERRY CAREFULLY PLACED her deck chair on the stern, half turned so she could look up and watch Dar at the controls of the boat. She settled into it as Bob took the seat next to her, and she resigned herself to a trip full of small talk. "So, Bob—you never did get around to saying last night. Were you on vacation?"

Bob leaned on the chair arm. "Vacation? I wish." He sighed. "No, it's..." he glanced around, "kinda stupid, really."

If he tells me he came out here looking for his one true love, I'll chuck up on him, Kerry thought, all the while keeping a pleasant expression on her face. "How stupid could it be?" she asked.

He edged a little closer. "Remember what I said about my grandparents?"

"From Boston," Kerry promptly replied, lest he repeat his tale.

"Yeah." Bob nodded. "My grandfather was lost at sea."

Kerry straightened a little. "Oh. I'm really sorry to hear that," she said sincerely. "How did it happen?"

"He was the captain of a...um...fishing boat," Bob admitted. "Not very glamorous, I know, but he was really successful at it," he added. "Anyway, he was out here on a trip to the islands and he just never came back."

Kerry leaned back in her chair and tucked one leg up under her. "Wow." She shook her head. "That's really sad. They never found the boat or anything?"

Bob gazed at her. "They know where it went down. This guy
who was a witness contacted my grandmother and sold her a map—"
"Sold her?"

Bob shrugged. "Yeah, I know, probably a sucker deal. But she
gave me the map, and I decided I'd come out here and see what I
could find."

Kerry frowned. "You don't even know if it's accurate."

"No, but it's something," Bob said. "Problem is, I came out here
and found out that the spot he supposedly went down has been
licensed by some salvage outfit."

One of Kerry's eyebrows hiked slightly. "Really?" she said. "A
salvage outfit, huh?"

"Yeah. I tried to talk to them, but they ran me out of there."
Bob shook his head. "Real bunch of jerks. Big-money types, you
know." He gave her a wry smile. "The kind that like to let you
know it."

"Uh huh." Kerry wondered if it was the same pair they'd run
into. "Were they sort of young, a thin guy and a bossy woman?"

Surprised, Bob nodded. "Yeah! You know them?"

Kerry got up and paced over to the cooler, opened it, and
removed a chilled bottle of iced tea. She was aware of Bob's eyes on
her back—could almost feel the heat between her shoulder blades—
and she briefly wished she'd put her overalls on over her sheer
bathing suit. "Not exactly," she answered his question. "We ran
into them back at that island. They were asking about a site Dar and
I dove that day." She returned. "I guess it was part of that area
you're interested in."

"Really?" Bob murmured. "So you're a real diver, huh? Got all
your own gear?"

Kerry nodded. "Sure." She opened her tea and took a sip.
"Dar's a master diver." She glanced fondly up at her lover, who was
leaning back with one bare foot propped up against the console.
"We've even got a compressor on board for refills."

"I always wanted to learn to dive," Bob said. "You got any
pointers for me?" he asked. "Hey, how about a lesson tomorrow?"

Eight-bit card, thirty-two bit bus. Kerry sighed inwardly. "Sorry,
we've got plans," she said. "But there are lots of places in St. Johns
that have certification courses."

"Yeah. I'd better get my insurance stuff straightened out
tomorrow, anyway." Bob sighed. "You staying anywhere special on
the island?"

"Dar made the reservations." Kerry smiled. "I can't remember
the name of the place."

"Oh."

Kerry spotted a fringe of land on the port side of the boat. She
got up and peered around the corner of the cabin. A low, beautiful

island stretched out before her, offering a semicircle of pure white beach backed by lush, green foliage. "Wow."

Bob came up behind her. "Yeah. It's beautiful, isn't it?" he murmured. "Hey, maybe I'll stick around a few days. Since I can't do anything else, might as well catch some rays, right?"

Kerry exhaled silently, rolling her eyes outside of his line of vision.

"Besides, I owe you dinner and a drink," Bob said. "You gotta at least let me do that, for what you did for me."

Yikes. Kerry watched the marina approach. "Dar, you want me to call in to the dockmaster?"

"Yep," Dar responded. "Looks like it's busy."

Kerry turned. "Excuse me." She waited for Bob to back off, then walked to the cabin radio. "St. Johns Marina, St. Johns Marina, this is the *Dixieland Yankee*. Over."

"That's a cute name," Bob offered. "Does it mean something?"

Kerry eyed him wryly. "She's the Dixie part and I'm the Yankee," she explained simply.

"*Dixieland Yankee*, this is St. Johns. G'wan."

Bob cocked his head, producing a puzzled smile. "Oh. You guys related?"

Kerry sighed and leaned against the cabin door. "St. Johns, we have a reservation for a berth. Please advise." She gave Bob a kindly smile. "You might want to sit down. Sounds like a busy dock."

"Okay." Bob wandered over and took a seat, leaving Kerry to finish her radio work.

"Gotcha, *Dixieland Yankee*. Tenth row, third berth. You've got 54 feet, yeah?"

"That's a roger," Kerry replied. "Thanks." She put down the radio mic and walked to the ladder, climbing up it as fast as dignity allowed and joining Dar at the console. "Row ten, slot three." She sat down and rested her elbows on her knees. "Dar..."

"How's your little worshipper doing?" Dar drawled, giving her a wicked smile. "He invited you to dinner yet?"

Kerry sighed. "Dinner, drinks, diving, you name it," she muttered. "Why do guys always do that?"

Dar eyed her. "'Cause you're charming and adorable?"

"Pffffttt." Kerry stuck out her tongue. "But you know something? He had a run-in with those 24 karat sleezoids we met on the island, too."

"Yeah?"

"Yeah. He's looking for the wreck of his grandfather's fishing boat. Supposedly it went down in that area they blocked off."

Dar frowned. "Busy spot of ocean."

"Mm."

They looked at each other. Kerry scratched her jaw. "Um. He really did ask me to dinner, to thank me for saving his life." She studied Dar's face. "Would you mind if I went?"

Dar's expression went still for a moment, only the tiny muscles on the sides of her eyes twitching. A silence fell between them as Dar glanced at the oncoming marina and adjusted their course. She watched the console for a moment, then returned her eyes to Kerry's face. She spoke very softly. "Yes, I would mind."

Kerry felt a mixture of surprise and pleasure. Surprise, because she'd expected Dar to profess a disinterest in preventing her from going, and pleasure because of the gut-level honesty of the actual reaction she'd gotten. "Good." She exhaled. "Because I would, if it were me."

Dar grinned briefly. "Jealousy's an interesting sensation," she commented, before she returned her careful attention to their approach.

"Mm," Kerry agreed, watching the island grow larger. "Ain't that the truth."

KERRY NUDGED OPEN the door to their room and peered inside. "Whoa." She chuckled as she entered and tossed her overnight bag down on the king size bed. "Definitely more colorful than your average Marriott."

Dar closed the door. She eyed the peach walls, strongly patterned carpet, and rich fabrics on the windows and bed with a half grin. "I like it," she decided. "Wouldn't want it in my bedroom, but it's nice for a change." She put her own bag down and reviewed the rest of the room. It had a high, peaked ceiling, with a fan and a dual vent to remove the hot air from the room. The windows were large and featured a gorgeous view of the half circle bay, and the atmosphere was light and airy.

Kerry went to the window and looked out. "Nice." She turned and leaned on the sill, watching Dar take off her sunglasses and toss them on the table. Much to Kerry's relief, when they'd docked Bob had scampered off to take care of his business, and she was looking forward to exploring the resort's interesting offerings. She'd spotted kayaks, among other things, and seen mention in the lobby of a rum-tasting demonstration.

Dar lifted the bottle of complimentary rum from the sideboard and held it up. "Very nice." There was also bottled water. "Use this," she cautioned Kerry. "I've had mixed results drinking from the tap."

"Ah. Thanks," Kerry said. "Not having phones was a surprise, though."

"Mm." Dar examined the discrete data port. "Internet access

but no phones. Incredible."

Kerry went to the locked, distressed leather briefcase Dar had put down on the chair. "I guess we've gotta bite the bullet, huh?" They'd agreed not to unlock the case, which held their cell phones and pagers, unless a full-blown crisis was at hand.

"Yeap." Dar tossed her the keys to the briefcase. "Probably better off using ours anyway." She watched Kerry unlock the catch and open the case, stick her hand inside, and withdraw one of their two phones. "I know there's phones outside in the lobby, but..."

"Yeah." Kerry tossed the phone to Dar, then she wandered back over to the windows, discovering a patio outside. "Hey." She opened the door and went out onto the stone edifice, alternately splashed with sunlight and the shade from nearby banana trees. It was quiet and peaceful, and the view of the water was quite spectacular. "Breakfast out here tomorrow, I think," Kerry mused, as a breeze off the water puffed her hair back out of her eyes.

With a satisfied grunt, she turned and went back inside their pleasant room, where she found Dar sprawled across the king size canopy bed with the phone to her ear. The sight was so attractive, Kerry decided to join her, and she crawled over to where Dar was lying, flipped over onto her back, and settled there as she watched the fan circle lazily overhead.

"That's right, Mark. Just run it for me." Dar inched her hand over and tugged a bit of Kerry's hair. "I don't have the registration number."

Mark's voice trickled from the cell phone's speaker. "Right, boss. How's the vacation going?"

"Aside from nearly being heaved to by pirates, and Kerry saving a drowning man in a storm, it's been pretty peaceful," Dar replied blandly. "How's it been there?"

A long silence ensued. "Did you actually fucking say pirates?" Mark asked. "Holy shit, Dar!"

"You didn't really think we could just have an ordinary vacation, did you?" Dar asked with an amused smirk. "You didn't answer my question."

"Huh?" Mark spluttered. "Oh, here? It's been dead," he told her. "Honest."

Dar waited silently. To pass the time, she blew gently in Kerry's ear and watched her torso shiver as she held back a laugh.

"Well, just the usual shit, you know, boss," Mark finally admitted. "Nothin' you guys need to worry about."

Kerry turned her head at that and her green eyes widened. "Mark?" She raised her voice. "You just made me really nervous."

"Um..."

Dar covered her eyes. "Mark, just spill it," she sighed.

"Honest, guys, just more of the usual," Mark insisted. "We've got some international lines down, and one of the northwest data centers crashed. I had to overnight them a bunch of stuff."

Kerry eyed her partner. 'Doesn't sound that bad,' she mouthed.

Dar shrugged. "Did the new DC nodes come in?"

"Yep." Mark sounded relieved. "Hey, listen, I'm glad you called for one thing — we got an early drop date for the new back-up IPC."

Kerry pumped her fist in the air. "Whoohoo."

"Incredible," Dar agreed. "I thought we'd be waiting until February."

"Well, boss — nothing came back on those guys," Mark said. "Not on the first run. You want me to keep going?"

Dar frowned. "Nothing?"

"Nothing on that name, no — or the two other names you gave me," Mark said. "But that's just a DMV and Marine reg. I'll do a deep run on 'em. You want me to give you a call back?"

"Yeah," Dar said. "We're going to..." She paused. "What are we going to do now, Ker?"

Kerry lifted both hands in the air and produced an engaging grin.

"We're gonna do something probably involving water and/or food," Dar said into the phone. "I'll keep the phone on. Let me know if you find anything, okay?"

"Will do, boss," Mark said. "You guys have a great time, huh? No more freaking pirates!"

"Do our best," Kerry called out. "Thanks, Mark. Tell everyone we said hi."

Dar disconnected the call and set the phone on the covers. Now that she'd set her query in motion, she felt satisfied to let it take whatever time it did, and in the meanwhile concentrate on resuming her vacation. "Want to just hike out and explore the place for a while?" she asked. "We're in the middle of the national park here."

Kerry nodded. "I like that idea," she said. "It's so pretty. Reminds me a little of that hammock down by Old Cutler we went to that one time." She sat up. "Okay, on with the hiking boots, then." She patted Dar's leg. "Let's go find us some pretty lizards."

LIZARDS, THEY FOUND in plenty, along with other assorted wildlife. Dar gingerly examined a vivid, bright green snake curled on a branch, taking care to keep her hands far away from it. "Did you see this?" she asked Kerry, who was busy taking a picture of some gorgeous flowers.

"See what?" Kerry trotted over and peered. "Oh!" She quickly brought up her camera and focused. "Hey, aren't you going to grab its tail and tell me what a beauty it is?"

Dar glanced down. "Does wearing khaki shorts and hiking boots require me to channel Steve Irwin?" she asked.

Kerry snickered. "Yes."

"Tell you what tail I'm gonna grab." Dar waited for her to snap the picture, then acted, grabbing onto Kerry's tail and making her hop forward with a startled squawk. "Isn't she a beauty?" Dar mimicked. "Lookit the bottom on that one!"

"Wench." Kerry reached behind her and tickled Dar's ribs, then continued down the path. They were surrounded by lush greenery, and a rich, organic smell filled her lungs as the wind stirred the branches. The jungle around them thinned ahead and revealed a mossy, stone-covered building. "Look, Dar." Kerry motioned toward it. "Is that one of the sugar mills?"

"Must be." Dar led the way toward the structure. It was just a pile of old stone now, a mixture of coral foundation and crudely made brick. They climbed onto it and looked around. Dar imagined she could still smell the tang of raw sugar cane, something she'd last tasted as a young child. "You ever chew sugar cane?" she asked Kerry.

"Me?" Kerry was kneeling next to a piece of machinery long overgrown with ivy. "You're kidding, right?" She looked over her shoulder at Dar. "One, I don't think it grows in Michigan, and two, my mother would have cut the hands off anyone giving it to me." She paused. "Have you?"

"Sure." Dar grinned. "The best is to get a nice piece, chew it a little, then dunk it in your lemonade."

Kerry's gaze went inward for a moment as she worked out the potential tastes; then she wiggled her eyebrows and licked her lips. "Mm." She got up and snapped a picture of the bit of machinery. "That does sound really good."

Dar wandered over to a row of old wooden basins nailed onto the walls with rusted iron spikes. The mill had made sugar for sale, and for the rum and molasses that had been the impetus for the island's colonization. Slaves had worked there under increasingly brutal conditions until they'd eventually risen up and conquered their masters, driving the plantation owners out and leaving the island to peacefully stagnate until modern times and modern tourism.

"Must have been brutal working here," Dar mused, touching grooves worn in the wooden sinks from countless wrists resting on them as they washed the cane.

"Mm," Kerry agreed, imagining the sweltering summer heat. "Maybe we should bring the staff over here when they start complaining about the vending machine selection."

Dar chuckled. "Just take lots of pictures," she advised. "Wow, did you see that?"

Kerry examined the huge wheels curiously. "What is it?"

"Grinding stone," Dar explained. "They put the cane between that and ground it up to get out the sugar syrup."

Kerry leaned over and sniffed the stone. "Just smells like mildew now," she said. "It's hard to believe that a place like this, as full of misery as it must have been, produced something so many people regard as a treat."

"Yeah," Dar agreed. "Speaking of which, want to stop and have our sandwiches?"

After Dar spent a moment making sure they weren't about to sit on any snakes or scorpions, they picked a spot on the edge of the coral foundation. Kerry opened the pack Dar had been carrying and removed a Thermos bottle and two neatly wrapped packages. She set down the Thermos and unwrapped the sandwiches, crusty French bread wrapped around spicy shrimp salad.

"Wow." Kerry handed Dar hers. "This looks great. All this hiking has made me hungry."

"Mmph." Dar had already taken a bite. She uncapped the Thermos and poured out a capful of its contents, took a sip, and passed it over to Kerry. "Coconut and passion fruit. Interesting."

Kerry washed down her mouthful and took another. "Very." She kicked her heels against the foundation and looked around, enjoying the food, the view, and the utter freedom of being in an unknown place with the person she loved best in the world.

"They've got horseback trails," Dar commented hopefully. "Interested?"

Kerry glanced at her knowingly. "Make a deal with you," she bargained adroitly. "Horseback riding one day, windsailing the next?" She didn't quite have the enthusiasm for horses that Dar did, but then Dar didn't quite share her love of wild water sports. However, compromise was good. It was a learning process, like everything else, and slowly they'd worked out a way to balance their differences. *Mostly*, Kerry acknowledged wryly. There were still some things they were working on. "Deal?"

"Okay." Dar wiped her mouth with a paper napkin. She leaned back against the ruined wall and relaxed while Kerry finished up her lunch, the blonde woman resting an elbow on Dar's knee. "A lot of people come out here and camp in the park."

Kerry watched an ant the size of a Jeep walk by. "Good for them," she said. "I admire their courage and fortitude."

Dar watched the ant, almost jumping when the tiny animal was suddenly attacked by an almost invisible lizard, whose tongue whipped out and tethered the ant before the insect could even twitch an antenna. The lizard sucked the ant in and casually chewed it, rotating an eye to peer up at Dar with benign disinterest.

"Ah." Kerry blinked. "Mother Nature in all her gory glory." She held a hand out toward the lizard, and it reciprocated by opening its jaws wide, displaying bits of dismembered ant as well as a double ridge of tiny razor teeth. "Yikes," she exclaimed. "Makes you feel really insignificant, doesn't it?"

Dar reached over lazily and, with a quick motion, captured the lizard. It struggled wildly as she brought it back over to her face. "Listen, buddy," she growled at it, "don't threaten my girl or I'll make lizard burgers out of you, got me?"

Kerry had to laugh at the bug-eyed look on the lizard's face.

"I don't care how many rhino-sized ants you suck up, you don't scare me," Dar warned, as the lizard stuck its tongue out at her. "So, beat it." She opened her hand and released the animal. It leaped off her hand and onto her shirt, then scampered up over her shoulder and onto the nearest bit of wall.

Kerry leaned against Dar's knee and gazed adoringly at her. Dar smirked and managed a self-deprecating chuckle.

"Hey, Dar?"

"Yeah?" Dar let her head rest against the wall.

"Anyone ever tell you you're a lot of fun?"

Dar considered. "No, no one's ever said that," she replied matter-of-factly. "I have been told I'm like being in a phone booth with a dozen porcupines in heat, though."

Kerry kissed Dar's knee, then laid her cheek against it. "My question to whoever said that would be, of course, 'how do *you* know?'"

"It was Eleanor."

"Ah. That explains a lot." Kerry grinned and gave Dar's leg a squeeze. "Well, you *are* a lot of fun, and I'm so totally enjoying this vacation."

Dar grinned back at her wholeheartedly. "Me, too," she agreed. "Even with the pirates." She leaned over and kissed Kerry gently. "I'm glad you're having as much fun as I am."

They rested a few minutes longer in the old cane mill, then resumed their hike. Dar shouldered the pack and cinched down the straps, and they started off up a path that was now getting noticeably steeper. "Hey," Dar observed, "it's a hill."

"Sure you can handle it, Dixiecup?" Kerry teased.

"Wanna find out?" Dar grinned. "Let's race." She broke into a jog.

"Pooters." Kerry sighed. "Someday I'll learn." She shook her head and chased after Dar, hoping it wouldn't be a really, really big hill.

"URGH." KERRY STEPPED under the pounding shower and scrubbed her body with a piece of natural sponge. She'd finished up their hike sweaty, covered in dirt, and with leaves stuffed down her shirt, courtesy of her lover, and the water felt heavenly as it washed away the grime. Kerry washed a smear of green off her shoulder and thought of how it had gotten there. They'd had so much fun.

After she'd chased Dar up the hill, they'd rolled down the other side, across a short swath of rich green undergrowth, and into a muddy embankment over a small creek. With a thumbful of mud, she'd painted tiger stripes across Dar's cheekbones, and they'd ended up going headfirst into the creek as they wrestled playfully.

Kerry soaped up her hair, which the mirror had reflected as closer to brown than blonde from the mud. She watched as the dirt rinsed away down the drain and her locks returned to their normal color. "Uck." She turned off the water and stepped out of the shower, toweling her body briskly before donning one of the thick, comfortable robes the resort helpfully provided.

Still ruffling her hair dry, Kerry opened the door and walked into their room. Dar was standing near the window talking on her cell phone, clad in nothing but a brief, though fluffy, towel that just barely covered her long torso from armpit to thigh. Her damp hair was slicked back, and it was all Kerry could do to keep from just walking over and removing the towel.

Instead, she merely sidled up to her partner and waited until Dar made eye contact with her. 'You look gorgeous when you're wet,' she mouthed, causing Dar to stop in mid-word and blink.

"Uh..." Dar paused, her train of thought completely derailed. "Sorry, what was that, Mark?" She reached out and tweaked Kerry's nose. "I got distracted."

"No problem, Dar," Mark said with a stifled yawn. "Anyway, the long run came up with a ton of crap. I think you'd better take a look at it."

"What is it?"

There was a long silence before Mark answered. "I think you'd better look at it. Maybe you can make more sense of it than I could."

"Hm." Dar glanced at the sun, which was painting the sky as it began its descent into the water's edge. "All right. Go ahead and bundle it and send it down. I'll pick it up when I get back from dinner."

"Gotcha," Mark said. "Hey, everyone says hi. Maria says to tell you everything's under control."

Dar gave Kerry a pointed look. "Good to hear," she commented. "Thanks, Mark."

"No problem," the MIS chief assured her. "Take it easy, Dar."

Dar closed her phone, then focused her attention on the robed figure in front of her. "You, Kerrison, are a little troublemaker."

Kerry grinned unrepentantly. "I learned from the best." She poked Dar in the belly. "Did Mark find something?"

"Yeah." Dar nodded. "Apparently he did, but he didn't want to discuss it on the cell."

"Uh oh."

"Yeah." Dar remained cheerful, however. "But I'd rather know what the hell I'm dealing with." She leaned on the window and gazed out. "Can I interest you in joining me at the Equator?"

"Is that the restaurant in the old mill?"

Dar nodded. "Seeing as you were so interested in the ruins, I figured maybe you'd enjoy eating in one." She picked up the colorful, cotton island shifts they'd purchased in the market. "And it'll give us an excuse to wear these outside our living room."

Kerry held one of them — in a flame red, green, and bright yellow pattern — up against Dar. "Oh yeah." She grinned impishly. "I want to see you in this, for sure."

Dar plucked wryly at the garish garment. "Only for you would I do this," she informed her lover. "I hope you realize that."

"I do." Suddenly overwhelmed by a wave of emotion, Kerry threw her arms around Dar in an unexpected hug. She squeezed Dar hard, scarcely able to breathe for a moment.

"Hey," Dar murmured, returning the hug despite her confusion.

"Dear Lord," Kerry was surprised to feel the sting of tears, "how did I get so lucky to have found you?"

"Um." Dar was caught flat-footed. "You got hired by a company ILS took over?" she offered hesitantly. "Besides, I thought I was the lucky one."

Kerry shook her head mutely, burying her face against Dar's bare shoulder.

Dar rubbed her back gently through the robe, simply holding Kerry until she felt her relax. "Sweetheart," she murmured, "I'm glad you feel that way."

Kerry sniffled and just squeezed her harder. After a few more minutes, however, she exhaled and tipped her head to one side, glancing up at Dar. "I'm not going crazy."

Dar stroked her hair back and removed the remnants of her tears with the edge of her thumb. "I never thought you were," she said. "We've just been through a hell of a lot together this year. You're entitled to a few freak-out moments."

They were, it seemed, exactly the right words. Kerry's face relaxed into a broad smile, and she gave Dar an affectionate pat on the side. "Thanks, Dr. Dar."

Dar Roberts, relationship expert and amateur psychologist. Dar felt a mental, slightly hysterical giggle coming on. She kissed Kerry's damp head instead. "Anytime, sweetheart. I'll always be here for you."

Kerry felt a quiet resonance as she heard those words. They touched something deep inside her, and she felt her spirit calm in response to them as a smile appeared on her face. "I know you will," she replied. "And I'll always be here for you." Her head lifted and she met Dar's eyes. "Thanks for understanding."

Dar felt like she'd been visited with a miracle, because in a very deep way, she did understand. Or, at least, she understood that Kerry was hurting, and that she had the ability to stop the hurt and heal some of the pain. That was a pretty damn nice feeling.

Kerry squared her shoulders and released Dar, holding her briefly by her shoulders before she picked up the shifts again. "Well then, let's get our garish duds on and go have some fun."

Relieved, Dar returned the smile. "All right, let's go." She leaned over and touched the floral basket. "You're not gonna make me wear one of these in my hair, are you?"

Kerry glanced at the flowers, then at Dar. A mischievous glint appeared in her eyes, but she demurred. "No, you get to escape that."

"Uh oh." Dar put her hands on her towel-clad hips. "I'm in trouble."

"Heh...but not too much." Kerry grinned, her spirits restored. "C'mon. Let's go."

The sun continued to dip lazily to the horizon, painting the sea in gold.

Chapter
Ten

THE RESTAURANT WAS charming; the sunset was gorgeous; the food was interesting and very tasty; and she was sitting across from what was definitely the best looking woman in the place. Kerry lifted her glass of wine and raised it in Dar's direction, then took a sip of it, savoring the slightly spicy, sweet taste. *There is really no more one could ask for, is there?* "Great choice."

Dar lifted her own glass, touched its rim to Kerry's, and smiled. "Nice place, but it's the company that counts."

Kerry accepted the compliment with a smile, then rested her wrists on the table and looked around. According to the menu, the building had once been a sugar mill overlooking the water. Parts of the structure still remained, and they'd cleverly fashioned the restaurant into it. The food was a mixture of Caribbean and American, and Kerry had just finished a bowl of extremely spicy shrimp gumbo. Dar had elected to try a Caribbean fruit mixture rather than soup, and they'd split a bottle of Chardonnay while they waited for the main course.

Kerry leaned back, enjoying the breeze as it brushed across her bare shoulders. There was a gently fluttering candle on the table, and she could smell the warm scent of the wax as it melted, which added to the atmosphere. A steel drum band was perched on a patio nearby, playing softly, and all around her a mixture of lilting accents wove in and out of the music.

She noticed that the guests were mostly just couples. There were very few families, and those that were there had older children. Most of the couples were traditional, but Kerry spotted at least two other sets of women and three other sets of men seated together, and she felt comfortable in the place. Even with the fact that Dar kept tweaking her toes under the table.

Kerry snuck a glance at her tablemate, who was studying the driftwood salt and pepper shakers, curiously turning them in her fingers. Dar wore her hair loose, and her brightly colored cotton shift clung to her body, very nicely outlining its muscular grace. The shift was pretty, but God, Kerry had to admit, it was so not

Dar. It was like putting a racehorse in a tutu.

Dar chose that moment to look up, and their eyes met. Dar's face creased into a grin as she put the shaker down. "Something wrong?"

"Not a damn thing." Kerry rested her chin on her fist. "That sunset is indescribable," she added dreamily. "You think it's this nice in Hawaii?"

"Hmm." Dar regarded the spectacle. "I don't know. I've never actually been there except on a layover on the way out to Micronesia. We'll have to go find out," she said. "I want to see a volcano up close."

"You're on," Kerry said. "How about mid-February?"

"Valentine's Day on Maui?" Dar chuckled. "Sure."

Kerry made a mental note to nose around for some reservations when they got home. Their waitress appeared at that moment and set down a tray with wisps of steam rising from it. She watched as a plate was set in front of her, containing a sizzling piece of broiled fish propped up with prawns half the size of their puppy Chino and drizzled with a tangy, citrusy sauce. "Ooh. Thanks."

The waitress set down a side plate of vegetables. "You're very welcome." She smiled at Kerry, then took Dar's plate from the serving tray and set it in front of her. "Anything else for you ladies?"

Dar inspected her surf and turf—a filet mignon nestled next to a lobster tail. "Nope. Not right now," she said. "Thanks." She picked up her fork and knife, separated the two items around the island of whipped yams, and started to cut the filet into pieces. "This looks great."

"Smells great, too." Kerry craned her neck to see. "What is that sauce?"

"Pineapple and coconut rum." Dar dipped a square of meat into it and then offered it to Kerry, who neatly took it off the end of her fork.

"Mm," Kerry mumbled approvingly. "I'll try that next time." She offered a taste of her fish in return, which Dar accepted.

"Tastes like Mandarin oranges," Dar commented. "Nice."

Kerry had taken one bite of her fish when her attention was captured by a couple who was just entering the restaurant. "Yrch." She caught Dar's eye and indicated the door. Christen and Juan Carlos had just stepped in, and were being greeted by the host.

"There goes the neighborhood." Dar nibbled a bit of her filet. "Wonder if she paid for that dress by the inch."

Christen was wearing an outfit of gold chain, which barely covered her tanned and very fit body from mid-thigh to chest. The outfit had gaps in the sides, and a jeweled belt hung below her navel. Juan complemented her in a gold silk shirt, a matte black silk jacket, and leather pants.

"Someone forget to tell them they weren't visiting New York?" Kerry leaned over and murmured, "Last time I saw clothes like that was out on South Beach at that TV chef's opening night."

The newcomers were led to a prime table near the edge of the open air seating. As Christen sat down, she spotted Dar and Kerry across the room. She put a hand on Juan Carlos' arm, then made her way over.

"Yip, yip yippee yahooey." Dar rolled her eyes, then assumed a cordially neutral expression as the woman neared. "Evening."

"Why, hello! Imagine bumping into you two here," Christen greeted them. "Visiting, or...staying here?"

"We're staying here," Kerry answered smoothly. "Did you just get in?"

"Last night," Christen replied with a smile. "Isn't it great? What a beautiful spot." She leaned on the balustrade next to them, the gold chains in her outfit clinking gently. "I'm glad we bumped into you again; I was afraid we'd lost you when you disappeared from the docks. You didn't get caught out in the weather, did you?"

Dar answered that one. "Just went on a cruise. We got back late."

"Really?" Christen was watching Dar closely. "Listen, some friends of ours ran into trouble out west of that little island. You didn't happen to see them out there, did you?"

Dar's ice blue eyes chilled and shaded. "Friends of yours?" she asked softly. "No. We didn't see anyone in trouble last night."

Recognizing the change in Dar's demeanor, Kerry kept quiet.

"Oh. Well," Christen replied. "I really didn't get the whole story, but they think someone might have run them aground. But that wouldn't have been really friendly, now would it?"

"Depends on what they were doing to make someone want to do that." Dar looked her right in the eye, suddenly projecting an air of surprisingly dark menace all out of character with her gaudy print dress.

They fenced for a moment, then Christen laughed a touch uncomfortably. "Well, who knows? Maybe they were mistaken, or...knowing them, they goofed in the navigation and are just trying to cover it up." She backed off a step. "Anyway, we'll see you around. Maybe we can do lunch?"

"Sure." Dar let the word roll off her tongue, keeping her eyes pinned on the smaller woman. "Anytime."

Christen beat a hasty retreat. Dar kept up her testy glower for a moment, then relaxed, hiking an eyebrow at the attentively watching Kerry. "Well?"

"You get a ten from the American judge." Kerry held up her napkin, peeking behind her to see Christen and Juan in close consultation, complete with uneasy looks in their general direction. "You know, Dar, for someone who's dressed like a passion fruit sundae, you really can scare the pooters out of people."

Dar snickered, then shook her head. "I shouldn't laugh. That probably wasn't funny." She eyed the two newcomers.

"You don't seriously think those goons'll try to find us, do you?" Kerry asked. "I mean, for running them aground. They were chasing us, Dar."

"I don't know." Dar sliced off a bit of her filet and ate it. "Let me get back to you after I have a chance to check out what Mark sent."

"Okay." Kerry went back to her dinner. She was a little surprised at how unworried she was about this new wrinkle. In fact, she felt more intrigued than frightened. Maybe she was turning into a little bit of a risk taker. She took in a forkful of the fish, enjoying the half-sweet, half-tangy taste, then washed the mouthful down with a long sip of wine. "Dar?"

"Hm?" Dar looked up from her task of decimating her lobster tail.

"You think this is dangerous?"

Dar paused, folded her hands, and rested her chin on them. "Dangerous?" she asked. "I think we bumped into some folks who are used to getting their own way."

"Mm." Kerry nodded.

"They shot flares at us last night," Dar went on seriously, "not bullets."

Ah. That is very, very true. "Shot them off the sides, too," Kerry realized. "So you think they're overbearing, obnoxious bullies, but only willing to go so far to achieve their goals?"

"Exactly." Dar went back to her plate with a satisfied look. "Unfortunately for them," she looked up from her dinner, "they're up against an equally overbearing, obnoxious bully who won't stop until she gets what she wants." She winked. "And I want a nice, peaceful vacation."

Kerry cocked her head and thought about that. "I don't think you're overbearing and obnoxious, and you're definitely not a bully," she finally stated positively. "But I do agree they've bitten off more than they can chew with us." She gave a brisk nod, then bit into a prawn and ruthlessly ripped it from its shell.

Dar merely chuckled and shook her head.

A SURPRISE WAS waiting for them when they got back to their room. Kerry warily eyed the basket of flowers and shot Dar a look. "You're the only person I'd welcome getting these from, but I'm guessing they're not from you."

Dar regarded the floral intrusion. "No." She searched the arrangement for a card. "For one thing, I know what kind of flowers you like," she said. "Tulips not being among them. Ah." She plucked a small square of cardboard from amid the greenery and held it to her forehead as she closed her eyes in psychic concentration. "The answer is...Bob." She handed the card over without looking at it.

Kerry sighed, took the card and peeked at it. "Can we rent you out to the Psychic Hotline?"

Dar shook her head. "Ker, you're just going to have to tell him straight out to back off, you're taken," she advised wryly. "He's one of those guys who can't picture two women together and think anything other than 'lunch.'"

"Yeah, I know." Kerry laughed helplessly as she removed the basket to the table near the door and plopped down onto the bed. "I figured while we were docking the boat, my referring to you as my partner and saying this was our delayed honeymoon would have clued him in, but I guess not."

Dar slid down beside her and plucked the card from Kerry's fingers, tossing it over her shoulder as she found something much more interesting to concentrate on. "Know what I like about these bawdy excuses for cut-up tablecloths?"

"Tch." Kerry smoothed her hand over Dar's hip. "You look cute in it," she protested. "But no, what?"

Dar closed her teeth around one of the ties holding Kerry's wrap closed and tugged on it, pulling it loose. "They come off easy." She peeled back one edge, exposing Kerry's chest, then went for the lower tie. She pulled it slowly, her eyes tracking up Kerry's body to meet her eyes. "See?"

Kerry felt Dar's hair brush against her thighs as she undid the fastening and laid her body bare to the soft breeze coming in from the window. She eased up onto her elbows, watching Dar's back arch as she prowled her way on up. "Sweetheart?" Kerry murmured.

"Yeees?" Dar rested her chin against Kerry's navel.

"I would love to spend the next few hours being ravished by you, but don't you think we should pick up Mark's stuff first?"

Dar sighed, a rush of very warm air that caused goose bumps to rise across Kerry's breasts. "No," she growled softly. "But..." She slid all the way up Kerry's body, bringing a rush of raw sensuality with her, then dipped her head to capture Kerry's lips for a long moment. "I guess we have to."

As Dar lifted herself up and off the bed, Kerry regretted having said a word. She exhaled and rolled over, then stood and trotted after her taller partner as she went to the briefcase tucked between the dresser and the wall. She waited for Dar to unlock the top, then slid her arms around her partner and started playing with the strings on Dar's shift as she pulled out the laptop and put it on the table.

Dar glanced over her shoulder. "Thought you wanted me to set this up."

"I'm helping." Kerry untangled a cable and plugged it in, still with her arms around Dar's body.

"Ah." Dar booted the laptop and flipped up its cellular antenna. "Thought we weren't bringing this."

"Yeah, I know." Kerry poked her head under Dar's left arm, watching the screen. "But I figured if something catastrophic did happen, and the office needed us, we'd have to have this to do anything about it."

"Good thought."

"And if they called us for something stupid, we could toss it overboard and make Mark get you a new one in that snazzy blue color you like so much." Kerry found another string to tug on, and Dar's shift fell as open as hers was. "Ooh... nice desktop."

"I could put this one on." Dar casually clicked a few keys and replaced her peaceful forest scene with one of Kerry on the beach. Naked.

"EEEK!" Kerry slapped at the mouse pointer. "Get that outta there, Dar!"

"Heh." Dar relented and switched back to the forest. "You're so cute." She started the laptop into its dial-up routine. "Now," she turned around and gathered Kerry into her arms, "before I was so rudely interrupted by logic, where was I?"

Kerry pressed her body against Dar's. "Here, I think." She wound a hand around Dar's neck and was about to kiss her when a knock sounded at the door. Kerry paused, looked at her partner, then at the door in visible outrage. "What the heck?"

"Hotel better be on fire," Dar muttered, then raised her voice. "Yeah?"

There was a moment of silence, then a voice answered, "H...hello? I'm looking for Kerry?"

Kerry fell forward against Dar's chest and shook her head. "Bob."

"Bob," Dar repeated. "You stay here. I'm gonna bob Bob." Dar headed for the door with determined strides.

"Ah...bu...bu...Dar!" Kerry scuttled after her, grabbed hold of her loose shift, and pulled her to a halt. "Whoa!"

Dar turned, her eyebrows lifting in outraged question.

Kerry tied the shift closed. "Blind eunuchs have it tough in the job market, sweetie," she whispered. "Let me handle him, okay?" She adjusted her own dress and slipped ahead of Dar, grasped the door handle, and turned it. "Yes?" She leaned on the jamb, opening the door just wide enough to make eye contact.

"Kerry! Great, I found you." Bob beamed. "Can I come in?"

Kerry got her thoughts in order and assumed one of her more no-nonsense expressions. "Bob, it's late. Is there something you need? We're pretty tired." She tried not to hear the low, vibrant growl that was buzzing the air behind her.

"I was hoping we could talk," Bob explained shyly.

Okay, Ker, Dar's right. Polite ain't cutting it this time. "About what?" Kerry asked.

The hallway was empty, though Bob glanced to either side just to be certain. He put his hands in his pockets and managed an almost engaging expression. "Look, I know we barely know each other..."

"Grrooowwwwll!"

Kerry felt Dar move closer, and the heat of her body warmed Kerry's back. "That's right," she answered Bob. "We don't."

"But I was thinking maybe we could see each other a few times, you know... I think you're a really —"

"Bob." Kerry opened the door a little wider and straightened, holding both hands out in a stopping motion. "Hold it."

"No, I know you're really modest, but I think —"

"Bob!" Kerry's voice lifted.

He peered at her anxiously. "Yeah?"

"Thank you, but I have a significant other," Kerry stated firmly. "One that I'm very attached to."

"Rowwwrrrll." Dar's growl turned to a purr.

Bob took a breath and gave her a determined look. "I figured you had a boyfriend, but I really think we can get to know each other better, after all —"

"Bob." Kerry sighed. "I don't have a boyfriend." She spoke slowly, enunciating carefully, "I told you before — I have a partner."

His brows contracted in puzzlement. "A partner?"

Dar's patience, never really extensive, snapped. She poked her head above Kerry's as she raised a hand over Kerry's shoulder. "That would be me."

Bob looked from one of them to the other, his head cocking to one side in patent confusion.

Kerry turned and looked at Dar. "See what happens when you eat too much Wonder Bread?" she asked, then turned back. "Bob, Dar and I are lovers," she painstakingly clarified for him. "We're gay. Am I making a connection here?"

Very slowly, comprehension dawned. "Oh," Bob finally murmured, turning a deep, brick red. "Sorry. I didn't...um..."

Kerry felt a little sorry for him. "It's okay."

"Okay, well then, have a good night. I'm sorry," Bob babbled, backing away. "Sorry." He escaped down the hallway, almost crashing into the corner in his haste to get out of sight.

"Mmph." Dar watched the last of him vanish and issued a satisfied grunt. "What an analog mindset."

Kerry nudged her backwards and shut the door. "Aw, he's not that bad. He meant well, Dar."

"No he didn't," Dar objected. "Kerry, did you hear what he said after you told him you had an SO? He didn't care! What a creep!"

Kerry chewed the inside of her lip. "Ew. Yeah," she admitted. "That was pretty scuzzy."

Dar shook her head and ambled over to where the laptop had finished downloading. She picked it up and took it to the bed, then rid herself of her shift and settled on the covers, stretching her naked body out as she studied the screen. After a second, she glanced up over the LCD and crooked a finger at Kerry. "C'mere."

Kerry put thoughts of Bob and his scuzziness out of her mind, removed her own clothing, and joined Dar in bed, snuggling up next to her lover. "What did he send?"

"Look." Dar pointed. They read together in silence, tanned faces outlined in the light of the screen.

Chapter
Eleven

THE NEXT MORNING, Kerry woke up first for a change. She let her eyes drift open as the sunlight poured in the slatted windows and made stripes across the bed. For a few minutes, she just lay there in a lazy half doze, watching Dar's chest move rhythmically. The sun made the soft, fine hairs on Dar's torso glisten, and Kerry rubbed her thumb over a few of them as she pondered the information they'd obtained the night before.

She'd expected...well, to be honest, she hadn't really had any idea what to expect. Maybe that the big black boat and the little white wiener following it were international jewel thieves, or something. Instead, what they'd discovered was that the boat was owned by a wealthy broker of art and collectables who was known for his aggressive acquisition and auction of just about anything he could get his hands on that was worth good money. *Nothing illegal about that.*

Kerry nuzzled Dar's shoulder, and her nostrils picked up faint traces of coconut from the tanning oil she'd spread all over Dar the day before. But they'd read some clips about how the man had forced his way into excavations and bought up rights for salvage, often taking valuable goods out from under the eyes of the original, and sometimes rightful, owners.

John DeSalliers. Not a nice guy. But that wasn't illegal, either. What Kerry couldn't figure out was why they'd been so set on chasing after her and Dar. After all, if they could get this information on who was registered to that boat, it was just as easy for the black boat to get the same information about Dar.

"I just don't get it." Kerry sighed. All they'd done was dive on a decrepit wreck. Surely they didn't think there was anything valuable on an old fishing vessel, did they? Why bother? It didn't make sense.

Their friends Christen and Juan turned out to be registered private detectives, apparently on a hefty retainer from DeSalliers. They were both very well off, and Christen was purportedly quite the wild woman of the world, if you believed the society gossip clips Mark had pulled off of God-only-knew-where.

But... Kerry kept coming back to the same question: why bother her and Dar? If they were looking for something, why take the time out to tangle with a pair of IT execs out on vacation? It just didn't make sense.

Dar's voice interrupted her musing. "Whatcha frowning about?"

Kerry tilted her chin up and looked at her newly awakened partner. "Trying to figure out what's going on."

"Ahhh." Dar nodded solemnly. "How about we figure out breakfast first?" She arched her back and stretched. "For one thing, thinking requires my brain to boot up, and for another, I'm not sure I want to waste the synapse firing on them."

"Even after what happened the other night?" Kerry asked.

Dar shrugged. "They ended up grounding their boat," she reminded Kerry. "We won. Why push it?"

Kerry eased up onto an elbow and studied Dar. "You're not curious as to why they did it?" Her voice rose in surprise. "Or what they're after?"

Another shrug indicated Dar's ambivalence. "Yes, I'm curious, but I don't know that I'm curious enough to waste part of our vacation on tracking it all down and sorting it out," Dar answered honestly. "If I really wanna know, I can find out when we get home and make their lives miserable retroactively."

Kerry ran her fingers through her hair as she considered that. "Well, yeah," she said. "I can see your point, but what if they do something else?"

Dar half turned on her side to face Kerry, and perched on an elbow, mimicking her posture. "I'd say they'd be stupider than I thought they were, but if they do, then we'll have to deal with whatever happens," she said. "But I'd rather forget about them until then."

Kerry's brow puckered. "I don't like it," she admitted, thinking about the angles as Dar waited for her with commendable patience. "I want to know what they were up to, and why they were chasing us, and what's so important about that patch of water."

Dar relaxed onto her back and put her hands behind her head. "Okay," she said. "How?"

"Hm?"

"Aside from chasing them down and demanding they tell us what they're up to, how do you figure on finding out what's going on?"

Kerry sat up cross-legged and rested her elbows on her bare knees. "Well..." she began, then stopped.

"We planning on following them around?" Dar inquired, with the barest hint of a twinkle in her eyes.

"No." Kerry shook her head. "I guess you're right. Unless they approach us again, there's really no way to do this." She looked up at Dar, who was gazing back at her. "You already figured all that out, didn't you?"

Dar pointed a finger at herself. "Me?"

Kerry poked her in the ribs. "Yes, you, little Ms. Ice-Cream-won't-melt-in-my-mouth." She sprawled across Dar's middle, pinning her to the bed. "It just bites my shorts to let those scurvies mess with us and walk away."

"They didn't," Dar reminded her. "They're probably laying out ten grand for patched fiberglass right now, remember?"

"Mm," Kerry grunted. "But won't that make them want to get back at us?"

"Maybe," Dar conceded. "I guess we'll just have to wait and see."

Kerry gracefully bowed to the logic of it. Dar's points were good ones. Unless they were willing to get the local authorities involved and press charges — of what nature she didn't know — there really was no investigating they could do outside of direct confrontation or some back alley skulking. She didn't feel like skulking, and while she had every confidence that they could present a very effective direct confrontation, she understood Dar's reluctance to engage in conflict. "Okay," she agreed. "Now, weren't we discussing breakfast?"

Dar grinned.

"How about we toss on some clothes and go foraging?" Kerry suggested. "I think I saw a little place out by the beach we could try," she said. "Right next to the windsurfing area."

"Ah ha." Dar chuckled good-naturedly. "I sense an ulterior motive." She took hold of Kerry's hand and held it, for no particular reason other than wanting the contact. "I don't want to hear you complaining tonight about getting bounced off the ocean the whole day."

Kerry smiled. "Yeah, but if I whine enough, you'll give me a massage," she countered. "Besides, maybe I'll have better luck than I did last time. I've been doing some upper body work at the gym."

Dar's eyes wandered over Kerry's upper body and a cheeky grin appeared. "I've never had a problem with that part of you," she drawled. "To hell with windsurfing."

"Wench." Kerry laughed. "You know that's not what I meant." She sat up and flexed both arms, showing off her biceps. "See?"

An even bigger grin creased Dar's face at the view. Kerry's arms and shoulders had gotten more defined, but the expression of uninhibited pride on her face was what really made Dar smile. "I surely do see," she agreed, giving Kerry's leg a pat. "Maybe you'll be pulling my butt out of the water this time. C'mon."

They rolled off the bed together in a tangle, only barely getting their balance before they ended up crashing into the wall. Taking advantage of their positioning by the windows, they peered out.

"Gorgeous day," Kerry observed, seeing the bright sunlight and the breeze blowing the branches nearby. "But we're gonna need sunscreen."

"Waterproof," Dar agreed, picking up the bottle from the dresser. "I slather you, you slather me?"

"You're on," Kerry replied. "Then let's go find some biscuits. I'm starving."

"With or without clothing?"

"Dar."

"Heh heh."

KERRY FOLLOWED DAR out onto the beach, feeling her stride change as they moved from the wooden boardwalk into the sand. "Ah, nothing like coming out to the islands to get some really exotic cuisine," she commented.

Dar chuckled. "I thought the bagels were pretty good."

"They were," Kerry agreed. "I just never figured on coming to St. Johns, AVI for bagel and lox."

"Playing to the marketplace." Dar guided her down toward where the windsurfing boards were stacked. "You want to stretch out for a few minutes, or start the torture now?"

"Tch." Kerry bumped her. "Hey, if you really don't want to do this, we don't have to."

Dar's lips quirked into a smile. "Nah," she said. "I just like spending time under the water more than skating on top of it. I'll live."

Kerry eased in front of her as they reached the kiosk, meeting the friendly grin of the man behind it with one of her own. "Two." She indicated herself, then Dar, then handed him her credit card. "We've done this before."

He took them through the safety drill anyway, Kerry noted. Possibly because he'd heard tourists claim bogus experience before. She listened attentively, checking out the rig to make sure there wasn't anything new or unusual on it. They'd windsurfed several times before—at the island, and the last time they'd gone to Key West. Kerry had really enjoyed it, though it had only been the last time that she'd been able to truly master the mast without getting pulled butt over teakettle by the wind. "Thanks." She acknowledged the end of the instructions and took hold of the crossbar. "Ready?"

Dar finished inspecting her board, then nodded. "Ready." Side by side, they moved into the shallow, crystal clear water and headed for the deeper sections. "Not that much wind today," Dar observed.

"Enough." Kerry felt the breeze flutter her hair. They were both dressed in shortie wetsuits, and she was looking forward to getting into deeper water because the neoprene was getting pretty warm in the sun. It had taken her time to get used to wearing the substance, and to the smell of it. The wetsuits fit snugly, zipped up the back, and after she'd taken the time to break hers in, it had gotten pretty comfortable. They did tend to squeak a bit when dry, though, and unless you were in the water, they were capable of sweating pounds off you if you weren't careful.

Their suits were mostly black, but Kerry's had purple shoulders and arms, and a flash of bright orange down each side. Dar's, in addition to being older and more broken in, had a soberly gray yoke with dark blue piping around her neck.

They reached deeper water and Kerry took the opportunity to duck under the waves, letting the ocean's cool penetrate her suit and cool her off. She stayed like that for a moment, then emerged, shaking her hair out of her eyes and spraying water across the crystal green, shimmering surface.

"Be careful." Dar gave her a pat on the behind, as she moved away a little and prepared to get on her board.

"Yes, Mom." Kerry splashed her. "You be careful, too. Don't fall on a jellyfish like last time."

Dar stuck out her tongue, then boosted herself up onto her windboard and got her feet set into the pockets, before she reached down and raised the sail. The wind caught the nylon at once and filled it with a fluttering rustle. "Last one down the beach has to buy the beer," she yelled back.

"You skunk!" Kerry scrambled up onto her board, catching her balance carefully before she attempted to pull up the hinged sail. That was the toughest part, really. Once it was up, you could use your weight to keep it up, but pulling it against the drag of the sea and the wind made Kerry really glad she'd spent the extra time in the gym recently. "When I catch you, you're sunk! Hear me!!"

Dar's laughter floated back.

"You laugh now, Dixiecup." Kerry felt the wind fill her sail, and the water started to slide by under her. "If I win, you're gonna owe me a lot more than beer!"

THE BEACH BAR was an open, tiki type structure, with a bar top made of a slice of wood taken right out of the heart of some native tree. Dar and Kerry entered from the beach side and settled on stools next to each other in the moderately busy place.

The bartender leaned on the other side of the bar from them. "Can I get something for you?"

Dar paused in the midst of unzipping her wetsuit. "Get the lady a nice, cold beer." She indicated her companion. "Pina colada for me," she added. "Since I'm buying."

"Heh." Kerry smirked. She pulled down the zipper on her wetsuit and peeled off the upper part, letting it drape down over her lower body. They were both wind and sunburned, and lightly dusted with sand collected on the walk up from the beach. Kerry rested her arms on the bar and reveled in the sensation of being a true beach rat, if only for a moment. "If you have anything amber on draft, that would be great," she told the bartender.

"Gotcha." The boy grinned at her and turned back to the taps.

Dar pulled down her wetsuit and adjusted the strap on the swimsuit she was wearing underneath. "I shoulda known I didn't have a chance if there was beer in the deal." She ran both hands through her damp hair and grinned. "What was that hopping about, anyway?"

Kerry stretched out her arms, feeling a pleasant ache in her shoulders. "I thought I saw a dolphin," she confessed with a chuckle. "I didn't want to hit it. Felt like I was on a bucking horse for a minute there, though."

"Ahh." Dar glanced up at the menu. "You up for a burger?"

Kerry heard her stomach growl at the mere suggestion. It was late afternoon, and breakfast seemed a very long time ago. "Sure." She grinned at the frosty mug the bartender plunked down in front of her and tugged it closer, then took a sip. It was nutty and very cold, and she sighed happily as Dar ordered them both lunch. "What a great day."

Dar was busy chewing the pineapple from her drink. She swallowed and turned toward Kerry. "That was a lot of fun," she admitted. "I can see why you want one of the motorized ones."

"Oh, yeah!" Kerry sat up and mimed holding the control rod. "Vroom! Vroom!"

"Wild woman." Dar offered her the cherry from her drink. "Here."

Kerry took the fruit neatly between her teeth and plucked it from its stem. "No fair." She sucked the cherry and rolled it around in her mouth. "I don't have one to give you."

Dar's eyes twinkled wickedly, and Kerry realized what she'd just said. She chewed and swallowed the cherry, then stuck her now reddish-colored tongue out at Dar. "Of course, you've always had mine anyway."

"Ahem." Dar cleared her throat slightly, glancing around as her skin turned a fraction of a shade darker.

Kerry lowered her voice, smothered a chuckle. "Oh, Lord. Don't tell me I just made you blush."

"I'm not blushing." Dar reassembled her dignity. "It's

sunburn."

"Uh huh." Kerry snickered. "I see that blush."

"It's not a blush."

"Heh."

Dar rested her elbow on the bar and half turned on her stool, assuming a seductive look as her eyes slowly, lazily made their way from the tips of Kerry's toes up to her top of her blonde head. By the time she hit Kerry's chest, it was bright pink.

"Now that," Dar met her eyes, lengthening the words out to a Southern drawl, "is a blush." She reached over and put her finger on Kerry's nose, which wrinkled as her lover couldn't prevent herself from smiling.

"You're such a troublemaker," Kerry sighed.

"You started it." Dar turned around and took another sip of her drink as they watched their pasteurized, processed milk product and half pound of chopped animal protein become a pair of nicely cooked cheeseburgers, accompanied by something called island fries. Dar inspected one and found it to be a French fry with a coating of spices and coconut. "Mm."

Kerry centered a slice of tomato on the top of her burger and placed lettuce over that, then dabbed some ketchup and mayonnaise on the bun before she replaced it. She was about to pick it up and take a bite when motion caught her attention from the corner of her eye. "Uh oh." She nudged Dar in the ribs.

Dar looked up, pausing in mid-munch as she spotted the small group of people walking across from the docks. Three women and two men, their clothing in some disarray, were being escorted by two policemen. They seemed very agitated, and one of the men had his arm around one of the women in a protective attitude. "Huh. Wonder what that's all about?"

The bartender nudged one of the waitresses, who had just come to pick up a bar order. "Another one?"

"Yeah." The girl shook her head. "Crazy pirates. Devils, I think." She picked up her tray and walked off.

Kerry leaned forward, projecting her voice. "Pirates?"

The bartender jumped a little, then turned. "Oh, it's nothing, ma'am. We were just—"

"Just not wanting to scare us, yes, but what about the pirates?" Kerry interrupted.

He looked like he'd been caught in headlights that rarely appeared on St. Johns. "Ma'am..." His eyes shifted around, but most of the patrons were eating at tables; Dar and Kerry were the only ones on that side of the bar. With a second careful look, he sidled over. "We're not supposed to talk about it," he explained.

"Sure," Dar said. "You don't want to scare off the tourists."

"Yeah." The boy grinned. "Glad you understand."

"We're not tourists," Kerry smiled at him, "so don't worry about it. Tell us about the pirates."

Reassured, the bartender leaned on his elbow near them. "Been six hijackings this month," he told them. "Boats comin' in, they get pulled over by these guys, and whap. No more boat, no credit cards, no cash; you name it."

Dar and Kerry exchanged glances. "Wow," Kerry said finally. "No wonder you don't want it to get out."

"Big money, you know?" The boy shrugged. "They just been lucky. Nobody's got hurt so far." He looked up as his name was called. "S'cuse me."

Kerry let her wrists rest on the bar. "Good grief, Dar!"

Dar watched the group cross into the resort building, a concerned look on her face. "How in the hell can they not tell people?" she said in outrage. "There should have been a goddamned travel advisory at least!"

"Six hijackings in one month?" Kerry shook her head in disbelief. "I know it's tough on the economy, but...Jesus!"

Dar interlaced her fingers and leaned her chin against them. Her eyes flickered rapidly over the interior of the bar, a sudden intensity to her demeanor that had been absent moments before, yet very familiar to Kerry. "Those people could have been us." She frowned.

"Well," Kerry took a bite of her burger, "it almost was, Dar, except it was you they were chasing, and you don't put up with pirates, right?"

"Mmph," Dar muttered. "Doesn't make sense. That guy's too public to be a pirate, and Charlie said..." She stopped speaking for a moment. "What was he trying to say?" she continued softly. "Maybe he was wrong. Maybe this guy's really running the pirates."

Kerry nibbled a fry. "Why?" she asked. "Dar, if that data is right, this guy's worth millions. Why run a bunch of boat hijackers in the Caribbean? I mean, yeah, okay—the boats are worth a lot, but can you imagine what it takes to do one over so you could sell it? And how much cash or jewelry could these guys be carrying anyway? It doesn't add up."

Dar scowled.

"Well, it doesn't," Kerry murmured.

"I know, I know," Dar said. "But what are the odds that we get chased down by someone who isn't part of the lowlife scum chasing down other expensive boats in the area?"

"Hm." Kerry sighed. "Yeah, that is kind of a coincidence." She lifted her mug and took a few swallows. "Do you think we should tell the police about what happened, though? Especially since we know who did it?"

Dar took a few minutes to finish off her cheeseburger before she answered, which also gave her time to consider the question. "I don't know," she finally admitted. "If the word's out not to tell anyone, how reliable are the police?"

"Maybe they're not the ones who are putting the lid on."

"Maybe," Dar murmured. "If we do tell them, then what? We're not going to press charges, not out here at any rate."

"He could buy them off anyway," Kerry replied with a hard-earned skepticism. "But at least if the police know, and if they are really trying to find these guys, they'll have the information."

"Would it make you feel better?" Dar queried. "Telling them?"

Kerry nodded, then her lips quirked a bit. "Besides, while we're telling them what happened to us, maybe we can get them to tell us what's going on."

Dar's eyebrows lifted and she gave Kerry an approving look. "Good point," she conceded.

Kerry blew on her nails, then buffed them on her bare shoulder. "Besides, they have something else in common," she added seriously, "those guys and the pirates. According to our friend the bartender, no one got hurt in the hijackings."

"Just like with us," Dar mused. "Once they had the boats, they could have just killed the owners."

Kerry nodded. "Not left any witnesses alive," she said. "Who knows, Dar, maybe this guy's got some angle on all this. Maybe he..." Her imagination kicked in. "Maybe he's taking these boats, revamping them, and selling them for twice what they're worth to the same guys buying that art stuff from him."

"Hm." Dar sucked on her straw as she considered the possibility. "It would be the right market," she said. "More money than brains."

Kerry chuckled. "You know, I've got relatives like that," she said. "In fact, you've met most of them." A ripple traveled through her at the words, as she recognized a certain sense of distance on hearing them. She realized that the rawness she'd felt over her father's death and the ugliness she'd faced with her family afterward were easing.

"S'okay." Dar gazed at her quietly. "You've met my contributions to the four-bit gene pool, too."

True. Impulsively, Kerry reached across the top of the bar and clasped Dar's hand, squeezing it briefly then letting it go. "Our family doesn't have that problem. Even our dog is a genius."

Dar chuckled. "I'll remind you of that the next time she steals your socks." She glanced around the bar. "You done?"

Kerry nodded. "Let's go find some trouble." She slid off the stool and followed Dar out of the tiki bar, toward the main resort building.

DAR UNLOCKED THE door to their room and pushed it open. "Might as well get changed first," she commented. "I hate talking to cops in a sandy wetsuit."

Kerry slipped past her and walked right out onto the porch, stripped completely out of her wetsuit, and left it on one of the chairs, inside out. "Give me yours and I'll rinse it," she called back over her shoulder.

"Sure." Dar pulled off the neoprene suit and slung it over her shoulder, then she stopped and looked around, warned by a faint prickling of her senses. The room was neat, as they'd left it, only the freshly made bed an indication that the maids had been in to tidy up. Neither she nor Kerry tended to leave things laying out, and before they'd left, they'd both tucked things away either in the drawer or in their bags. So, nothing was out of place. And yet... Dar frowned, then looked up as Kerry stuck her head back inside. "Here." She walked over and handed her the wetsuit. "Something's bugging me about this place."

Kerry ducked outside, then eased her entire body back in the room, standing inside and watching Dar curiously. "What is it?"

Dar turned in a circle. "I'm not sure." Her eyes swept the room, searching for whatever it was that was bothering her. Nothing was missing; everything was right where she'd left it, including her laptop sitting on the table, its theft warning label bold on the outside.

Curious, she walked over and flipped up the top, breaking the log-in sequence and rattling off a series of commands to the operating system. No, the machine hadn't been touched since they'd left. It wasn't the computer; it wasn't their things... Then she realized that it wasn't something visual at all. Her nose twitched, and the alien scent she'd detected came back to her as her mind tried to identify it. "You smell that?"

Kerry stepped inside and shut the outside door. "Smell what, hon?"

Dar waved her hand vaguely. "In the room. Something that isn't us."

Resisting the urge to walk over and check Dar for fever, Kerry dutifully sniffed at the air. "Well, I can smell salt water, neoprene, and sunscreen. I guess that's us, right?"

Dar nodded.

Kerry walked around near the bed. "Sorry, Dar. I don't..." She paused. "Wait, you mean that sort of roseish, alcoholy kind of smell?" It seemed vaguely familiar, but nothing immediately popped into her mind as to why.

"Yeah." Dar circled near the dresser. "It's strongest here," she stated positively.

"What is it?" Kerry asked. "It's not cleaning solution; I know what that smells like. All hotels use the same kind."

"Perfume," Dar replied quietly. "Our little friend Christen's perfume."

Kerry stared at her. One blond eyebrow lifted slightly. "Are you sure?" she asked. "I didn't even notice she was wearing any."

"I noticed," Dar replied. "Because I hate the brand. It's the same one Eleanor uses."

"Ah!" *Bingo.* Kerry slapped her head. "No wonder it seemed familiar." She paused. "Are you saying she was here in our room?"

Dar sat down on the bed, letting her elbows rest on her knees. "Can't think of any way for her perfume to get here without her, so yeah."

"Ew."

"Yeah." Dar frowned. "I'm going to go check the boat." She got up and headed for the door.

"Dar." Kerry unzipped Dar's overnight bag. "Here. Not that I mind you storming around like an escapee from the swimsuit competition of the Ms. Aggressive America, but..." She tossed her lover a long black T-shirt with a snarling tiger on it.

"Thanks." Dar pulled the shirt on over her bathing suit and picked up the pouch in which she'd carried their keys. "Be right back."

"Be careful," Kerry called after her, watching as the door shut behind Dar. For a moment she just stood there, then she put her hands on her hips and shook her head. "Boy, this sucks." She opened her own bag and riffled through its contents, wondering what the creepy woman had been looking for. They'd only packed a few shirts, their swimsuits, and some other casual wear, and even the most avid of detectives probably couldn't have gotten much information from their choice of bathroom toiletries, other than the fact that they had a preference for mint toothpaste and apricot body scrub.

Of course, the laptop was a mine of information, but it might as well have been in Fort Knox for all the good its presence could have done anyone. The security on the machine that held the keys to the company was so anally extensive, even Mark couldn't break into it. Even removing the hard drive wouldn't do a thing for the potential hacker. Without Dar's encryption algorithms, the data was scrambled past recovery, and she never kept much locally anyway. *So, if not information, what were they looking for?*

Another thought occurred to her. *What if they weren't looking for anything? What if they planted a bug?* "Son of a bitch." Kerry sat down and flipped open the laptop, and waited for the log-in to come up. When it did, she logged in, waited for it to validate her, then started up the broad spectrum data analyzer program Dar kept on the drive.

Bugs weren't really that complex, and one of the first things Dar had taught her was how to find them. She'd felt a little funny knowing how frequent their use was in their particular trade, but competition was fierce, and salesmen were not above using them to get any advantage they could.

Dar, she'd been told, never bothered with them. Sometimes when she knew a bug was there, she'd have fun with the planter by passing along the most outlandish information, then waiting for it to come back in a bid meeting — which it sometimes did.

The program started up and she configured it, setting it to scan using two specialized ports for all frequencies across the bandwidth used for radio transmission. She started it running and propped her chin on her fist, waiting. You could do that with cell phones, too, and anything else that used electronic signals that went through the air — like wireless networks, which was what the program had really been designed to analyze.

It showed nothing until she started reciting the pledge of allegiance. Then the program picked up scans on two frequencies, and Kerry shook her head in irritation. She left the program running and slowly walked around, continuing her oration and watching the screen. Near the ornate lamp, the signal peaked. Kerry regarded the lamp, then she simply unplugged it, picked it up, and carried it outside. She set it in the far corner of the porch and went back inside.

Now the program showed a clean scan again. Kerry gave it the acid test — she started singing. Even at her top volume, the scan remained quiet. With a nod of satisfaction, she went back outside and picked up the small hose attached to the spigot, turned the water on, and rinsed off their wetsuits with careful thoroughness.

There is nothing, Kerry sprayed the inside of the suits, *nothing on earth that smells worse than a dirty wetsuit.*

After a moment, she glanced over, then sprayed the lamp for good measure. *Except scuzzy, rose water wearing, obnoxious detectives, that is.*

DAR HEADED FOR the docks, conscious of a growing anger. She hadn't been asking for trouble out there; in fact, she'd gone out of her way to avoid it, but damn it, the bastards kept coming after them and now she was starting to get really pissed off about it. She made her way down toward the slip in which they'd docked and used the key she'd been given to unlock the steel gate that blocked off the slip. It appeared undisturbed, but so had their hotel room door, and Dar wasn't stupid enough to think whoever got paid off to let the slimebags in there hadn't also done the same for the gate at the marina.

The boat was floating quietly, tied to its pylons — the umbilicals plugged into dockside power to run the few things they'd left on, like the refrigerator. Dar stepped onto the deck and dropped down onto the stern, looking around carefully before she went to the cabin door.

It was a small brass lock, not really intended for serious security, and Dar fitted her key in and turned it without encountering any resistance. She peered at the brass plate, then pushed the cabin door open and slipped inside, quickly closing the door after her.

She relaxed at once. Just as the faintest hints of strange perfume had triggered her senses in the hotel room, the absence of anything she hadn't expected reassured her here. Dar inspected the interior anyway, moving into the very front of the bow, then checking the master bedroom where the scent, since the hatches were closed, was definitely very familiar to her. "Well," she spoke into the silence, "as long as I'm here, might as well shower and change."

She went to the dresser and took out a pair of stone-washed shorts overalls and a dark blue shirt, leaving them on the bed as she went into the bathroom and flipped on the water. She slid out of her swimsuit, ducked under the water, and quickly scrubbed the salt off her skin. A moment more, and she'd rinsed the soap out of her hair and was stepping out of the shower, turning off the water, and grabbing one of the towels draped over the holder in the small space. She dried herself off and wrapped the towel around her, then emerged and headed back to the bedroom.

Now that she was sure the boat was secure, she started considering both what had happened, and her options. She dressed as she thought, tucking the shirt into her overalls and buckling the shoulder straps. When she finished, she reviewed the results in the mirror. "Cute and conservative. You're starting to look like Kerry." Dar sighed, then unsnapped one of the shoulder straps and let the front of the garment rakishly hang half down. "That's better." She added her wraparound sunglasses, then grunted, satisfied with her changes.

As she passed back out through the living area, she paused, then sidetracked to the equipment locker. She opened the top, moving Kerry's shotgun aside to get to a blue milk crate underneath. Inside there was a thick piece of hardened steel chain and a padlock. She pulled out the chain and looped it around her neck, then picked up the padlock, hefting it as she left the cabin and locked the door behind her.

On the deck, she paused, acknowledging her territorial reaction over the boat. It wasn't as if they had anything truly valuable on board — or even that personal, but she regarded this vessel as part of their private space and the thought of anyone invading it made her hackles stand right up.

With a slight snort, she stepped up onto the side of the boat, then leaped to the dock, landing lightly and padding barefoot back up to the gate. Hearing voices on the other side, she slowed as she approached it, then stopped when she recognized one of the speakers as Juan Carlos. He was standing with a security guard on the other side of the gate, and they both stopped speaking when they looked through the bars and spotted Dar.

Dar leaned on the gate and stared steadily at them from behind her sunglasses. "Something I can do for you?" she asked in a tone usually reserved for budget meetings.

The security guard looked, if anything, relieved. "Ma'am, this gentleman was asking to be let into your slip."

Dar kept her stare on Juan Carlos, who was stone faced. "Why?"

The security guard turned to him questioningly. "Sir?"

"I have reason to believe some of my property is there," Juan Carlos said smoothly. "I wish to look."

"Then call the cops," Dar replied calmly. "File charges, and let them get a search warrant instead of trying to bully the staff into doing something you, and they..." she gave the guard a look, "know is illegal."

"This does not have to get nasty," the detective said.

"It already is," Dar said. "And it's going to get a lot nastier when I get over to this resort's corporate offices and file a complaint, not only for this, but because they let your little partner into our hotel room."

Imperceptibly, the security guard edged closer to Dar and farther away from Juan Carlos.

"Ms. Roberts, I do not think you know who you are dealing with."

Dar smiled, then she pulled off her glasses and pinned him with a stare. "No," her voice dropped to a low rumble, "I don't think you know who *you're* dealing with." She pulled the gate open and emerged onto the dock. "So take your slimy boss, your stinky partner, and whatever idiotic business you're involved with, and get all of it out of my sight unless you want more trouble than you know what to do with landing right on your ass." She pointed at Juan Carlos' chest. "Now move it."

"If you force us to take this to the authorities, you will regret it," he said, apparently not intimidated. "I can get a search warrant, and I will." He turned and walked away slowly, assuming an air of casual disinterest.

Dar shook her head. "What a moron." She turned and wrapped the chain around the gate. "How much was he offering you to let him in?" she asked suddenly, turning to the guard who was still standing there watching her.

The guard had the grace to look embarrassed.

"C'mon." Dar leaned on the gate. "Pencil neck like him wouldn't scare someone like you."

The guard shifted his brawny shoulders, responding to the compliment with a sheepish grin. "Twenty dollars," he admitted. "He was about to go to fifty when you walked up."

"Cheapskate." Dar finished putting the lock on the gate, closing it with a distinct click. She opened the pouch she was carrying and removed two bills, reached over, and slid them into the guard's khaki shirt pocket. His eyes widened at the amount. "I can buy his boss for petty cash," Dar said. "So you tell everyone if they get an offer from them, look me up first. I'll do better."

"Yes, ma'am!" the guard responded enthusiastically. "I'll make sure everyone knows!" He gave her a little wave, then trotted off down the dock, taking a moment to examine the contents of his pocket as he ran.

Dar dusted off her hands, then followed him. "When you care enough to buy the very best," she muttered, shaking her head. Now things were getting to the point where she knew she had to do something about them. The question was, what?

Well. Dar considered as she walked. Usually she solved problems by cutting to the chase and going to the very top. She didn't know where John DeSalliers was, but she bet if she went high enough at this resort, someone did. And she bet she could make them tell her.

Chapter
Twelve

KERRY RAN A brush through her damp hair, peering at her reflection in the room's mirror. She'd showered and slipped into a pair of neatly pressed khaki shorts with a pristine, white T-shirt tucked into them. The fabric made a nice contrast with her tan, and she smiled back at the face in the mirror as she pulled out her chain and let the ring threaded on it rest against the hollow of her throat.

The sparkle caught her eye, and she studied the ring, running her fingertip lightly over its brilliant stone, pondering again whether she should remove it from the chain and wear it. The idea appealed to her but she hesitated, frowning a little at her reflection and leaving the chain where it was. She didn't want Dar to feel pressured into doing the same thing, and she knew how much her partner disliked wearing anything on her hands.

"Ah well." Kerry met her eyes in the mirror. "Probably better to leave it off since we're out here. I don't want to lose it, either." The sound of a key in the lock made her look around, and she stepped back from the mirror as it swung inward, admitting Dar's tall figure. "Hey."

Dar turned a pair of stormy blue eyes on her, then put a finger to her lips.

"Already found it," Kerry replied in a normal tone of voice. "It's outside." She stepped forward and gladly accepted the heartfelt kiss on the lips. "Hey, I had a great teacher."

Dar gave her a hug as well. "Good work. I just prevented her slimy partner from searching the boat."

"You look cute," Kerry observed, flicking the hanging strap on Dar's overalls.

"Cute wasn't what I was going for." Dar sighed. "They think we've got something of theirs."

"Really?" Kerry took her hand and led Dar into the room, sitting on the couch and pulling Dar down with her. "What?"

"I have no idea." Dar propped one bare foot up on the table and studied it. "I was going to just go right up to the manager's office and start yelling at people, but I realized I don't have enough data to yell intelligently."

"I hate when that happens."

"Me too," Dar agreed. "So I decided to come back here, and maybe between the two of us, we can start figuring this thing out."

"All right." Kerry felt a surge of pride at the statement. It felt good to hear the confidence in her in Dar's voice. "I could use some coffee. You?"

"Yeah."

Kerry got up and went to the well-stocked coffee maker on the dais near the window. She busied herself starting a pot while she assembled her thoughts. "Okay. First off, here's what we know."

Dar squirmed around and got comfortable, stretching one arm out along the back of the couch as she listened to Kerry.

"First, we encountered a large vessel, acting in a very rude manner, crossing the Florida Straits," Kerry began, as she set up two cups. "Despite your giving them a friendly warning, they rejected the warning without consideration."

"Right."

"Second, we encountered a smaller vessel circling us after we dove that little wreck not far off Charlie and Bud's island. The boat did not approach or contact us, but appeared to be watching what we were doing."

"Right," Dar agreed again.

"Third, after we get to Bud and Charlie's island, the small boat follows us there, and two people get off and question us about where we were diving." Kerry turned and leaned against the credenza as the coffee brewed. "But they don't ask us specifics, they just make a claim to that area."

"Exactly."

"Fourth, when we are out in that same area having dinner, we get accosted by what appears to be the same large rude vessel, and the crew attempts to board us. We also get chased by them, without explanation."

"But they don't shoot at us," Dar added.

"Even though they must have seen me on the stern with a loaded shotgun." Kerry nodded. "Okay, fifth — we pick up a man from a capsized boat who just coincidentally is here apparently trying to recover something from the exact same small wreck you and I happened to dive on the day before."

Dar's eyebrow lifted.

"And, who just coincidentally happens to have tangled with the two people from the small boat, and probably whoever is in charge of the large boat over that spot of the ocean."

"Yeah," Dar murmured.

"Are these coincidences all piling up for you like they are for me?"

"Oh yeah."

"Sixth, now we get here, and coincidentally find the people from the small boat staying at the same resort we are, and snooping in our hotel room and trying to search our boat for some undisclosed reason." Kerry turned and poured out two cups of coffee, stirring them and bringing them both back over to the couch. She handed one to Dar and sat down cross-legged next to her. "So, what the hell is going on?"

Dar sipped her coffee thoughtfully. "Well, I think it's safe to assume they think we pulled something up from that wreck," she said. "Question is, what could we find in an old fishing trawler that would interest anyone?"

"There wasn't much to see, Dar," Kerry said. "Just some old crates."

"No, there wasn't," Dar recalled. "It's not a bad wreck. There's a lot of good coral there, but why it's of interest to a bunch of..." She stopped speaking, her brow creasing thoughtfully. "We did bring up something."

Kerry stared, then exhaled. "The box." She would have slapped herself if she hadn't been holding a cup of coffee. "But, Dar... it's just an old wooden box, half covered in coral," she protested. "We couldn't even open it it's so encrusted."

"I know," Dar agreed. "You and I know that, but if someone saw us bringing up the catch bag and looking at something, how would they know what it was?" She got up and paced. "So the question is — what is it they're really after, that they think we might have found?"

What indeed? Kerry cupped her hands around her coffee and slowly drank from the cup. "First off, we need to find out more about that fishing trawler, right?"

Dar smiled at her. "Right. More about that, and more about your friend Bob's grandfather, who ran it." She picked up the laptop and sat down next to Kerry again. "I think we need to start collecting ducks, so we can pin them down in a nice, neat row."

Kerry snuggled closer, putting an arm around Dar and leaning against her shoulder as the laptop booted up. Dar's log in came up and her partner put in her information, then they both watched as the autonomic systems kicked in and started establishing a satellite cellular connection to their world-wide network.

It took less time than most people would expect. After about sixty seconds, Dar was presented with the same desktop she usually saw on her machine in the office, right down to the collection of broadcast messages sent to their local Miami group ranging from parking violations to a test of the fire alarm system. Dar started up her database parsing program and cracked her knuckles as she waited for the screen to come up. When it did, she typed in her request.

"Is that the boat's name?" Kerry asked.

"*Lucky Lady*? That's what the dive maps have it as," Dar answered, adding a few other details. "Did Bob say what his grandfather's first name was?"

"No," Kerry said. "You're not going to ask me to go talk to him to find out, are you?" She gave her partner a mournful look.

Dar chuckled dryly. "No. Let's see what this comes up with first."

"Good." Kerry rested her cheek against Dar's shoulder. The long day on the water in the sun was starting to take its toll, and she found herself getting a little sleepy as the rattle of Dar's keystrokes lulled her. "They were really trying to get on the boat?"

"Uh huh," Dar murmured.

"Slimy."

"Yeah."

"What if they try again?" Kerry asked.

"I fixed that," Dar said, watching the response on the screen. "Damn. Nothing on that name." She shook her head, then typed in another command. "Okay, we do this the hard way. Gimme all the maritime incident reports in this sector... damn." Dar cursed, closing her eyes. "What the hell were the coordinates of that blasted wreck."

"Oh." Kerry stirred, then got up and trotted over to her notebook. She opened it to her dive log and studied the page. "Here you go. I logged it." She recited the longitude and latitude.

"You rock." Dar typed in the numbers and hit return. "That'll take a few minutes," she said, putting her arm around Kerry as she resumed her seat. "You know something?"

"What?" Kerry curled up against her, one hand stroking Dar's thigh absently.

"We are one damn good team."

Kerry's eyes twinkled happily. "We are, aren't we?"

"Yes, we are." Dar kissed her on the head. "I couldn't ask for any better."

"Me either." Kerry relaxed, putting her head back down on Dar's shoulder. She watched the scanning markers on the screen, her eyelids drooping shut after a few minutes of it.

Dar heard the faint change in Kerry's breathing and she glanced over, suppressing a grin at her dozing partner. She carefully shifted a little to a more comfortable position and rested her head against Kerry's, content to let her well-designed program do its job.

In her sleep, Kerry seemed to sense Dar's emotion. Her fingers curled around Dar's arm and clasped it, creating a warm band around her forearm.

"KER?"

DAR'S VOICE nudged her out of a very pleasant dream, one that involved her, Dar, and a bunch of grapes. Kerry let her eyes drift open slowly, complacently taking in the glistening sunset for a moment before her mind kicked in and fully woke up. "Oh." She lifted a hand to stifle a yawn. "Sorry."

"For what?" Dar inquired. "Sleeping's not a punishable offense, even in our division."

"I know, but we're supposed to be solving a mystery here." Kerry peered at the laptop. "Anything?" She could see a table of information in Dar's usual structure on the screen.

"Lots," Dar said in a dry tone. "I managed to exclude all the non-relevant shipwrecks. That took me forever, because they're a dime a dozen around here." She brought the laptop closer. "The wreck has to be this one."

"*Lucky Johnny?*" Kerry read the screen. "Oh, I can see where they'd confuse that with *Lucky Lady*." She observed. "Wonder if they have a thing about sexual confusion around here."

Dar eyed her, both brows lifting.

"Well, if they thought Johnny was a lady, I mean."

Dar chuckled soundlessly.

Kerry rubbed her eyes. "Okay, so maybe I should go back to sleep," she admitted. "Anyway, what else is there?"

"Mm." Dar pulled up a screen. "Problem is, there's nothing special about the damn thing. It was just a forty foot working trawler, out catching crabs."

"Ah." Kerry read the details. "Storm?"

"Uh huh," Dar confirmed. "Capsized and sank. Two survivors, both mates. Captain went down with the ship." She brought up another screen. "This is Bob's grandpa."

Kerry peered at the whiskered, scraggly looking man in the blue Macintosh. "Holy pooters, it's Popeye's Pappy!" she yelped. "Is there a picture of Grandma? You take a bet it's Olive Oyl?"

"That explains a lot." Dar chuckled. "He mostly trawled the North Atlantic. I don't know what brought him all the way down south, but the boat couldn't take it. It was his first, and last, Carib run." She studied the picture. "Nothing on him—just a working sailor."

Kerry's head cocked to one side. "Yeah? I thought Bob said his family had money, though. At least that's the impression he gave me," she added with a touch of droll humor. "How'd they make that from a rig like this?"

"Well." Dar tapped a few more keys. "He didn't lie. According to this tax filing, old Popeye left a ton of cash to Mrs. Popeye, and they've got a place that's worth another small fortune up in Maine." She scratched her jaw. "Maybe he already had wealth and just decided to fish for a living because he could."

"Maybe down here, Dar." Kerry shook her head. "I've spent time in Maine. No one does that if they've got a choice. It's a hard, dangerous life—fishing the North Atlantic." She moused through the results Dar had called up. "Hm. You're right, though. I know that neighborhood. Outhouses go for a quarter mil."

Dar glanced at her. "You'd think places that expensive wouldn't use outhouses."

"They're very traditional," Kerry replied blithely. "I think they just got three- pronged forks."

"Huh?"

Kerry chuckled and leaned her head against Dar's shoulder. "Never mind," she said. "My snobby upbringing getting the better of me."

"Okay." Dar sent off another probe, this one into financial databases. "We'll see what we can come up with for Popeye in Duks' side of the house." She leaned back. "Still doesn't explain why a storm wreck is stirring up all this interest, all this time later."

"No," Kerry agreed. "If there was something really important in that wreckage, you'd think they'd have come after it before now."

Dar drummed her fingers lightly on the keyboard. "That's true," she mused. "Unless..." The screen beeped and she looked up at it. "Huh."

Kerry peered over her shoulder. "Wow," she murmured, running a fingertip along the data. "Those must have been incredible hauls."

"Mm." Dar frowned. "But it's still not making sense, unless he took a pile of that money, converted it to gold coin, and it went down with him in the storm," she said. "Why would they be interested in that hulk now, is the question."

They both were quiet for a moment.

"Unless the 'why' behind those numbers went down with him." Dar spoke slowly. "And now that 'why' is worth something."

"Has the family become society now?" Kerry asked suddenly.

Dar gazed at her with a droll smile. "I don't know, hon. Where do you check for that kind of thing?" she said. "They didn't teach that in my redneck hacking classes."

Kerry slid her hands between Dar's and started typing. "That's easy." She hit a few keys. "The local newspaper, and let's hope they actually use public archives."

"Let's say they are nouveau riche," Dar said. "You think it has something to do with the whole thing?"

"I think people will do a lot to avoid family embarrassment," Kerry stated in a quiet, very flat tone. "Especially if they have something to lose by it."

Dar put her arms around Kerry and pulled her closer, not saying anything.

Kerry pushed the laptop away a little and accepted the comfort. "You know what I think about the most, when I think of what my father did to me last year?"

"What?" Dar asked.

"How awful it felt knowing I was such a disappointment to him," Kerry whispered. "When I woke up in that psych hospital, how ashamed I felt." She paused. "Before I got so ripping mad that I put that aside."

"You've got nothing to be ashamed of," Dar said.

Kerry sighed. "I know that now," she said. "Heck, I knew that then, but it brought home to me how family and love can take second place to image and ego."   She watched the screen. "Pride does strange things to people." Her finger traced a headline on the list that popped up. "So, maybe you're right. Maybe what went down with that boat is information — a secret someone doesn't want anyone to find out about."

"Uh huh." Dar studied the screen. "If that's the secret they think we brought up from that wreck, we could be in a whole new ballgame right now," she said. "And where, I wonder, does Bob fit in?"

Kerry untangled herself from Dar's embrace, but not before giving her a healthy hug. She stood up and stretched, working a kink out of her neck. Then she walked to the window and opened it, letting the ocean breeze blow against her face. After a moment, Dar joined her, perching on the sill and gazing out over the water. "So, what's the plan?" Kerry finally asked.

Dar folded her arms and thoughtfully nibbled the inside of her lip. "We've got a couple of choices," she said. "We can just get the hell out of here and leave them to their games."

"Mm."

"We can call in legal, make a mess for them for the bugging and the attempted pullover."

"Mm."

"We can play it by ear and see if we can find out what the real story is, then decide what we want to do about it."

Kerry grinned.

"Yeah, that was my choice too," Dar admitted. "But we could be playing with fire, Ker."

The blonde woman's lips twitched into a faint grin. "We could be," she acknowledged. "But I love a good mystery. I'd hate to just walk away from this and not know what the deal was."

Dar leaned back against the window frame. She had no real desire to get deeply involved in what seemed like a big mess, but she also found herself curious. "Let's see what we find out," she said. "Maybe it will be enough to convince them to leave us alone."

"You think they'll make the next move?" Kerry asked. "Or will they wait to see what we do?"

Dar considered the question. "I'm guessing they're waiting for us," she said. "So why don't we get moving and go find us some calypso dance music, and see what happens?"

"You're on." Kerry held out a hand. "They're not gonna know what hit 'em."

They shut down the laptop and walked out the door hand-in-hand, heading down the path toward the casual, beachside restaurant from which they could already hear the sound of drums rising. "Hey, Dar?" Kerry suddenly asked. "Remember what I said about rum and the samba?"

Dar eyed her. "Yeeesss?"

"This could get dangerous."

"Ker?"

"Yeees?"

"I never did tell you what happens when *I* get into too much rum, did I?"

There was a thoughtful pause. "No, I don't think you ever mentioned that," Kerry allowed. "I guess this might get *really* dangerous, huh?"

"Only to your reputation."

"Wh.... Oh." After another pause, she stammered, "You mean you...might get, um..."

"You do like the way I kiss, doncha?"

"Way too much." Kerry grinned rakishly. "Maybe we'd better stick to beer."

As the light faded to twilight, they joined a string of people headed in the same direction. In the shadows behind them, two other figures slipped in, trailing them with watchful eyes.

KERRY FELT DAR'S hands come to rest on her shoulders as she stood in the doorway trying to spot an open table. The tables were rough and wooden, and the atmosphere casual and very relaxed. She'd spied a free table and started easing her way through the crowd, when Dar's hold on her tightened and pulled her to a stop. Curious, she turned and looked up at her. "What's up?"

Dar pointed to a small table near the window. "Let's sit over there."

"There?" Kerry squinted. "Oh." She recognized the faces at a nearby table as the people they'd seen escorted by the police that afternoon.

Dar led the way over, taking the rearmost seat against the wall

as Kerry settled in across from her. She glanced casually at the
table next to them, where the five hijacking victims sat. They still
looked shaken and not very happy, and as she watched, Dar
realized one of them seemed familiar. She leaned back and searched
her memory, trying to place the oldest man's distinctive profile.

"Two of whatever this rum special is," Kerry told the cute
waitress who stopped by with her tray at the ready. She put down
the drink menu and looked over at Dar. "Boo."

With a start, Dar glanced back at her. "Sorry." She rested her
elbows on the table and indicated the next table with a jerk of her
head. "One of those guys looks familiar."

Kerry's eyes shifted. The people at the next table were somber,
hands clenched around nearly empty glasses, and there was a sense
of tense shock still about them that she attributed to their ordeal.
One of the women was about her age, also blonde, but with tightly
curled hair and wide, amber eyes. She seemed to be the most
shaken, and even in the low light of the restaurant Kerry could see
she'd been crying. "Those people who got hijacked, you mean?"
she asked, lowering her voice.

"Mm." Dar turned her head slightly, studying the other table
without appearing to. Kerry did the same, but none of the men
looked familiar to her so she turned her attention back to Dar,
lifting a brow in question. "Not to me."

"No." Dar shook her head. "I think..." She leaned back on her
chair arm and called out to the older man, "Jacob?"

The man started a little, and then peered at her uncertainly.
"I'm sorry, I don't..." He leaned a little closer. "Good heavens...
Dar?" He swiveled in his seat and extended a hand, an honestly
pleased expression crossing his face. "Dar Roberts!"

Dar took his hand with a firm grip. "How are you, Jacob? It's
been a long time." *Very long*, Dar realized. She'd last seen Jacob
Wellen over six years earlier at a technical convention in Las Vegas.

"It certainly has." Jacob smiled. He was a man of medium
height and build, with wiry gray hair and a closely trimmed beard
and moustache. "What a great surprise. Here." He turned to his
friends, who had turned to look at Dar. "Folks, this is an old
colleague of mine, Dar Roberts," Jacob said. "Dar, this is my wife
Minnie and her brother Richard, and this is my son Todd and his
fiancée Rachel."

"Pleased to meet you," Dar replied courteously, and then half
turned. "This is my partner, Kerrison." To Kerry, she said, "Jacob
and I survived the last great reorg you've heard so much about."

Kerry stood and took Jacob's hand. "My sympathies." She
grinned. "I've heard." Her eyes shifted to the rest of the table.
"Hello." The return greetings were cordial, if a little restrained.
Kerry wasn't sure if that was due to their circumstances or her

introduction as Dar's partner, but she gave them the benefit of the doubt and assumed the former.

Jacob shifted his chair over. "Why don't you pull that table over and join us, Dar," he suggested. "We have plenty of room."

The others shuffled their chairs to either side while Dar edged their smaller table over, then everyone sat back down again. "What a coincidence, bumping into you here, Dar," Jacob said. "You out here on business?" He turned to the rest of his family before Dar could answer. "Dar's the CIO of ILS now. One busy lady."

"Nope," Dar replied, lacing her fingers and resting her chin against them as she propped her elbows on the table. "We're on vacation, as a matter of fact. What about you? Still working out in Australia?"

"Just got back," he said. "Thought we'd take a tour through the islands before we settled back in the States again." His face crumpled into a frown. "Bad idea that turned out to be."

"Dad," Rachel murmured.

"Why?" Dar asked. "Seems like a nice place."

"Yeah, well, looks can be deceiving, as many folks found out about you, huh?" Jacob sighed. "Let me tell you what happened to us last night."

"Dad!" the young man interrupted. "They said not to talk about it."

"Thanks, kid, but I know what I can say and who I can say it to," Jacob told Todd with a tolerant smile. "Dar here may look about your age, but she's got more savvy up top than anybody I ever met."

Dar snorted. "You only say that because I saved your butt in Paris."

The waitress returned with Dar and Kerry's drinks. She took in the table arrangement without blinking, then caught Kerry's eye. "Get you something to eat?"

Kerry glanced over the small menu. "Can you get us two bowls of the stew, two baked yams, and some of this?" She pointed to the bread.

"Sure." The woman smiled at her, then took the menu and disappeared into the crowd. Kerry turned her attention back to the table, interested to hear Jacob's version of what had happened. She noticed furtive glances from the younger pair, and she returned the looks with mild amusement. Another thing to add to her coincidence list—one of the people the pirates chose to attack just happened to be an old colleague of Dar's. What were the odds of that, really? Certainly, ILS had a huge employee base, and they were a worldwide organization, but sheesh!

Jacob rested his arms on the table. "It was like something out of a really bad movie of the week."

"Been there, done that," Kerry murmured under her breath.

"We were out off the big reef just north of here, fishing," Jacob went on. "It was getting on to dark, so we were about to pack it in and come in to dock, when this big, racy boat came up to us."

"Black?" Dar hazarded.

"No." Jacob shook his head with a frown. "White with blue trim, why?"

"Just curious."

"Anyway, I figured they needed some help, or their radio was out, you know."

"Sure." Kerry nodded. "You want to help people if you can."

"Right," Jacob said. "So I let 'em pull up and tie on, and next thing I know, the damn bastards..." He glanced up. "Pardon me, ladies." He gave them an apologetic look and then returned his attention to Dar. "Damn bastards jumped on board and pulled out guns!"

Dar affected a surprised look. "Guns? For what? What did they want?"

"Everything," Rachel muttered. "And boy, were they obnoxious about it." She shook her head. "They scared Todd's mother, pushed us around. It was awful."

Kerry gave her a sympathetic look. "I bet it was. That's just lousy."

"Wouldn't have been so tough without those guns. They were just punks," Todd added.

His tone was sullen, and it was obvious, at least to Kerry, that his pride had taken a beating. "Did they say anything to you? Who were they?"

Jacob took up the story. "Didn't say. Just told us they were taking the boat, and left us on a sandbar with a handheld radio and nothing else." He shook his head in disgust. "Punks. Todd's right. They were just two-bit Johnnies with a couple of rifles."

"They took your boat?" Kerry asked.

"And everything on it," Jacob agreed wryly. "Did I feel like a jackass? You betcha." He sighed, picking up his drink and draining it. "Good thing there was a marine patrol that came by about a half hour, forty five minutes later, and rescued us before the tide came in."

"Wow," Kerry murmured.

"Did they say what they were doing it for, Jake?" Dar asked. "Just for money, or what?"

The older man shook his head again. "Didn't say a word, Dar. Just told us to get off the boat, that they were taking it. No reason — no *ifs*, *ands*, or *buts*."

At that moment, the waitress returned with a large tray. She set down food for both tables, and the conversation ceased while everyone got their plates.

Dar pulled her plate over and inspected the bowl nestled beside a steaming baked yam that smelled of vanilla and nutmeg. The waitress put a basket of hot bread in the middle of their table, and then set down another round of drinks for Jacob's party. Dar held up her own glass, and indicated Kerry's, and the woman took them with a smile as she retreated back toward the kitchen.

"So," Dar took a piece of the bread and dunked it into the stew, then bit a piece off and chewed, "what'd the cops say?"

"Bah." Jacob waved a hand in disgust. "The usual. Asking us a million questions, telling us how shocked they were, that this never happens, blah, blah, blah."

Kerry looked up and met Dar's eyes. One of her pale brows lifted.

"They did, huh?" Dar murmured. "Let me guess. They told you to just file a claim as quickly as you can with your insurance, and they'd do their best to find the boat before it left the island, right?"

Jacob looked at her with honest surprise as Todd blurted, "Yes, that's right. How'd you know?"

Dar's eyes narrowed and a faintly unpleasant smile appeared on her face. "Let's just call it a hunch," she said. "So, what's your plan now? You going to head back to the States?"

Jacob was cutting into a steak, and he put his knife down before he answered. "Nah. Figured as long as we were here, we might as well stick around for a few days, get some fun out of the whole damn thing." He patted his wife's hand. "Give Minnie here a chance to get over all the nastiness."

"It was dreadful," his wife agreed softly. "Ms. Roberts, you can't imagine how awful it was. Those men were acting like it was one big game to them, like we were just toys."

Kerry forked pieces of meat out of her stew and ate them as she listened, turning the new information over in her mind. The meal was very good, and she followed Dar's example in dunking the hot, herb-infused bread into its broth. Jacob and his family seemed to be relaxing a little, and she guessed that after a few days, the horror of what had happened would probably fade.

The pirates, though seemingly scary, had effected their plan in a quick, efficient manner. They hadn't risked keeping the family on board; they'd just found a convenient spot and simply taken them off, retaining possession of the boat and all its contents. She suspected they'd taken the vessel around to some sheltered cove to rummage through it at their leisure. Quick, efficient, and practiced. It was obvious to Kerry that they'd done the deed before, and had their routine down pat. From Dar's earlier comment, she suspected her lover had come to the same conclusion. She wondered if there was anything they could actually do about it.

"Jake, you didn't keep a maintenance log on your boat, did you?" Dar asked suddenly.

Everyone looked at her curiously.

Jacob finished chewing and swallowed, wiping his mouth hastily. "Well, not me, no, but my captain did, I betcha. Why?" he asked. "Hey, speaking of—you flew out here, didn'cha?"

Dar shook her head. "No. We're docked out in the marina. Did your captain keep the log on the boat, or back at home?"

"Boy, you better be careful," Jacob said. "Don't you be going out far around here, Dar. I'd sure hate to have what happened to us happen to you."

Kerry had to muffle a smile at the irony. "We're always very careful," she said.

Jacob shook his head. "Well, anyway, I think Rick kept the log with his gear, and I can't be sure if he left that on shore or not," he said. "Why, Dar?"

"If he's got part numbers, and the pirates try to sell the boat, it can be tracked," Dar remarked mildly. "Might take a while, but—"

"That's a great idea," Todd burst out enthusiastically. "Then we can find those creeps!" He turned to his father. "I bet Rick has that book. We should give it to the police."

"Now, Todd—"

"We can't let those guys just get away with this, Dad!" the young man protested. "That's what they all want us to do, just go away, and lick our wounds, and forget about it. No way!" He slapped his muscular hand on the table.

"Todd!" Minnie frowned at her son.

"He's right," Dar interjected. She waited until all of them looked at her in surprise. "It is what they want. You're not the first victims, and I'm betting you won't be the last." She rested her forearms on the table. "So, if you do have that log, it'll help. But don't give it to the cops."

They stared at her in shock for a long moment after she finished speaking. "Not the first?" Jacob said hesitantly.

"No." Kerry took up the conversational ball, giving Dar a chance to eat. "There've been a number of hijackings around here recently, but no one wants to talk about it because it would scare people off," she explained. "I think that Dar thinks..." she glanced at her lover, "it may be a local gang doing it."

Dar nodded.

"Well." Jacob looked aghast. "Son of a bitch."

"Look," Todd leaned closer to Dar, "whatever you think of doing to maybe stop them, count me in. We need to do something," he said. "I'm gonna call Rick as soon as we're done in here, and I'll see if he's got that book."

"Do you really think..." Minnie spoke up hesitantly. "Perhaps the authorities would be better to deal with this, wouldn't they?"

"You heard her. They're probably in on it." Todd stood up. "I'm so mad, I gotta go kick something. C'mon, Rach." He held a hand out and assisted his fianceé to her feet. "Let's go."

The two young people threaded their way out of the restaurant, disappearing into the crowd.

"Damn hothead." Minnie's brother Richard spoke for the first time, removing his face from his beer mug. "What in hell's got into that kid, Jacob?"

Jacob shook his head, still visibly upset. "Dar, I can't believe the people here know this is going on and they just let people keep coming in. That's...that's..."

"Piracy," Dar supplied succinctly. "Yeah, well, maybe the cops aren't in on it, maybe they just don't want the tourist boat rocked, but something doesn't smell right to me about the whole thing." She finished up the last bit of her stew, wiping the bottom of the bowl with a bit of bread and munching it.

"We don't want any trouble," Richard muttered "I think we should just leave and go the hell home." He looked around. "This place gives me the creeps anyway."

"That's 'cause you can't cope with any place that doesn't have slot machines in the bathroom," Jacob snorted. "Just relax, would you?" He turned to Dar. "Listen, Dar, he's right about one thing. We're not looking for trouble here. If the local cops don't want to stir things up, neither do I."

Dar leaned her chin on her fist and regarded him.

"Dar, don't give me that look," Jacob sighed. "I know what you're thinking."

Dar's eyebrows lifted visibly.

"I'm not a crusader. Never was," the man stated. "I've got my family here, and if that's the deal and this is all a scam, then I'm willing to do my part and go file my claim and let 'em have it. Damn thing leaked anyhow."

"Damn right," Richard agreed. "Minnie doesn't need any more trouble, either."

Minnie looked profoundly relieved.

Dar rolled her eyes toward Kerry and they exchanged looks. "That's okay." Kerry gave them a gentle smile. "We understand."

Jacob relaxed a little. "It's not that I think it's right," he stated.

"Of course not," Kerry said. "It's better you leave it for Dar and me to handle."

Jacob blinked at her. "Come again?"

"We'll take care of the pirates. No need for you to get involved. After all, you've been through a lot, and I'm sure you just want some time to rest."

Minnie leaned forward a little. "Honey, those men are dangerous."

"Life is, sometimes." Kerry smiled kindly at her. "But Dar and I have a knack for getting through things." She looked up as the waitress returned. "Sometimes you just gotta go for it. Can I get two of the Island Volcano sundaes and another rum punch?"

"Sure." The waitress beamed at her. She glanced at Dar. "Anything for you, ma'am?"

"I think one of those sundaes is mine," Dar replied dryly.

Kerry grinned and then returned her attention to Jacob. "Anyway, don't you worry about a thing. We can handle this on our own."

"Now, wait a minute," Jacob protested.

Kerry held up a hand. "No, no — we understand completely." She sucked the rest of her rum punch down to the bottom, feeling the beginnings of a mild buzz. It surprised her, and she tried to figure out how many beers were the equivalent of one of the punches. *Two? Three? Yikes. That means I've already drunk as much alcohol as there is in six beers. Maybe I should pass on the next rum punch.*

"Well, now, you listen, Dar," Jacob was saying.

Was it six?

"I know what I said, but if you two really think we should do something..."

Or was it only four?

"You can count on us."

"Jacob!"

Heh. Gotcha. Kerry chuckled silently to herself.

An overwhelming smell of chocolate suddenly snapped her out of her musing. Kerry blinked as a bowl was put in front of her: ice cream, fudge, more ice cream, more fudge, a brownie, maybe another brownie, covered in a chocolate shell whose top had a flame coming out of it. "Wow," she said. "This damn thing's as big as my head!"

Dar chuckled at her. "I want to do some more checking around, Jake, before we decide what to do," she said. "But I'll keep your offer in mind."

"You do that," Jacob said.

Kerry contentedly doused the flame of her volcano, and cracked the chocolate shell keeping her from the ice cream inside. Casually, she glanced around the room, glad not to see the familiar faces she half expected. Maybe the goons had decided to take the night off.

The waitress set down her third rum punch and took away the empty. Kerry eyed it, wondering if chocolate possibly counteracted rum. *Hm. Guess I'll find out.*

DAR SCRUBBED HER teeth, flicking the occasional glance into the mirror as she worked. She rinsed out her mouth, then poked her head around the corner of the bathroom door and peered over at the bed. Kerry was sprawled across it on her back, looking extremely relaxed.

"Hey, Paladar," Kerry drawled. "Get your butt over here."

Drat. Dar sighed. *The times I choose to leave my voice recorder at home.* She eased around the door and entered the room, settling down on the bed next to Kerry. "Yeees?"

One green eye opened and looked at her. "You let me get drunk. Bad girl." Kerry poked Dar in the side. "Boy, are you gonna be sorry."

Dar grinned at her. "You're really cute when you're drunk, did you know that?" She touched Kerry's cheek, and felt the pressure as Kerry leaned into her fingers. "Besides, you were due."

"Uh huh. See if you say that when I'm sick as a three-day-dead toad tomorrow," Kerry warned her. "Hope you like cleaning up."

Dar slowly stretched out alongside her. "I'll take care of you, don't you worry," she promised.

"I ain't worried," Kerry said, reaching over to play with a bit of Dar's hair. "I got you." She watched Dar's face through half-closed eyes. "Y'know how cool that is?"

"How cool what is?" Dar asked.

Kerry turned her head and regarded the ceiling for a few moments. "First time I ever really got drunk was when I moved here," she said. "I think I went nuts for a while."

Dar wriggled a little closer and curled her arm around Kerry's. "After leaving home? Lots of people do that."

"S'true," Kerry agreed. "Nobody telling me what to do, who to talk to, where to go. Felt great." She looked at Dar's hand, resting casually on her shoulder. "Like I was an animal, out of my cage."

Dar chuckled softly. "I'm sure you weren't that bad."

Kerry met her eyes. "Yeah, I was," she admitted. "Then...one night...I still don't remember it a whole lot, but I woke up in my car—half on the beach near a tree—and didn't know how'n the hell I got there."

Dar's brow contracted.

"Couldn't remember a thing," Kerry murmured. "Scared the shit out of me."

"I bet." Dar moved closer.

"I remember sitting there, kinda wondering what the whole damn point was?" Kerry shook her head a little. "I felt so empty." She turned and looked at Dar. "I felt like...if I'd kept driving, right into the water, no one would have given a crap."

Dar merely gazed at her compassionately.

"Just another sordid back-page story: senator's kid, drunk off her ass, drowns."

"Ker."

"S'true, and you know it." Kerry smiled sadly. "I had no clue what it felt like to really matter to somebody." She interlaced her fingers with Dar's. "Didn't know what it would be like to be a part of someone's life."

"Well," Dar studied her face, "you do now."

Kerry grinned easily. "Yeeeahh, I sure do." She rolled onto her side unsteadily and pulled Dar's hand close to her. "That's what's so cool," she said. "I got you."

"You got me," Dar agreed, carefully gathering Kerry up into her arms and hugging her. There was no resistance in her lover's body; Kerry meshed her limbs into Dar's embrace with total abandon, humming softly in delight as Dar rocked them gently on the bed. "You got me, Ker, I got you, and that's how that is."

"Uumrrrmm. I love you so much," Kerry warbled, her breath warm against Dar's neck. "You make my life rock."

Dar was surprised to feel tears welling up in her eyes. She blinked, and they spilled out over her cheeks, disappearing into Kerry's pale hair as she swallowed the lump in her throat. She stroked Kerry's head and kissed her, knowing a moment of pure joy so intense there were no words for it. True happiness was, she'd discovered somewhere in the last year, in making someone else happy. A damn simple concept, really, that somehow escaped all the laboriously written motivational manuals. All that crap about inner balance. Millions of dollars made on a bunch of bs when a single line on a cocktail napkin would do it. *It's love, stupid.* Dar sniffled.

Kerry squirmed around to look up at her. "Hey, BooBoo..." She reached up and gently wiped Dar's eyelids. "What'samatter?"

"Nothing." Dar's lips quirked. "Booboo? You been watching too many cartoons again, Kerrison?"

Kerry poked out her lower lip and grinned sheepishly. She hid her face in Dar's shoulder as a giggle escaped. "I am so tanked," she muttered, "I'm channeling an animated bear."

Dar chuckled. "Tell you what, Yogi, let's get your clothes off and get you into bed."

"Is that a plan or an invitation?" Kerry giggled again, but she eased back and rolled over, covering her eyes with her arm. "Too bright in here."

Dar started with her sneakers, untying them and tugging them off, then working Kerry's interestingly striped socks off her feet.

"Ooo." Kerry wiggled her toes. "Can I get drunk more often? I like being undressed."

"You do, huh?" Dar slid back up her lover's body and unfastened the button on her shorts, moving the zipper down.

"Well, just so happens I enjoy undressing you, so that works out great." She eased the shorts down, aided by a helpful wiggle of Kerry's hips, then pulled them off and tossed them over onto the chair. "Half down, half to go."

Kerry put her hands behind her head. "Do your worst," she grinned.

Dar slipped her hands under Kerry's T-shirt and slid them up, pulling the fabric with. She leaned over and gently kissed Kerry on the lips, before she bunched up the shirt and eased it over her head, returning for another kiss as she finished.

"Mmm." Kerry had her eyes closed. "I definitely like being undressed."

Dar tossed the shirt towards the chair. "I'll have to remember that." She slid her hands behind Kerry's shoulders and rolled her over onto her side so she could undo the catches on her bra. She felt a tug at her waist, and then heard the soft sound as Kerry unbuttoned one of her overall buttons. "Hang on a minute here."

"Hang on?" Kerry tangled her fingers in the straps and pulled. "Okay."

Dar chuckled as she eased her partner's grip. "Let me get you some water."

"Water?" Kerry folded her hands on her now bare stomach, watching amiably as Dar moved her half-clad body towards the credenza. "We never needed no water before."

"To drink." Dar poured from the bottle on the dresser into a glass, then returned to the bed.

"Is it warm water?"

"No. It's cold water."

"I'm cold. Don't want no cold water."

Dar set the glass down, then pulled down the covers on the bed and knelt, sliding her arms under Kerry's knees and shoulders and shifting her over. She pulled up the covers then handed her the glass. "Sweetheart, you gotta trust me on this one. Drink."

Kerry clasped the glass, studying it seriously. She peered at Dar over the rim, her blonde hair partially in her eyes. "Okay," she finally said. "If you tell me how come you were crying before."

Dar blinked, not expecting the question. "Oh." She cleared her throat a little. "It was just...um...you said something that really touched me, I guess."

"I did?"

Dar nodded. "Yeah."

"In a good way, right?"

"Right."

Kerry stuck her nose in the glass and drank its contents, lifting it up and letting the last drop drip into her mouth before she handed it back to Dar. "Now what?" she inquired. "Do I turn into a pumpkin?"

"You turn into a beautiful sleeping princess." Dar quickly stripped out of her own clothing and joined Kerry under the covers.

Kerry giggled. "Does that make you the frog?"

"C'mere." Dar gathered Kerry into her arms again, and turned the light out. It was quiet for a moment.

"Hey, Dar?"

"Mm?"

"I'm gonna really regret this in the morning, ain't I?"

"Eeerrrrmm, probably."

"You are too, huh?"

"Eh." Dar rubbed Kerry's neck. "We'll survive."

"Dar?"

"Hm?"

"I love you."

Dar smiled into the darkness. "I love you too, Ker." She let her eyes close, hoping she could remember her father's old hangover remedy by the next morning. Though, she wasn't sure whether Kerry would consider it better or worse than what it was supposed to cure. Or if they had Bosco syrup on St. Johns.

DAR PROWLED THROUGH the aisles of the small grocery, one of the few customers so early in the morning. She had a small basket hanging off her arm that already had a quart of milk in it, along with a box of Oreo cookies. She spied a bottle of chocolate syrup and snagged it, studying the label. *Ah well, it will have to do.*

She made her way to the soda aisle and selected two bottles, then analyzed the contents of her basket and retraced her steps to the refrigerated case, swapping her quart of milk for a half gallon. Satisfied, she walked up to the single register and set down her selections.

The cashier picked up each item and punched its price into the old-fashioned cash register. "Got you some kids, huh?" She smiled at Dar.

Dar peered at her over the top of her sunglasses. "No." She handed the woman a twenty dollar bill and accepted her change. "It's my breakfast."

The woman looked at the bag, then at Dar.

Dar pushed her sunglasses back up and took her bags, heading for the door as a young couple entered, stopping short when they recognized her and reacted.

"Hi," Todd said. "Sorry about last night."

In an instant, every ear in the place seemed to turn their way. Dar suppressed a wry grin. "Don't worry about it."

Rachel put a hand on Todd's arm. "We've heard a lot about you."

Erf. "I can imagine," Dar replied. "Take it with a grain of salt."

"Well, we just came in to get some breakfast." Todd glanced around. "Maybe if you're not busy later, we can sit down and talk?"

"Sure." Dar eased around them and slipped out the door.

Rachel gazed after her. "She's weird, Todd."

Todd steered her towards the grocery aisles. "No, she's not. You're just freaked out because she's gay."

"I am not," Rachel protested, noticing the looks they were getting from the cashier. "Don't make like I'm some white-bread JAP."

"Oreos on the left there." The cashier pointed helpfully. "Got lots of 'em."

Todd and Rachel exchanged puzzled glances, then shrugged.

DAR WRAPPED THE handles of the plastic bags around her hands and started on her trek back to the room. She'd left Kerry asleep, though they'd both stirred before dawn and she'd heard the pathetic moan as Kerry regretted opening her eyes.

It was clouding over, Dar noticed, and far off she could hear a faint rumble of thunder. That was good, because a stormy morning gave her a chance to pamper her ailing sweetie and not have Kerry feel too awful about missing out on any fun.

Dar glanced up as a faint, first spattering of rain hit her shoulders. She gauged the distance back to their section of the resort, and broke into a jog. She took a tighter hold on the bags to keep them from swinging, and crossed the expansive grounds at a very fair clip. She hurdled a hedge, taking it in stride, and then turned toward the building. Halfway there, seeing someone coming in the opposite direction, she moved to one side of the path. The tall man, however, saw her shift and moved directly into her way, holding up a hand.

Dar contemplated simply running him down. He was tall, but relatively thin, and she calculated she probably outweighed him. She studied his face as she approached, seeing a chiseled, hawk-like visage, clean-shaven, with a cap of graying dark hair. The suit he was wearing was silk, and his attitude projected the fact that he expected her to do whatever it was he wanted.

Dar grinned recklessly and didn't slow down. She focused her gaze on the man and kept up her pace, her hands slowly curling into fists without conscious direction. She got closer, but his expression didn't change and he didn't so much as flinch, so Dar steeled herself for the impact, ready to twist her body to the right and lower her shoulder. Her dad had taught her to play chicken right around the time she'd gotten her first bicycle. The roadblock waited until she knew he could feel the vibration of her footsteps, and then just as it almost became too late, he jumped aside.

Hah, Dar snorted silently, brushing past him without a word. She almost missed seeing the quick lunge as he reached for her, but he'd misjudged his grab, and her speed, and she was already past him by the time he made the attempt. She waited until she was certain he knew he'd screwed up, and then she slowed and stopped, turning to regard him icily.

He seemed surprised. "You don't take direction well, do you, Ms. Roberts?"

Dar just laughed. "Not in this lifetime," she replied. "You want something, or do you just grab women for fun?"

He collected himself and put his hands behind his back. "My name is John DeSalliers," he announced. "And I believe we need to talk."

Dar peered at him and then glanced up. Rain spattered her sunglasses. "Maybe, but not now." She turned. "I've got important stuff to do."

"Ms. Roberts."

Dar looked over her shoulder. "If you want to deal with me, you do it on my terms," she told him flatly. "Have a great day." With that, she started off toward the building again, picking up speed as the rain started to come down harder. As she reached the door, the skies opened, and she ducked inside just in time. Turning, she looked back and saw a satisfying vision of DeSalliers bolting through the rain, running awkwardly in his silk trousers. "Jackass." She let the door close with a snick and hastened back to the room.

It wasn't really the way she'd wanted to approach, or deal with DeSalliers, but sometimes, Dar had learned, you just had to take what life offered and make the best of it. She slid her key into the door lock and turned it carefully, pushing the door open and slipping inside.

It was dark. Dar had prudently closed the shutters before she'd left, leaving the room in soothing dimness. She set the bags down on the credenza and took her sandals off, then she padded silently over to the bed and knelt down.

Kerry's eyes were still closed and she was sleeping on her side, one arm wrapped around her pillow. Her mussed hair half-obscured her face, and Dar only just kept herself from smoothing it back. Instead, she stood up and tiptoed back to the credenza, removing the items from it and trying very hard to keep the Oreo bag from making noise.

"Uugh." A soft groan came from the bed.

"Hey, cute stuff." Dar set down a glass and opened the milk.

"Ugh." Kerry lifted her head a little and peered around. "S'dark in here," she muttered. "What time is it?"

"Eight." Dar continued mixing her potion. "I closed the blinds."

"You're a goddess." Kerry rolled onto her back, throwing her arm over her eyes. "Jesus. I feel like a horse kicked me in the head."

Dar finished mixing and picked up the glass, crossing back over to the bed and sitting down on the edge of it. "I've got something to make you feel better."

Kerry peeked at her, seeing the glass. "Noooooo." She pulled the covers over her head. "No...no...not...stuff."

"C'mon." Dar gently untangled the covers. "Kerry, honest — it'll work."

"Dar, if I try to put anything in my stomach, that and everything already in there is coming up into your lap. Wanna risk it?"

"Yes. Just take a sip," Dar coaxed.

Kerry rolled onto her side, giving Dar a piteous, miserable look. "I can't."

Undeterred, Dar put the glass down and eased her partner into more of an upright position. Then she picked up the glass and offered Kerry the straw she'd stuck in it.

Kerry stared dubiously at the mixture. "What is it?" All she could see was foam and dark streaks. "It doesn't have Worcestershire sauce in it, does it?"

"No."

Kerry put a hand over her stomach. "Dar, I really don't think I can."

Dar studied her, seeing the pale tinge to her skin. "Give it one try," she requested. "Just one sip. You need to get fluids into you, love."

Kerry sighed in resignation and maneuvered the straw over. "How can I resist when you ask me like that?" She held her breath and took the tiniest sip possible, hoping to swallow it before her system had time to analyze what it was.

It was cold and effervescent, and it slid down a lot easier than she'd imagined it would. Cautiously, she inhaled, and then licked her lips. The taste was sweet and rich and bubbly, all at the same time, not at all what she'd expected. "What is that?"

Dar was cautiously pleased with the response. "Something my daddy taught me to make."

Kerry took another sip, swallowed it. "Have I mentioned lately how much I love your daddy?" She felt her stomach settle and she took the glass, leaning against Dar as she sucked at its contents. "You know what? I don't care what it is. It's great."

Dar grinned in satisfaction. "Glad you like it." She set to work gently massaging Kerry's neck and shoulders. "Looks like it's fixing to storm out there for a while."

"Mm?" Kerry kept drinking, peering around Dar's body at the closed shutters. A rumble of thunder rattled them, and she settled back against Dar with a contented grunt. The concoction really was helping, and she felt the aching nausea ease, along with the painful cramps that had almost sent her diving for the bathroom. And why wouldn't it? she reasoned. Along with its other ingredients, the concoction had been laced with love.

Her head still hurt, though, a dull pounding that thrummed through her body and made her resolve never to experiment with rum again. "Stick to beer, Kerry," she murmured. "Worst thing that does is make you piddle."

Dar massaged Kerry's neck, working out small knots she could feel with her sensitive fingertips. "Guess who I met on the way back?"

"Not those scumbucket sneaks?"

"No. Their boss," Dar informed her. "He wanted me to stop and talk to him."

"And?" Kerry inquired.

"I had other things to do," Dar told her. "But I think he'll be back."

"Hm." Kerry finished her drink, sucking the last drops from the bottom of it. She gazed mournfully into the empty glass for a moment, and then looked up at her solicitous partner. "Any chance of getting another one of these?"

"You bet." Dar grinned, very pleased with her successful plan. "Coming right up." She took the glass. "Think you can take some aspirin for your head now?"

Kerry thought about it. "Yeah." She curled up on her side and watched Dar work. "What's in the bottle?"

"Chocolate syrup."

Kerry had to smile. "That's a chocolate milk soda you just made."

Dar brought it back to her. "It's an egg cream," she corrected.

Kerry took the glass. "But there aren't any eggs in it."

"Or cream," Dar agreed amiably, handing her a couple of pills. "It's kind of like Welsh rabbit."

"Ah." Kerry swallowed the aspirin and then settled back against the headboard. Rain rattled against the window, and she was more than glad to be nestled in the dim room, with Dar to keep her company. "So you think he'll be back, huh?"

"Yep." Dar chuckled softly. "Then maybe we'll get closer to the truth of this."

Kerry listened to the thunder, her fingers idly stroking the arm Dar had curled around her. *Maybe we will,* she agreed silently. *But not right this minute.*

Lightning flashed, outlining the closed shutters.

Chapter
Thirteen

IT JUST KEPT raining. Kerry was actually kind of glad, feeling they both needed a little down time after the excitement of the previous few days. She was curled up on the bed, with her neatly bound writing diary in front of her. A half finished poem was scrawled across one page and a steaming mug rested on the nearby bedside table.

Dar was sprawled across the couch, one long leg draped along its back, the other propping up a book. She had a glass of milk nearby, and next to it, the bag of Oreo cookies sat neatly peeled open. On the table, her laptop was busily working, streams of data flicking across the screen at an alarming rate.

Kerry nibbled the end of her pen as she watched Dar read, her eyes tracing down the page, then pausing while long fingers turned it. She was dressed in a pair of soft cotton shorts and a T-shirt, and somehow managed to make even that seem attractively sexy.

How does she do that? Kerry wondered. She cocked her head and regarded her lover with bemused curiosity. What really struck her about Dar, she realized, was just how nicely proportioned she was. Though she was tall, and her arms and legs were long, her body was also, and everything seemed to fit together just right. The white cotton showed off her tan, and as she scrolled down another page, the subtle shift of muscle under her skin was visible to Kerry's appreciative eyes.

Kerry sighed and put her chin down on her arm, still feeling a little knocked out from the partying the night before. Her stomach wasn't in the mood for more than tea, and her head hadn't quite stopped throbbing. The discomfort was making it hard for her to concentrate on her writing, and besides, it was really a lot more pleasant just to lie around and look at Dar.

She has such a nice profile. Kerry blinked dreamily. It was all angles and clean, sharp planes, with a nice nose and well shaped lips. *And the eyes, of course.* Kerry smiled.

"Ker?"

Uh oh. "Hmm?"

"What's that goofy grin for?"

"Was I goofily grinning?" Kerry rolled onto her back and tugged the covers over her pajama-clad body. "I can't finish this poem." She changed the subject. "I got stuck in the middle."

"What's it about?" Dar slipped a bookmark into her book and put it down, turning on her side and focusing her attention on Kerry.

Ah, those eyes. Kerry suddenly found herself lost in them, until the rising brow over one made her realize she was staring like a loon. "Sorry, what was the question?"

"You still feeling the rum?" Dar asked curiously.

Kerry put her head down on her arm. "Maybe," she admitted. "I just feel a little silly, I guess."

Dar got up and walked over to the bed. She sat down next to Kerry and rubbed her midriff through the covers. "Want to try some toast or cereal?"

Kerry curled herself around Dar instead, and rested her head on Dar's thigh. "I think I just want you." She planted a gentle kiss on the tan skin and closed her eyes.

Dar had never considered herself a sentimental person, but since she'd met Kerry she'd felt like she was living inside a circle of perpetually adorable Golden Retriever puppies all the time. It worried her sometimes. Dar felt parts of the image she'd always had of herself falling away and disappearing, and it was a little unsettling to know it was happening and be helpless to stop it.

Ah well. Dar draped her arm over Kerry's shoulders and resigned herself to it. "Tell you what," she said. "Let me go get my laptop, and we can take a look at what we've got so far."

Kerry reluctantly released her and sat up. "Okay."

Dar got to her feet and retrieved the device, then returned. She sat down on the bed and leaned back, resting the laptop on her thighs. Kerry squirmed over and settled next to her. They both looked at the screen as Dar smoothly keyed in a request.

"Okay." Dar reviewed her programmatic results. "What I was looking for—"

"Was a link between the piracy and DeSalliers," Kerry murmured, reaching out and touching the screen. "Nice code, honey. I like that recursive parse."

"You always say such romantic things to me," Dar remarked. "I love that."

"Nerd."

"Thanks." Dar smirked at the screen a little. "Let's see what it found." She brought up two screens and locked them into concurrency, scrolling down evenly and looking from one to the other. "That bartender said there had been six; there've been more than two dozen. Damn."

Kerry was shocked. Two dozen hijackings in the area, and no one had said anything. That information bordered on substantiating a definite collusion. "Are those from the police files?" she asked, pointing to the piracy records.

"You're joking, right?" Dar looked at her. "No. Those are the insurance filings." She nudged a key. "Ah. Looks like the insurance underwriters are starting to get suspicious. This one's pending investigation."

"Hm. So the hijackers will get their money, but the guy they hit might not?"

Dar shook her head. "No, they'll have to pay out, unless they think the owner's in cahoots with the pirates just to make a claim. Most of the guys who can afford to buy boats like that wouldn't bother." She ran a cross-check. "I was hoping I'd see a correlation between DeSallier's salvage operations and the missing boats, but it looks like this is the first time his bunch has shown up in this area."

"Mm." Kerry frowned. "Yeah." She rested her chin on Dar's shoulder. "Can you plot the piracies graphically?"

Dar studied the data, then she brought up a code screen and started typing rapidly, stopping only to tab to a different window and clip some data before she resumed programming. After a few minutes, she ran the program and a new window appeared with a somewhat rough outline of the islands, the space around them dotted with ominous little plus signs. "Ain't pretty, but there ya go."

"Hmmm." Kerry studied the graphic, then sighed. "No real pattern, huh?"

"Nope."

"We're hitting big nulls here, Dar."

"Yeah," Dar had to admit. "So much for being a nerd."

A knock startled them both. Kerry felt Dar's body stiffen, and she put a hand on her arm. "I'll get that." Before Dar could protest, she rolled off the other side of the bed and walked to the door, running the fingers of one hand through her hair self-consciously. She peered through the peephole, relieved to see one of the hotel staff outside. Kerry opened the door and issued an inquiring smile. "Hi."

The man held up an envelope. "Ma'am? I have a note for a Ms. Roberts?"

"I'll take it." Kerry extended her hand.

Reluctantly, he gave it to her. "The gentleman said to make sure Ms. Roberts got that note."

"She'll get it. I promise." Kerry pulled her head back inside and closed the door firmly. She turned and nearly jumped right out of her T-shirt when she found Dar standing silently in back of her. "Yipes! Jesus, Dar!"

"What?" Dar took the note. "You didn't expect me to be in the room? What's up with that, Ker?"

"I didn't hear you come up in back of me, you fink." Kerry peered past her shoulder as Dar opened the envelope. It was standard hotel stationery, and the note was written in black ink in a distinctively strong script. "Who's it from?"

Dar's eyes dropped the bottom, then lifted. "DeSalliers," she answered briefly. "Looks like he wants to set up a meeting to talk."

Kerry read the note. "Arrogant SOB, isn't he?"

"I nearly knocked him on his ass outside," her partner murmured. "I don't think he likes me much."

Ms. Roberts.

I will omit any polite preambles. I have business to discuss with you. I will be available this afternoon to meet with you and determine if this business can be handled between us, or will be remanded to the authorities. Be at my dockside at three.

J. DeSalliers.

"You should have knocked him on his head. Maybe it would have let some sense leak in." Kerry shook her head. "Did he forget he was chasing us?" she added. "Or is this something else?"

Dar folded the note and put it back into the envelope. "Guess we'll find out," she remarked. "Though, if you're not feeling up to it—"

"Ah ah ah." Kerry clapped a hand over her mouth. "Don't you even try that," she said. "You're not leaving me behind." Blue eyes widened above her fingers and Kerry removed her hand. "Isn't going onto his boat a little risky, though?"

"Might be," Dar acknowledged. "We'll have to play it by ear." She tossed the envelope onto the desk and went to the window, gazing out at the still stormy weather. *Am I crazy to be doing this at all?* They were away from home, and operating all by themselves. Dar wasn't stupid, and if she had to look logically at the scenario of two women executives out in the Caribbean playing with fire like this, she'd be forced to admit it wasn't the smartest idea in the world.

Damn it. Dar knew herself to be a risk taker, and she had a lot of confidence in her judgment and ability to take care of herself, but was this taking it too far? Was she just indulging her own ego?

"You know what?" Kerry had wandered over and leaned on the sill next to her. "I think we're just natural troubleshooters."

Dar looked at her.

"We're so used to problem solving, we never really stop to think about it, even if the problem really should be solved by someone else."

A little unsettled, Dar turned and folded her arms. She was surprised to hear her own thoughts so eerily echoed back at her. "You think someone else should be solving this one?"

Kerry kept her eyes on the horizon and nodded slightly. She turned to face Dar. "But the people who should be the solution might be part of the problem," she said. "That's what you think, isn't it—that the cops are in on it?"

Dar nodded. "I think they are, yeah."

"Everyone's attitude seems to be to hush it up. Let the fat and happy tourists keep coming, and if a few get hit, well, then that's okay because most won't and we need their money," Kerry said. "They didn't hit us, so we could go along with that, Dar. Just take our boat and cruise on out of here. Let them solve their own problems."

"We could."

The green eyes glinted. "Fuck that."

Dar smiled.

"I lived the first twenty-six years of my life maintaining the status quo, Dar," Kerry said, in a firm tone. "I want to rock boats and make a difference, even if that means taking a risk." She pointed at Dar, poking her in the arm. "And you, Paladar Roberts, are a natural-born caped avenger, no matter how much you deny it."

Dar rubbed her neck. "I'm not sure I'd put it like that," she protested. "But I like to fight the good fight, and win it, if that's what you mean." She glanced out the window. "And I don't trust people to fix things just because they're supposed to."

"I know." Kerry eyed her with gentle amusement. "I always get a kick out of seeing your log-in checking up on me." She saw Dar stiffen and realized she'd caught her flat-footed. "It's like passing a senior exam," she went on quickly. "Because I know if you don't say anything to me, I did it all right."

Dar turned, her expression a mixture of consternation and sheepishness. "I trust you," she said. "You just do things so differently than I do, it's..."

"Dar, we've had this argument already," Kerry interrupted her quietly. "It really is okay. You're my boss, and it's your job to make sure things happen." She sensed the upset in the woman next to her. "I know you trust me."

"It has nothing to do with trust," Dar muttered. "I was just curious." She sighed. "I like to know how things work, so I was curious as to how you did what you did. So, after you were all done, I went in and looked."

Kerry blinked. "You mean you weren't—"

"No." Dar shook her head. "I'm sorry you thought that."

"Oh." Kerry sat down on the sill, her head cocking to one side as she absorbed this new information. "Wow."

"I checked up on you the first couple of times, but that was before you went to closure on anything," Dar said. "So if there was a problem, I could fix it. After that...no." She sat down next to Kerry. "You didn't do things the way I would have, but it worked, and that's all I really care about in the long run."

Kerry scratched her jaw. "Um." She cleared her throat. "Sorry for assuming."

"S'okay." Dar sighed. "It's a reasonable assumption to make."

They looked at each other. "I think we got a little sidetracked there," Kerry suggested. "So, are we going to go after this creep?"

Dar exhaled. "Yeah, I think we did get a little off course," she agreed. "Let's go see what he wants. Maybe we can just talk to him and cut through some of the crap."

Kerry nodded. "Okay."

They both sat there for a few moments in silence. Then Kerry took a breath. "So, did I—"

"You did great," Dar cut in. "You impressed the hell out of me," she added. "Or, as your boss, I would have said something."

Kerry kicked her heels gently against the wall. "I figured that. But it's nice to hear it."

Dar made a mental note, again, to work on her positive feedback. It was so easy to tell everyone when they did something wrong, and she often forgot to take care of the flip side. Bad mistake. She knew better. "Sorry I didn't take the time to let you know," she told Kerry. "I'll try to do better."

Kerry peeked at her. "Thanks, boss."

They looked at each other. "Aren't we supposed to be on vacation?" Dar asked plaintively.

"We are," Kerry replied. "Sorry about that."

Dar gave her a wry look, then chuckled. "Let's get dressed. We can go get you some soup for lunch."

"You're on." Kerry leaned over and gave Dar a one-armed hug. "Let's go be crusaders."

Rolling thunder boomed an enthusiastic endorsement.

KERRY STOOD JUST inside the door to the verandah of the restaurant, watching the rain fall. She'd managed a bowl of cream-of-something bland soup with some crackers for lunch, and her body seemed to have settled back down to near normal.

Dar had been very quiet since they'd left the room, though, and Kerry sensed there was still a little strain between them from their abrupt foray into the business side of their lives. *There are times*, she admitted privately, *when I wish we didn't work so closely together.* She didn't mind having Dar as her supervisor—as far as corporate officers went, Dar was better than most in that department. It was just that as their relationship deepened and evolved, separating their lives at work got tougher and tougher on both of them.

In this case, she knew she'd made Dar feel bad about her assumptions, even though Kerry didn't actually mind if they'd been true. The first time she'd spotted the log-on, she'd been a little unsettled, but after that, she'd watched for it with a sense of anticipation. "Dar's final check-off" became a way for her to put closure on a project, and she knew once she'd seen it, she could put that puppy to bed and not have to worry about it coming back to nip her in the butt. It was a very safe feeling.

Kerry sighed. *Ick.* Though, now that she thought about it, the fact that Dar took the time to review her techniques, evaluating them and learning how she did things, was extremely flattering. However, she realized that her thinking Dar was snooping after her wasn't. So... She heard footsteps behind her, and Dar emerged onto the porch, standing quietly as she sucked on a mint candy. Kerry backed up a step and leaned against her, feeling Dar's body relax as she felt the contact. She curled her fingers around Dar's and squeezed them, and smiled a little as the pressure was returned.

"You doing okay?" Dar asked.

"Almost," Kerry replied, turning her head to look up at Dar. "Are you okay?"

Dar gazed back at her with a quizzical expression, then her face relaxed into a smile. "I'm fine," she reassured Kerry. "But do me a favor, wouldja?"

"Anything," Kerry replied sincerely.

"Next time, ask me."

Kerry understood what she meant. Ask instead of assuming. It was a key concept she thought she'd learned from Dar from the very start; she'd just seldom needed to apply it to her very straightforward boss. "I will," she promised.

"Okay." Dar gave her a pat on the hip. "You ready to go meet our mysterious adversary?"

"Ready as I'll ever be." Kerry felt her insides unknot as they pulled their jackets closed and zipped them. Then they walked together down the steps and into the rain. The drops hit her shoulders heavily, beating a gentle tattoo across them as she put her head down and kept walking.

Dar threw an arm over Kerry's shoulders and pulled her casually closer, turning slightly to take the brunt of the rainfall on her taller form. She focused her attention on the approaching docks. Spotting the ominous form of the big black boat at the very end of them, her pulse raced.

There were two men guarding the gangplank when they arrived. Dar stopped comfortably short of them and put her hands into her pockets. She stared at them until they got uncomfortable, then she pulled the envelope out of her pocket and frisbeed it over to the nearer one, smacking him in the chest with it.

Ten points for style. Dar returned her hand to its dry haven and waited.

The guard scrambled for the envelope and snatched it before it hit the ground. He gave Dar a threatening look, then opened it and unfolded the paper. After he read it, he turned away and spoke into the radio clipped to his shoulder.

Kerry rocked up and down gently on her heels, taking the opportunity to study the boat. The bow near the waterline bore fresh paint, and she gauged they'd had to patch at least ten feet of the fiberglass. She chuckled silently, but looked up as she heard the guard coming closer.

The lackey spoke gruffly to Dar. "Come with me. Just you."

"Kiss my ass," Dar replied in a pleasant drawl. "Tell your boss if he wants to talk, c'mon out here."

The guard just looked at her.

"G'wan." Dar shooed him off. "Yes or no, sixty seconds."

The man snorted, then turned away again and spoke into his shoulder.

"Don't you get a stiff neck after a while like that?" Kerry whispered to Dar.

"You start doing it even when you aren't wearing the damn thing," Dar whispered back. "Like in the supermarket. There ya are, buying milk next to a guy talking to his arm."

"Is that like 'talk to the hand, buddy, talk to the hand?'" Kerry snickered as she moved her fingers in a puppet-like motion.

Dar shook her head. "These guys are like cartoon characters." She indicated the guard approaching them again, his bodybuilder's physique flexing like a Macy's balloon.

"Mr. DeSalliers says he doesn't have time to play games with you," the man announced.

"All right." Dar lifted a hand. "Hasta Manana, jackass." She turned and started back down the dock. "If he changes his mind, we're in slip 30."

"Bye." Kerry waggled her fingers at the men before she ambled after Dar. She caught up to her partner after a few steps and they strolled along together. "So," she commented. "Now what?"

Dar glanced down at the keychain watch looped through her belt. "Give it a minute."

It really was a big game, of sorts. Kerry had gotten used to the delicate and sometimes not so delicate maneuverings of the boardroom. This didn't seem that different.

"Ms. Roberts!"

Kerry clucked her tongue. "Ooh, you're good."

Dar paused and looked over her shoulder, her eyes hidden behind sunglasses despite the rain. *Ah.* DeSalliers himself was trotting down the dock after them, his blue blazer getting spotted with rain. Dar turned fully and waited, having gotten what she'd asked for. "Yes?"

"Ms. Roberts, Ms. Roberts." DeSalliers sighed. "You know, I think we really did start off on the wrong foot." His attitude, completely reversed from the morning's, was almost friendly. "All we do is keep getting more and more hostile. Can't we turn this around?"

Dar regarded him warily. "You're giving me bullshit whiplash."

"Please," DeSalliers continued, "let's just go inside, out of this blasted rain, and talk."

The risk seemed acceptable, Dar reasoned, considering everything. "All right," she agreed.

"Great." He started to lead them back toward his boat. "I'm sure we can come to a better understanding of each other, if we just put a little effort into it." Only then did he seem to notice Kerry's continued presence. "Sorry. I don't think we've met?"

Kerry promptly extended a hand. "Kerry."

"Ah." DeSalliers took it and pressed it briefly. "And you are?"

"Dar's American Express card," Kerry replied smoothly. "She never leaves home without me."

Dar had to bite the inside of her lip to keep from smiling. "We're partners," she supplied succinctly.

They passed the two guards, both of whom glared at Dar as she brushed by them. Dar ignored their attitude and followed DeSalliers up the long gangplank to the deck of his boat, stepping neatly down after him onto the vessel.

Kerry eased off after Dar, looking around the deck of the big boat as they moved around toward the cabin. The deck floor was covered in plush-looking, all-weather Astroturf, and there were two more guards who were braced on either side of the deck, hands clasped behind their backs. They were big and healthy looking, and reminded Kerry irresistibly of cattle. "Moo," she uttered, under her breath. She saw Dar's shoulders twitch in a silent laugh.

They followed DeSalliers inside the cabin and found a space as ostentatiously well-appointed as the exterior deck suggested. It was full of dark leather furniture and teak wood, and smelled very masculine. On one side there was a bar, complete with a ceiling-mounted glass rack with pivots. Across from the bar was an entertainment center with a circular viewing lounge. Toward the rear was a spacious galley, and behind that, a closed door that led to the more private areas of the boat's cabin.

The windows were so tinted that light barely penetrated. Most of the illumination was provided by recessed fixtures near the walls, and one searingly bright beam that splashed over the dining room table, highlighting a crystal vase with a single, perfect red rose in it.

"Please, sit down," DeSalliers said as he crossed to the bar. "Can I get you both a drink?"

"No thank you," Kerry replied. She waited quietly near the door, looking around.

Dar was circling the cabin, examining the oriental-themed, framed mats on the walls. "Nothing for me, thanks." She stopped in front of a small painting near the galley, leaning forward a little as she recognized the style. Her eyebrows rose behind her glasses.

"Nice piece, isn't it?" Their host spoke up behind her. "I have a much larger one in my home. Truly captures the majesty of the sea."

Dar straightened. "Very nice." She pulled off her sunglasses and turned, chewing on the earpiece as she regarded DeSalliers. "I'll pass your compliments on to my mother."

The man froze in place. His brows contracted fiercely, giving him an almost comical look as he paused in the act of pouring himself a glass of what appeared to be scotch. "Excuse me?"

Dar's thumb gestured over her shoulder at the small painting. "That's my mother's work," she replied mildly. "Seascapes are a favorite theme of hers."

DeSalliers put down the glass and rested his hands on the bar. "Well, well," he murmured. "You are a veritable Pandora's box of surprises, aren't you, Ms. Roberts?" He picked up his glass and swirled the contents, circling Dar. "I send out an inquiry expecting, at best, some rich brat tooling about the Caribbean, and what do I come up with? The CIO of the largest computer services organization in the world." He paused. "What a surprise."

Dar shrugged. "We're even. I go out tooling about the Caribbean on a simple vacation, and what do I come up with? Assholes chasing my boat, breaking and entering my hotel room, and vague, useless threats sent by courier," she countered. "What a surprise. All I was expecting was reasonable weather and a few spiny lobster."

DeSalliers sighed. "I thought we were trying to get on a better footing."

Dar spread out her hands, both of her eyebrows lifting. "I come up from a damn dive, and the next thing I know, your half-witted goons are chasing my ass down."

"Now, Ms. Roberts…" The man held a hand up soothingly. "I realize now we came at you the wrong way."

"You mean, after the intimidation tricks didn't work, then you decided to find out who you were chasing?" Kerry commented from her spot near the doorway.

DeSalliers shot a glance at her and apparently decided the gracious host scam wasn't working. "Let's cut to the chase."

"Finally." Dar chewed on her sunglasses again, then she sauntered over to the nearest comfortable leather chair and sprawled in it. Kerry caught the almost imperceptible signal and joined her, perching on the chair's arm.

"Okay." DeSalliers adapted again, taking the chair across from them. "Here's the deal." His entire attitude changed, becoming tough and businesslike. Almost like Dar, in fact. "I have a piece of ocean on which I own the rights of salvage. You dove that piece of ocean and removed something from it. I want it."

Kerry took the lead. "Okay. First off, you didn't mark the salvage site." She ticked off her fingers. "You didn't post a buoy, you didn't put up a diver flag, and there were no tags on the wreck."

He took a sip of his drink. "We were about to."

"But you didn't," Kerry said. "So how were we supposed to know you were going to salvage it? ILS doesn't hire psychics."

"That's not the point," DeSalliers said with a frown. "The fact is, you were down there."

"What's so important about this wreck?" Kerry asked. "I saw it. It's an old fishing freighter with more coral than steel."

"That's none of your business."

"Then," Dar picked up the conversation, "for your records, we picked up a conch shell and brought it topside. You don't have salvage rights on marine invertebrates or their calciferous exterior structures."

The man's fingers drummed nervously on his knee, which jiggled slightly with tension. "I'm very sorry," he remarked quietly, "but I don't believe you."

"Why not?" Kerry asked suddenly. "Excuse me, but what the hell would we care about marine salvage? We're nerd sport divers." She stood up and paced. "That's what I don't understand about this entire scenario. What makes you think we give a rat's patootie about whatever junk you're searching for?"

DeSalliers gazed at her through hooded eyes. "Who are you?"

Dar leaned forward and caught his attention. "What are you looking for?" she asked in a low, vibrant tone. "If it's what we took from the sea, we'll tell you."

His dark eyes bored into hers. They stared at each other for a long moment. "I can't tell you," DeSalliers finally said.

Dar started to get up. "Waste of time."

"Ms. Roberts," he also stood, and held up a hand, "I mean it. I *can't* tell you, not *won't*."

"You don't know what it is," Kerry realized. "You have no idea what you're looking for, do you?"

DeSalliers relaxed back into his chair with a disgusted sigh.

Dar settled back and crossed her ankles. "I'm not getting this." She shook her head. "How the hell can you stake a salvage claim on an unknown object?" she asked their host.

He rubbed his temples. "Did you ever get hoisted on your own petard, Ms. Roberts?" he inquired. "Hung out to dry by your own reputation?"

Dar considered the question. "No," she replied. "Not yet, anyway."

Kerry walked over and knelt next to his chair, resting her arm near his. "Talk to us, Mr. DeSalliers. Tell us what the heck is really going on. Maybe we can help." She gave him a quiet, sincere look. "We're better friends than enemies, believe me."

He hesitated, then took a breath, as if to speak.

The door slammed open and one of the guards rushed in. "Sir! Sir! He's out there! They're diving the wreck!"

"Shit." DeSalliers jumped to his feet. "I'll kill that little bastard. Cast off!" He started to leave the cabin, then apparently remembered his guests. "Sorry. Hope you enjoy the ride."

Dar and Kerry were both on their feet and heading for the door. DeSalliers popped through it before they could reach it, and the guard slammed it shut, facing them with an air of muscular menace.

"You ladies better sit on down," the guard said gruffly.

Dar handed Kerry her sunglasses. "I suggest you move," she replied to the guard in an even tone. "We're leaving."

"Sit down," the guard repeated, pointing.

Dar advanced on him. "Move." She pinned him with an ice-cold gaze.

"Lady or not, I'm gonna break your ass if you don't sit down," the guard told her.

"Try it." Dar didn't miss a beat. She felt her body react to the danger, adrenaline kicking in and bringing a surge of blood to her skin as she came up over her center of balance. The guard was twice her size, but in that moment she could have cared less. He was between her, and safety for her and Kerry, and he was moving. The boat engines rumbled to life. Dar's hands flexed, and she let the dark energy inside her uncoil as she started for the door.

The guard reached for her, cursing. They grappled briefly, then he threw Dar against the wall, coming after her with one hand extended and the other curled into a fist.

Dar grabbed his hand and swiveled, lashing out with a sidekick that caught him right in the jaw. His head snapped back and she jerked him off balance, then whirled and levered him over her shoulder, throwing him to the floor. With a snort, she grabbed the door handle and yanked it open, just as Kerry hopped over the stunned man and joined her.

They looked out to see the dock receding, blue water between them and it. Two guards were scrambling toward them. "Feel like a swim?" Dar asked, already starting for the stern railing.

"Anywhere you go, I go." Kerry dodged an outstretched arm and they both bolted across the deck, hearing DeSalliers' yell behind them as they leaped to the railing, then dove off together into the churning water.

Chapter
Fourteen

DAR SURFACED, COUGHING to clear her lungs of a hastily mis-swallowed mouthful of seawater. She swiveled around, shaking the hair out of her eyes as she frantically searched for Kerry. A moment later, the blonde woman popped up nearby. Kerry spotted her and swam over with quick, efficient strokes. The water was choppy, and the downpour made it hard to see, but she made it through the swells to Dar's side. For a moment, they treaded water and just looked at each other. Dar shook her bangs out of her eyes again and squinted through the rain. "C'mon." She stifled a cough. "Let's get to the boat."

Between the tide, the rain, and the chop, it was a tough swim. Kerry found herself really missing her fins as she struggled to make progress. A crawl stroke didn't do much, so she switched to a frogman style of swimming, keeping just her head above water so she could breathe. Her strength, though, started giving out when they were about three quarters of the way back to the docks, and she slowed to catch her breath.

Dar seemed to sense it. She stopped and turned in the water, then swam back to her. "What's wrong?"

"Tired," Kerry admitted. "Give me a minute."

"Hang on." Dar offered her arm, her legs moving powerfully under the waves and keeping her upright.

"No, it's okay." Kerry felt a little better. She started moving forward again. Dar stayed close by her side as they battled inside the seawall, the rain coming down harder and harder. Kerry felt Dar slow just inside the wall, and she reached out to grab onto the rocks, resisting the waves that were trying to bash her against them.

"Not much farther." Dar pointed to the rocking form of their boat, dimly seen through the rain. "Are you all right?"

Kerry felt her second wind kicking in. She nodded positively. "Yes. Let's get over there." She pushed off the wall and started swimming, feeling the strong current fighting her, pulling out with the waning of the tide. Grimly, she pushed against it and kept at

Dar's shoulder with determined effort. The chop washed over her, making her eyes sting, and she tasted salt in the back of her mouth more than once. Her focus narrowed down to the chilling water, the beat of the rain, and the tall body moving just ahead of her. Something not water brushed against her, and she felt stringy somethings trail over her body. She jerked and twisted, then gasped as a searing pain across her midriff nearly shocked her senseless. "Damn." She held still with great effort, and felt the strings drift off, and then she started forward again, grimacing at the jolts going through her body.

Jellyfish. Kerry cursed under her breath. *Just my luck.* After a moment, though, the pain faded a little, and she pushed it out of her mind as she struggled on. Her breath was coming short and her muscles were burning painfully when she heard the distinctive sound of the waves slapping against fiberglass nearby. Kerry looked up to see a white surface arcing over her head. She reached out and grabbed the barnacled edge of the dock as she watched her companion approach the side of the boat. With a powerful surge, Dar emerged from the water, arms extended toward the railing that ducked toward her at the last moment and obligingly slapped itself into her hands.

Dar grabbed on and hung there for a moment, visibly gathering her strength. Her wet clothing clung to her body, and Kerry saw her chest expand as she took a deep breath. Her upper body contracted, pulling her up to the railing and then over it, but Kerry could see the effort it took, and given how she herself felt at the moment, considered it a testament to Dar's very sturdy constitution.

She knew she wasn't going to be able to duplicate Dar's feat any time soon, so Kerry pushed off again and stroked for the stern, the lowest part of the boat, where the dive ladder was clamped in place. By the time she got there, she heard the clanks as Dar unhooked the hatch and freed the ladder. The next thing she felt was a light sting as the aluminum tubing hit the water next to her and quickly submerged. Gratefully she grabbed onto the steps, riding the ladder in the chop until the boat dipped again, then getting her feet on the bottom step and pushing upward. Dar's grip suddenly fastened around her arm and she was unceremoniously hauled aboard the boat, landing on the stern deck in a soggy lump as Dar pulled up the ladder and closed the back hatch.

Buh. Kerry discovered that sitting still was a very good thing. She didn't even mind the rain pelting her, rinsing the salt water off her body as she struggled into a cross-legged position. Her arms and legs felt numb and weak; she kept her head down as she rested her elbows on her thighs and simply worked on catching her breath.

Dar dropped down next to her, seemingly just as glad to just sit still. She extended her long legs out and rested her hands on her knees. "Son of a fucking bitch."

Kerry's head lifted and she regarded her lover bemusedly. "Are you thinking maybe next time we should just go to Las Vegas on vacation?"

Blue eyes framed in a mess of dark, wet hair peered at her. "With my luck, a computer virus would take down the entire city while we were there." Dar exhaled. "You okay?"

Kerry nodded. "Just wiped. And I think I swallowed half a gallon of salt water. My tongue is pickled." She raked her hair back out of her face. "Dar, that sucked."

"Uh huh." Dar blew out a breath. "Might as well get out of the rain." With a slight grunt, she pushed herself to her feet and gazed out past the marina entrance. It was hard to fathom what had just happened. One moment they'd been getting somewhere with DeSalliers, the next minute she'd found herself in an almost dangerous situation. Which, she considered thoughtfully, she'd actually handled damn well.

"Dar?"

Dar turned, to find Kerry holding up a hand with a wry expression.

"Mind giving me a tug up?"

Dar clasped her hand and leaned backward, pulling Kerry to her feet. "Wonder who he took off after?" she mused as they moved toward the cabin door and she fished in her pocket for the key. "Damn, if we'd only had a minute more."

"Yeah," Kerry agreed. "We were close. Did you hear what he said, about his reputation? What was that all about, I wonder?"

Dar paused, holding the door open. "Want to go find out?"

Kerry looked up at her. "You mean, go out there after them?" She watched Dar nod. "That's totally insane, Dar." An eyebrow quirked wryly at her. "Let's do it."

"Go in and change. I'll cut us loose." Dar gave her a pat on the behind, and then disappeared up onto the deck.

"Aye aye, cap'n." Kerry entered the cabin, shaking her head and chuckling bemusedly. "No one's gonna believe this," she told the empty room. They'd brought their things down from the hotel before they'd gone for lunch; their bags and Dar's laptop were resting on the table where they'd left them.

Kerry stripped off her soaking wet shirt as she continued through the cabin and into the head. She hung it up on the shower rail then added her shorts to it, tossing her sneakers into the shower itself, along with her socks and underwear. The rumble of the engines starting thrumming through her bare feet, and Kerry slipped out of the head and into the bedroom, giving herself a cursory glance in the mirror on her way to the dresser.

"Wow." She pointed at her reflection. "Check out the drowned rat." Her skin showed a few light scrapes and the red mark where she thought she'd been stung by a jellyfish. It still throbbed, and she winced as she pressed lightly against the spot.

The boat moved and she grabbed quickly at the dresser, holding her balance. She waited for the turn to be completed and the bow to straighten out, then she tugged dry clothes from the dresser and slid into them. She grabbed a rain slicker from the closet and pulled it over her head, pausing to chuckle when the garment fell all the way to her knees. "Whoops." She started to remove it, then stopped in mid motion and resettled the rubberized fabric around her.

Without really stopping to think about why she'd done that, she walked to the galley and grabbed a bottle of water from the small refrigerator. Twisting the top open, she sucked down a few gulps to get the taste of the sea from her mouth, then headed for the door.

Dar settled soggily into the captain's chair, wincing at the uncomfortable dampness of her clothes. She adjusted the throttles and guided the boat away from the dock, reasoning that she could get Kerry to take the helm long enough for her to change once they were out into open water. The rain beat steadily down on the roof covering her, and Dar leaned forward to see better through the plexiglas as she guided the boat out into the channel. She turned at the buoy and nudged the engines forward, setting off after the disappearing speck that was DeSalliers' craft.

She'd barely had time to relax when she heard Kerry climbing up the ladder. Dar turned to see her lover appear on the flying bridge, dressed in a blue slicker obviously not her own. "Nice jacket," she commented as Kerry scooted under the bridge cover and pushed back the hood on her raincoat, exposing disheveled blonde hair.

"You like it?" Kerry presented her with the bottle of water and then draped her arms over Dar's shoulders. "I think I got stung by a jellyfish, Dar."

"Yeah?" Dar set their course and then turned her attention to Kerry. "Where?"

Kerry pulled up her overlarge jacket and then her shirt, exposing her belly. "There."

Dar peered at it, gently touching the angry red mark. "Does it hurt?" She looked up at Kerry's face. "Not just sting, actually hurt?"

"A little," Kerry admitted. "It's sort of throbbing. Otherwise I wouldn't have even mentioned it, Dar. I mean, I've gotten hit by men o'war before."

"Did you clean it off with anything?"

Kerry shook her head. "Didn't think I needed to; do I?"

"I don't know." Dar frowned. "Did you see what kind of jellyfish it was?"

"No." Kerry sat down next to her. "It's okay, I think. It hurt a lot when it first happened, but now it's just annoying." She scanned the horizon. "What's the plan?"

Dar opened the small cabinet under the console and removed a brown bottle and a small packet of gauze bandage. "Pull that jacket back up," she ordered, opening the bottle of alcohol and wetting the gauze.

"Shouldn't you be watching where we're going?" Kerry teased gently, "instead of playing with my navel?" Nevertheless, she hiked up the fabric and the shirt underneath, sucking in a breath as the gauze touched her skin and burned. "Ow."

"Some of those stupid things leave stinging cells," Dar told her. "Hold the wheel while I do this."

Kerry curled her fingers around the metal, keeping them on course as she felt Dar carefully clean the still-painful spot on her belly. The throbbing seemed to be getting a little worse, but she figured that was because Dar was touching it. "What are we going to do when we catch up to them?"

Dar finished her task and gently pulled Kerry's shirt down, then arranged the rain jacket over it. "Just watch," she said, giving Kerry a little pat on the side. "Maybe we can maneuver him into revealing what his game is."

"I hope so." Kerry sat down with a sigh.

Dar glanced at her. Kerry's profile seemed tense, and she could see tiny creases around her eyes. "Hey."

Kerry looked over, her green eyes visibly bloodshot. "Hm?"

"We don't have to do this."

The blonde woman cocked her head. "Huh? I thought you wanted to go after them."

"You don't look so hot."

Kerry swallowed, her brow contracting. "I'm fine," she insisted.

Dar looked doubtfully at her.

"Dar," Kerry's voice took on a hint of impatience, "I'm not a little kid."

"I didn't say you were." Dar fiddled with the controls, fidgeting over the throttles. "I'm just wondering if being out here chasing down a nutcase in the rain is such a good idea," she said. "Maybe we should just drop it, Ker."

Kerry propped one bare foot against the console and studied it. She could hear the upset in Dar's voice and knew she was at the root of it. "I think..." She paused, and really considered her words. "I think if we'd dropped it at the very start, that would have been okay."

Dar watched her out of the corner of her eye.

"But now, I think we have to see this through. You know?" Kerry said. "I don't like the idea of running away, and if we just ducked out now, knowing what we know, then that's how I'd feel."

"Mmph," Dar grunted grudgingly. "This was supposed to be a relaxing vacation," she grumbled. "For both of us."

Kerry reached out and circled Dar's arm with her fingers. "Do you want to stop?" she asked with quiet sincerity. "Sweetheart, if that's what you want, we'll do it." Her hand tightened slightly.

Dar fastened her eyes on the horizon, pondering in silence for a very long minute. She felt torn between her desire to know the truth, and her equally powerful desire to protect Kerry.

"Dar?" Kerry uttered softly.

"Yeah?"

"Why don't we compromise? Let's not follow them. Let's circle around the other side of Charlie's island and watch from behind that point on the west side. "

Dar adjusted the throttles a little. "And?" She probed the idea cautiously.

"That way, we don't force a confrontation, and we can just sort of satisfy our curiosity," Kerry reasoned. "And if there's nothing going on, we can...um..." she plucked gently at Dar's damp sleeve, "get a lot more comfortable downstairs."

It was an acceptable plan, Dar decided. "Okay," she agreed. "I can go with that."

"Cool." Kerry grinned briefly. She slid over on the seat and leaned against Dar's damp body, laying her head on Dar's shoulder. The throbbing from her sting seemed to be getting worse and she now had a headache, but she reasoned that it was nothing a little relaxing in Dar's proximity couldn't cure.

The boat shot on in the rain, now in a curving path that left DeSalliers to disappear over the horizon.

THE SECOND TIME she felt the chill, Kerry realized something was wrong. Despite the protection of her rain slicker, she felt cold, and her throat seemed to be closing, making it hard to swallow. She debated trying to ignore the feeling, but her better sense intervened. "Dar?"

Her partner looked quickly at her. One hand lifted and touched the side of her face. "You okay?"

Kerry's lips twitched. "I don't think so. I feel kind of lousy," she admitted. "I'm cold and my throat hurts."

Dar put a hand on her forehead and cursed. She turned and surveyed their surroundings with anxious eyes. They were nearing the north side of Charlie's island, but otherwise they were in a large patch of quiet, empty sea. She slowed the engines and then stilled them, checking the depth meter as they drifted.

"Wh..." Kerry stopped, finding it a little hard to breathe. "What are you doing?" She watched Dar work the boats controls, and realized suddenly her hands were shaking. "Dar?"

"Need to get you below." Dar spoke quietly, a world of tension in her voice. "I'm going to drop anchor." She did exactly that, and the rattle of the deploying anchor was suddenly loud as she cut the engines. "C'mon. I've got a kit downstairs I think we're gonna need."

Kerry wasn't really sure what was going on, but she stood, holding on to Dar's arm when her knees suddenly threatened not to hold her. "Oh boy."

"Hang on to me." Dar clasped her around the waist, and guided her to the ladder. "I think you're having a reaction to whatever stung you."

"Oh." Kerry shivered, feeling like she was trying to breathe underwater. "My throat...feels kinda thick." She saved her breath for climbing, feeling the utter security of Dar wrapped around her. "Feels funny." They reached the deck and Kerry's legs buckled under her. "D..."

"I've got you." Dar picked her up and carried her into the cabin, kicking the door open and taking Kerry from the confusion of the rain and warm air into the cool quiet.

Kerry sucked in air, hearing the rasp in her own breathing, and it occurred to her suddenly that she should be scared. She felt the cool fabric of the couch against her lower legs as Dar put her down. "D...Dar?" She clutched Dar's arm in shivering fingers as she felt Dar slide a pillow under her head, propping her up a little.

"Just stay quiet and try to relax. I'll be right back," Dar assured her.

Kerry just watched, her breathing now coming in shallow heaves. She felt like there wasn't enough oxygen in the air, and as Dar came back and knelt next to her, she noted that her fingers and toes were tingling. An unreasoning fear swept over her, and she started to panic.

Dar's voice penetrated the haze around her. "Ker...Ker...take it easy."

"Da... I can't breathe," she panted.

"Sweetheart, I know. Just give me a minute. Hang in there."

Kerry suddenly felt something cold against her arm. "Wh..." She turned her head and saw Dar bringing a needle close to her, its length quivering as Dar's hand shook. Kerry looked up at Dar's face and saw a fierce, intent mask, eyes widened in fear, and that terrified her. *Am I going to die?* A soft cry escaped her throat. She felt a sting and her arm jerked, then a solid bolt of pain made her struggle, panting, unable to draw in a decent breath.

Dar's weight pressed against her abruptly, pinning her down. Kerry felt panic take over and she fought the hold, grabbing at Dar and pushing hard against the powerful body laying over her. One arm was grabbed and held tightly, and she felt another prick, then a chill, then a hot, strange sensation under her skin where the needle had entered. Then it was gone, and she thought she heard a clatter of something going across the room. The weight came off her and the cabin whirled up and around, and she couldn't breathe, and it was cold and...

"Kerry!"

The voice penetrated her confusion. Kerry coughed, and then inhaled in reflex, surprised when she was able to suck in a lungful of air. The bands of pressure around her chest eased and she shivered, huddling close to the source of warmth now wrapping itself around her. Slowly, the tingling in her hands receded and she flexed them weakly. She could still feel harsh chills shaking her body and it was very hard to think straight, but she did know she was being held securely and she could feel Dar's breathing against her back. At least she could breathe. Kerry sucked in air gratefully, feeling completely drained. "Wow," she whispered. "That sucked."

She felt the faint jerk behind her as Dar almost laughed. She could hear the hammering of Dar's heart where her ear was pressed against her chest and she coughed a little, hearing a rattling in her lungs that unnerved her. "Ungh."

"Easy." Dar finally spoke, easing back against the couch and cradling Kerry closer. Kerry's face had taken on a pale gray tinge, and she could feel the shivers working their way through her body. Now that the injection, a stimulant she always carried, had been administered, there was not much more Dar could do other than just be there. There would be time later for her to curse herself for not seeing the signs. Time later for her to be angry she hadn't checked Kerry's sting further, or taken more precautions, or...

Dar exhaled. Kerry had never had a reaction to a sting before. Truth be told, Dar kept the shots on board for herself, since she'd gotten stung once at age ten and had almost gone into convulsions. "Easy, honey."

Kerry simply lay there quietly, her head resting against Dar's chest. Her hand rested limply on her partner's, her thumb moving ever so slightly. "Dar?" she murmured.

"I'm here."

"Am I dying?"

Dar felt her blood pressure shoot up so high she got lightheaded and saw sparkles in front of her eyes. "No, sweetheart," she answered softly. "Please don't even think that."

It was like listening to constant thunder. Kerry almost couldn't count the beats. She rolled her head to one side and looked up fuzzily, seeing the stark fear written across her lover's face. Her hand lifted to touch Dar's jaw, and she felt it quiver under her fingers. No. Kerry blinked. She couldn't die, now could she? Dar needed her. Wanted her. "Never felt like that before," Kerry burred. "What happened?"

Dar swallowed hard and then impatiently wiped her forearm across her eyes. "You reacted to that damn fucking sting."

Kerry's eyebrows lifted slightly. "Ouch. Never did that before." She felt another chill take her and she burrowed into Dar's embrace, seeking warmth. Her arm ached, and she looked at it with a frown. "Ow." She touched the sore spot.

"Sorry." Dar shifted. "Had to stick you pretty fast." She drew in a breath. "How about I get you into bed? Bet the covers'll feel good." Her voice sounded a little rough. "Should get you to the hospital on St. Johns."

Hospital. Kerry's nose wrinkled. *Ick.* "How 'bout we start with bed?" she conceded. "But only if you come in with me."

"You're in no position to be bargaining, Kerrison." Dar's tone had gentled, and Kerry could hear her heartbeat slowing down and steadying. "You need a doctor." But she carefully stood up, letting out a little grunt of effort as she picked Kerry up and cradled her. She walked slowly into the bedroom, turning sideways to get them both inside the door and then putting Kerry down on the bed.

Kerry gazed at her through half-closed eyes as Dar examined her. "Urmph."

With a sigh, Dar unzipped the raincoat Kerry was still wearing and pulled it off. Then she drew the covers over her partner's body, tucking them in carefully around her. The blonde woman's skin still had an unhealthy tinge, and she was shivering. "We're heading back," Dar told her.

Kerry reached out and caught her hand, holding it. "Don't leave me."

Dar's brows contracted. "Kerry, I've got to drive the boat."

"Don't leave me," Kerry begged softly. "Please?"

Indecision seared its way across Dar's face, as she found herself caught between two overwhelming urges. Her better sense was telling her to get Kerry to a doctor's care. However, she knew St. Johns was a long ride away, and by the time they got back there Kerry's symptoms would most likely have faded.

"Let me get you something for your fever," Dar temporized.

"And get those wet clothes off," Kerry teased weakly. "We don't both need to be sick."

The coherence in her partner's eyes reassured Dar immensely. "Okay. Don't go anywhere," she warned, as she turned and eased out of the bedroom.

"I won't." Kerry watched her go. She relaxed a little and pulled the covers more closely around her, relieved to feel her body starting to feel more normal. Her arm hurt where Dar had injected her, and the sting throbbed, adding that discomfort to her fever, but she could now breathe easily and all the feeling had returned to her hands and feet.

"Son of a biscuit," Kerry remarked to the cabin ceiling. "That was not funny." Not funny at all.

DAR WALKED INTO the galley and stood for a moment, then she slowly leaned on the counter and cradled her head in her hands. *Son of a bitch,* she thought silently. *Son of a fucking bitch, that was too close.* With a sigh, she straightened, letting her hands drop to her sides. She felt completely drained and her legs were still shaky, but she forced herself to walk over and pick up the teapot. Hot tea would not do anything particularly medicinal, but she knew Kerry liked the beverage. Besides, it gave her something to do.

Dar filled the pot and put it on the galley stove, then opened the cabinet and removed a bottle of Tylenol. She shook out a couple of the tablets and set them down, then removed Kerry's mug from its hook and put it down next to them. She studied the items, then shook out a few more tablets and palmed them, putting a little water in Kerry's cup and using it to swallow down the pills. Then she turned and leaned on the counter, folding her arms across her chest as she waited for the water to boil.

The dampness against her forearms reminded her she'd forgotten to change. With a sigh, Dar pushed off the counter and walked over to where their bags were still resting on the table. She unbuttoned her shirt and removed it, draping it over the chair, then pulled off her sports bra, wincing at its clammy dampness. Dry clothes felt good against her skin, and she felt a lot warmer as she crossed back over to the galley and poured the boiling water over the herbal tea ball she'd placed in Kerry's cup. Steam rose, carrying with it the scent of blackberries. Taking a small jar of honey from the refrigerator, she drizzled some into the cup and carefully stirred it.

When she was satisfied that it was perfect, she picked up the Tylenol, tucked a water bottle under her arm, and secured the teacup. With a glance around the cabin, she headed back for the bedroom, entering the door and sweeping her eyes over the bed with badly hidden anxiety.

Kerry was right where she'd left her, curled on her side with her arm wrapped around her pillow. Her eyes were half open, watching the door, and they widened as Dar entered.

"Ah. There you are."

"Here I am," Dar agreed, setting her burden down on the bedside table. "How are you feeling?"

"Feeling like I want my Dar." Kerry reached out and fingered the soft cotton of Dar's shorts.

Dar sat down on the edge of the bed and put her hand on Kerry's forehead. It was warm to the touch, and her color was still definitely off. "Sit up a minute and swallow these." She helped Kerry sit and handed her the pills, then uncapped the water bottle and held it while Kerry suckled a mouthful, then swallowed.

"Thanks." Kerry leaned against her. "Jesus, I feel like hot boiled trash."

"Hm." Dar put her arm around her. "I bet."

Kerry shivered. "That was really scary."

"Oh yeah." Dar picked up the cup of tea and offered it to her. "I was scared."

Kerry cradled the cup in her hands, savoring its warmth. She took a sip of the sweet, hot tea and sighed. "I know," she said. "I think that scared me the most."

Dar eased off the bed and knelt in front of the dresser, opening the lower drawer and rummaging in it. She found the small case she'd tucked inside when they'd boarded in Miami and picked it up, bringing it with her as she resettled herself on the edge of the bed.

"What's that?" Kerry watched her curiously. Her eyes followed the zipper as Dar unzipped it, then the eyebrows over them lifted sharply as she saw the blood pressure cuff inside. "Where in the hell did that come from?"

"Dr. Steve," Dar replied quietly. "Gimme your arm."

"Dar."

Ignoring the mild protest, Dar fastened the cuff around her lover's toned arm and started pumping it.

Kerry sighed. "Do you actually know how to use that?"

"I can manually reprogram the flash bios of an IBM mainframe; I think I can figure it out," Dar replied, watching the small gauge on the gadget.

Kerry exhaled unhappily and her shoulders drooped.

Dar glanced up and caught the expression. "He made me bring it," she explained gently. "I wasn't gonna use it, but since I had to give you a damn bucket of stimulant..."

Kerry peeked at the gauge. "Hmph." She tapped it with her other hand. "Damn."

One sixty. Not good. Dar released some of the pressure and checked again. *Over one hundred.* She unfastened the cuff from Kerry's arm and rubbed it in attempted comfort. "Probably from the stimulant, sweetheart," she offered. "Why don't you lie down?"

Still visibly unhappy, Kerry meekly complied.

Dar tossed the device onto the dresser and stretched out next to her partner, gently combing Kerry's disheveled hair with her fingers.

"Bah," Kerry muttered.

Dar gave her a sympathetic grin. "I bet when I check it later, it'll be fine."

Kerry eyed her dourly and then held out a hand. "Gimme that." She pointed to the cuff.

Dar reached over and snagged it, then handed it over, surprised when Kerry wrapped it around her arm and started pumping. "Um..."

"Ah ah." Kerry continued her task. "Fair's fair, Dar. I thought your heart was going to come out of your chest earlier." She finished pumping and observed the results. "Hah." She gave Dar a look. "Higher than mine, darling. Park your head on the pillow."

Dar blinked in real surprise, looking down at her arm, then she gave Kerry a sheepish grin and wriggled into a more comfortable position next to her partner. "I was stressed," she commented. "You matter to me."

Kerry tossed the cuff into the corner and wrapped her arm around Dar as she put her head down on her shoulder. "I guess we're letting DeSalliers go, huh?" she murmured. "Are we in this over our heads, Dar?"

Dar had her eyes closed, and she welcomed the easing of the headache throbbing across the back of her skull. She considered Kerry's question for a few minutes. "I don't know. Maybe." Her body shifted a little and she pulled Kerry closer. "Let's take it easy for a while, then head back to St. Johns." She rubbed Kerry's back. "I'd like them to check you out, just in case."

A green eyeball rotated up and fixed on her in faint accusation.

"I know, I know." Dar sighed. "I'd be kicking and screaming at the mere suggestion."

Kerry snorted softly. "Yes, you certainly would be."

"Humor me," the dark-haired woman requested. "Please?"

Having made her point, Kerry grunted. "Okay." She closed her eyes again.

Dar put her arms around Kerry and hugged her. "Atta girl," she said, then paused as she heard the sound of a motor approaching. She exchanged a quick glance with Kerry. "Let me go see what that is."

Kerry hitched herself up on an elbow and watched as Dar got up and left. She considered following her, but her body protested, unwilling to move. Instead she fluffed the pillow up behind her and settled back, tucking her feet up and picking up her teacup, inhaling the fragrant steam.

DAR THREADED HER way through the cabin and went to the door, opening it and looking outside. A medium-sized fishing boat was approaching them, with two men on the flying bridge and several others standing in the stern. For a moment, she stared at them, and then comprehension dawned. *Pirates*?

Dar didn't see any real fishing gear on the boat, and the men were clustering together, watching her. Her heart rate started to increase, and for a single brief moment she wished she and Kerry were back in the office dealing with a multiple-layered, international cluster fuck. With a soft oath, she pulled her head back inside and bolted for the bench seat, yanking it open and pulling out the case. "Ker!" she yelled. "Keep your damn head down!"

She opened the case and removed the shotgun, loading it hastily as she heard the engines outside throttle down. With a savage motion, she chambered a round, then jumped to the door and threw it open.

Two men were about to jump on board from the fishing boat's bow. Dar braced herself and threw the gun up to her shoulder, sighting along the barrel as her finger curled around the trigger. "Hold it!" she barked loudly.

The men in the stern had guns. She could see them from the corner of her eye. But her immediate problem was the men on the bow.

"All right, lady! Take it easy! Nobody gets hurt!" the man closest yelled at her. "You got one gun, we got ten. Now put that down, okay?"

"Fuck you," Dar snarled back. "Touch the boat and I'll blow your damn cock off!"

The man lifted his rifle casually. "I'm telling you, lady, put it down!"

Dar didn't budge. She tightened her finger on the trigger, feeling the cold metal warm to her touch. "Back off!" she yelled at the man. "Get your asses out of here, you pieces of pirate shit!" A hand touched her back and she almost jumped through the bulkhead. "Grrrr!"

"I'm calling the Coast Guard," Kerry told her in a low voice. "Tell them that."

"G'wan, jump! She won't shoot you! All talk!" the man on the stern yelled. "Hurry!"

Dar felt her heart lurch as the man on the bow prepared to leap. She trained the barrel of the shotgun on him and swallowed hard, not sure she was either willing or able to pull the trigger.

"Dar." Kerry's voice was tense.

I have to protect her. Dar's inner voice spoke quietly. "Stay back," she called over her shoulder, and then faced forward. The man tossed a rope over to the deck and climbed up onto the railing. Dar steeled herself, and pulled the trigger. The gun bucked powerfully, jerking against her shoulder. Yells erupted. Then she pulled it again. Splinters of white erupted all over the water as both shots blew through the hull of the pirate's boat near the waterline. She pumped the shotgun and loaded two more shells into the chamber.

"Crazy bitch!"

"Shoot her ass!"

"Look out!"

"Get the fuck back! Get back! Holy shit!"

"Next one's gonna put chum in the water," Dar bellowed, "instead of fucking fiberglass!" She swung the shotgun toward the stern, since the two men on the bow had dived into the water for cover. One of the men facing her brought his gun up and sighted down it, and their eyes met across their gun sights.

And in that moment, with her life on the line, Dar felt her fear drop away as the predator inside her woke. Her eyes narrowed and a smile etched itself across her face, and she knew way down deep that she not only could pull that trigger...she would. Her finger tightened on the trigger.

"Get the fuck outta here, man! We're fucking sinking!" One of the men from the bow had climbed over into the stern and grabbed the wheel.

"Coast Guard, Coast Guard, mayday, mayday." Kerry's voice came from behind her. "This is *Dixieland Yankee*, a US registered vessel being attacked just north of AVI B21."

"Fuck! They're calling the Coast Guard! Get moving!" The man pointing the gun at Dar dropped his muzzle and ducked behind the cabin. "Move! Move!"

The fishing boat wallowed in the water, then its engines cut in and the bow turned away from them. They gunned the motor and the bow lifted, two holes now visible against its white curve. As they left, one of the men on the stern lifted his rifle to his shoulder and pointed it at them.

"Shit." Dar jerked back through the doorway, trying to get the door closed.

One of the man's companions knocked the muzzle up, then cuffed the man in the back of the head. The gun carrier angrily smacked his crewmate with the butt of the rifle. They struggled, shoving each other as the boat retreated, curving widely toward the southern shore of the island just north of Charlie's.

"We better get out of here," Dar uttered tensely. "In case they come back." She turned to find Kerry watching her with a pale face and widened eyes. "You okay?"

Kerry set down the microphone, leaned against the cabin wall, and exhaled. "Yeah." Her voice held a rough note. "But heading back to some place where I can just..." she took a breath, "take a nap would be very cool."

Dar guided her over to the couch and sat her down, then put away the shotgun. "Curl up here, sweetheart. I'm pulling up the anchor and we'll dock over by Charlie and Bud's," she said. "Bud's a medic."

"Bet his bedside manner's a peach," Kerry muttered as she lay down on the couch. She watched Dar's face as she closed the shotgun case, seeing the tension etched across it and the restless shift of her jaw muscles. "Hey, Dar?"

"Yeah?" Dar didn't look up.

Kerry reached out to stroke Dar's leg. "That was really impressive," she said.

Dar's hands paused in their work. The dark head turned and their eyes met. Dar closed the bench seat and sat down next to Kerry, resting her forearms on her knees. "Was it?" she answered softly. "It just sounded like a bunch of pompous yelling to me."

Kerry smiled. "It worked," she said. "That was a great idea to put a hole in their boat."

Dar gazed at the floor between her bare feet. Her mind drifted back to the feeling she'd had when the gun had centered on the man on the bow. There had been no fear, no confusion in her. She'd centered the sights on his chest. Why hadn't she pulled the trigger? What had sent the muzzle lower, to target the boat instead?

"Dar?"

Dar lifted her head and turned. "Yeah? Um...thanks." She managed a smile. "I'm not sure it was all planned, but I'm glad I ended up doing the right thing." She pushed herself to her feet. "Call me if you need anything, okay?" She ruffled Kerry's hair, then walked to the door and eased through it.

Kerry felt her brow furrow. Her instincts told her something in Dar's voice...in her manner...just wasn't right. She heard the engines start up, followed by the clank of the anchor retracting, felt the motion as the boat headed toward the island. Later, they'd have time to talk. Kerry put her head down on the arm of the couch and let her eyes drift shut. Then she'd figure it out.

Chapter
Fifteen

DAR WAS IN turmoil. The rain had stopped, and a weak splash of sunlight dusted her forearms where they rested on the control console of the boat. Things were just happening too fast, she decided. She was in a place where she was purely reacting instead of driving what was going on, and she wasn't used to that.

"So I react like a freaking nutcase. Nice." She stared glumly at the controls. "What the hell was that? A gun? Shooting people? What the hell is going on with you, Roberts?" Shaking her head, she turned the wheel a little, arcing the boat toward the end of the island. "I think I'm losing it."

"Honey?"

Dar jumped in startlement, and then picked up the microphone. "Right here. Everything okay?"

"Well..." Kerry's voice crackled through the intercom, "you've got the mic keyed open, and it's kind of tough for me to listen to you yelling at yourself when I'm not there to kiss you and make it better."

"Oh." Dar felt herself blushing. "Sorry," she muttered. "I'm just a little rattled, I guess." Her eyes lifted to the horizon and adjusted their course again. "Be glad to be in port."

"Me, too," Kerry replied.

Dar felt a pang of anxiety. "You feeling worse?" Pure instinct caused her to hit the throttles and increase their speed. On top of everything else, worry about Kerry's physical condition was gnawing at her.

"No," Kerry replied, a touch of warmth in her tone. "I just had some more tea, matter of fact. I think the fever's down," she said. "I think I just need some processing time."

Dar relaxed a little but her body still twitched, her leg tensing and releasing in a nervous tattoo. "Yeah," she agreed. "Just take it easy, okay?"

"I will if you will," Kerry's wry retort came back.

"Mmph." Dar released a gusty sigh. "Almost there," she commented. "Might want to radio ahead to see if... Crap." As they cleared the northern point of the island and headed southwest, her gaze found a profile on the horizon. DeSalliers' boat was hunched in front of the channel leading into the island's dock, trolling in a tight circle.

"What?" Kerry answered, then after a rustling while she moved to where she could see out a porthole, she said, "Oh, fudge. What the hell is he doing, Dar?"

Dar's face tightened in anger. She felt a wash of rage flood through her, focusing a dark energy on the boat squatting arrogantly in her path. "He's pissing me off," she growled softly. "And he's going to regret it."

She turned the boat directly toward the harbor and gunned the engines. Almost immediately, the radio crackled to life. "Approaching vessel, stand off and remain clear of our position."

Dar clicked the mic. "Kiss my ass. You're in my way; I suggest you get out of it," she barked into the instrument, putting some of her tension and a lot of her pent-up frustration behind the words. She could feel her temper flaring to the flashpoint, and curiously, she had no desire to squelch it.

"Do not approach this vessel! We are conducting a search!"

"Get..." Dar let her voice deepen and intensify, "out of my way." There was a moment's silence, during which she directed the bow of the *Dixie* right for the center of DeSalliers' hull.

"Roberts!"

Dar grinned unpleasantly. "Not in the mood, buddy." She clicked the mic. "I'm going into that harbor."

"Listen to me," DeSalliers replied. "You can't come through here. We're in the middle of — "

"You're the one not listening," Dar told him. "I don't give a damn what you're in the middle of. Move, or I'll go right through you."

"You're insane!"

It was, if you looked at it, pretty crazy. Dar snarled and rethought her words. "No. I've just got a sick passenger and I need a medic. You're between me and that."

There was a short period of silence and she didn't slacken her speed, though she set her hands on the throttles. She almost jerked them backwards when the intercom crackled, aware of the dire tension running through her muscles.

"Hey, sweetie."

She could hear the anxiety in Kerry's tone. "Hang tight, love. I think I'm gonna win this point," she uttered. "Jackass."

The main radio blasted static at her. "All right, Roberts. We'll clear you a channel past us, but slow down for Christ's sake."

Dar watched the other boat carefully, and saw the bow dip slowly toward her as it moved. With a satisfied grunt, she pulled the throttles back, diminishing the rumble of her diesels and slowing the boat. There wasn't much room in the channel for even DeSalliers' boat, and as she got closer she could see they were trawling a net along the length of the big vessel and blocking the path into the harbor.

What in the hell is he doing? Dar shifted the *Dixieland Yankee* to the far southern part of the channel, protected by two seawalls of coral that stretched out into the sea. There would be, she realized, just barely enough room for her to squeeze by, and any shift in the waves would send her against the coral.

DeSalliers' small boat circled behind it, with a diver's flag out. Dar could see faces turned her way, full of anger and resentment as she approached their position. She reduced speed to almost an idle, wishing she could better see what they were up to.

Two of the men pointed at her and shouted, and Dar's quick hearing detected the distinctive sound of a camera shutter closing. Occupied with the delicate task of maneuvering the tiny path she'd been given, looking wasn't possible, but by the looks on the faces on that boat, she could guess what Kerry was up to.

Gotta love her. Dar watched her depth meter anxiously, tapping the throttles to get them past a bulge in the seawall.

The small boat cut toward them and got in her way. Dar slowed and let out a warning blast on their air horn. The men yelled and pointed at Kerry. Dar raised her middle finger to them and tapped the throttles. As the boat skimmed closer, Dar glanced behind her to where the stern of the *Dixie* cleared DeSalliers' boat, the bow emptying of people as Kerry's lens swept over them. "Kerry, hang on!" she yelled back, as she threw the boat hard to one side, then gunned the engines and reversed course, building a wake that smacked into the smaller boat and sent it half onto its side.

One of the men on the boat catapulted over the side and the boat swerved, its occupants screaming at her in words that the wind ripped away into incoherence. Dar wrapped her legs around the captain's chair and swept past them into the island's small, protected harbor. A flush of wild triumph washed through her, muting the anger and forcing a chuckle from her throat at her successful maneuver. They left DeSalliers behind, and she pulled slowly into the cramped dock.

He wasn't finished, however. "Roberts."

Dar eyed the radio with a smirk.

"You only think you got away with that."

Dar eased the *Dixie* into an open slip, not a difficult task since most of them were unoccupied. She picked up the radio. "You only think you let me," she replied. "Have a great day." With that, she dropped the mic onto the console and shut down the engines, leaped to her feet, and headed for the ladder.

Kerry was standing on the stern deck, wrapped in a jacket and pale faced. She turned as Dar slid down the ladder and let the camera looped around her neck rest on her chest. "Wow," she exhaled.

Dar hopped to the railing, then onto the dock to secure their lines. "Wow wasn't the word I had in mind," she responded, as she leaped back onto the deck. "Stupid son of a bitch. I don't know what the hell he thinks he's doing, or who he thinks he is, or what the hell he's looking for, but..."

A loud clank made them both jump. They froze for an instant, then moved to the other side of the boat and looked down.

"Me," a bedraggled, ragged figure was hanging on to one of their buoy lines, "is what he's looking for."

Kerry gripped the railing and blinked. "Bob?" she uttered.

Dar gaped at him. "Son of a..."

Bob tugged off his mask and coughed, his face pale and strained. "Fifty psi left." He looked completely drained. "He almost got me."

Dar and Kerry looked at each other. Kerry rubbed her eyes, very obviously at a complete loss. She gave Dar a plaintive, sheepish look and lifted both hands in appeal.

Dar scratched the back of her head and then shook it, having nothing really to add to the emotion. Substituting action for reaction, she leaned over the railing and extended a hand. "Gimme your gear," she directed. "Come 'round to the back. There's a ladder."

Bob gave her a wry look. "Thanks." He unbuckled his BC and tank, and lifted them high enough for Dar to grab. "I know I'm not what you wanted to find hanging off your lines." His eyes shifted to Kerry, then dropped.

"At this point..." Kerry walked over to the deck chairs and sat down on one, despite its dampness, "if Harry Houdini showed up clipped to the rudder, it wouldn't surprise me." She slumped in the chair, the fever and residual effects of the jellyfish poison taking over as the adrenaline faded.

Dar set Bob's scuba gear in the corner and let the ladder down. She put a hand on Kerry's shoulder and squeezed it gently. "I'm going to go see if Bud's at home. Hang in there, love." She started to jump to the dock, and then paused, pointing a finger at Bob, who had just emerged wearily onto the deck. "Mess with her, and I'll tie you to that pylon and call your friends to come pick you up. Got me?"

Bob froze, and looked at her, wide eyed. "Yes, ma'am," he squeaked, at the menacing scowl directed at him.

"And when I get back, you're gonna tell us what the hell's going on," Dar added in a growl. "So get your story ready." She turned and leaped for the dock, landing gracefully and stalking toward the shore.

Bob sat down on the stern rail and blinked at Kerry, who gazed wanly back at him. "I can guess what you must be thinking," he murmured awkwardly.

"No, you can't," Kerry sighed, putting aside images of bubbles and hot fudge. "Really."

"Oh." Bob studied the deck. "Hey, listen, I'm sorry I—"

Kerry gently cut him off. "It's okay."

Bob peeked up at her, noticing her pallor. "Are you sick or something?"

"I got stung by a jellyfish," Kerry told him. "It's been kind of a crappy day." She exhaled, turning her eyes toward the shore and willing Dar to reappear. "Hopefully, it won't get worse."

Prudently, Bob kept his thoughts strictly to himself.

BUD STRAIGHTENED, RESTING his hand on the edge of the bed as he knelt next to it. On the bedside rested a small, olive-drab kit, a coiled stethoscope sitting snakelike on top.

Kerry was lying quietly on the bed, the covers pulled up to her waist. Her eyes moved between Bud and the visibly restless Dar lurking behind him, and a faint smile crossed her face. "Find anything?"

"Jelly sting's fine." Bud issued a half shrug. "Ain't much you can do for that 'cept what Dar did." He glanced behind him, then looked back at Kerry. "Fever's from a bug. Here." He tossed a packet onto her chest. "Penicillin. Take one now, then every twelve hours for two days." He paused. "Unless you're allergic to it."

"I'm not." Kerry shook her head slightly. "Thank you, Bud. I really appreciate this."

He got up and turned to Dar. "You wanna tell me what the crap on the radio was all about?"

Dar considered the question. Bob was tucked away in the spare room across the hall, keeping silent. She wanted to get to the bottom of his story, but she knew Bud deserved some kind of explanation, especially since he'd dropped everything to come and check Kerry out. "Sure."

Behind them, Kerry was swallowing one of the tablets Bud had provided her, drinking down the rest of the bottle of water that had been sitting at her bedside. Her nose wrinkled a little at the pungent scent of the antibiotic, but she was glad to trade that for the chills wracking her again. "Why don't you go grab some coffee, Dar? I'm just going to lie here and vegetate for a while."

Dar studied her, pale blue eyes shadowed and the brows over them tensed and lowered. After a moment, however, she nodded.

"Sounds good to me. Bud?"

Bud picked up his kit and grunted. "Java works." He looked briefly at Kerry. "Drink water. It'll get that crap out of you." With that, he turned and followed Dar out of the bedroom.

Kerry pulled the covers up higher and looked up at the open hatch admitting a splash of sunlight that brought out the warm colors in the comforter. She still felt lousy, but knowing what the problem was eased her mind and erased some of the fear that had started to nibble away at her composure. She'd been afraid that the fever had been connected to the sting, and that maybe the sting had been something other than a jellyfish. She'd read enough horror stories about marine snakes and their venom for all sorts of bad ideas to begin circulating, but Bud's words — along with the fact that the sting mark was fading — reassured her immensely.

As the tension faded, fatigue replaced it and she found she couldn't keep her eyes open. Though she wanted to hear Bob's explanation, she knew it would have to wait until Bud left. Kerry felt the gentle rocking of the boat soothing her and she surrendered to it, allowing sleep to finally claim her in its healing embrace.

"SO," BUD EXAMINED the cup of coffee Dar had provided him, "what's the gig?"

Dar had seated herself across from him, and she took a swallow from her own cup before she answered. "Guy who chased us the other night," she said, "he's a big-money treasure hunter."

Bud sipped his coffee, holding the cup in his whole hand rather than by the handle. "DeSalliers. We heard," he said. "He's a right bastard."

"Mm," Dar agreed. "He wants something off that wreck we dove the other day," she said. "He wouldn't say what." Her eyes studied Bud's face. "The kid we picked up the other night's also after something on the same wreck."

Bud's grizzled eyebrows lifted in surprise. "No shit?"

Dar shrugged.

The retired sailor leaned back, his attitude relaxing and opening a little. "It's just an old trawler. I've dived it," he said. "Got some nice holes for lobsters, but that's about it." He frowned. "Though..." His voice trailed off. "Now, hold on."

Dar leaned forward, cocking her head.

Bud tapped his forehead with two powerful fingers. "Remember a story I heard some years after that damn thing sank," he muttered. "Somethin' about how maybe some kinda fight on board made it go under in the storm." He got up and prowled through the cabin, his muscular body shifting under the light tank top he wore. "Didn't really pay attention to it."

Dar watched him stop and study a picture on the wall, then turn and look out the window. "But that was years back."

Bud nodded. "Yeap, it was." He turned and regarded her. "So, why drag it up?" he asked. "Cops just buried it back then. No one cared." He walked back over and sat down. "Charlie'd remember. He listens to all that crap."

"He around?" Dar asked casually.

"Be back 'round sunset," Bud replied. "Had to go over to the big island for something." He leaned back, seemingly relaxed. "Hey, listen. Charlie told me about what you offered. Thanks." His eyes met hers. "I know I act like a jerk sometimes. Sorry."

Dar eased into a more comfortable position. "Going to take me up on it?" she asked directly.

Bud shook his head. "We're fine." He dismissed the idea. "I worked something out." His eyes roamed over the inside of the boat again. "So now what?"

"With DeSalliers?" Dar asked.

Bud nodded. "He took off out of the harbor. Headed east."

Figures. Dar leaned her head against the back of the chair. "I dunno," she mused. "First thing's first—Kerry needs to get well." She looked over at him. "Thanks for checking her out."

Bud issued a rare smile. "She's a nice kid," he allowed. "Sweet."

Dar felt her own face relax into a return grin.

"Never figured you to get all wrapped up like that," Bud drawled. "Thought you'd end up a lonely old salt and not ever been in the Navy for it."

Dar's nostrils flared slightly. "I thought I would too," she admitted. "Life's weird sometimes."

Bud nodded, then set his cup down and stood up. "I gotta get the kitchen cranked up for Charlie," he said. "Heard some weather's brewing up east of here."

"Great." Dar sighed. "Next time, I swear I'm gonna go skiing."

Bud snorted. "Holler if Kerry's feelin any worse." He put the cup down in the galley sink. "I'll send Rufus down to let you know when Charlie gets here."

"Thanks." Dar stood and walked him to the door. They were about the same height, and his slight rolling swagger reminded her strongly of her father. She was glad Bud's attitude had softened a little. Maybe he'd just needed a little while to think things through.

They emerged onto the stern deck to a wash of late afternoon sunlight filtering through the trees. The air bore the sweet scent of gardenias, and a sense of quiet peace pervaded the scene. In somber contrast to the chaos of the previous hours, now the sleepy spell of the tropical sea surrounded them as the tide lapped gently at the docks.

Bud stepped off the boat and lifted a hand, then turned and walked back up toward the buildings without a word or backward glance.

Dar leaned against the cabin and watched him for a moment. A few more puzzle pieces seemed to have been delivered to her, and now she took them, juggling them mentally as she went back inside the cabin to collect a few more. "Now," she eyed the spare bedroom, "let's put two and two together and see if we get something other than zero." With a determined look, she headed for Bob's hiding place.

THE SUN WAS setting, slices of reddish gold light peeking through the hatches and splashing across the hardwood floor. Kerry gazed fuzzily at them, then blinked her eyes open wider and stifled a yawn. Hearing low voices nearby, she cocked her head to listen, recognizing them after a moment as Dar's and Bob's.

Her head seemed clearer, and it hurt less. Kerry stretched, grateful for that. She could still feel a little chill and there was an ache in her bones, but she found her curiosity prodding her past the discomfort and urging her to get up and go find out what was going on.

Accordingly, she eased out of bed and padded over to the dresser, removing a sweatshirt from the bottom drawer and tugging it on over her head. She paused a moment, sniffing the distinctive smell of home in its folds, then pulled it down into place. She stopped by the dresser and peeked at her reflection. "Uck." She picked up Dar's brush and ran it through her hair, settling it into some kind of order. Then she eased out the door and into the main cabin. Dar was sitting in one of the easy chairs, facing Bob. Dar's eyes lifted as Kerry entered and her face shifted into a warm smile, which Kerry returned. "Hey."

Bob turned around. "Oh. Hi."

"How're you feeling?" Dar asked.

"Eh." Kerry cleared her throat. "What's going on out here?" She went into the galley and retrieved a bottle of juice, pulling off the top as she trudged over to where Dar was seated and plopped into the chair next to her. She tucked her feet up under her and leaned on the arm, sipping her juice quietly.

"I was...um...just kind of getting into why I'm here," Bob said. "But first, I'd kinda like to apologize for getting you both mixed up in all this," he went on. "When I came out here, I thought I could get in and get out, and no one would be the wiser."

Dar reached over and scratched Kerry's back lightly. "All right, let me get this straight," she said. "Your grandfather was the captain of that fishing trawler that went down just west of here."

Bob nodded. "Right."

"He left a fortune."

"Right."

"The fortune went to his eldest son, your uncle," Dar continued.

"Right."

"Nobody else got anything."

Bob nodded. "My uncle is tighter than a ten-year-old girdle."

"I knew money had to be at the root of this," Kerry muttered in disgust, getting a startled look from Bob. "Let me guess — grandpa took a treasure chest with him, and you're trying to find a few pieces of eight to raise a family on, right?"

"Um. No." Bob exhaled. "Actually, I'm trying to prove my uncle killed my grandfather, and get him charged with murder."

Two perfectly still faces with identical expressions of startlement faced him for a long beat, then Dar and Kerry looked at each other. "O...okay," Dar said. "You have reason to think he did it?"

Bob nodded. "If I can prove it, the will's broken and the rest of the family will take over the inheritance," he said. "Oh, I won't pretend to altruism. I'm due for about a tenth of it. I don't want to spend the rest of my life behind a desk, and that'll keep me in style."

Kerry sipped on her juice to keep herself from commenting. "What the hell are you looking for?" Dar asked.

Bob gave her a wary look. "I can't say," he said. "It's very confidential."

Kerry rolled her eyes.

"It's something of my grandfather's," Bob said hastily. "We thought it had been destroyed in a fire at his house, but just recently we found out it hadn't." He ran a hand through his hair. "So, I decided to try and find it. I figured the wreck was the only place left to look."

"You weren't the only one, I guess," Kerry finally commented. "And, I guess you won't be needing those scuba lessons, huh?"

Having been caught in his earlier lie, the young man cleared his throat and looked away. "DeSalliers boasted he was the best in the business, and my uncle hired him to salvage every speck of the wreck. He's paying him a king's ransom," Bob admitted. "And his reputation is at stake."

"That's what he meant," Kerry murmured, "about being hoisted on his own reputation."

Bob stared at her. "You talked to him?"

"Long story," Dar cut him off. "Your plan sucks. He almost caught you today, and if he's got a few more days to get a salvage barge in place, you're sunk."

Bob blinked. "Um...well, yeah," he confessed. "I thought I'd have more time. He surprised me." He sighed. "I don't know. It was probably a bad idea to begin with."

Kerry scratched her jaw, her green eyes in wry agreement with him. "Even if you could find whatever this is, do you really think you can make a case against your uncle?" she asked skeptically. "People with lots of power and money don't give it up that easily."

Bob sat up. "I'm sure the police will help us, once they see the evidence," he told her. "That's their job."

Dar snorted. "Well," she got up and walked to the door, "good luck." Her eyes searched the dimming horizon, streaked with gentle orange light. "You're gonna need it."

Bob stood up and peered out the window toward the west. "I know I can do it," he said. "I just need the time to look. If I could only get that bastard DeSalliers off my back for a few days." He straightened up and turned. "Well, anyway, thanks again. I know you didn't mean to rescue me for the second time, but boy, I appreciate it."

Dar remained staring out at the sunset.

"I'm glad we were in the right place at the right time." Kerry gracefully picked up the ball. "Where are you going now? You can't try the wreck again. He'll get you next time."

Bob sighed. "Yeah," he said. "I don't know. Maybe I can check out the drift shops on the islands. Maybe what I'm looking for has already been picked up, and it's there."

"Hm." Kerry made a noncommittal sound.

"Hey, maybe I'll ask those buddies of yours. They're pretty savvy," Bob suddenly added. "Bet they've been around...a while, haven't they?"

Kerry frowned. "Well, I guess. I just met them. They're old friends of Dar's, really. Probably they know where to start looking, though."

"Yeah," Bob answered briefly.

"Don't you think DeSalliers has thought of that?" Dar asked from the doorway. "I bet his little gumshoes are looking right now."

Bob smiled. "He would, if he knew what he was looking for." He eased past Dar, then turned with a faint, half-crooked smile. "But he doesn't." He picked up his gear and stepped off the boat onto the dock. "Thanks again," he said to Dar. "Hope Kerry feels better soon."

He turned and started walking up the dock, slinging his gear over one shoulder as he carried his tanks in the other.

Dar turned and went back inside the cabin. She found Kerry waiting, one leg slung over the arm of her chair as she finished her juice. "He'll never find it," she said. "Whatever *it* is."

Kerry wiggled her toes. "Probably not," she agreed. "You think there's anything to his story?"

Dar sat down on the couch and extended a hand out to her. "C'mere." She wrapped her arms around Kerry when she complied, pulling her down into her lap and leaning back on the couch. "I don't know," she answered. "Right now, I don't really care."

Kerry put her arms around Dar's neck and nuzzled her cheek. "What a mess." She found Dar's ear invitingly close by, and despite the fact that she still felt like heck, she gently suckled the tasty looking earlobe. Dar's arms tightened around her and she laughed softly.

"Mmm," Dar hummed. "Feeling better?"

Kerry gave her a kiss on the cheek. "How could I not feel better?" Her lashes brushed Dar's skin, tickling it and making the dark-haired woman smile. "How about you?" she whispered into Dar's ear. "You sounded kinda torked before."

Dar hesitated, then sighed. "Yeah, I'm okay," she said. "Just too much going on at once, I guess," she admitted.

Kerry nuzzled her cheek again. "I think we're due a vacation from our vacation, Dixiecup."

"Mm." Dar thought about the trials of the day, then decided dismissing them and simply immersing herself in Kerry's presence was a much better idea. There was really no point in dwelling on it all anyway. It was over, and in the past. Things had worked out all right. Kerry was okay. She was okay. They knew what was going on. Now they could take off and leave it all behind. They were out of it. Kerry suckled on her earlobe again, blowing gently into her ear. Dar closed her eyes and smiled. *Yeah. Everything is all right.*

Chapter
Sixteen

DAR WOKE TO the soft clang of the buoy sea bell at the edge of the harbor. She blinked the sleep out of her eyes and looked around in slight confusion, taking a moment to recognize the dim interior of the boat around her. She and Kerry were lying together on the small couch, limbs entangled. Dar had no idea what time it was or how long they'd been sleeping, and she found herself quite willing to let her eyes close and drift back into peaceful oblivion.

Not that she could have gotten up even if she'd wanted to. Dar observed the slow, rhythmic rise and fall of Kerry's chest up close and personal, since she was pinned under her lover's sturdy form. Luckily for her, it wasn't nearly as uncomfortable as one might expect, and after she stretched her body out a little, she settled back down and amiably resigned herself to pillow duty. However, after a few quiet minutes, Kerry stirred and made a tiny grumbling sound.

Dar scratched the back of her neck gently. "Shh...go back to sleep."

Kerry opened one eye and peeked at her. "Thirsty," she muttered with a hoarse edge to her voice. "Damn pills."

"I'd get up and get you some water, but, um..." Dar reviewed their tangled bodies.

"But I'm squashing you." Kerry got her hands on the couch and pushed herself upward, awkwardly getting to her feet. "Ooof." She wavered a minute, then sat down again, putting her hand to her head. "Whoa."

Dar immediately sat up. "Hey."

"Just a little dizzy," Kerry muttered. "I got up too fast," she added. "I think."

"And you also haven't eaten anything since that soup and crackers at lunch," Dar realized.

"Neither have you." Kerry got to her feet a little more cautiously, then she held a hand out to Dar. "C'mon. Let's go raid the fridge together." She looked around. "What time is it?"

Dar picked up her cell phone as she stood to join her partner. "Eleven thirty." Her eyes lifted to the cabin door. "Huh. Bud was supposed to send Charlie down when he got home. Guess he got caught up." She tossed the cell to the table, then reached up to put her hand across Kerry's forehead. "Ah."

"No chills," Kerry acknowledged. "Now I just feel like a dishrag."

"Maybe we should call you terrycloth, then, instead of Kerry," Dar teased, relieved at feeling no fever in her partner. "C'mon."

They walked together to the galley. Kerry slipped inside first and retrieved a water bottle from the fridge, popping it open and sucking several mouthfuls from it. She turned to find Dar rummaging the shelves, and put a hand on her partner's shoulder. "Nothing exotic, honey. Just some yogurt, if it's there."

Dar retrieved a container and handed it up. "How about some toast to go with that."

Kerry cleared her throat experimentally, feeling an ominous scratchiness. "I think my bug is migrating," she informed Dar mournfully. "Ice cream would work better."

"Ah." Dar stood and gave her a sympathetic look. "How about some soup?"

"Mmph." Kerry had popped the top on the yogurt and spooned up a mouthful. It was plain and cool, and it made her throat feel better. "Only if you're having some too,"she replied, bumping Dar lightly with her hip.

Dar felt her stomach growl at the thought. "Deal," she agreed, searching in the cupboards for the appropriate cans.

Kerry took her water and yogurt and retreated to the table, sliding behind it and sitting cross-legged on the bench seat. She nudged the indirect light on and sat there quietly munching. "If we both get sick, this is going to so suck, Dar."

"Eh." Dar shrugged, busy emptying things into one of the pots. "In that case, I vote we just find an empty beach, stake it out, and let the sun take care of it."

Kerry sighed.

"Relax. At worst, we spend a couple days in bed together." Dar chuckled softly. "Is that so bad?" Taking a small oil candle from the cabinet, she lit it and walked over to set it down in front of Kerry. It made a friendly, warm flicker between the two of them, and Dar watched it a moment before she went back to her task.

"If you put it like that, no." Kerry played with her yogurt, making small mounds of it with her spoon as she consumed it. Out of the corner of her eye, she watched Dar in the galley, her profile quiet and somewhat somber as she heated up the soup. Absently, she lifted a hand and pushed a bit of hair behind one ear, then fiddled with it, a sure sign Dar was preoccupied with something. "This has sure been a day, huh?" Kerry asked.

Dar glanced over with a half smile. "Yeah."

"Those pirates had me a little spooked," Kerry said. "Glad you knew how to handle them." Her ears detected a hitch in Dar's breathing and a soft clank as her spoon whapped against the side of the pot. "I know they didn't hurt those other people, but getting tossed off the boat the way I was feeling...wow."

Dar eased past the galley entrance and came over with two bowls of something steaming in her hands. She set one down in front of Kerry, then took the seat next to her.

"Mm." Kerry sniffed. "Chicken noodle."

Dar dabbled her spoon in her soup, propping her head up on her fist. "I wasn't gonna let them take the boat," she said. "But what was more important to me was protecting you."

Kerry took a spoonful of the hot soup and swallowed it, feeling a blessed sense of relief as it soothed her cranky throat. "You did." She ate a small bit of carrot. "Protect me, that is."

"Mmhm." Dar nodded. "And anyway, you know how much I hate having anyone tell me what to do. I wasn't going to let those scrungy bastards do it."

"Aaabsolutely not." Kerry smiled. "Not my Dar."

That got a smile from Dar, and she stopped twiddling her spoon.

"So...why is that bothering you?" Kerry asked softly.

Dar looked up at her. "Did I say it was?" she asked in a deceptively mild tone. Kerry just looked her in the eye without saying anything. After a moment, Dar's lips tensed into a wry half grin, and she ate a spoonful of soup to give herself time to think about her answer.

It wasn't something she wanted to talk about, but if she couldn't talk to Kerry about it, then who? There was no one on Earth closer to her than her partner, not even her father. Andrew, though, might well understand what she'd felt; Kerry surely wouldn't.

Kerry simply waited, and ate her soup. Dar would either tell her, or she wouldn't—further probing didn't seem like a good idea.

Dar started to speak, then stopped, a mildly bemused expression on her face. She shook her head. "It's actually pretty stupid."

A blonde eyebrow lifted. Stupid wasn't a description Dar usually applied to herself. "Hm?" Kerry made a small encouraging noise.

"When that guy on the boat pointed that gun at me, I almost shot him."

Kerry waited, but when nothing else seemed to be forthcoming, she leaned on her elbows. "Okay," she accepted. "And?"

Dar was sucking on her spoon. "For a minute there, I wanted to." Her eyes fixed on something past Kerry's head with a pained, almost lost expression. "I wanted to kill that guy."

"He was pointing a gun at you, sweetie," Kerry answered matter-of-factly. "For that matter, I wanted to kill him too. It's a good thing for him *you* were holding the shotgun." She gazed at her lover. "Because if I saw anyone threaten you with a gun like that, I would kill them."

That wasn't quite the response Dar had been expecting. She regarded her adorable soulmate with bemused eyes, watching her slurp her soup. "So, you don't think that was a strange reaction, I take it?"

"To someone pointing a lethal weapon at you? No!" Kerry snorted. "Do you?"

Dar reconsidered. "It just surprised me, I guess," she admitted, remembering that moment of dark joy, and the fire that had seemed to fill her from within. Maybe it was normal, or at least the alternative to dissolving into a puddle of fear. With Kerry's obvious acceptance of the subject, the tension inside her eased and she attacked her soup with greater gusto.

Kerry grinned to herself and picked up her bowl, drinking from the side of it. "Now this, on the other hand," she commented, after swallowing a mouthful, "is guaranteed to send you straight to hell, if you believe my family." She drained the bowl, then licked her lips. "Heh."

Dar chuckled, a great deal more easily this time.

Kerry offered her a carrot. Dar's eyes narrowed and she bared her teeth. They both laughed as Kerry relented and ate the vegetable herself. "You know, I like this."

"Carrots? I know," Dar replied, slurping a noodle.

"No, this." Kerry indicated the flickering oil lamp. "It's romantic. Almost like being around a campfire."

Dar eyed the tiny flame, then looked at Kerry. One eyebrow lifted.

"Okay, so it's a campfire for gerbils," Kerry admitted. "I still like it."

Her eyes went to the clock on the wall, then she remembered something. "Be right back." Kerry slid out from behind the table and disappeared into the bedroom. After a minute, she returned, her hands behind her back, and walked over to where Dar was seated and rested her chin on Dar's shoulder. "Hi."

Dar turned her head so they were nose to nose. "Hi," she replied.

Kerry removed her hands from behind her back and set a small box down in front of Dar. "Happy birthday, my love." She leaned in and gave the shocked Dar a kiss on the lips. "You forgot, didn't you?"

Dar stared at the box. She had completely forgotten that it was her birthday the next day. She and Kerry had agreed to exchange Christmas presents when they got home, so she'd figured... "Yeah, I did," she answered softly. "Kerry, you didn't have to—"

"Ah ah ah ah ah." Kerry put her fingers over Dar's mouth. "Just open it. Humor me; I'm a sick woman." She slid back into her seat and watched as Dar examined the box, turning it over in her hands before she started to unravel the thin, lacy ribbon around it.

Dar's face was a study in concentration as she carefully untied the knots and laid the ribbon open on either side of the box. Then she held the bottom steady with one hand and lifted the top with the other, setting it down before she removed the light layer of cotton batting just under it.

Kerry waited. She saw the motion as Dar's jaw muscles relaxed and the sudden reflection of the dim light on her widened eyes. "You're tough to shop for." She spoke quietly, more to give Dar a chance to collect herself than anything else. "And you're one of the most conservative non-traditionalists I know. So, I thought you'd like something like this."

Dar carefully lifted the gift out of the box and cradled it in her hand. She released a long held breath and looked up at Kerry. "It's gorgeous."

Kerry smiled.

Dar looked back down at her gift. Resting in her palm was a pocket watch, its cover etched in fine gold and silver filigree over a darker base. From the top, a twisted link, silver chain trickled through her fingers. She gently opened the facing to reveal a face with large, crisp numbers and a briskly sweeping second hand. There was engraving on the inside of the cover. Dar tilted her head to read it. *Because you make every moment of my life worth living.* She stared at the words until they blurred and she had to close her eyes to blink the tears from them. Without a sound she put the watch back into its box and reached for Kerry, who readily squirmed into her arms for a hug.

Kerry felt the shudder as Dar inhaled, and the soft gasp as she buried her face against Kerry's shoulder. She held the moment carefully in her heart, understanding deep down that she could have written the words on a napkin and it wouldn't have made a difference. "I love you," she whispered in Dar's ear, hugging her tightly.

Dar drew in a breath, held it a moment, and then exhaled, sniffling a little before she spoke. "Sorry. Didn't mean to get you all wet."

"Honey, you always get me all wet," Kerry teased gently, rubbing Dar's shoulders with both hands. She felt her lover's body shake again, but this time it was with laughter. She rocked Dar back and forth, just loving her.

So what if she had a bug? So what if their vacation had turned into a bad television movie? She had Dar, and they had each other, and there was nothing else anywhere that could top that. Nothing.

The soft sound of the waves trickled through the windows on a breeze that ruffled the oil lamp and threw a single dancing shadow against the wall.

Chapter Seventeen

DAR WHISTLED SOFTLY as she worked on the stern deck, tidying up the boat from their ordeal the day before. It was about an hour past dawn. The sunlight poured over her swimsuit-clad body, warming her shoulder blades and allowing her to appreciate the brisk breeze.

Kerry was tucked in bed with a cup of hot tea for her still-sore throat. Despite that, the blonde woman had seemed much more chipper when they'd woken up, and Dar suspected Kerry would not stay in bed that long. But that was okay.

With a grin, Dar finished her task and re-entered the cabin. The scent of fresh coffee greeted her and sure enough, behind the galley counter she found one of Santa's own little elves making it. "Ah hah."

Kerry looked up, producing a sunny smile for her partner. "Merry Christmas and happy birthday, honey."

Dar prowled into the galley behind her. "Thought you were resting."

"I was," Kerry replied. "Now I'm cooking. It's a serial processing kind of thing." She tapped Dar's chest with a mixing spoon. "I feel a lot better. Now go over there and let me finish my pancakes."

"Pancakes?" Dar's voice rose in surprise. "Mmm." She inclined her head and kissed Kerry on the lips.

"It's a tradition." Kerry put a hand up and touched Dar's cheek. "Now scoot."

Instead of obeying, Dar slipped her arms around Kerry's body and caught her up in a powerful hug, lifting her up off her feet.

"Urgh." Kerry reveled in it, enjoying the unexpected side effect of feeling her spine relax and realign itself. "Ooh... Thank you." She felt Dar's hands rub her back briskly as she was set down again. When she leaned back and looked up, she was glad to see Dar's face completely open and happy—lacking the worried tension of the previous day. She patted Dar's belly through the thin swimsuit fabric and gave her another hug, then gently nudged her out of the galley so she could finish making breakfast.

Dar reluctantly retreated to the couch and dropped onto it, stretching out on her side and crossing her ankles. "So, are we in agreement about ditching DeSalliers and company?"

Kerry pushed a bit of hair out of her eyes. "You mean, just take off and let them all sort out their own problems?"

"Mmhm."

"Yeah." The blonde woman nodded. "I mean, there's really nothing we can do, is there?"

Dar examined a faint scar on her upper thigh. "Not really," she said. "Sometimes it pays to know when to just close the books and walk." She gave Kerry a rakish grin. "Besides, that family feud sounds ugly."

Kerry had occasion to know more about that than most people. She merely grunted in agreement as she poured pancake batter onto the small griddle, getting the temperature just right for the creamy substance to immediately start bubbling at its edges. She reached over to a dish and removed a handful of chocolate chips, sprinkling them evenly into the batter.

She could only imagine her mother's reaction to her choice of breakfasts. For more years than she could count, breakfast at home had been dry toast, perhaps an egg white, and a bowl of healthy cereal with skim milk. Of course, that had only spurred her to find a way to grab a candy bar before first period at school and resulted in her developing an intense dislike of Grape Nuts.

Living with Dar was definitely different. If she felt like having a milkshake for breakfast, the only comment she'd get from her partner was likely to be "Where's mine?" Dar had a very secure and relaxed attitude toward her own body and that extended to Kerry's as well, easing Kerry's initial shyness considerably.

To be fair, most of the time she and Dar ate relatively healthily, and somewhat to her surprise, the last time Dr. Steve had checked her cholesterol, it had actually gone down forty points. She suspected all the extra time in the gym was responsible for that, but she wasn't about to argue with the results. Not when she was finally getting to indulge herself and not have to worry about comments around the dining room table.

Ah well. She turned her attention back to her task. Pancakes took practice. Kerry maneuvered the paper-thin flipper under the cakes and expertly turned them, exposing nicely golden bottom sides. The scent of the cooking batter as well as the melting chocolate filled the air, and she felt her mouth start to water.

Well, at least my appetite's back. That's a good sign. Kerry reached over and turned a few slices of bacon that were sizzling nearby. Her throat was still bothering her a little and she still felt "off" — her body ached and her head felt slightly stuffed. But she had no fever and she was hungry enough to eat a raw fish, so she figured she was probably getting better.

Besides, it was Dar's birthday. Kerry found herself smiling as she remembered her gift-giving the night before. She glanced over at the couch, charmed to see Dar studying her new watch, a grin tugging at the corners of her mouth as she turned it over in her fingers. She turned back to the griddle and got a plate ready, deftly transferring four of the hotcakes and several slices of bacon to it. She set it to one side and put the rest of the food on a second plate, then turned off the heat and set two covers on the plates. "Dixiecup, can you come over here and give me a hand?"

Dar chuckled as she set aside her watch and strolled over. "You know, if anyone had told me before I met you that I'd ever put up with someone calling me that, much less liking it, I'd have clocked them."

Kerry gave her a charming smile and handed her the plates. "Let me get the biscuits and the coffee."

"And the syrup," Dar reminded, setting the plates on the table and returning to duck past Kerry and retrieve a jug of juice from the refrigerator. They sat down together and Dar lifted the cover off her plate, inhaling the scent of the chocolate chip pancakes. "Mm."

Kerry drizzled a little syrup neatly over her stack and separated a forkful. "You know, if anyone had told me before I met you that I'd be scarfing down pancakes and bacon without any guilt, much less enjoying them, I'd have just laughed," she said. "So, I think we're neck and neck for making positive changes in each other's lives." She winked at Dar.

Dar slid closer, and they traded forkfuls of breakfast. Kerry licked a bit of syrup that had somehow ended up on the tip of Dar's nose, and they toasted each other with coffee.

"Okay, so if we're not crusading, and me sticking my head underwater isn't a really good idea, what did you have in mind for today?" Kerry asked after a few minutes of peaceful munching. "Shopping?"

A nice quiet stroll through some of the eclectic shops of St. Thomas? Dar suddenly found that appealing, if for no other reason than that it provided an activity they could do that wouldn't compromise Kerry's health. "All right," she agreed. "When we're done with breakfast, I'll run up and tell Bud and Charlie so long, and we'll head out."

"Ooh...you're letting me take you shopping on your birthday. You're in so much trouble, Paladar," Kerry chortled, crunching a piece of bacon between her teeth. "I'm going to spoil you to within an inch of your life."

"Uh oh." Dar covered her eyes. "What have I gotten myself into?"

"Heh."

DAR STROLLED UP the beach toward Bud and Charlie's place, feeling mellow and a little lazy after her favorite treat, despite the threat of shopping hanging over her head. The island was very quiet — only a few seagulls noted her presence as she climbed up the slope to the restaurant. She stepped up onto the porch and peered inside the screened door.

Inside, the restaurant was silent and still — chairs were upended on tables, and the floor mats piled near the door. It was still very early, though, so Dar didn't consider that unusual. She pulled the iron handle experimentally, a little surprised when the door readily opened towards her. "Hello?"

Her voice echoed in the empty room, but there was no answer to her call. With a slight shrug, Dar entered and crossed the wooden floor, pushing the kitchen hatch open and peeking inside.

The place was also empty — pots hanging spotless and empty on ceiling hooks, and stoves standing cold and barren. Dar crossed through the somewhat cramped space and through the doors in the back, finding herself in a small corridor with closed rooms to either side. She knew Bud and Charlie lived in the back of the restaurant, and now, suddenly, it occurred to her that maybe they'd closed the restaurant for the holiday and were sleeping in.

"Whoops." She ducked back inside the kitchen, looking around until she found an ordering pad with a pencil tied to it. She picked it up and bent her head over it, writing for a few minutes before she studied the results, then tore the top page off the pad. Leaving the pad where she'd found it, Dar went to the inside door and stuck the note on it, facing in toward the inner rooms. Anyone coming into the kitchen would see it, and she felt reasonably sure either Bud or Charlie would do just that sometime that morning.

She regarded the note with a touch of bemusement, remembering certain rainy days when she and Kerry had played hooky from work. *Okay, maybe sometime this afternoon.* With a smile, she turned and walked back through the restaurant and out the back door.

Chapter
Eighteen

KERRY REGARDED THE charming streets of Charlotte Amalie with a grin, enjoying the colors and the displays of local handicrafts. She wore a pair of dark, mid-length shorts with more pockets than was really safe, and a crisp white shirt tucked into them, and she felt properly touristy and ready to shop.

Dar ambled along next to her, sporting snug-fitting, black bicycle shorts and a bright red muscle T-shirt. With her sunglasses, and her dark hair tied back in a tail, she looked like a walking advertisement for a bad attitude.

Kerry loved it. She kept catching people looking at Dar, who strode through the crowd with an air of cool disregard. She had on a light backpack, which contained the laptop and their cell phones, since the marina wasn't what Dar considered very secure, and the straps pulled the fabric of the shirt taut against her muscular body.

Very butch. Kerry's grin wrinkled her nose, and she suppressed a chuckle.

"What's so funny?" Dar inquired, peering at her from over the tops of her wraparound sunglasses.

"Nothing," Kerry assured her. "This place is so cute." She indicated the market. "Want to see if we can pick up some of those straw baskets? I think your mom would like them for her painting stuff."

Dar regarded the stacked wares. "Lead on," she replied. "Hey, maybe I can pick up a pair of pearl earrings while we're here."

Okay. Kerry linked arms with her. *Not so butch.* "How about some of those nice miniature seashell ones? They'd look pretty on you."

"Think so?"

"Absolutely."

AFTER A TOUGH afternoon's shopping, they ended up in a little outdoor café on the street overlooking the harbor. Dar's backpack had gotten heavier by several packets, and Kerry had a woven hemp bag resting at her feet. "This is nice," Dar commented, sipping from a cup of fragrant cappuccino. The breeze was coming inshore, and she stretched out her long legs and enjoyed it.

Kerry had both hands clasped around a cup of hot tea. "It sure is," she agreed. "Hey, you want to spend the night up there at that Blackbeard's Castle? It looked really cute."

Dar tipped her head back and looked up at the hill above them. "Yeah." She smiled. "That did look like a fun place. Sure." She turned back to look at Kerry, spotting the imperfectly masked sigh. "Running out of steam?"

Darn. Kerry cleared her throat. "My bug is still bugging me, I guess," she admitted.

"To the inn with you, then." Dar put some money down on the table and extended her hand. "Let's grab a cab and get us a room up on that there hill." She caught a motion out of the corner of her eye, but as she turned to look, several men brushed by and distracted her, and by the time she refocused on the spot, there was nothing there.

Probably just the waiter, Dar considered, shouldering her pack and pushing in her chair. She pulled out her cell and checked it. Seeing no activity, her brow creased. "Don't tell me they're still in bed."

"Huh?" Kerry cocked her head.

"I asked Bud to give me a shout when he got up. I need to ask him something," Dar explained. "He hasn't called."

"I thought they didn't have a phone," Kerry commented as they walked along the street toward the crossroad. "That's what they told Bob."

"That's what he told Bob," Dar repeated wryly. "They've got a cell. They just don't like using it. They pay by the minute." She shook her head, then looked up a number in her cell's memory and dialed it. It rang several times, and then politely informed her that the cellular customer she was trying to reach was unavailable. Dar closed the phone. "Probably has it turned off."

"What did you want to ask him?" Kerry inquired, as they stopped and she lifted a hand to hail a cab. Incredibly, the car slowed and pulled over, its driver sticking his head out and regarding them with a very cheerful expression. "Hi," Kerry greeted him. "We'd like to go up to the castle."

"Anywhere you lovely ladies want to go, I take you," the man replied immediately. "Come, come."

"Thanks." Kerry eased the back door open. "I think," she added, under her breath.

Dar merely pushed her sunglasses up a little and followed. As she closed the door behind her, she caught something in the corner of her eye again, and this time turned quickly to see what it was.

Nothing. The street corner behind her was empty. Dar frowned and faced forward, crossing her arms over the pack she'd taken off her back and wondering if the rum smoothie she'd drunk at the last shopping stop was making her see things. Or imagine them.

"OH, THIS IS adorable." Kerry looked around their small room approvingly. "I'm glad they didn't have room in the big resort, Dar—this is much, much more quaint." They were staying in the small inn that circled the tavern, with a view that overlooked the harbor. Kerry walked over to the plush, four-poster bed and sat down on it, bouncing a little, then falling back and spreading out her arms. "Whoof."

Dar set her pack down and put her hands on her hips as she inspected their assigned quarters. "Nice," she agreed, with a smile. "Tell you what. You hang out here and relax, and I'll run down to the boat and pick up a change of clothes for the both of us," she said. "Order up some hot tea and enjoy the view."

Kerry considered arguing, then her better sense took hold and she waggled her fingers at Dar in peaceful acquiescence. "You rock."

With a pleased smile, Dar waved back, and then she turned and slipped out the door and closed it behind her.

"Ahh." Kerry exhaled, glad to be lying still. As the day had progressed, her body had protested more strenuously, though she'd enjoyed their shopping trip. Now she had a quiet night in this cute, snug little room to look forward to. It had a small balcony with a table, and she suspected a light dinner, a bottle of wine, and the two of them were just the right size to fit there.

A nice end to Dar's birthday, she decided. A smile crossed her face as she thought about her partner, and how much she'd enjoyed their day rambling around together. Maybe if she felt better tomorrow, she'd fulfill her half of their bargain, and they'd go horseback riding up in the hills. She'd seen advertisements for a nice looking stable at the hotel's check in desk.

Yeah. A nice ride, maybe a picnic together. Maybe we'll find a nice quiet spot and I'll write a poem about it. Kerry imagined a patch of green, fragrant forest, with birds singing around her. She could almost smell the rich scent of the earth. *Yeah.*

With a yawn, she rolled over and crawled to the edge of the bed, retrieving the leather-covered room service menu and opening it. "Ah." She spotted the tea section, pleased at having more than one choice. "Mango. Let's try that." She picked up the room phone and dialed.

DAR DECIDED TO forgo a cab, preferring to jog down to the boat instead. The crowds were thinning out as sunset approached, and the cafés she passed were starting to gear up for dinner. The air held hints of an eclectic mix of foods — hickory smoke mixed with a dash of tomato and garlic, crossed with a jolt of jerk spices. Dar took an appreciative breath of it, and acknowledged she was damn glad they'd decided to cut out and leave Bob and his family problems behind.

DeSalliers had annoyed her, true, Dar admitted privately. It wouldn't have bothered her to knock him off his pedestal. But the man had been hired to do a job, and while she didn't particularly like his style or his attitude, his methods were efficient and very business oriented. *And, Dar, admit it — that's how almost everyone describes you, isn't it?* She chuckled a little in wry self-knowledge.

Bob's story had seemed a little too pat to her, she decided, as her path took her down a fairly steep incline toward the dock. Did she really buy that convenient emergence of a clue after all this time? It seemed a lot more likely to her that Bob had run out of cash, and had gotten together with all the other family wannahaves and cooked up a plot to cause trouble. He was probably banking on a settlement of some kind, if he could stir up enough chaos.

Of course, Dar dodged a man on a moped, *it could also be that I don't like Bob because he tried to hit on Kerry.* She wondered briefly if he had simply seen a cute girl he was interested in, or if he was interested in Kerry because of her obvious financial resources.

She turned a corner and jogged between two buildings. As she passed a garbage dumpster, a flash of motion made her turn her head, but before she could react, a body hit hers and drove her into the wall. "Hey!"

Hands grabbed her and threw her against the wall again, and then a heavy weight pinned her and she got a blast of not very nice breath in her face. "All right, you bitch. Don't move."

Dar blinked, and a heavy, pockmarked face swam into focus. Her attacker had his forearm pressed against her throat and his weight holding her against the wall. Her senses, shocked at first, recovered, and she felt her wits settle back into place. "Who the hell are you?" she asked.

"Shut up." The man shoved against her throat, cutting off her air. "I ask, you answer."

A wash of red swam unexpectedly over her vision, and Dar felt her temper snap before she could get a handle on it. A low snarl erupted from her throat and her body convulsed, shoving against the wall and arching with all her strength. She got her hands up against the man's chest and pushed hard, getting him off her long enough for her to take a bouncing step forward.

He cursed and grappled with her, grabbing her throat with

both hands, but made the mistake of letting Dar lean forward at the same time as he was spreading his legs for balance. Dar immediately brought her knee up with explosive force, slamming her kneecap into the pit of his groin.

He choked and released her, reaching down in pure reflex to protect himself. Dar took the opportunity to duck past him and whirl, then turn sideways and kick out, catching him in the buttocks and sending him hurtling into the wall head first. She whirled as she sensed someone else coming, and her hands came up into fists at shoulder level as she spotted another man close by.

He held up his hands, but they were palm out. "Whoa, tiger."

Dar glared at him. "Don't you know when the fuck to leave people alone?" she asked. "What the hell does it take, DeSalliers? A damn court order?"

"Well, damn it, Roberts. You keep showing up in my business; what the hell am I supposed to do?" DeSalliers answered. "If you'd mind your own, and get the hell out of my way, I'd be glad to never set eyes on you again!"

Dar put her hands on her hips. "You're nuts," she stated flatly. "You wanted your spot on the ocean? Fine. We left. We came over here, and haven't thought about you all the damn day long. So what are you talking about?"

DeSalliers eyed her suspiciously. "You're searching the shops for what I'm after."

Dar rolled her eyes. "We were searching the shops for pearl earrings. You into that? I never woulda guessed." She backed a step to keep her attacker in her sight, since he was now getting to his feet.

"You're lying."

"You're a jerk. I guess we're even," Dar shot back. "Now get the hell out of my way before I call the cops." She pointed at him. "We don't want any part of whatever the hell you're after."

"How much did he offer you?" DeSalliers countered, as though he hadn't heard a word she'd said. "I'll double it."

Dar glared at him. "You're really pissing me off," she warned.

"Triple it. What will it take?"

It got to the point where it became, oddly, funny. "Okay." Dar held up her hands. "I give."

DeSalliers folded his arms. "I knew I could find your price."

"English isn't working," Dar went on. "What language would you like me to tell you to fuck off in next, one you'll understand?"she asked. "Sprechen Sie Deutsch? Habla Español? Parlez-vous Français?" She held up her left hand, middle finger extended. "American Sign Language? What?"

With a sudden motion, she closed on him and grabbed his shirt, twisting her hands in it before he could jerk away. She lifted up and pushed him against the garbage dumpster, surprising him with her strength. "I DO NOT WANT ANYTHING TO DO WITH YOU OR YOUR BUSINESS!" she bellowed at the top of her lungs. "DO YOU UNDERSTAND ME, MISTER??"

His eyes were as big as saucers, Carvel flying saucers, in fact. "Roberts, I don't think you want to do this."

"All I want to do," Dar's voice dropped to a low rumble, "is go get some clothes, go back to my hotel, and spend the night necking in the moonlight with my partner." She got nose to nose with him. "And you, mister, are all that's between me and what I want." She shook him. "*You*...are the one who doesn't want to do this. Trust me."

"Boss, you want me to shoot her?" The thug behind her spoke in a voice that was a touch hoarse.

"Put that away, you idiot," DeSalliers snapped nervously. "She can probably catch the bullet."

Dar snorted. She released the man's shirt and let him up off the dumpster. She looked over her shoulder at the thug, who was uncertainly juggling a small handgun. With a shake of her head, she returned her eyes to DeSalliers. "What will it take to convince you I don't want any part of this?" she asked in a normal tone. "We got involved by accident; I got uninvolved on purpose."

He studied her. "All right," he said. "Explain why you had your people jump my men out on St. Richard last night, and maybe I'll believe you."

"My people?" Dar stared at him.

"Pity we had to hurt them." DeSalliers gave her a thin smile. "They didn't get what they were after. Maybe you," his long finger poked Dar in the chest, "should take a lesson from that." Now his tone turned dark. "You listen to me, Roberts. Keep out of my way. If you get in it again, I'll take you out. Permanently." With that, he turned and stalked off, his thug trotting behind him.

Dar stared after him. "My people?" she whispered. "What in the he..." Her mind went back to an empty restaurant and a quiet, still home that morning. She pulled out her cell phone and recalled Bud and Charlie's number from memory, then dialed it. It rang three times, then went to voice mail. Dar waited for the beep, then spoke. "Hey. It's Dar. Give me a ring when you get this. I need to talk to you guys." She hesitated, then hung up, closing the phone and tapping it against her chest. "This is getting to be like a bad episode of Twilight Zone," she muttered. After a moment of indecision, she headed toward the boat. She'd pick up their clothes, then go back to the hotel and let Kerry in on what had happened.

And then? *Christ.* Dar shook her head in honest bewilderment. *Who the hell knows what then?*

KERRY DIDN'T REALLY remember falling asleep. One moment, she was looking at the little area guidebook she'd found in the inn room, the next moment she felt a warm hand on her shoulder. She rolled over and blinked up at Dar. "Oh, Jesus. Did I conk out?"

Dar sat down on the bed next to her. "Apparently." She smoothed Kerry's hair back and felt her forehead. It was cool. "Might have been better if I'd stayed here and joined you."

"Uh oh." Kerry gazed up at her, seeing the turmoil in Dar's expression. "Now what?

"DeSalliers."

"Again? What the hell is it with that guy?"

Dar collapsed next to Kerry and spread her arms out across the covers. "He's a self-absorbed, megalomaniacal moron."

"Well, yeah, but besides that."

"He and one of his goons chased me down on the way to the boat. He still thinks we're part of this stupid game he's playing."

"Chased you down?" Kerry sat right up, wide-awake, her eyes going big and round.

"Easy, slugger," Dar drawled, faintly amused at the always surprising ferociousness Kerry displayed on her behalf. "Yeah, we yelled at each other, and he left." She sighed. "Problem is, he also hinted that he'd run into friends of ours, and they'd gotten hurt." She lifted her phone. "I left a message for Bud, but there's been no answer."

"Yikes." Kerry became concerned. "Dar, this isn't funny. I think it's time we called in the cops."

Dar nodded. "Me, too," she said. "I stopped by the police station on the way up here."

"And?" Kerry settled back down next to her.

"It's Christmas Day." Dar gave her a wry look. "There was only one man in the place, and he was cleaning it. I think the rest of them are out on patrol." She paused. "At least, I hope so."

"Crap." Kerry frowned. "Is there anyone else we can call?"

"All the US offices are closed." Dar drummed her fingers on the covers. "I don't know if there is anything we can do before tomorrow. I wish Bud would call me, though. "

"Stupid jerk."

Dar's eyebrows lifted. "He's not that bad."

"I meant DeSalliers." Kerry scowled. "Should we go back to Bud and Charlie's island? What about Rufus?" She eased over onto her side. "Dar, this sucks."

"I know." Dar gazed at the ceiling, considering. "We could go back there, but what if they didn't? It's a big ocean, and there's dozens of islands around here."

Kerry sighed. "No, it sucks because, damn it, I wanted to

celebrate your birthday with you tonight," she complained, plucking at the fabric underneath her. "God, that sounds so selfish, doesn't it?" A faint laugh was forced out of her.

Dar reached over and scrubbed Kerry's back with her fingertips. "Nah."

"Urmph." Kerry arched her neck. "Yes, it does," she grumbled.

"Well," Dar snuggled closer and nuzzled the side of Kerry's face, "it's on my behalf, so you're excused."

Kerry slid her arms around Dar's body and drew her closer, detecting a hint of wood smoke on her clothes. She tucked her head into Dar's shoulder and exhaled, simply wanting the comfort of her lover's presence.

Dar was more than glad to oblige. She gently rubbed Kerry's lower back while she gazed at the ceiling, trying to figure out what to do next. It was almost dark outside, and with only the dim bed light on, the room settled into a peaceful twilight.

So quiet, that Dar's cell phone going off nearly caused both of them to jump right off the bed. "Shit." Dar scrabbled for the ringing cell. She flipped it open and held it to her ear. "Yes?"

Kerry put her head back down on Dar's shoulder, willing her heart to stop trying to climb out her ears. She'd been half asleep, in that hazy place just before you went completely out, and her body was feeling a sense of shock at being jerked so rudely out of it.

"Yes." Dar's voice was serious. "All right. We'll be right over." She folded up the phone and set it on the bed, letting out a long breath.

"What is it?" Kerry asked.

"Charlie," Dar murmured after a moment. "He's in the hospital, here, on St. Thomas." She turned her head and looked at Kerry. "It's not pretty."

Kerry could easily have lived her entire life without seeing another hospital. She gave Dar's side a pat and hitched herself up on an elbow. "Let's get going, then," she said. "Like it or not, we're buying into this, aren't we?"

Dar sat up. "Looks like it. Yeah." She got up off the bed and clipped the phone to her waistband. "You can stay here if you want, Ker. If you're not feeling well, no sense in both of... Ah."

Kerry had gotten up and was running her brush through her hair. "Sweetie, if I can't spend the night with you in that bed, then I'll take what I can get." She tossed the brush to Dar. "Besides, I like Charlie. I hope he's okay."

Dar brushed her hair, hoping the very same thing.

Chapter
Nineteen

THE HOSPITAL WAS busy. It was a relatively small group of buildings not far from the town they'd been staying in. Dar led the way inside and they went to the front desk. Giving Charlie's name, they were directed upstairs.

Exiting onto the third floor, Dar spotted Bud near the end of the hall. She called out in a low voice and he turned, closing his cell phone and walking toward them.

Kerry drew in a breath. Bud's face was half-covered with an ugly bruise, though he appeared oblivious to it. His shirt was ripped, exposing his shoulder, and the back of one hand was scraped raw.

"What happened?" Dar asked quietly.

Bud looked up and down the corridor, then motioned them over to a bank of chairs. He sat down in one and let his elbows rest on his knees. He studied the floor as Dar took a seat next to him. "You ever hear of something being too stupid for the Navy?"

Dar stifled a wry chuckle. "Heard that around my house growing up a time or two, yeah."

"Well," Bud's voice was very soft, "I done something too stupid for the Navy." He glanced at the back of his hand. "I stuck my mug someplace it didn't belong, and got Charlie hurt for it."

His pain was evident. Kerry settled in the chair on the other side of him and put a hand on his back, rubbing it sympathetically. "I'm sorry."

"Not half as much as I am," Bud said. "And you know, it kicks my ass to admit being this stupid." He turned his head and regarded Dar. "Shoulda taken you up on your offer. Worst that'd caused is givin' me a week's heartburn."

Dar managed a relatively sympathetic look. "What'd you get into?"

Bud appeared to struggle with himself for a moment longer, then he shook his head. "That damn kid offered us a chunk of change to go on and dive that site. We did."

"The wreck?" Kerry asked. "The kid... You mean, Bob?"

Bud nodded. "He approached us the other day when you dropped him off at the island. Said it was a dark dive — get in, get out. Didn't seem too dangerous to me. No big deal," he said. "They caught us out there, but we got on the boat and headed out."

"They followed you?" Dar hazarded.

"Chased our asses all the way back here." Bud nodded. "We didn't want to go back home." He exhaled. "They caught us." His eyes lifted toward a set of doors. "They had pipes and bats. Charlie's got a busted kidney. He couldn't get away from them, 'cause of his leg, and I—"

"Stayed with him," Kerry said.

"Something like that, yeah," Bud admitted. "That piss-ant kid ran. Took the boat and left us there."

Kerry's eyes narrowed. "That skunk."

Dar rubbed her temple. "How much did he offer you?" she asked quietly.

"Doesn't really matter," Bud muttered.

"HOW MUCH?" It was amazing how much force Dar could project in her voice without raising its volume.

Bud blinked. "Ten grand. Why?"

"That what the nut is on your place?"

Bud nodded.

Dar checked her watch, then dialed a number on her cell phone. She waited for it to connect, then she started punching in numbers, leaning back and concentrating on what she was doing.

"So, how is Charlie?" Kerry asked.

Bud turned his eyes from Dar's simmering form. "He got hit all over. They ripped his prosthesis off. Belted him in the kidney. That's the bitch. He's had problems with that one."

Dar tapped him on the knee. "This place taken care of?" She indicated the hospital.

Bud straightened. "I ain't looking for no handout," he snapped at her. "We're fine."

Dar leaned closer to him and narrowed her eyes. "If I have to, I can dial into this place and find out if you've got insurance or not, so just answer the damn question and don't give me a hard time."

Bud's eyes dropped.

"That's what I thought." Dar stood up. "Okay. I've had it. That stupid mother bastard DeSalliers is so damned convinced I'm a part of this, he's gonna get what he asked for." She put her hands on her hips. "Can we see Charlie?"

Bud looked like the subject changes were giving him whiplash. He put his hand on his jaw. "Yeah, I think so."

"Good," Dar said. "You got a place to stay out here?"

Bud shook his head.

"Rufus taken care of?"

"Yeah. He's staying with a buddy."

Kerry pulled a slip of paper out of her pocket and got up, heading for a nearby pay phone. "I'll call the hotel," she told Dar. "You want me to start calling around to find our friend Bob?"

"Wait until we get back to the room," Dar instructed. "I need my laptop."

Bud looked between the two of them, a little taken aback. "What are you doing?"

"We," Kerry told him, covering the mouthpiece of the phone, "are doing what we do." She glanced at Dar's fierce expression, then went back to the phone. "Yes? Yes. We have a room, I know. I'd like a second one."

Dar waited for Kerry to finish. They entered Charlie's room, walking quietly into the softly blinking machinery that surrounded him.

Dar closed her eyes. The beating her friend had taken was hideous. *DeSalliers, you bastard. You don't know what you just stirred up.* She laid her hands on the iron rails and gazed at Charlie's battered form. "Hey."

His eyes were mere slits, but they opened a little wider on seeing Dar.

Bud gently clasped his hands around Charlie's, chafing them. "Called in the Marines, Punky."

A faint hint of a smile pulled at Charlie's lips. "So I see."

"Take it easy." Dar leaned on the rails. "I'm in charge now, and I make the rules," she said. "They giving you good drugs?"

Charlie nodded slightly.

"Good." Dar wrote her cell phone number on the pad sitting on the small bedside table. "You need anything, call." She put the pen down. "I'm going to stop at the desk when I go out. You'll get taken care of."

"B..." Bud straightened.

Dar just looked at him, and Bud subsided with a tired sigh. "I've got a wire transfer coming in tomorrow," Dar went on. "We'll get your Uncle Guido taken care of, then I'm gonna go after DeSalliers."

"What are you gonna do?" Bud asked.

"Find out the truth first, then I'm gonna give him exactly what he asked for," Dar said. "You staying here for a while," she asked Bud.

Bud nodded.

"Inn at Blackbeard's Castle. We've got a room for you," Dar told him.

Charlie made a muffled sound that sounded suspiciously like laughter.

"You hush," Bud growled at him. "I can stay right here."

Kerry leaned over and gave Charlie's arm a squeeze. "Chase him out, okay?"

Charlie nodded, still chuckling. "Runnin' some tests or suchlike on me. Checking my guts out," he explained. "Hell, if they get their asses done, I'll drag him over there m'self." His bruised eyes went to Dar's face. "Damned if you don't sound just like your daddy."

Dar straightened. "Thanks." She gave him a gracious nod. "C'mon, Ker. Let's go light some fires."

Kerry's eyebrows went up. So did Bud's and apparently Charlie's, but it was hard to tell.

Dar cocked her head. "What?"

Kerry circled the bed and took Dar's arm. "You can light my fires anytime, honey," she assured Dar. "But you don't need to brag about it."

Dar opened her mouth to answer and saw the smirks. She closed her jaw and gathered her dignity, sweeping it around her like a cloak as she followed Kerry's lead out of the room.

Bud glared at the door for a minute, then he released a sigh. "Son of bitch, I hated doing that."

"Buddy, Buddy, Buddy..." Charlie squeezed his hand. "She's a friend, yeah?"

Bud stared at the bleached linen.

"We got any other friends who'd do what she's doing?"

"It twists my shorts," Bud ground out. "I ain't a charity case!"

"Bud," Charlie's voice gentled, and he stroked Bud's cheek, "for her, it ain't charity," he said. "She's Navy; she's family. That runs deep, you know. If anyone from back then asked, and we could, wouldn't we do it?"

"Almost anyone," Bud muttered. "But..." He slumped a little. "Yeah."

Charlie ruffled his hair affectionately. "Well then, they gotta let me outta here, 'cause damned if I ain't gonna stay with you in Blackbeard's Inn."

KERRY PUT THE phone down into its cradle and closed the room service menu. Dar was seated across from her with her laptop open on her lap, its cellular antennae poking up along the side. "Hey, sweetie?"

"Uh?" Dar looked up, blinking at her.

"Could I bribe you to do that from here?" Kerry patted the bed next to her.

"Sure." Dar got up and carried the laptop with her, dropping down onto the bed and waiting as Kerry fluffed the pillow up behind her. She leaned back and was rewarded with not only a backrest, but a body pillow that propped up her arm and twined between her legs. "What'd ya order?"

"It's a surprise." Kerry put her head down on Dar's shoulder and examined the screen. "What's that?"

"Police reports." Dar scanned them. "Not that I really know what I'm looking at. I need a lawyer."

"Sorry." Kerry stifled a yawn. "Though, that was actually one of the acceptable alternative careers my family would have allowed me." She reviewed the cryptic comments on the screen. "They were hedging their bets. I think they knew Mike wasn't going to cut it."

Dar rubbed the side of her thumb against the laptop, trying to imagine Kerry as a lawyer. "What kind of lawyer would you have been?" she asked curiously.

"No kind," Kerry informed her. "I never even considered it." She scrolled with the thumb pad and clicked. "First thing I wanted to be was a fireman."

Dar held back a chuckle. "That shoulda told them something."

"Mm." Kerry chuckled softly. "Yeah, now that I think about it," she agreed. "Then I wanted to be a research scientist, but I realized in high school that I didn't have the aptitude for it." She clicked again. "Then I found computers, and went... Ah hah!"

"Ah hah." Dar examined the screen. It was a complaint filing, apparently by Bob's grandmother at the time of his grandfather's death. In the stark, impersonal language used by the police, the complaint involved the woman's accusation that Bob's uncle had somehow been involved in the sinking, and detailing why. Threats had apparently been made. The police had not been impressed, and merely had noted the complaint along with the comment that the woman had been extremely "emotional" when the statement had been taken.

"Hm." Dar drummed her fingertips on the laptop keyboard. "What do you think?"

"Well," Kerry exhaled, "at least it wasn't just some bs story Bob made up on his own," she said. "Which does not excuse him from skunkhood for leaving Bud and Charlie behind."

"Mm. Think you can find him? Where do you figure he went— back to St. Richard?"

Kerry rolled over and squiggled across the bed, reaching for the island directory. The squiggling intrigued Dar, who enjoyed it as Kerry squiggled on back and opened the book.

"I'm betting he's here in St. Thomas," she said. "It's bigger and busier than St. Richard." Her finger traced a column of hotels. "Let's see if we can find the little stinker."

Dar watched in bemusement as Kerry selected a number and dialed it on the room phone. "He's probably not registered under his real name," she commented.

"Last name, no," Kerry agreed, waiting for an answer. "Hello... Hi, um..." Her voice shifted to a slightly different tone. "This is kind of crazy, but I met this guy today... Yeah... I'm trying to find him again, and I only know his first name. Can anyone help me?" She paused to listen. "Oh, thanks. You're wonderful."

Dar folded her arms over her chest.

"Hi, yeah. No, his name's Bob, and he's really cute... Oh, right, um...he's got red, curly hair, and he's really well built... Yeah, about that age. Yeah...okay, I'll hold." Kerry hummed under her breath. "No? Oh, what? Oh, I see... You did? Wow... Thanks!" She hung up. "They're full. They sent their overflow to a different hotel, and she thinks Bob was one of them."

"A different hotel?" Dar laughed.

"This one." Kerry found the name on her list and proceeded to call it. "Want me to try Southern belle, next?"

"Is that how you conned those circuits out of Southern Bell last month?" Dar was still laughing.

Kerry grinned. "No, but...I'll have to remember that." She cleared her throat. "Howdy there... Ahm lookin' for a real cutie I met down on the beach t'day... Kin you help me?"

Dar covered her mouth and continued her scrolling, keeping one ear on Kerry's best efforts to sound like Dolly Parton. The information she'd recovered was straightforward enough, but the problem was, it was hard to tell if there was any truth to any of it. What to do? She really felt in need of an expert to at least look at the case and give an opinion as to who was more likely to be telling the truth, if any of them were. The uncle had answered through a lawyer, in a tone almost insulting in its dismissal of the insinuation, and she instinctively favored the grandmother, but... *Grandmothers can be sneaky, too, and maybe she was trying to hold on to her husband's money.* Dar sighed. She checked her address book and looked up a number, then dialed it on her cell phone.

It rang twice, then was answered. "Hello?"

"Merry Christmas, Richard," Dar said. "It's Dar."

"Dar!" Her family lawyer sounded pleased, if a bit puzzled, to be hearing from her. "Merry Christmas and happy birthday, lady!"

"Thanks," Dar replied. "Listen, I need a favor." She paused. "More or less a professional one."

Richard Edgerton's gears switched. "Well, sure, Dar," he answered briskly. "You're not in any trouble, are you? Hard to believe."

"No," Dar answered without thinking, then considered. "Well, not me personally, that is."

He hazarded a guess. "Kerry?"

"No. We're on vacation," Dar explained.

"Uh huh."

Dar could hear rustling, and she guessed Richard was getting a pad to write on. He was a very good lawyer, and he knew estate law like the back of his hand. "Don't ask me how I got involved in this, but I am," she began.

"Uh oh." Richard chuckled. "Let me hold onto something. This should be a doozy."

Dar sighed. "You don't know the half of it."

"He's here," Kerry's voice interrupted her. "He's staying in this hotel."

"Hang on, Richard." Dar looked at her. "Invite him over for a drink," she said. "Tell him we'd like to chat."

Kerry nibbled her lip. "I won't let him know we know about Charlie and Bud."

"Not yet, no." Dar smiled grimly. "Wait until he gets here."

Kerry nodded and went back to the phone. Dar did the same. "Okay, Richard, here's the deal. We're out on St. Thomas—"

"Nice place to spend Christmas," Richard replied amiably.

"Right. We ran into a guy who told us a horse's tale about trying to prove his uncle murdered his grandfather to inherit the family fortune."

A long silence preceded the lawyer's response. "Dar, have you been at the rum?"

Dar sighed. "Yes, but not today," she said. "Listen, if I shoot something over to you in email, will you just look at it and tell me what you think? It's a pile of legal crap I don't have time to figure out."

Richard chuckled. "Sure, Dar, send it over. I was stuck watching my second cousin's vacation video from Mexico. It's a great rescue."

Dar packed the files into an archive and sent it. "Thanks. You can call me on the cell once you see what you think."

"What's your percentage in this, Dar?"

Hm. Good question. "Like I said, I got dragged into it," Dar replied. "Now some friends of mine got dragged in too, and they got hurt. I need to know what side the angels are on, so I can figure out what to do."

"Ah, I see," Richard murmured. "It's your crusader side coming out, eh?"

"Why does everyone keep calling it that?" Dar whined. "It's not crusading. This stupid asshole just won't leave me alone!"

"Uh huh," her lawyer replied. "Lemme take a look, Dar. It sounds like some typical sordid, family in-fighting over money, but I'll give you my best opinion on it."

"Thanks, Richard." Dar smiled. "I owe you one."

"How about letting me handle your investments?" Richard shot back with cheerful mercenary humor. "You know, I hate to admit this, but you made me a bundle investing in ILS last quarter."

Dar chuckled. "We'll talk."

"How are your mom and dad doing?" Richard asked. "I heard some scandal that they were living out on a boat?"

"A sixty-foot Bertram, yes," Dar replied dryly. "Having the time of their lives."

Richard laughed heartily. "Good for them! I love it!" he chortled. "I'll have to come down and see it sometime. Listen, let me get to this and I'll be back to you, okay?"

"Thanks, Rich." Dar hung up the phone and turned to Kerry. "Are we set?"

"Hook, line, sinker, and a tin can off the bottom." Kerry nodded. "He'll be on his way over in a little while. He's just finishing dinner." She scratched her nose. "He sounded really happy to hear my voice for some reason."

Dar gave her a very wry look. "With the Southern Comfort, or without?"

Kerry stuck out her tongue. Dar obligingly leaned over and caught it between her teeth. She slowly released it, then fastened her attention on Kerry's lips instead. "Mm," she drawled softly as they parted. "Much as I want to get this nailed, I'd be lying if I said I wanted it to be tonight." She tilted her head and kissed Kerry again, then moved her nibbles down Kerry's throat to feel her pulse thrumming against her lips as she suckled the soft skin.

"Guess you see my point then," Kerry murmured, her hand slowly gliding beneath Dar's shirt to explore the warm surface underneath. "About feeling selfish."

Dar set her laptop on the floor and then rolled over, shoving the island guide and phone aside and wrapping her arms and legs around Kerry's body. "Oh, yeah," Dar growled, continuing her assault. "Call me selfish. I want you all to myself."

"Ooh." Kerry felt her heart rate speed up and a warm flush tingle her skin. There was a faint pressure at her waistband, then Dar's touch slid beneath her shirt and traced up her ribcage. She laced her fingers through Dar's hair and nuzzled her ear, nibbling lightly on her earlobe. She could feel Dar's breath against her neck, then the soft, insistent tug as Dar's teeth undid the top button to her shirt. Kerry cupped her hand along Dar's cheek, stroking it as her thumb traced Dar's lip.

Dar unbuttoned her shirt slowly, and Kerry felt the cool air from the room brush against her, raising goose bumps along her belly. Dar's lips intensified the sensation, and Kerry rapidly lost any thought of their problems. All that mattered now were the teasing touches on her breasts, the warm, sun-filled scent of Dar's skin, and the need for Dar's body that made her hands push aside the soft cotton separating them with bold impatience.

"Grrrrrowlll..." The low rumble tickled her skin. Kerry felt Dar's teeth close gently, teasingly, on the skin around her belly button. "Mine."

Definitely. Kerry's back arched and she wrapped her arms around Dar, feeling the powerful muscles along her spine bunch and move. They pressed together briefly, a jolt of heat before Dar shifted lower and her hand dropped to stroke Kerry's thigh. *Oh, definitely.*

"THANKS." KERRY SIGNED the check and shooed the room service waiter out of the room before his eyeballs could skitter out of his head and ramble across the floor. She shut the door behind him and turned, regarding the bed with a wry grin.

Dar was sprawled across it, the sheet just barely covering what was very obviously a naked body. She had the laptop propped on one thigh, but the other was outside the linen, extending its long, tanned length across the white surface.

Shaking her head, Kerry went over to the table and investigated the tray, peeking under one cover and grinning at what she saw. "Hungry, sweetie?"

"Not anymore," Dar drawled.

"Heh." Kerry hitched up the edge of Dar's red muscle T-shirt, which she'd stolen and donned after they'd finished their lovemaking. She perched on the edge of the table, arranging a few of the plates on it. "Well, okay — we'll start with this, then." Taking one of the plates, she walked over to the bed and knelt down.

"Happy birthday to you...happy birthday to you..."

Dar looked up in alarm to see a beautifully made chocolate-something with more chocolate inside and chocolate topping, with berries surrounding it on the plate. In the center was a single candle. "Awww."

"Happy birthday dear Dar...happy birthday to you," Kerry warbled.

Dar sniffed at the plate, licking her lips appreciatively. She blew out the candle with a single puff of air. "Share?"

Kerry sat down on the bed and picked up the fork, cutting off a gooey piece and feeding it to Dar.

"Ooo.. I like that," Dar mumbled. "I just got a data dump from Mark," she informed Kerry. "DeSalliers' stats — financial and otherwise. I figured out why he's so desperate."

"Why?" Kerry fed her another forkful of cake as she peered at the screen.

"He's broke." Dar munched. "He invested in two capital ventures that went belly up, and the banks called in some of his loans when they figured out he had paper that wasn't worth the paper it was printed on in his accounts."

"Ahhh." Kerry nodded. "Yeah, that makes sense. So old Uncle offers him a windfall to...to what, Dar?" she asked. "Not bring up something. That's the last thing he'd want to do."

Dar gazed at the screen. "No. He'd want him to scuttle the wreck," she realized. "Jesus...that's what it is. He's gonna cannibalize it."

Kerry had the fork in her mouth. She drew it out and swallowed the rich mouthful. "Are you saying he's going to wreck something that's already wrecked, to keep anyone from getting anything out of it?"

Dar nodded. "Yeah, but..." she flipped to another screen, "he's got a problem. It's in AVI territorial waters, and he can't just go in there and set off dynamite."

Kerry portioned off another forkful and handed it over. "How do you light dynamite underwater, Dar?"

Dar chewed and typed in silence, then swallowed. "Did you get any—"

"Milk? Yeah." Kerry set the plate down and went to retrieve it.

"I don't know." Dar answered the previous question. "You'd have to ask my father. His specialty used to be called UDX, underwater demolition."

As if by some supernatural invocation, Dar's cell phone rang, and when she checked the caller ID, it was familiar. With a tiny, surprised grunt, Dar flipped open the phone. "Hi, Dad."

Kerry, on her way back with the milk, goggled. "Wow," she murmured. "Spooky."

"Hey there, Dardar." Andrew Robert's cheerful voice came through the phone. "How's the vacation going?"

Truth? Dar had microseconds to decide. "Great," she finally said. "We ran into pirates, we're involved in a possible murder case, and Kerry got stung by a jellyfish, but other than that, it's been very cool."

It wasn't often that Andy Roberts was rendered speechless. "Son of a biscuit," he finally spluttered. "Damn, Dar, what the hell you two getting into out there?"

Dar sighed. It was such a long story at this point.

Kerry took the phone from her and put it to her ear. "Hey, Dad?"

"Howdy, kumquat."

"I've got sort of a running diary of it. Want me to email it to you on Dar's computer?" Kerry offered. "I think that'll be easier than us trying to explain it. I'll set it to print out on the printer."

"Ah would appreciate that, kumquat. Mah wife is rattling her eyebrows at me wondering what the hell's going on."

Dar took the phone back. "It's not that bad, Dad," she

explained. "Just...complicated." She lifted her hands off the keyboard as Kerry crawled into bed next to her and pecked out a few commands.

"Uh huh," Andrew grunted. "Well, anyhow, you having a happy birthday?"

Dar examined the blonde sprawled in her lap. "Yeah, it's great," she replied. "Kerry and I have been shopping and...um...relaxing all day."

"Relaxing?" Kerry murmured. "I certainly wasn't relaxed... Yipe!" She squirmed as Dar pinched her. "Stop that." She ran a finger along the inside of Dar's very bare thigh, snickering when she heard Dar's voice break.

"N...no, Dad, honest. We're fine." Dar cleared her throat. "I've got everything under control." She bit the inside of her lip as Kerry tickled her thigh again. "Almost everything."

"Wall, you be careful," Andrew warned. "Hang on."

The phone rustled, then a lighter voice came on. "Dar?"

"Hi, Mom," Dar said.

"I'm not going to pretend I have a clue about what's going on, so I'm just going to wish you a happy birthday."

Dar chuckled. "Thanks."

"And I hope you're having a good, annual, hyper-commercialized, forced exchange of personal resources, too."

"Merry Christmas to you, too, Mom."

"Merry Christmas, Mom!" Kerry leaned back and called out. "Good Solstice."

"Tell Kerry I said thanks, and thank her for the card," Ceci said. "You kids be careful, hear?"

Kerry finished her transmission, then scooted out of bed and ambled back over to the table, before Dar's close, bare proximity spurred her to further amorous adventures.

"We'll be fine, Mother," Dar exhaled. "How's Chino?"

"She's just fine," Ceci assured her. "The place is fine, the island hasn't sunk, your stock is up two dollars, and I do believe your father has just opened a bottle of champagne, so I'll just have to let you get on with your celebration."

"Have a great night," Dar told her. "Call us if you need anything."

"How about you call us if *you* need anything?" Ceci countered. "G'night, Dar."

"Night."

Dar had just closed the phone when a knock came at the door. "Ah. Bet that's our friend," she commented. "Let him in."

Kerry turned, putting one hand on her hip. She gazed at Dar with both eyebrows lifted.

Dar stared back at her, then realized what she was looking at.

"Oh." She put the laptop aside and stood up, shedding her bed sheets and padding across the wooden floor. She opened her bag and pulled out a pair of shorts and a shirt.

Kerry went to the door and leaned on it. "Just a second," she called, peeking through the eyehole to make sure it was Bob and not something even skunkier.

"Okay." Dar returned the bed and retrieved her laptop, then settled into an armchair.

Kerry opened the door. "Hi." She stepped back to allow Bob to enter. "C'mon in."

He was dressed in pressed chinos and a neatly ironed polo. "Hi." He gave Kerry an eager smile, his eyes flicking over her head to Dar and then back. "Thanks for calling me. I was hoping I could find you guys again. I really need to talk to you."

"Ah," Dar murmured. "That's good, because we need to talk to you."

Bob hesitantly walked over and took the seat across from Dar. "I'm sorry, I'm interrupting your dinner?"

Kerry had returned to the table. "It's okay. We're used to eating during business meetings." She examined Dar's plate, then walked over and handed it to her. "Bob, you know, I'm really pissed off at you."

Dar set the plate on the arm of the chair and continued her work, letting Kerry do the talking as they'd planned.

"M...me?" Bob sounded very surprised. "What did I do?"

"You left two friends of ours in a really bad place last night." Kerry gazed seriously at him. "They got hurt." She sat down on the edge of the window and rested her elbows on her knees. "Why did you do that?"

For a moment, the only sound was the soft, rapid-fire rattling of Dar's laptop keys.

"I thought they'd be fine," Bob finally muttered. "I thought the thugs would come after me, not them." He shifted uncomfortably. "I didn't mean for them to get hurt."

Well, Kerry considered, *that was actually marginally logical.* "Why did you think they'd go after you?" she asked.

Bob got up and paced, visibly nervous. "Why? I'm the one they're after. I'm the one who keeps trying to get down to that wreck. If we'd gotten anything, it'd have been on that boat. Sure, I thought they'd go after me."

"But they didn't," Kerry said.

"No, I..." Bob stared out the window. "I thought I got lucky." He turned. "Hey, it'd be the third time, you know? Besides, Bud and Charlie looked like they could take care of themselves. What could I have done, anyway?"

Kerry stared steadily at him.

"Hey, I admit it—I'm no hero." Bob lifted his hands. "I'm not like you. I'll save my own skin first, and that's just the truth, okay?"

Kerry looked at Dar. Dar rolled her eyes and shook her head. Kerry sighed and took a bite of her dinner. "So, why were you looking for us, then?" she asked. "Did you need another diversionary target?"

Bob apparently felt his grilling was over and that he'd won a point. "No." He gathered his confidence again. "Look, I realized I was going about this the wrong way. I need resources, and help." He faced them. "So, here's the deal."

Dar rested her elbow on the chair arm while Kerry leaned forward attentively.

"I want to make you my partners," Bob said. "Is that a good deal or what?"

Blue and green eyes met across the inn room. Kerry sighed. "Bob?"

"Yeah?" He grinned at her. "I know, it's a big sacrifice for me, but—"

"Did you get dropped on your head a lot as a kid?"

"Huh?"

"I should have stayed naked," Dar commented, shaking her head sadly. "He'd never have noticed."

"Huh?"

"Another explicit reason why stupid people shouldn't breed."

"What are you guys talking about?"

"I think we should just tie him up and leave him in the closet," Kerry decided.

"Hey!"

Chapter
Twenty

"OKAY. HERE'S THE scenario as I see it." Dar paced in front of the window, her hands in her pockets.

Bob was sitting in the corner, keeping as far away as he could from Bud, who'd arrived not long before. Kerry was seated on the bed cross-legged, and the only thing missing was a whiteboard and markers.

Dar was actually quite a good situational analyst, as Kerry had decided some time ago. She tended to toss out all the irrelevant details and concentrate on the core issues, and if you were smart, you let her finish before you asked any questions.

"But, wait." Bob spoke up. "Don't you think I should explain my part of this first?"

"No," Dar said. "As I was saying...here's the scenario." She paused. "We have a ten-year-old wreck in pretty rough condition, just east of Charlie and Bud's place. We have one certifiable nutcase trying to bring up bits of it, and another certifiable nutcase trying to blow it up."

"Hey!" Bob protested.

"Shut up," Bud drawled. "Or I'll stick a chair leg down your throat."

"Nutcase two has the resources to achieve his objective." Dar consulted a piece of paper on the table, now cleared of its tray. A pot of tea, however, squatted mutely in the center. "He also has the easier task." She turned to Bob. "Are you ready to tell us what you're looking for?"

Bob squirmed a little as all eyes fastened on him. "Um." He swallowed, an audible sound in the silent room. "Well, you know, that's a... Y'see, I don't know if I can, um..."

Dar walked over and put her arms on his chair, fixing him with her dourest look. "Kerry risked her life to save your ass. Don't even think about not trusting us."

"Uh." Bob leaned back in the chair. "It's not that, it's... just...I..."

"You don't know, do you?" Kerry spoke up. "You have no idea

what you're looking for."

Dar looked at Kerry, then looked at Bob. The expression on his face spoke volumes. "Is that true?"

"Um." Bob gulped. "Sorta."

Dar straightened and walked over to the window, lifting both hands and letting them drop in eloquent silence.

"Son of a bitch," Bud snorted. "No wonder you told us to show you everything we done brought up," he said. "I thought that was a weird-ass story about lookin' for pieces of some puzzle."

"See." Bob sat up. "I told you I shoulda explained first. Here's the deal." He took a breath. "My grandma—"

"She's not your grandmother," Dar interrupted. "You're not even related to her. You're trying to impress her granddaughter, who you want to marry."

Bob looked at her in consternation.

"You're from Ohio," Kerry added with a brief smile. "Your family raises alpacas."

"Who are you people?" Bob asked, looking from one to the other. "Cops?"

Dar snorted. Kerry just laughed.

"Okay." Bob sighed. "Yeah, I'm a fraud."

"Now there's a damn news flash," Bud muttered.

"But it's in a great cause. Listen," Bob recovered, "it's true, about Tanya's grandpa. He hated his kids like poison. Wanted to find a way to screw 'em over any way he could. So his will—"

"Left most everything to charity and his wife," Dar broke in. "Except after he drowned, the family brought a suit claiming he was nuts, and they had the will invalidated." She lifted a sheet of paper on the table. "Everything went to the eldest son."

"Right." Bob wrested control back of the conversation. "And he's a jerk."

"Common problem we've been encountering lately," Kerry murmured. "Maybe it's the water."

"He controls everything, and the worst part is, he took all Tanya's grandmother's money away from her because he got the courts to say she's incompetent," Bob went on. "Tanya helps her out, but it's really tough. Her uncle says it's just too bad, since she, Grandma, I mean, supported Grandpa and didn't want him to leave any money to the rest of them."

That, Dar acknowledged, seemed to be the truth according to the two-page, neatly formatted answer she'd gotten from Richard. The uncle, Patrick Wharton, was apparently really the asshole Bob was describing. Richard had added several footnotes in which he'd laid out the players. None of them seemed to be sterling citizens, but of them all, Wharton was the worst, and apparently the grandma was a witchy, but basically innocent victim.

The fact that Bob actually wanted to marry into that nest of unpleasant invertebrates sealed his idiocy, so far as Dar was concerned. However... "Okay." Dar sat on the windowsill. "So we don't even know if this thing, whatever it is, exists."

"We think it does. Well, it did," Bob said. "The thing is, we're looking to prove old Grandpa Wharton wasn't nuts, and maybe Uncle Patrick had something to do with his drowning."

"Do you really think he did?" Kerry asked.

Bob shrugged. "I dunno, but he's the type that coulda."

Bud got up and messed with the teapot. "Bullshit chase." He shook his head.

Dar was inclined to agree. "What makes you think there's anything on that boat that can prove anything? It's been sunk for a decade."

At last, Bob smiled. "'Cause Putrid Pat thinks so," he said. "After they shipped the old lady off to a nursing home, they pulled apart the old man's house. Right after that, Pat went nuts and started trying to hire DeSalliers to go check out the wreck." His fingers tapped the arms of the chair. "Tanya found out, and that's how the whole thing got started. We figure he must know something or else why bother?"

Kerry propped her chin up on her fist. "That makes sense," she admitted.

"So DeSalliers must know what he's looking for," Dar murmured.

"And he thinks maybe you found it, that first time," Bud commented. "Maybe that's why he keeps pestering you."

Kerry got off the bed and walked over to the table, examining the pages Dar had printed out. "But we didn't. All we brought up was an old wooden cigar box, falling to pieces. It was so coral-encrusted, it looked like a piece of sea garbage. There wasn't anything there."

"But...he doesn't know that." Dar leaned back against the sill. "And he's panicking, because unless he can bring back positive proof to Wharton that no evidence exists, he doesn't get paid. He doesn't get paid, he's tapped, and I doubt he can afford the gas to get back to the States."

"Okay." Kerry joined Dar by the windowsill, settling next to her shoulder to shoulder. "So there are two different things here. I guess the proof that he was involved in a murder would be more important to the uncle, but if there's anything proving that Grandpa wasn't nuts, I don't think that would be something that would have been on that wreck."

"No," Dar agreed. "We have to figure out why Popeye was all the way down here in the tropics, and what he was after."

"We were hoping to find his log," Bob explained. "He kept a

diary, but it was a paper book, so...unless someone salvaged it and it's in somebody's house, or in a shop somewhere..."

Bud sipped his tea, glaring at everyone over the rim of the cup. "Can ask around," he said. "We know the freelance salvagers 'round here."

Dar grunted, giving Bud a brief nod. "All right," she decided. "First thing we do is scuttle DeSalliers. I'll call Pat Wharton tomorrow, tell him I think I've got what he wants, and see what he says about it."

Everyone looked at Dar in surprise. Dar looked back at them. "What? I'm sick and tired of that bozo smacking my friends around and ruining my vacation."

"He could freak out," Kerry suggested.

"He could grow tail feathers and fly to Bermuda, too," Dar replied. "Meantime, Bud, if you'll check with your buddies and see if you can find out what the old captain's gig was, maybe we can make heads or tails out of this stupidity and I can go back to windsurfing."

"Yeah, I can do that," Bud agreed grudgingly. "They figure on letting Charlie out of the hospital tomorrow. He's got a bigger little black book than me. We can call more then."

"All right." Dar folded her arms. "I'll pull as much regulatory information as I can on the old man's business contracts. I've got someone unraveling his public trust filings." She exhaled. "Meanwhile, we'll visit the government offices tomorrow and see what they have on record for him and that damn boat, and what was filed when it sank."

Bob gazed at her. "Who are you people?" he asked again. "C'mon. I came clean, now it's your turn. Are you government agents or something?"

"No," Dar told him with a severe look. "It's worse. We're rampaging techno-capitalists." She put an arm around Kerry's shoulders. "Dilbert on steroids, only classier, and with a much cuter dog."

Kerry snorted, turning and burying her face in Dar's shoulder. "Honey, stop it."

Dar shrugged. "He asked."

"Right," Bob murmured. "Okay, well...what do you want me to do?"

"Nothing," Dar told him curtly.

"Really," Kerry adopted a slightly kinder tone, "we've got it covered. If DeSalliers sees you around, it's just going to complicate things."

Bob looked at her. "You're really a spy, aren't you?" he accused. "Or some international police or something ?" He snapped his fingers. "I've got it; are you a DEA agent?"

"No." Kerry sighed. "I'm a nerd," she told him, causing Bud to muffle a smirk. "Really."

"Oh." Bob still looked very confused. "Like a hacker?"

Kerry was about at the end of her patience. "No. Dar's the hacker; I'm just a nerd."

"You really a hacker?" Bud asked Dar with interest.

Dar started chuckling. "Sometimes, yeah," she confirmed. "A very, very expensive one." Her hands drifted over the laptop keyboard. "Okay, I think that's enough intrigue for one night. Kerry needs to get some rest." She glanced up at Bud. "You let us know tomorrow how Charlie's doing?"

Bud nodded. "Yeah." He fiddled with the room key. "He about chewed that doctor's arm off when he said he couldn't come outta there tonight."

"Know how he feels," Dar said. "I'll give you a call in the morning after I call Wharton."

"What about me?" Bob whined.

"We'll call you, too," Kerry told him, trying to ignore the low growl behind her. "Dar's right. We should all get some rest. I'm sure tomorrow's going to be busy." She gently herded them out and shut the door, then she turned and faced Dar, who had taken a seat in one of the armchairs. "Why do I feel like I'm trapped in a bizarro Agatha Christie mystery novel?"

Dar held out a hand and Kerry crossed over to the chair and sat on an arm. "I figure, we get rid of DeSalliers, dig up whatever stuff we can here and give it to Bob and get rid of *him*, and then we can get back to having fun."

Kerry leaned over and kissed Dar on the head. "Sounds like a plan, boss." She only hoped it would work.

Chapter
Twenty-one

KERRY STRETCHED OUT her legs, and then propped them up on the railing of the porch outside their room. The day had dawned bright and sunny, and she had decided to spend the time waiting for breakfast by attempting a little poetry. Dar was off picking up something at the hotel's sundry shop, and she had a few minutes to simply look out over the harbor and revel in the gorgeous view.

And it was truly gorgeous. High up on the slope as they were, the harbor stretched out below her and curved to either side, cupping a crystal aqua circle of water with just the lightest visible chop on it. Around her, she could hear the rustle of trees, the cry of gulls, sounds from the harbor, but very little traffic or bustle. The air mostly bore the scent of foliage and salt air, and Kerry felt a sense of peaceful well-being as she relaxed in the warm sunlight.

With a smile, she returned her attention to the book balanced on her lap and the heavy, injected-ink writing pen Dar had given her. The pen was hardwood, and warm from her hand, and it balanced well in her grip as she flexed her fingers around it. Thoughtfully, she regarded the page and then added two more lines to the several already there. A knock on the door, however, interrupted her.

With a resigned sigh, Kerry put down her book and went inside, going to the door and peeking through the eyehole. "Oh, crap." Seeing the female half of DeSalliers' gumshoe team outside, she considered not answering it. Then she figured she was likely to get more info from the woman than the woman was going to get from her, so she opened the door. "Yes?" Her tone made no pretense of being friendly, and the woman took a half step back.

"Oh, hello, Kerry," the woman recovered. "I was hoping to talk to you."

"Why?" Kerry asked bluntly.

"Just because I think we can help each other."

Kerry had to wonder briefly if stupidity was contagious. Perhaps Christen had spent a little too much time with Bob. "Help each other do what?" she inquired. "So far, all you people have done is help me get a migraine."

Christen sighed. "Look, can I just come in and talk?"

"No," Kerry replied. "I'm not sure what it's going to take to get across the fact that we don't want anything to do with you, your boss, your stupid mission, or the people you represent. I'm out of options. Should I hire a flying banner plane?"

"The fact is, honey, you are involved." Christen's attitude changed, became harder. "So either you let me in and give me what I want, or—"

"Or what?" Kerry found it almost funny. "Are you going to pull a gun on me?"

"No."

"Are you going to make like Jackie Chan and start yowling Japanese haiku while striking kung fu poses?"

Christen didn't answer.

"Are you going to try to hit me?" Kerry's nose crinkled up in amusement. "Threaten me with a lawsuit? What?"

"You think this is a game, don't you?"

"Hey, you're the one making the threats." Kerry laughed, and then got serious herself, jabbing the air in Christen's direction. "You listen to me, you half-baked excuse for a high-priced, snoopy lackey. You'd better just back off and go back where you came from. Stop messing with us."

"Or?" Christen threw the comment back at her.

"Or I'll call the president of your agency and file a complaint of harassment without cause," Kerry replied.

Christen laughed. "You think he'll care?"

"When he gets a call from the executive VP of the company where he gets all his data? Yeah." Kerry smiled. "He'll care," she assured the now not-smiling Christen. "And if he doesn't listen to me, he'll listen to Dar." She watched Christen's face. "Tch... didn't do your homework, did you?"

"Your inquiry came back totally negative."

"Not surprising." Kerry smiled. "Try it with a last name of Stuart." She started to close the door. "You, on the other hand, provided us with a lot of information. You and your little partner really should work a little harder, you know? That last job of yours was a real disaster."

Christen had turned brick red.

"So don't you mess with me, lady," Kerry warned her seriously. "You're an amateur. It offends me that you actually get paid to be an amateur. My Labrador Retriever would do better as a detective, and as far as I'm concerned, you're just a flashy poser. Scoot."

She slammed the door with a sense of guilty satisfaction. "Jerk." She turned and started to walk away, then stopped as a knock came at the door again. With a growl, she whirled and yanked open the door, a further stream of invective ready and waiting. Which she swallowed when she found herself facing a doe-eyed, uniformed, room service waitress. "Oh." She stepped back. "Hi. C'mon in."

Christen was nowhere to be seen. Kerry allowed herself a moment of regret for her outburst, wondering belatedly if she shouldn't have just let the woman in to have her say. Maybe she could have learned something from her.

Ah well. Kerry watched the waitress set the tray down. *Too late now.* She walked over and took the check, reviewing it and then signing. "Everything looks great. Thanks. "

The woman smiled shyly. "You are welcome. You are good customers," she said. "So many bring sandwiches with them, just make a mess."

Kerry grinned, her good humor restored. "Well, we've got sandwiches on the boat, but one of the nice things about visiting other places is getting to sample their culture and foods. You can't do that with peanut butter."

The woman nodded agreement, then slipped to the door, backing in surprise when it opened inward to admit Dar. "Oh."

Dar regarded the woman with a raised eyebrow, then moved aside to let her out. She closed the door after her then walked over to Kerry, setting a colorful, print bag on the chair. "Hi." Her blue eyes went to the table. "Looks like I'm just in time."

"Yes, you are," Kerry agreed, lifting the covers and revealing some intriguing dishes involving eggs, fruit, native spices, and seafood. "You just missed our friend Christen."

"No, I didn't." Dar sniffed appreciatively. "She crashed into me on her way storming out of the building." She sampled a bit of papaya. "Mm."

"I think I pissed her off."

"Good. I made it worse. She fell on her ass," Dar replied. "What'd she want?"

Kerry sat down "Unfortunately, I have no idea. I was too busy insulting her to find out." She gave Dar a mildly regretful look. "In hindsight, maybe that wasn't such a good idea. She wanted to talk to me, said she could help me out."

"Out of what?" Dar asked, setting her napkin aside and pouring Kerry some passion fruit juice.

"Well, that's what I don't know," Kerry said. "I told her she was a fraud and sent her packing, actually. I told her if she didn't leave us alone, we'd call her boss."

"Ah." Dar investigated her fluffy shrimp and pepper egg cup. "Well, I don't really blame you," she admitted. "I'm just waiting for it to be nine a.m. over in the States before I put in a call to Wharton.

Maybe after that, they'll just disappear." She opened a crusty brown roll and put some butter on it. "Damn, these people are a pain in my ass."

Kerry slowly chewed a piece of star fruit. "What do you think he'll do?" she asked. "Wharton, I mean? From the background information we pulled on him, he seems pretty rough. Is there a chance this is going to backfire on us, Dar?"

"Eh." Dar put a bit of her eggs on her roll. "I was thinking about that. Maybe I should keep it anonymous instead of telling him who I am."

"Hm," Kerry murmured. "Just tell him you're out here, and you found something? Will that be enough for him to call off DeSalliers and the wonder twins?"

In the light of day, Dar had been wondering the same thing. Her plan last night had seemed simple and straightforward, but now she was starting to have doubts. "I don't know," she answered honestly. "Maybe I'd feel better if I actually had something under my belt before I call him."

"You want to visit the government offices first?" Kerry asked. "Maybe we can dig up some stuff there, and you can just fax it or something. Maybe that'll be enough."

And then what? "Okay, that sounds good," Dar agreed. "You know, Ker, I was thinking — what if the old man *was* nuts?"

"The thought had crossed my mind," Kerry admitted. "But leaving your fortune to charity doesn't sound very nutty to me, Dar. If he'd left it to Greenpeace after spending a life trolling a net, maybe, but...I checked out the charities. Fisherman's Home, local firefighters in Boston...a lot of community stuff," she said. "So I don't know — maybe he had reason to cut the kids out."

Dar selected a strawberry, took a bite, and then offered the rest to Kerry. "Money sometimes ruins a family," she observed. "It changes everything, doesn't it?"

Kerry didn't answer immediately. "I guess it does," she said. "In my family, it was kind of taken for granted." She sounded a little surprised. "No one really thought about the money part of it. It was the power that attracted the attention." A faint chuckle emerged from her throat. "You know something? They're executing my father's will this week, and I never even thought twice about being cut out of it."

"What would you do if you weren't?" Dar asked curiously. "I mean, if you found out you were getting something?"

"Donate it to charity," Kerry answered instantly. "I don't...want anything from him, from them." She studied her fork. "I have everything I've ever wanted or needed in you."

Dar reached over and clasped Kerry's hand. "Ker, you know I feel the same way. But don't be shocked if you end up with something in that will after all." She spoke softly. "But it might not be money."

Kerry was briefly silent, then she lifted her eyes and met Dar's. "Do you know something, or are you just guessing?" she asked quietly.

Dar shook her head. "Just guessing."

"Or is it because you have the father you do, that you cut mine some slack?" Kerry rested her chin on her hand. "People are bastards, Dar. Fatherhood doesn't grant them nobility if they didn't already have it in them."

"True," Dar said. "But most people aren't either totally good or totally bad. You never know." She eased off the subject, seeing Kerry's discomfort with it. "At any rate, I think a visit to town is probably a good idea. I'll hold off contacting Wharton until we've got more data available to us."

Kerry wasn't quite ready to abandon the conversation, though. "Do you really think my father had redeeming qualities?" she asked Dar seriously.

"I think he was your father, and that's enough of a redeeming quality for me," Dar replied.

Kerry sighed. "I used to think that," she said. "Maybe part of me still wants to believe it. But...if I believe that, then it makes it all the more difficult for me to accept what I did."

"Mm." Dar chafed Kerry's fingers with her own.

"So it's easier for me to believe otherwise," Kerry went on. "I'd rather hate him than hate myself." She sighed heavily. "So, frankly, I hope I get a sack of coal if I get anything, Dar."

Ah. "I gotcha." Dar squeezed her hand.

"Maybe after some time's passed, I'll feel differently. But right now, I can't deal with it."

"Okay."

Kerry looked at her. "That's pretty chickenshit, isn't it?"

"No."

"Yes, it is," Kerry said with a wry chuckle. "But you know, that's the first time I've been able to talk about that since he died, so maybe it's okay to be a chickenshit for a while." And it was, she realized. It was as though she'd taken a step back and gained at least a tiny measure of perspective. Was it part of some healing process? Maybe. Kerry felt obscurely better all of a sudden, and she picked up her fork and went after the remainder of her breakfast.

"I've got to go to the bank and get that cash out," Dar suddenly remembered. "Damn, I forgot about that." She took a mouthful of eggs and chewed them. "Get that done before we go hunting for information."

"I can't believe you got Bud and Charlie to agree to let you do that." Kerry smiled. "I'm glad you did, though."

"Well, it's going to be a loan. They won't let me get away with giving it to them as a gift," Dar said. "But the terms'll be a hell of a lot better than they had." She shook her head. "Want to come with me?"

"You bet your butt I do." Kerry finished her fruit juice and stood up. "Be right back."

Dar watched her duck into the bathroom, then concentrated on clearing her plate as the sound of running water filtered through to her. The decision to do some data mining before confronting their putative adversary was, she thought, a good one. They might find some facts. Dar liked facts. She put them in her pocket and used them like darts, flipping them out and nailing people with them when they least expected it. Facts were good.

Dar drained her coffee cup. She didn't mind bluffing, but bluffing was always easier when you had something to fall back on. She stood and wiped her lips, then dropped her napkin on the table. Her backpack stood mutely in the corner. She went over and lifted it, then slipped it over her shoulders. Kerry came out and joined her at the door and they left the room, heading off to find some facts. Or some trouble. Or maybe both.

DAR HELD OPEN the door to the Chase Bank, waiting for Kerry to enter and then following her inside. The bank was on the way to the police station and courthouse, so they'd decided to stop there first. Dar pulled off her sunglasses and looked around, then walked across to a small desk with a receptionist behind it.

"Good morning." The receptionist greeted them with a professional smile. "What can I do for you ladies today?"

"I have a wire transfer I need to pick up," Dar explained. "It was generated last night."

"Sure." The woman glanced behind her to a single desk with a young man at it. "Mr. Steel? Are you free?"

The man looked up. "Yes, I am."

Dar and Kerry walked over and sat down at the man's desk. Dar removed her driver's license from her wallet and handed it to him. "I requested a wire transfer last night," she repeated. "From Florida."

Mr. Steel took the license and put it in the desk, then typed Dar's name into his computer. He waited, then nodded. "Yes, Ms. Roberts, we have it." He leaned closer to the screen. "For... ten thousand American?"

"Yep."

"Would you like that as a draft, ma'am?"

A draft. Dar considered her memory of Cheapside Guido and sighed inwardly. "Cash," she replied. "Gimme it in hundreds."

The bank officer frowned. "Ma'am, it's not a good idea to carry that much currency on your person," he objected. "Really."

"I know," Dar agreed. "But I won't be carrying it long, hopefully."

The man still didn't like it, but he tapped in a request and hit enter. "Okay, let me just get that for you." He stood and walked to a locked door, keying in a code and disappearing.

Kerry looked around at the empty bank with its one remaining teller. "Quiet."

"Mm." Dar leaned back. The bank's outer door opened and two men came in, bypassing the receptionist and heading for the teller. They were tall, and there was something vaguely familiar about one of them that set Dar's mind to itching.

The man was dressed in typical island fashion—surfer-type shorts and a loose print shirt. He was wearing deck sandals and a red baseball cap, and carrying a worn bank deposit bag.

Dar frowned. A lot of people on the island looked just like this guy. So what was it? The walk? The attitude...

"Dar." Kerry's voice broke into her concentration.

"Yeah?"

Kerry lowered her voice to a whisper. "I think that's one of the pirates that attacked us yesterday."

Oh. Duh. "Guess that's why he seemed familiar," Dar whispered back.

They watched the man push several things across to the teller, seemingly relaxed and at ease. The teller took them and processed them, smiling at the man, apparently familiar with him.

"What are we going to do?" Kerry murmured. "If we recognized him, he'll probably recognize us."

Dar gauged the distance between them. "He didn't on the way in," she said. "Let's just turn around and see what happens."

Kerry shifted in her chair and looked at Dar. "Okay, but what are we going to do after that?"

"Maybe we can find out what his name is."

"And report him to the police?" Kerry glanced quickly behind her, then back. "Dar, he's obviously a known quantity here."

"Uh huh." Dar didn't seem surprised.

The inner door opened and the bank officer reappeared. He was carrying a small box, and he looked around as he crossed back to his desk. His eyes fell on the two men. "Ah. Morning, Mr. Chasiki."

The man turned at his name and smiled, then his eyes slipped past the banker and focused on Dar's face.

Uh oh. Dar thought fast, meeting his eyes briefly, then moving on, hoping she was projecting an air of profound disinterest. She'd seen the recognition as he looked at her.

"Yeah, yeah," the man answered the bank manager. "Great holiday, yeah?" His voice was tense.

"Very good, thanks." The officer sat down and put the box in the center of his desk. He pulled over some paperwork and filled out a few forms. "All right, Ms. Roberts, let me just fill this out and you'll be all set."

"Thanks." Dar rested her elbows on the desk and resisted the urge to turn and look at the pirate. Next to her, Kerry was leaning back with her arms folded, her back mostly toward the teller. The blonde woman looked tense, a furrow creasing her brow.

"Here you go. Please sign here" Mr. Steel indicated a space on the form. "I've made a copy of your driver's license, and here's that back." He handed her the card.

Dar picked up the pen and studied the form, her ears cocked as she heard footsteps approaching them. They stopped just behind her, and she watched the officer's eyes from the corner of her own, seeing them go up and over her shoulder curiously. She signed her name on the form.

"Something you need, sir?" the officer asked.

"Nah. Just thinking." The pirate spoke from just behind them. "Later." The footsteps receded and the door opened, letting in the sound of wind and the street.

Dar pushed the paper back over to the officer. "There you go." She leaned back, feeling the tension relax from her shoulders. "Always quiet like this here?"

Mr. Steel took the paper. "Oh, mostly," he said. "Fridays, payday, it gets a little hectic." He smiled, then looked curiously at Dar. "Beg your pardon, Ms. Roberts, but did you know Mr. Chasiki, the gentleman who was just here?"

Dar glanced Kerry's way. Kerry's eyes widened slightly and her pale brows lifted. "He seemed a little familiar," she temporized. "Why?"

"Oh, he was staring at you, and I was just wondering," the officer said easily.

Dar turned and gazed at the closed door, then looked back at Mr. Steel. She shrugged. "Who is he?"

The banker shrugged back. "He's known to be a ladies' man," he said. "Bit of a rogue, but a generous one." He handed over the box. "Here you go, Ms. Roberts. I hope you do take care and put this somewhere soon. It's really not a good idea to be carrying it."

Dar stood and lifted her backpack, then opened the box and transferred the bound stacks of bills to the pack. "Thanks for the warning." She finished stashing the cash and zipped up the pack, handing him back the box. "Nice doing business with you." She shouldered the knapsack, adjusting it around her shoulders and pulling the straps tight. "Ker?"

Kerry gave the officer a brief smile, rising and joining Dar as they headed for the door. She put a hand on her partner's arm as they exited the bank, both of them looking left and right as the sunlight hit them. "Dar, that was creepy."

"That was very creepy," Dar acknowledged. "C'mon. I want to get hold of Bud and get rid of this cash before we do anything else." Her senses were jangling. "Last thing we need is for that Chasiki to follow us and hold us up."

Kerry looked around nervously. "You really think he would?"

"I'd rather not find out." Dar took out her cell phone and opened it. She dialed Bud's number. After two rings, he picked up. "Bud, it's Dar." Dar spoke into the receiver crisply. "Did you get hold of your friend?" She waited for the answer. "Good. We're heading back to the hotel now." She closed the phone and clipped it to her belt. "We'll take care of that, then ..."

"Seeing the pirate kinda throws a wrench into things, huh?" Kerry asked. "At least we have his name now."

"And he has mine," Dar reminded her. "Kerry, I don't know if going to the police here is a good idea." She started walking back toward the hotel. "I just don't know who we can trust. If we go to the cops and tell them, and they're in on it, then what? They're gonna want to protect him."

Kerry sighed. "Yikes."

Dar shook her head as they crossed the street and headed for the long climb up. They'd walked for just a few minutes when Dar heard footsteps behind them. She used an appreciative look around to glance behind her, and sure enough, two men were meandering up the slope after them. "Son of a bitch."

Kerry looked. "Cripes," she muttered. "Maybe they're not following us, Dar. We could just be a little paranoid."

True. Dar swerved, and the smell of coffee and hot dough hit her. She pulled Kerry into a shop they were passing and went over to the counter. "Two johnnycakes and two coffees, please."

The man behind the counter handed both over readily, accepting Dar's cash and giving her change. Dar picked up one of the cakes and handed Kerry the other, then took her coffee. She strolled casually to the entrance and leaned against it, waiting. Kerry eased up behind her.

At first there was only silence. Then abruptly, the two men passed the shop, talking casually to each other and not giving Dar so much as a second glance.

Kerry released her held breath and took a bite of her cake. "Mm," she murmured.

"Good call," Dar complimented quietly. "C'mon."

They eased out of the shop and continued up the stepped street. "This would be a great morning workout," Kerry commented, almost dizzy with relief.

"Oh yeah," Dar agreed. She finished her cake and dusted off her fingers, then took a sip of the coffee. "Ugh. Gross." She stopped dead and looked for a garbage can.

"I was wondering when you'd realize you took it from there without any cream or sugar." Kerry smiled. "I figured we were going to toss the stuff in those guys' faces. I never dreamed you'd try to drink it."

"Yeah, yeah." Dar disposed of the offending beverage and resumed her climb. She was still uneasy, and the inn at the top of the hill seemed a very long way off. Three-quarters of the way up, she heard footsteps again. She glanced at Kerry, and they both looked around. Six men were coming up after them. They looked at each other. "Race ya," Kerry murmured, increasing her pace to a jog.

Dar followed suit and they powered up the steps. They heard the men behind them speed up as well. Twenty more steps to go and they'd be at the inn level. Ten, and they heard the men catching up. Five, and Dar could hear the heavy breathing. Then they topped the steps and were in front of the inn. Dar spotted Bud waiting in front of the door for them and she headed in his direction, Kerry sticking to her like a flea on a dog.

The steps behind them stopped. Dar slowed her pace and risked a glance behind her, only to see the men clustered at the top, apparently in an argument. Bud watched the two women curiously as they approached, cocking his head as they pulled up next to him. Bud looked past them to the men. "What's up?"

"Tell you later," Dar said. "Let's go inside."

Bud was staring over her shoulder, his eyes narrowed. Dar turned to look, but the six men were melting back down the stairs and were out of sight a moment later. She glanced back at Bud. "You know those guys?"

Bud looked at her.

"Let's go inside," Dar repeated.

CHEAPSIDE GUIDO WAS waiting as they entered the lobby. He spotted Bud and nudged the big gorilla he had with him, then his eyes fell on Dar. A disagreeable smile crossed his face as Dar, Kerry, and Bud reached them. "Bring your girlfriends? You switched sides, there, Buddy?"

"You want your money? Then shut up," Bud replied gruffly. He indicated a small side room with a couple chairs in it.

"Oh, so now you're telling me to shut up?" Guido snorted. "You little horse's ass."

Dar was already very much on edge. Her temper was at the

breaking point, and for a moment she felt all better sense leave her as she stalked toward the nasty, greasy man. She'd only taken two steps when she felt a hand gripping her shirt from the back, and then an even firmer grip on the back of her shorts.

"He's not worth it." Kerry spoke in an almost normal tone. "You'll just get your hands dirty, and it'll take a week to wash off the stench."

Guido spun and looked at her, then tilted his head up and found Dar's set, angry face confronting him. He looked like he very much wanted to laugh, but a second look convinced him to just walk into the room behind Bud. "Figures you have girls protecting your pansy ass."

Bud went stone-faced. "You got the papers?"

"You got the money?" Guido tossed back at him. Bud looked at Dar. Guido turned. "Oh, right. Well, chickie, I don't take no friggin' Platinum cards."

Dar studied him, then she unhitched the pack from her back and set it on the small table in the room. "You're right," she said to Kerry. "Definitely not worth it." She pulled out several stacks of hundreds and tossed them at Guido. They hit him in the chest, and he grabbed at them. She pulled out three or four more stacks and chucked them as well.

"Hey!" Guido lost one and it bounced off the floor. "Cut that out, freak!"

Dar whipped the final two stacks at him. They hit him in the face. She turned her back on him and zipped up her bag, trying to let her raw nerves settle before she had to turn back around and continue the conversation. She heard the rustle as he captured the bound bills.

"Where's the papers?" Bud asked in a toneless voice.

"Hold on to your pecker. You should be usta that," Guido muttered. "I gotta count this."

Dar turned and sat down in the nearest chair, her knees finally giving out as the adrenaline stopped pumping. Kerry settled on the arm of the chair and Dar curled a hand around Kerry's knee, the touch soothing her nerves. Guido had given his muscle man most of the stacks, and he was laboriously counting one. The thug was watching Dar with a dour glare.

Bud sat down in one of the other chairs, mostly focusing his gaze on the floor.

Kerry put a hand on Dar's neck, her fingers working gently at the rigid muscles. She could almost feel the vibrating tension in her partner, and though she completely understood Dar's silent rage, she'd been called worse by far better than that little greasy punk. "If you're going to have to take your shoes off for that, let me know so I can get the window open," she remarked casually.

Guido looked up at her. "Shut up."

"Why?" Kerry asked. "I've talked to animals since I was a kid. Most of them were better looking than you, though."

"You looking to get hurt, chickie?"

Kerry smiled charmingly at him. "The both of you together aren't a quarter of the man it would take to do that."

Dar chuckled and rubbed the bridge of her nose.

"You got a big mouth," the thug told Kerry.

"That's all right. You've got a pea brain," Kerry responded. "And I can always shut up."

"Huh?"

"All right." Guido finished counting one stack. He took another and pressed it down with his thumb and forefinger, matching it against the one in his hand. They were exactly even. He repeated the process with the rest of the stacks, then handed the money back to the thug. "Sucker girlie. What'd he promise you for this? Don't tell me a good time." Guido pulled a wad of papers out of his back pocket and threw them at Bud. "You got real lucky, fag. One more week and we'd have torched that shithole."

"Guess I did," Bud answered softly.

"Not nearly as lucky as *you* did," Dar remarked flatly, giving Guido a level, cold stare.

Guido snorted. "Lousy doing business with you. Don't call again." He stuffed the cash into a plastic bag the lackey had in his pocket and motioned him to leave. They walked out without looking back, heading for the front door to the hotel.

Dar slowly let a breath out. "That sucked," she enunciated with precision.

"Mm. Glad it's over," Kerry agreed, moving her hands around to give Dar's shoulders some serious attention. "Makes me wish we'd had them embed dye packets in the bills."

Bud glanced at her. "You're pretty damn funny."

Kerry grinned back. "I'm really, really glad we could do this for you," she told Bud honestly. "No one should have to deal with assholes like that." She felt Dar's muscles unlock under her hands.

Bud looked down at the papers again, slowly shaking his head at them. "It was a hard choice to have to make," he admitted. "I hate taking help from anyone."

"Yeah." Dar spoke up at last. "I know the feeling." She stretched out her legs and slumped in the chair. "I can't do it either," she said. "Ask for help, I mean."

Bud glanced at her, then looked at Kerry, who was still industriously kneading. "Right."

Dar caught the look. "She doesn't count," she said. "Besides, she doesn't wait to be asked."

Kerry leaned over and gave Dar a kiss on the top of her head.

"Okay," she said. "Now that's over."

Bud shifted, giving her a wary look.

"Talk to me about pirates," Dar said. "At the bank, I spotted the guy running the pirate boat that tried to board us. He was making a deposit."

Bud chewed his lower lip. "Can we talk upstairs?" he finally said. "Charlie's supposed to call any time."

Upstairs sounded good. Dar felt exhausted. A pot of strong coffee and a nice milkshake were really what she wanted, and she figured room service could probably take care of that for her. "Sure." She got up, glancing at Kerry when Kerry took the backpack. "Hey."

"It's okay, honey." Kerry gave her a kiss on the shoulder. "I can handle it, really."

Kerry was, Dar realized, handling the entire thing a lot better than she was. She thought about that as they walked up the short flight of stairs to their room. Was she letting the stress get the better of her? Was she too much out of her element? *Better get your damn head on straight and stop reacting to everything. What the hell is wrong with you, Dar?*

"Hey, Dar?" Kerry glanced back. "Are you going to try calling Wharton?"

Dar studied a point in the middle of Kerry's shoulder blades. "Let's wait 'til we get to the room, and let me sit down and think," she said. "I don't want to complicate this whole damn thing even more than it already is."

"Okay." Kerry nodded. "Good, because I was just getting a really bad feeling about you calling him. He's just...it's too unknown a quantity. This whole thing is just getting weird."

Dar felt slightly relieved. "Oh, so it's not just me," she muttered, as they stopped in front of their room and she unlocked the door with the large iron key.

Kerry pushed the door open and walked in, then stopped short. "Son of a bitch."

Bud peeked past Dar's shoulder as Dar edged into the room in back of Kerry.

The room was in total shambles. Everything had been ripped apart as though a tornado had blown through the place.

"Damn," Bud uttered. "They mess up your stuff?"

Kerry let out a disgusted breath. "We didn't have any here." She lifted her hands in utter exasperation and let them fall. "One bag, with two pairs of jammies and some toothpaste."

Dar moved through the room, shaking her head. She walked over to the phone and picked it up, waiting for the operator to answer. "I need to speak with the manager." There was a pause. "Your name? Mr. Brack. Well, Mr. Brack, we have a problem. Our room has been ransacked." After another pause, she said, "The door wasn't broken into. So whoever on your staff was paid off to let someone in here..."

Kerry could hear a loud voice protesting all the way across the room.

"Would you like to come up here and explain how else they got in?" Dar asked. "Good. See you shortly." She dropped the phone into its cradle. "If those bastards have gone anywhere near the boat, they're toast."

"I'll go check." Kerry started out the door, only to be hauled to an abrupt halt. 'Whoa!" She turned to find Dar hanging on to the back of her shirt.

"Not by yourself," Dar told her quietly. "And before you say it, yes, I know you're a big girl and you can take care of yourself, and I'm being an overprotective ninny."

Kerry shut her jaw and her face scrunched into a wry grin.

"I'll go," Bud interrupted, going to the door and exiting before Dar could reply.

"B..." Dar looked at the closed door. "Damn."

"Bet he wanted to get out of talking about pirates." Kerry sighed. "Dar, would you look at this place? What a bunch of jerks." She walked over to their one bag and examined it. The contents had been pulled out, then carelessly shoved back in, and she felt her blood begin to boil.

A soft knock came at the door and Dar went to it, pulling it open to find the hotel manager and a man in a security guard's uniform standing there. She stepped back and gestured to them to enter. "C'mon in."

Both men entered and looked around. The manager's eyes widened at the state of the room. "This is..." the manager started, then stopped. "I've never had..."

The security guard seemed just as bewildered. "Sir..." He cleared his throat. "Ma'am, when did you find this?"

"Sixty seconds before I called you," Dar stated. "I want an explanation." She folded her arms over her chest and gave the manager a cold stare.

Mr. Brack collected himself. "No one but security and the housekeeper have the keys," he said. "We have checked the security logs, and no one was allowed into this room. I have called the chief housekeeper. Perhaps she can shed some light on what has happened."

"Oh!"

They all turned to see a small, wizened woman in the doorway, dressed in a neat, gray uniform. Dar guessed this was the housekeeper. The woman entered slowly and looked around, wide-eyed.

"What has happened here? Why was this done?" She looked at
Dar. "What have you done this for to the nice lady's room?"

The manager drew breath. "Constantina, this room is
registered to these two ladies here. What do you mean?"

The woman drew back in dismay. "These ladies? Oh...but..."
She twisted her fingers together. "Oh, sir, I am so sorry. A very nice
woman came to me when I was cleaning, and she said she left her
key inside the room. You know so many guests to do that, so..." Her
eyes moved over the room. "She said this was her room."

The manager frowned. "And you didn't check?"

"She was a nice woman, sir," the housekeeper protested. "Nice
clothes, with rings, and why should I think she was not telling me
the truth?"

The manager looked like he'd swallowed a live cockroach and
it was crawling around inside his stomach. "Constantina, go to my
office and wait there for me," he said with quiet restraint. "Jan,
please bring your camera up here and take photographs of
everything." He turned to Dar and Kerry. "I will have you moved to
a new room immediately while we start our investigation. I will
also be calling in the police."

The housekeeper's eyes widened.

"We can give you the probable identity of the person you're
looking for," Kerry said. "We've been pestered by some people
since our arrival in the islands." She added, "I'd like a chance to
discuss that with the police as well."

The manager nodded. "Certainly. Constantina, please." He
grasped the woman's arm and steered her outside. "The bellman
will be up to move you in just a moment."

"It's okay. It's just this." Dar held up the bag. "All the damage
was done to your hotel, not our property."

A facial tic started on the manager's face. He left and took his
two employees with him.

For a moment, the room was silent. Dar and Kerry looked at
each other, then at the same time, lifted their hands in a shrug and
let them drop. "This is nuts," Dar sighed. "This is just nuts."

Kerry's eyes narrowed. "You got that guy Wharton's phone
number?"

Dar regarded her warily. "His office, yeah."

"Gimme."

Dar removed a slip of paper from the backpack and took out
her own cell phone. "I'll handle it." She took a breath and
composed herself.

"Dar—"

"I know," Dar cut her off. "I know you can do this, but I really,
really want to."

Kerry subsided.

Dar opened the cell and dialed, then put the phone to her ear.

A low, growling voice answered.

Dar started off with being civil. "I need to speak with Mr. Patrick Wharton."

"Where the hell did you get this number?"

Okay, so much for that. "Does it matter? You Wharton?"

"Who the hell is this?"

Dar listened to the voice. It was middle-aged, had a slight rasp, and a distinct New England accent. "Someone who's been just east of St. Johns," she replied. "Now, are you Wharton, or not?"

There was silence before the voice grudgingly said, "Yeah."

"Good," Dar answered. "Then maybe you can explain why I've got your hired hands crawling all over my last nerve."

"Look, lady, I don't know who the hell you are—"

"*You...*" Dar barked at top volume, "don't have to know who I am, mister!" She drew in a breath. "All you need to know is that the two-bit amateur you're paying top dollar for couldn't find his way out of a paper bag with instructions printed on the inside of it in twenty-four-point black letters."

"What?"

"I..." Dar dropped her voice to a low purr, "have what you're looking for."

"Who the devil are you!"

"You wouldn't know who I was if I told you my name," Dar told him quietly. "And I'd have been a much happier person if I'd never heard your name or the name of the jackass you hired, trust me."

"Now you listen here—"

"No, *you* listen to me." Dar overrode him. "You get your little paid pirate the hell out of here or I'll go to the cops and blow your little scheme wide open."

There was silence, and then a click.

Dar eyed the phone. "Hung up on me," she commented.

Kerry scratched her nose. "Well, honey, I think you got across the message you were going for."

"Did I?" Dar mused, as Kerry walked over and slid an arm around her waist.

"Yep," Kerry assured her. "I wouldn't want to be a fly on DeSalliers' boat walls, unless I could swim really well."

"Ma'am?" The security guard was back with a smaller man. "Jasar will take you to your new room, okay?"

Kerry picked up their overnight bag. "Lead on."

Grumbling, Dar put the phone away and followed, shouldering the backpack. Her conversation with Wharton hadn't been very satisfactory, and she ran over the brief exchange in her head as she walked down the hallway. Should she have started out more

professionally, explained who she was? Full of self-doubt, Dar felt
her brow furrowing. Maybe she should have let Kerry handle it
after all. Dar felt very off balance, and she wasn't even sure why
she felt that way. She didn't like it.

They stopped in front of a door, and the desk clerk opened it
for them. "Here you go, ladies." He stood back to let them enter,
then followed them in and shut the door.

This room was on the corner of the cliff, and roughly three
times the size of the other. It had a wraparound balcony and a
general sense of plushness the other room, though comfortable, had
lacked. "The manager said he would be up shortly, with the police,"
the desk clerk said softly. "Is there anything else we can get you?"

Dar dropped her backpack on the couch then sat down next to
it. "Yeah," she said. "A pot of strong coffee and a big chocolate
milkshake."

"Make that two," Kerry added. "Thanks."

"Right away." The desk clerk left.

Kerry took her time exploring the new room. She opened the
door next to the bathroom, exposing a hot tub neatly sunken into a
wooden deck. "This is nice," she concluded, peeking out the
window. "I guess this is the 'please don't sue us' suite." She turned,
leaning against the windowsill and regarding Dar. "Okay, so where
are we?"

Dar let her head rest on the back of the couch. "I wish I knew,"
she admitted. "Well, one thing — that idiot woman wasted her time.
Did she really think we'd be stupid enough to leave
something...anything...valuable in that hotel room?"

Kerry exhaled. "Good question." She got off the sill and
crossed over to sit down on the couch next to Dar. "Maybe she
didn't. Maybe she was just trying to prove a point. I got...ah...kinda
nasty with her earlier."

Dar's brow rose. Kerry didn't usually go the nasty route. "You
did?"

"Yeah." The blonde woman looked a touch sheepish. "I was
just so pissed off at her, at them, at..." She let out a disgusted sigh.

Dar turned and leaned forward, gazing at Kerry. "Is this whole
thing driving you nuts?"

Kerry nodded.

"So it's not just me?"

Kerry shook her head. "No," she said. "I'm just so upset."

Dar edged closer and took her hands. "About what,
sweetheart?" She was more than glad to focus her attention on
Kerry rather than their perplexing problem.

"Well it's... I feel really stupid saying this, but I'm just really
ticked off that they're messing with our vacation," Kerry confessed.
"I feel like they're robbing me, robbing us, and it's making me very

mad." Inexplicably, she felt tears welling up. "It's not fair, Dar. I know we didn't get into this on purpose, and we've just been reacting to all this stuff, but..."

Reacting. Dar felt a puzzle piece slip into place. "I know," she murmured. "I think that's part of the problem: we're not in control of any of this; it just keeps rolling over us."

Kerry sighed. "It's not that I don't want to solve this stupid thing."

Dar decided Kerry needed a hug. Accordingly, she slid an arm around her and pulled her closer, then enfolded her in both arms. She felt Kerry's exhalation warm against her skin. "All right," she murmured. "Let's hold on a minute and see if we can get a handle on this."

"Buh." Kerry buried her face into Dar's shoulder. "I want my milkshake."

Dar chuckled faintly. "Listen."

"I'm listening."

"We fixed Bud and Charlie's problem."

Kerry nodded. "Right."

"We ticked off Wharton, and maybe now he'll call DeSalliers on the carpet."

"Right."

"Here's what we're gonna do. The cops are on their way here to talk to us. We're gonna tell them the whole seven-layer Mexican bean dip these last couple days have been. The pirates, DeSalliers, the works."

"Okay."

"Then we're gonna go out, and dive a gorgeous blue hole and see that cave I was telling you about before we left Miami."

"Ooh. This is getting more interesting."

"Then we're gonna have dinner on the boat under the stars." Dar rubbed Kerry's ear gently. "And when we get back here, we're going to enjoy that hot tub with a bottle of cold wine and a big bowl of strawberries."

"Mm." Kerry relaxed against Dar's body. "That sounds awesome," she said. "But you know what?"

"What?"

"I'd be just as happy to spend the entire time just like this instead," Kerry said. "I like the idea of telling the police everything, Dar. Even if they are in on whatever is going on with the pirates, it would make me feel better just to say it."

Dar nodded. "So here's how I think we should play it." She felt a little more stable. "Let's not mention that we know who the pirate is, or that we know it's not the first time. We'll do the outraged-American-executives-on-interrupted-holiday routine."

"Gee, that's a stretch." Kerry chuckled.

"You know what I mean."

"Like we did with the hotel manager." Kerry nodded. "I get it." She considered. "Because if we tell him all we know, the first question they're going to ask is why didn't we come forward before?"

"Mm."

"And, why we didn't just leave the island and get out of the situation."

Dar sighed.

"Wish we had?"

"Yeah." Dar nodded. "But you know what? Once they'd gotten it into their damn stupid heads that we had something from that wreck, I'm not sure we could have."

No. Kerry thought back over the last few days. Their big mistakes were diving the wreck, and saving Bob. She straightened a little inside the circle of Dar's arms, not sure she would have avoided either event, despite what they were going through now. She thought about Dar's observation. "You know, I think you're right."

Dar grinned. "However, if you want to go on feeling crummy about it, I'll be glad to sit here and comfort you all day long."

Kerry started laughing. "God, you know, this whole thing is just so ridiculous," she said. "The only thing that could top it, is if it started snowing."

Dar glanced at the window in pure reflex. "Right." She unclipped her phone and dialed a number. "Better tell Bud what room we're in." She listened, but after two rings the phone switched to voice mail. "Hm." Dar waited for the beep, then spoke. "Bud, it's Dar. Give me a buzz when you get this, and I'll tell you where we are." She closed the phone.

Kerry eyed her. "You don't think he's going to run off, do you? He seemed really spooked about those men who were following us up the hill."

"I don't know." Dar cocked her head as she heard footsteps approaching. "Ah. That's either room service or the cops." She reluctantly released Kerry and went to answer the knock. "Or both."

Outside the door were the manager, a tall, thin man in a khaki uniform, a room service waiter, and most importantly, two chocolate shakes and a pot of coffee. Dar opened the door and waved them all in, neatly stealing one of the shakes as the waiter passed by.

The manager waited until the waiter put down the tray and Dar signed the check. After the man left, the manager cleared his throat. "Ms. Roberts and Ms. Stuart—this is Captain Alalau, who is in charge of the police. I have asked him to come and investigate this destruction of our property and of your peace of mind."

Kerry almost applauded at the speech. The police captain seemed reserved, but politely friendly. "Captain, why don't you sit down? This might take a few minutes to explain,"she said. "And you too, Mr. Brack."

"Thank you, Ms. Stuart," the policeman answered in a gracious tone. He and the manager sat down. "You are most kind. I understand how upset you and Ms. Roberts must have been to come and find your room in such disarray."

"After the week we've had?" Dar came around the couch and handed Kerry her shake, then sat down next to her on the couch facing the two men. "You could say that, yes."

The officer leaned forward. "Mr. Brack tells me you knew this woman? Is this true?"

"We think so," Kerry said. "Based on the description from the housekeeper, she's one of two people who have been bothering us while we were here on the island."

"Ahh." Captain Alalau nodded. He had a handsome, finely sculpted face, and almost nonexistent hair. "That would be Mr. DeSalliers' two employees, would it not?"

Dar's eyebrow twitched. "You know him?"

The captain produced an almost imperceptible sigh. "Ms. Roberts, there are few here who do not," he said. "He is a very well-known, well-connected man here, and is used to getting his way. His agent came to speak with me today, in fact, to lodge a complaint."

Dar's other brow lowered. "Against us?" she hazarded a dour guess.

The officer pressed his lips into a faint smile. "No. Against another man they claim is encroaching on a wreck they are attempting to recover."

"Ah," Kerry said. "Bob."

Now it was the officer's turn to look surprised. "You know this man? We have been searching for him. There are charges being pressed." He looked from Kerry to Dar and back. "I have a warrant for his arrest."

"Ah."

The manager glanced between them, obviously at sea. "If they are after this other man, why then did they come into your hotel room?"

Dar leaned back. "All right." She lifted one hand. "Let's just start from the beginning, shall we?"

The officer took a pad and a pencil from his pocket. He scribbled a few notes. "That is an excellent idea," he said. "I am sure we can clear up this unfortunate situation once we have all the facts."

Kerry sucked on her shake and tried not to smile, hoping the facts didn't, in fact, send the man off screaming. She liked this policeman. Besides, she really wanted to hear what he'd been told about Bob.

Chapter
Twenty-two

"YOU KNOW SOMETHING, Dar?" Kerry was sprawled on her back on the big, comfortable bed. "I didn't realize just how wild the last couple of days had been until we told someone about them and watched their brain dribble out their ears."

"Errff." Dar made a small sound of bemused agreement. "I thought he was going to fall over when we told him about shooting at the pirates. Did you see that?"

Kerry nodded. "He knows something." She looked at Dar. "You were right. He was really relieved when you told him no one appeared to have gotten hurt."

"And did you see how fast he changed the subject?" Dar cracked her knuckles. "All right. So now they know everything."

"And boy, I bet they wish they didn't."

Dar smiled. "The captain said he was going to haul in our detective friends if he could find them, and he's contacting DeSalliers to make sure he leaves us alone."

"I think we put in a few points for Bob," Kerry mused. "But we'd better warn him to lay low." She drew up her knees and stretched, arching her back. "But I'm really glad we got the police involved. I feel a lot better now."

Dar's ears twitched approvingly at that. "Yeah, even if he did look at us like we'd dropped a ticking bomb onto his desk," she agreed. "So, you up for a dive now that we've put things to bed?"

Kerry folded her hands across her stomach and considered. "Yeah," she said after a moment. "I don't feel sick at all today. A dive would be nice." She turned her head. "What did you mean about a blue hole?"

Dar grinned and held out a hand. "Come with me, Yankee. I'll show ya."

Unable to resist that kind of invitation, Kerry rolled up off the bed and joined Dar, taking her hand as Dar shouldered the backpack and they headed for the door. "Make sure you lock it." She had their overnight bag in her hand, just in case.

Dar snorted. "I'm willing to bet anyone who opens this door for someone gets their fingers cut off." She opened her cell phone and dialed Bud's number again. "C'mon, Bud, you damn big chicken. Answer the phone."

But still, it went to voice mail. Dar shook her head. "Bud, we're heading out for some water time. Let us know how Charlie's doing, okay?" She considered a moment. "We just got finished telling the cops everything. I think we're clear now. Gimme a call." With a frown, she closed the phone and restored it to her belt. "Damn stubborn old mackerel."

"Give him the benefit of the doubt, Dar," Kerry chuckled. "Maybe he's getting Charlie out of the hospital. If it were me, I wouldn't be answering my phone either."

"Mmph." Dar rocked her head from side to side. "He doesn't call back in a little while, I'll call the hospital and find out what's going on."

They walked together to the lobby and out the front door. The sun was out, and everything seemed peaceful and quiet, back to the sleepy friendliness of normality again. They made it down to the dock without incident.

The docks were fairly busy; boats were pulling in and out. Dar noticed there was no sign of DeSalliers' monster. They reached their slip and she paused to check the boat over before they boarded, but the vessel seemed untouched, floating in its assigned space. "Looks okay."

Kerry hopped over and jumped to the stern deck, going to the door and peering inside.

Dar unlocked the door and pushed it open, and they entered to find it reassuringly just as they'd left it. Even the apple Kerry had left on the countertop was still in place, beckoning invitingly to her as she crossed the floor and took possession of it.

Dar continued on and poked her head into the rooms in the bow, then returned looking satisfied. "Well, if they did search the place, they didn't leave any marks."

Kerry nodded and took a bite of the apple. It crunched pleasantly, mostly sweet and a little tart against her tongue. It felt good to be back on board their traveling home, and she felt herself relaxing and looking forward to their dive. "Tell you what. You go get the gerbils hustling, and I'll check out our gear. Deal?"

"Deal." Dar circled her and leaned in for a kiss. The brief notion lengthened as Kerry put her apple down and returned the kiss with gentle passion. When they parted, she rested her forehead against Kerry's and nibbled the tip of her nose affectionately. "I think things are looking up."

"I think they are, too." Kerry tilted her head up and brushed her lips against Dar's again, coaxing her into a longer, deeper exploration. "Oh, definitely," she whispered, lifting her hand to caress Dar's cheek. She felt the skin under her thumb move as Dar smiled.

They loitered together a few minutes longer, then reluctantly parted and went about their separate tasks. Kerry ducked down into the gear room and set aside their buoyancy compensators. She felt the engines rumble to life as she carefully checked Dar's regulator, connecting it to a single tank they kept strapped to the wall for exactly that purpose and pressurizing it.

Cocking her head to one side, she listened for leaks, then shut the valve and repeated the process with her own equipment. Satisfied, she slung both regulators over her shoulder and picked up the BCs on her way out the door.

The boat shifted as she traveled, her body compensating almost automatically for the motion. The view out the windows changed as Dar directed the vessel out and away from the docks. Kerry caught a breath of cool, sea air as it rushed through the portholes, and she found herself smiling broadly as she stepped out onto the stern deck.

What a gorgeous day it was. She tipped her head back. The sky was clear, deep blue, with only a couple of fluffy clouds down on the horizon. There was a nice breeze, and as they headed out across the water the spray from the boat's wake whisked through the air and dusted Kerry with its damp richness.

With a chuckle, she went to the tank cabinet and opened it, removing two of the tanks inside and lifting them with a grunt. She carried them over to the bench and set them in their holders, letting the BCs slide down onto the bench next to them. "Hey, Dar?"

"Yeah?" Dar's voice carried down from the flying bridge.

"This blue hole thing a good place for pictures?"

Dar laughed.

"I'll take that as a yes." Kerry finished readying their gear and trooped back inside to get her camera and its waterproof housing.

DAR SLOWED THE boat as she approached the lee side of the island, its overhanging cliff structures circling them with wild grandeur. The sun poured in over her shoulders, reflecting off the glittering surface of the sea in molten darts, and she could see the pale green of the shallow waters deepening to a deep clear blue as it neared the cliffs. Since the open topped cave wasn't a popular choice with the beginning divers who peopled the cattle boats, the few other dive boats nearby were smaller ones. Dar picked a spot in relatively open water and circled it. "Ker?"

"Yeah?" Kerry was on the bow, peering avidly at everything.

"What have I got under the keel?"

Kerry looked down, shading her eyes. "Sand."

"You sure?"

Kerry leaned over, coming perilously close to examining the surface in a real, personal way. "Yeah. Go ahead; let it loose."

Dar hit the switch for the anchor and heard the rumble as it released and plunged into the water. Then she cut the engines and stood up, stripped off her shirt and let it drop onto the back of the chair. She adjusted the strap on her swimsuit and made her way to the ladder, climbing down it to the lower deck. Now that the engine was off, she could hear the lap of the water and the rustling crash of the waves against the stone walls of the cliffs nearby. Kerry joined her a moment later, and they stood side by side near their gear.

"Weren't you going to call about Charlie?" Kerry suddenly remembered. "At the hospital?"

Dar paused in the act of fastening her regulator to her tank. "Damn. You're right." She shook her head. "Hang on." She walked over to the cabinet near the door, and then stopped in realization. "I don't think I have the number."

Kerry had connected her tank to her BC. "Is there Information out here?" she wondered aloud. "Or, the hotel probably would know the number."

"Good thought." Dar dialed the number of their hotel, listened, and then scowled. "Busy." She tapped the cell phone against her neck as she thought. "Well, let's go under, and when we come back up, I'll try it again."

Dar put the cell phone in the drawer of the cabinet and closed it, then walked over and got into her BC, fastening the belly strap and standing up. The heavy tank shifted and she had to make a few adjustments, then she buckled the front buckles and turned, waiting for Kerry to stand.

Kerry preferred to buckle everything first. "Okay, ready." She stood upright, then hopped a little, getting everything settled over her center of balance as much as she could. "Let's go."

They each picked up fins and mask and walked to the back of the boat. Dar let down the dive ladder and opened the back gate, then rested her hand on the gate as she slipped on her fins. "We're gonna go in, then just go down for ten feet or so. We've got to swim over to where the water changes color."

"Okay." Kerry felt a little excited and a touch pleasantly scared. "I'll be right behind you."

Dar settled her mask over her face, pulled her hair out from under the rubber, and seated the seal firmly. Then she winked at Kerry and inserted her regulator in her mouth, took a big step off the back of the boat, and plunged into the water.

Kerry followed, clasping one hand over her camera case and one over her mouthpiece and mask as she stepped off the deck and entered the ocean. *Ooh.* Not expecting the relatively mild chill of the water, she opened her eyes wide in surprise. She'd been used to the almost bathtub warmth they'd been in so far, and this was definitely a change. Briefly, she wondered if putting her shortie wetsuit on over her swimsuit would have been a good idea, but after a moment her body adjusted and she let herself drift down to the shallow bottom in water so clear it was almost like glass.

Dar was resting on her knees on the sandy bottom, her dark hair floating freely about her head as she waited for Kerry to descend.

Kerry hugged her arms and rubbed them, giving Dar a wry look from behind her mask.

Dar slapped her head, then held her hands up in apology and pointed to the surface with a questioning look.

Kerry shook her head and pointed toward the rocks.

After a moment's hesitation, Dar flipped over and started swimming slowly, glancing behind her as Kerry caught up. They finned along, side by side, over the sandy bottom, moving through schools of colorful fish that scattered at their approach then re-formed behind them.

Kerry looked ahead to where she could see a rocky escarpment that rose almost to the surface. The waves were breaking over it, churning up the water and sending bits of debris tinkling down to the ocean floor. As they swam closer, Kerry could feel a current of cooler water and see the faintest hint of a shimmer. She unstrapped her camera and took a few shots of the approaching wall.

Dar swam ahead of her to the wall and caught hold of it, reaching out to grab Kerry as she came closer. She grinned around her mouthpiece and mimed snapping a shutter near her mask, indicating that there was about to be a good photo op. Kerry lifted her camera, but Dar held her hand over her eyes.

Oh, c'mon Dar. But Kerry humored her, covering her eyes as she trustingly allowed her partner to maneuver her over the escarpment. She sensed the rocks moving under her, felt her fins brush against them, and heard the sound of the waves close over her head. Then Dar pulled her hand away, and she could see.

For a moment, Kerry simply stared. Beyond the escarpment was a vast chasm in the sea, filled with the deepest blue water that was yet clear enough for the sunlight to penetrate down for what seemed to be hundreds of feet. It was gorgeous. She could see divers far off down the rocks, exploring the sides of the underwater canyon. Swarms of fish darted past them, reflecting the sun. Quickly, she lifted the camera and snapped off a few shots, then looked at Dar and simply pointed imperiously downward.

Dar smiled and pushed off the wall, letting the air out of her BC and sailing downward. Kerry shoved off after her, feeling a wash of cooler water ease past her as she descended. It was like floating into a fantasy world. The rocks on either side were crawling with life — schools of small fish and crustaceans hanging within the crevices. A swordfish whisked past her and she barely focused in time to catch it, only to have Dar tug her arm.

She turned to see a dark, gray figure lazily moving through the water and her eyes widened. She didn't need the up-thrust fin to identify the newcomer as a shark, and she quickly looked at Dar to gauge the danger.

Dar seemed quite relaxed. She pointed to her right. Kerry looked and saw a grouper bigger than she was nibbling at the wall; then they both jumped as two clown fish chased each other between them, brushing their legs as they sped toward the rocks.

They were still drifting down. At the bottom of the abyss, Kerry could now see a cave with a ripple above it. The water also seemed to mist. She pointed at it and looked at Dar in question.

Dar tapped the water bag Kerry had strapped under her tank, and mimed a gush of something welling up.

Oh. A freshwater spring. As they drifted closer, Kerry saw a crab making its way along the rocks. She turned and set the lens for a tight focus, then got a good shot of its blue-black shell against the tan rock. Looking down, she saw the bottom coming up. She turned and looked across the space, watching it fill with swarms of fish. As they swam in and out of the sunbeams, she could barely take one shot before another presented itself.

Lowering her camera for a brief moment, she checked her dive computer. At 120 feet, it was the deepest she'd ever been, but with the clarity of the water, it hardly seemed like more than a regular reef dive. She looked at Dar, who was watching her with a visible grin. Kerry held up three fingers, then made an O with her thumb and forefinger, then three fingers again. *Wow.*

Knowing that she only had about ten minutes at that depth, Kerry was determined to make the most of it. She moved off toward the underwater spring, and swam over the gap in the rock through which fresh water gushed. She put a hand into its path, feeling the pressure, and then she took a picture of it.

Turning, she saw Dar relaxing nearby, idly playing with a blowfish. The creature had blown itself up into a spiky ball, and Dar was bouncing it gently from hand to hand as she floated. Kerry quickly snapped a picture of them.

A flounder wafted past. It watched Kerry out of one eye as she turned in the water and photographed it. A sand shark squiggled below her, and she jumped a little, getting out of its way. Then she flipped over onto her back and took several shots looking straight up, through the clouds of fish to the surface.

Gorgeous.

Kerry felt lines of poetry erupt into her mind, and she just floated there for a moment, exulting in the sheer wonder around her.

At last, with an almost apologetic look, Dar swam over and tapped her wrist. Kerry nodded reluctantly, and they started drifting upward. She shot the rest of her roll of film on the way up, and wished she had a second.

DAR'S HEAD BROKE the surface, and she grabbed the boat's ladder. With a grunt, she pulled herself on board and dumped her fins and mask, then turned to help Kerry up out of the water as she felt her weight on the ladder.

Kerry barely waited to get her body clear of the sea before she pulled her regulator out of her mouth and squealed like a pig. "Eeeeeeeeeeehyhoooo!" She jumped onto the deck and hopped a few times, despite the fact that she still had her gear on. "Dar, that was by far the most awesome thing I've ever seen!"

Dar dumped her tank and dropped her mask and snorkel into the water well. "Guess I picked a good one, huh?" she asked with a grin. "Gimme your stuff."

Kerry unbuckled her vest and turned, shrugging out of it as the weight of the tank lifted. "Oh my freaking God!" She set her camera down and went to the cabinet to grab a towel to dry her face. As she opened the door, she heard a chirp. "Your cell's squeaking," she told Dar. "Bet Bud called back."

Dar turned from where she was putting up the gear. "Good. I'll get it in a minute."

"That place is great." Kerry walked over and dried Dar's face for her. "Did you see the caves that kind of went on from the bottom?"

Dar nodded. "I did. But you really don't want to go in there unless you've had cave training. It's dangerous."

"No problem." Kerry reached into the cooler and pulled out a bottle of water, uncapping it and drinking deeply. "I loved looking up and seeing the sun all that way up. Jesus!" She still felt exhilarated. "Dar, that was worth the entire damn trip."

Dar turned and walked over, wearing a very pleased grin. "Glad you liked it."

"Liked it?" Kerry put down the water and threw her arms around Dar instead, hugging her fiercely. "Errrooof. I loved it," she told her partner. "I got some fantastic pictures. I think I'm going to do a series of underwaters from this trip for the cabin."

"Mm." Dar exhaled in satisfaction. She liked underwater shots. She liked the cabin. She loved Kerry. So far as she was concerned, it all seemed to be falling together perfectly.

Kerry gave her one last squeeze and then released her. "How

about I make you a special surprise for dinner?"

"Surprise?" Dar inquired. "Like what?"

"Hardly be a surprise if I told you, sweetie." Kerry winked. "Trust me. You'll like it."

"Okay," Dar agreed amiably. "But as hungry as I am right now, you could serve me pureed asparagus on wheat toast and I'd like it."

Kerry chuckled. "I'm going to go shower and change." She gave Dar a pat on the side and disappeared into the cabin.

Dar wiped off her hands and picked up the still-chirping cell phone. She opened it and dialed her voice mail, listening to the phone as she dried herself. Her brow creased at the voice. Instead of the expected Bud, it was Charlie.

"Hey, Dar? This is Charlie. Listen, they let me loose from this joint, and I'm trying to get hold of Bud to come pick me up. Gimme a call here if you've seen him. Cell's not answering, and I'm figuring he got stuck in some damn poker game or something. Thanks."

"Huh." Dar studied the phone. "Now what the hell is going on?" She dialed the number Charlie had left and waited. "Charlie?"

"Hey, Dar?" Charlie's voice sounded relieved. "Glad to hear ya. You know where Buddy is?"

Dar took a breath. "Charlie, we thought he was with you," she said reluctantly. "He left our room this morning, and he was just going to check on the boat. Haven't heard from him since. I left him a couple of messages, but no answer."

Hearing voices, Kerry stuck her head out of the door. "What's up?"

'Bud's missing,' Dar mouthed.

"Well, damn," Charlie said. "Where the hell can he be?"

Good question. Dar ran her hand through her damp hair. "I don't know," she admitted. "Listen, we can..." Her eyes shifted to Kerry. "Um..."

"Go back, pick up Charlie, and find Bud." Kerry completed the statement with a wry smile. "Lift the anchor, Cap'n Dar." She patted Dar's arm and disappeared again.

"Charlie, stay put. We'll swing back by and get you," Dar relayed. "We're out off the western side of St. Thomas, so it'll take a little while." She acknowledged the grateful response and then closed the phone. She made her way to the ladder and climbed up, her mind turning thoughtfully to the new problem. Bud was a loner, no question about it. The fact that he'd disappeared someplace didn't really surprise her, but he hadn't told Charlie where he was, and that did.

He could just be in a bar somewhere, but Dar didn't think so. Too many things had been going south on her lately for it to be something as simple as that. In fact, she was beginning to think their vacation was cursed.

All we wanted was a week of peace and quiet. Dar sighed as she adjusted the throttles. Instead, they'd found nothing but trouble and more stress than she'd bargained for. Just wasn't damned fair.

DAR LOOKED UP as she heard Kerry climb the ladder, her motions slower and more hesitant than usual. "Kerry!" She grabbed for the throttles, slowing the boat as she watched her lover balancing an armful as she attempted to get up onto the upper deck. "You're gonna kill yourself!"

"Shh. I'm fine." Kerry managed to get her footing. "Relax and keep your eyes on the road, honey."

Dar increased her speed, but couldn't resist keeping one eye on Kerry as she made her way over and settled next to her. "What's that?"

"Well," Kerry set down a big covered plate, "we don't have time for me to make what I wanted, so I compromised." She uncovered the plate, revealing two neatly made peanut butter and jelly sandwiches and some cookies.

"Mm." True to form, Dar went right for the cookies, her eyes widening when she felt them. "They're warm!"

"Well, yeah." Kerry slid an arm around her. "I just made them. Thank goodness for Pillsbury." She put a Thermos on the console. "I figure we'll just have time to have lunch before we pull back into dock."

"You didn't have to do that."

Kerry leaned back, the wind blowing her pale hair off her face. "Of course I didn't. But we've gotten so little time to relax on this so-called vacation, I thought I'd better get in some lunch before we have to run off and save the world again."

"Mmph." Dar regarded the horizon with a grumpy expression. "I was just thinking about what a crock this vacation turned out to be."

"Well," the blonde reached over and gave her partner a scratch on the back, "at least we're together."

Dar made a low, grumbling noise.

"Honey, we're trouble magnets."

"Mm." Dar made a face.

Kerry's eyes twinkled a little. "We attracted each other, didn't we?"

"You saying we're both trouble?"

"Consider the last couple of days. What do you think?" Kerry asked wryly.

She had a point. Dar leaned back a bit, relaxing her tense grip on the throttles.

"PB and J?" Kerry nudged her and indicated the plate. "Get 'em before they blow away."

Dar agreeably selected half a sandwich and bit into it. "Wonder what the hell's going on?" she mumbled. "Bud just being a jerk, or..."

"With our luck on this trip?" Kerry laughed wryly. "Or. Definitely or. Maybe he tangled with that nasty shark we paid off this morning. They sure didn't seem friendly, and that thug seemed like the type to hold a grudge for no real reason."

Possible. Dar nodded as she chewed. "Might be. Or maybe he's checking on Rufus and the damn battery on his cell died."

They looked at each other and Kerry sighed. "You don't really believe that, do you?"

Dar shrugged and took a cookie. It was a nicely browned, chocolate chip cookie, Dar's favorite, despite Kerry's experimentation with many other exotic types. "Guess we'll just have to find out the hard way."

Her phone buzzed, making them both start. Dar frowned, put the cookie down, and picked up the phone. The caller ID showed a private number, making Dar's eyebrows hike up. She opened the phone. "Hello?"

"Hello, Roberts." DeSalliers' voice sounded cold and smug, not a good combination at any time.

"What the hell do yo—"

"Shut up!" the man bellowed. "You just shut up and listen to me, you bitch, if you want to see your little fag friend again."

Dar felt Kerry move closer, as she heard the words even over the rumble of the engines. A sick feeling washed over her and her nostrils twitched, but she carefully bit her tongue and withheld a retort. Her heart rate sped up, making a faint thunder in her ears as she waited.

Kerry slid an arm around Dar's waist and pressed her ear against the other edge of the phone.

"Roberts?"

"You said to shut up and listen." Dar heard the icy clip in her own tone, though her voice had dropped to almost its lowest register.

"All right," DeSalliers replied with a verbal smirk. "This is very simple. I kept it very simple so you'd understand it."

Dar's eyes narrowed but she remained silent. Beside her, Kerry made a noise halfway between a spit and a growl.

"You will give me what you found. When you do that, I will give you your friend," the man said. "If you call the police, I will kill this piece of trash. If you mess with me, I will kill this piece of trash. If you do anything that makes me think you're crossing me, I will not only kill him, I will drag him over the reef to kill him. Do you understand me?"

"No," Dar said. "That would require a graduate degree in animal psychology, which I don't possess. Where do you want to make the trade?"

"Just for that, bitch, he gets two smacks with a pipe," DeSalliers told her. "I'll let you know where to bring my property."

The line went dead. Dar licked her lips and put the phone down on the console, gazing at it in honest consternation. Kerry slowly let out a breath, her head still resting against Dar's shoulder. The sound of the boat's engine filled the air for several very long moments as neither spoke.

"Oh boy." Kerry finally exhaled. "We are so—"

"Fucked." Dar completed the thought succinctly. "Oh yeah. Big time." She slowly released a breath and concentrated on driving the boat for a moment. Her stomach was clenched in knots, and she struggled to catch hold of the thoughts whirling in her mind.

"You..." Kerry cleared her throat. "You think he was serious?"

Dar replayed the conversation in her head. DeSalliers' voice had been very different than she remembered from their previous encounter. It had held an edge that was making Dar very nervous. "He might be, yeah," she answered softly. "I think we may have pushed too hard by stirring up Wharton."

Kerry exhaled. "Dar."

"Yeah, I know. I feel like shit," Dar said in a small voice. "I didn't think this through at all."

Kerry rested her head against Dar's shoulder as the island's marina grew ahead of them. "My God, what are we going to do?" she asked. "Dar, we don't have anything to give him!" Dar didn't answer. "He won't believe us if we tell him that," Kerry went on, her tone rising. "Jesus!"

"Okay," Dar said. "Freaking out is not going to help."

"I'm not freaking out," Kerry objected. "I'm just..." She paused. "Okay, maybe I am freaking out. But I think it's justified."

The buoy approached and Dar steered past it, aiming for their slip. Her hands trembled on the throttles, but she focused on what she was doing. The last thing she needed to do was take out the dock and have that to worry about on top of everything.

Kerry seemed to realize that, and she kept quiet while Dar maneuvered the boat into its place. "I'll go tie us up," she muttered softly, using that as an excuse to burn off the churning of nervous energy in her belly. She climbed down the ladder, a thousand screaming thoughts fighting to gain the upper hand in her mind.

Horrified pity for Bud was uppermost. Despite the fact that she'd started out not liking him, seeing him talking to Charlie at the hospital had softened her attitude. The thought that they'd put him in mortal danger mortified her. How could they have been so damned irresponsible? Couldn't they see how strung out DeSalliers was getting? How desperate? What made them think he'd just go running away if they challenged him? *Damn.*

With a sigh, she climbed onto the dock and secured their lines, glancing up to the flying bridge as she did so. Dar was still seated at the console, her head buried in her hands. Her heart lurching, Kerry finished her task and jumped back on board, scaling the ladder and approaching the still figure. "Dar?" She put her hands on her partner's shoulders. Dar had been right. Freaking out wouldn't help. "Hey." Slamming themselves or each other wouldn't either.

Dar lifted her head and rested her chin against her clasped hands. "Yeah?"

"We'll figure out what to do." Kerry leaned against her back. "C'mon. Let's go meet Charlie, and then we'll all come back here and just talk this out."

Dar straightened and let her head rest against Kerry's chest. "How could I have been that stupid, that wrong?" she asked in a soft, plaintive voice. "What's wrong with me?"

Kerry put her arms around Dar's neck, and kissed the top of her head. "There's nothing wrong with you," she said. "We're just way out of our league, Dar."

Dar blinked a few times. "Are we?"

"Well, I can't speak for you, but they never taught megalomaniacal fruitcake avoidance in my IT classes at Michigan," Kerry said, taking a deep breath. "Sorry I freaked out."

The dark head tipped back and pale blue eyes searched her face. "Don't be. You were right; it's justified," Dar said. "I put someone's life in danger with my own arrogant stupidity."

"Hey." Kerry slid around the console and sat down next to Dar. "Someone I know once told me when you make mistake, know it, then move on and get it fixed." She took Dar's hand. "We made a mistake. Let's just go figure out how to fix it."

Dar stared at the console morosely. "What if we can't?"

"Dar, if anyone can, it's you," Kerry murmured. "We'll find a way, somehow." She rubbed Dar's shoulder, worried at the pained, lost expression on her lover's face. "C'mon."

Dar visibly pulled herself together, rubbing her face with one hand and straightening. "Okay," she sighed. "We'll see what we can come up with to fix this cluster." She shook her head. "God knows it could have been worse." She moved to stand up.

Kerry moved with her. "How's that?"

One hand on the console, Dar paused, and then she looked at Kerry. "He could have taken you." She eased past her lover and pulled her head close as she did, kissing it. "Let's go."

Jesus. As she turned to follow Dar mechanically, Kerry sucked in a shocked breath. *She's right. She stopped me from coming down here alone to check the boat.*

She tried to imagine what that would have been like, a flash of her time in the mental hospital appearing stark and vivid in her mind's eye. How angry she'd been. How ashamed at being taken like that, by her own father. What would Dar have done if it had been her? Kerry watched Dar carefully lock the cabin door. "Hey, Dar?"

Dar turned, apparently having recovered her composure for the time being. "Yes?"

Kerry took her arm as they crossed onto the dock and started the long uphill walk to the hospital. "I was just thinking about what you said." She folded her fingers around Dar's. "I was thinking about what I would have done, if it'd been you DeSalliers took instead of poor Bud."

Dar looked at her. "And?"

"And I think I would have gone after his ugly ass with that shotgun," Kerry admitted with a wry, brief smile. "I can see me doing a Rambo and getting my fool head blown off."

Dar squeezed her hand. "Nah."

"Yeah," Kerry said seriously. "So, I know this really sucks, and it's going to be tough on both of us, but I'm selfish enough to be glad I don't have to be thinking about you locked up someplace in that guy's clutches."

"Well," Dar kicked a pebble out of the way, watching it skitter down the docks past two men working near one of the boats, "I think you know that goes double for me." She squared her shoulders. "I guess we need to figure out what our assets are, what advantages we have, and decide what to do."

Kerry felt a tiny sense of relief. "Right."

They walked along in silence, passing the other boats and collecting a few curious glances from the men working on them. They left the dock and headed up the road. "Kerry?" Dar finally said when they'd passed the marina and mounted the first of the steps up the hill.

"Mm?"

Dar paused and put a hand on Kerry's shoulder. "I wouldn't have gone after him with that shotgun."

"Oh?" Green eyes searched her face.

"I would have just used my bare hands." Dar spoke the words with eerie calm. "And ripped his heart out of his chest."

"Ah."

They resumed walking.

"We'll find a way to fix this," Kerry stated firmly. "I know we will."

Dar grunted softly in response, her eyes fastened on the hospital on the slope above.

CHARLIE REMAINED SILENT for a while after Kerry finished speaking, a look of shock on his face. His eyes slowly went from her to Dar, who was sitting in the chair on one side of the hospital room.

The dark-haired woman had her elbows resting on her knees, her clasped hands resting against her chin. She lowered her gaze to the floor, tacitly accepting responsibility for the situation in which they found themselves. "So, our plan was to get you out of here, then figure out what the hell we're going to do."

"Son of a bitch." Charlie sighed deeply.

Dar's shoulders hunched just slightly. This was a failure of self that was eating a hole inside her, and she knew it. There had been very few times in her life when she'd known down deep that she'd committed an unfixable error, but this surely seemed to be one of them. Even Kerry's gentle reassurance wasn't helping.

She heard Kerry's footsteps approach and then felt a hand come to rest on her back. Between her shoulder blades, Kerry's thumb moved slightly, giving her a comforting rub. She would never blame Dar, but she also knew the truth about what had caused Bud's abduction, and knowing that Kerry knew, that made Dar feel hollow inside. Hollow and empty and sick to her stomach.

Dar could hear Kerry continuing to speak, but the words just seemed to slip past her and without really realizing it, she rested her head against Kerry's hip and let her eyes close, shutting out the sight of all that disappointment.

"I know this is pretty tough to hear," Kerry said. "Believe me, I wish I wasn't here saying it."

Charlie glanced at the silent figure next to Kerry. His lips twitched slightly. "Y'know, I told that damn fool he shoulda listened to you in the first place, Dar," he said, with a sigh. "Too damn stubborn, that's what his problem is; always was."

Kerry could feel Dar's breath warm against the skin of her leg. "About the loan, you mean?"

Charlie nodded. "Don't blame yourself, Dar. We got ourselves into this mess. We went after that kid's offer instead of doing the smart thing and accepting the hand of a friend," he said. "We never'da been here otherwise."

Kerry scratched Dar's back, running her fingertips over the tense surface. She could almost feel how upset Dar was. It was like a gray baseball sitting in the pit of her stomach, and she really wanted her lover to shake off the darkness so obviously clouding her mind. "Honey?"

The truth was too much to shrug off. Dar looked up reluctantly and inhaled. "I know," she muttered. "What ifs, what ifs. What if Kerry and I had just gone to another island, or picked a different damn wreck to dive..."

"Look." Charlie collected himself and eased off the edge of the bed onto his newly restored prosthesis. "Bud's a big boy. I ain't sure they don't have themselves a bigger problem than they started out with, grabbing him."

"Mm." Dar straightened up a little. "They ready to cut you loose?" she asked. "We figured we'd head on back to the boat and regroup."

"Good idea." Charlie nodded. "After what you told me about what happened at that inn, I don't trust them people further than I can pitch 'em off the cliff."

Dar stood up, feeling very tired. "All right. I'll go downstairs and get us a cab." She gave Kerry a simple, brief hug, then left them to collect Charlie's things.

Kerry exhaled.

"Dar's taking it pretty hard, huh?" Charlie asked.

"Yeah." Kerry glanced at him shyly. "She hates being caught by surprise." Her eyebrows contracted together. "So do I, actually."

"Life does that." Charlie stuffed the last shirt into the small, battered canvas bag and slung it over his shoulder. "She done all right. Guy's nutters." He limped slowly toward the door. "Whole thing's nutters."

"Well, I thought so." Kerry opened the door for him and followed him out. "But Dar's pretty big into situational responsibility."

Charlie grunted. "Just like her daddy."

Kerry thought about that. "That's true," she mused. "Dad does like to make sure everything's just so." She looked up to see Charlie glancing back at her. "I appreciate that about him. I'm glad Dar inherited it."

"He put up with you calling him that?" The ex-sailor seemed amused.

"What?" Kerry asked. "Dad?"

Charlie nodded.

"Sure." Kerry walked slowly next to him. "I don't have a very good relationship with my own family. Dar's folks treat me more like a daughter than my parents ever did, and they know I love them for that." She found a surprising lump in her throat and had to take a moment to swallow it. "Besides, I never got the feeling he minded being a daddy."

"No." The older man smiled briefly. "Andy wore one of Dar's nappy pins on his gear for years, and nobody dared say boo to him about it."

Kerry had to smile at the vision. "She'll be all right," she assured him. "She just has to finish kicking herself, and then we can figure out what the heck we're going to do about this mess." Her hand curled around the door handle at the end of the corridor and she pulled it open. "I'll feel a lot better when we're back on the boat, though."

"You and me both, Kerry." Charlie limped toward the front door of the hospital. Dar's distinctive form was visible through the half glass. "Me and Bud have some friends out here. Maybe we can get some help from them."

They emerged into the warmth. Dar was standing with her hands in her pockets, her sunglasses effectively hiding her eyes. A battered cab was waiting nearby.

Kerry followed Dar over to the cab and got in, while Dar held the door open so Charlie could ease gingerly into the front seat. Dar joined Kerry in the back and they drove off, navigating the winding streets in silence.

DAR WENT BEHIND the galley counter and poured herself a glass of milk, then went into the bathroom and took a couple of aspirin from the bottle in the medicine chest. She swallowed them as she emerged to rejoin Kerry and Charlie in the living space of the boat. Kerry patted the seat next to her on the couch, and Dar detoured from the chair she'd been aiming for and settled next to her partner instead. Now that the shock had worn off a bit, and despite the headache she'd developed, her problem-solving instincts were beginning to kick in again. Facts were starting to sort themselves out from the chaos.

"Okay." Dar took a sip of milk. "First off, Wharton's got no home base here in the islands, right?"

"Not that we know of, no." Kerry had the laptop fired up and had been doing some quick data searches. "Not that he couldn't be anywhere," she added with a sigh.

"True," Dar agreed. "But if he's on the islands somewhere, we should be able to find a record of him doing business." She looked over Kerry's shoulder. "See who has the telecom contract for St. Thomas."

Kerry's fingers moved and then she pointed. "There."

"Do we have a reciprocal with them?"

Dar's voice had started sounding more normal, and Kerry took a moment to be grateful for that as she searched out the information her lover was asking for. "Better." She suppressed a smile. "We're the outsource."

"Okay." Dar nodded. "Give me the laptop."

She traded her milk for the machine and settled it onto her lap.

"All right. Let's start solving this problem by using our heads instead of our asses for a change." She started up her programming language and began constructing a script. "I'll capture traffic to Wharton's area code and match it against his telco's records database."

"What'll that tell you?" Charlie asked curiously. "We don't much care, do we? They ain't sent Bud all the way over there, did they?"

Dar shook her head. "Probably not. But if we get a hit on Wharton's number, coming from this island, chances are the originating number is DeSalliers'."

"He probably has a cell," Kerry stated quietly.

"If he does, it's probably a sat cell like ours." Dar finished her task, then opened a connection to the managed switches and inserted the program into place. "Pretty simple," she muttered. "I'll just have it dump to a log, and email me with it every hour."

"Is all that legal?" Charlie inquired.

Dar glanced up at him. "What, data parsing? Technically it's all part of the internetwork I'm paid to manage, so if you mean do I legitimately have access, yes. Should I be dipping into that data stream for my own purposes? No."

"Oh."

Dar continued to type. "The cops can request this, with a court order. But we can't call the cops and we're not in a position to petition the courts, so I'm just doing what I have to do." She opened another window and considered it, drumming her fingers lightly on the keys. "Let 'em sue me."

"Assuming we find it, what are we going to do with the information?" Kerry asked. "Chances are, when he calls back, he'll tell us where to meet him anyway."

"True," Dar agreed absently. "But we've been waiting for someone to make the next move the entire week. I'm over it. I want control back." She opened her cell phone and typed a number off the back into the new script she was building. "When he calls me, this'll locate him to his nearest relay point station." She linked the script to a mapping module.

"Won't do no good to call the cops anyhow," Charlie remarked. "He'll just buy 'em, if he hasn't already."

"Like the pirates have?" Dar asked without missing a beat. "Just before he left, Bud was fixing to tell us about your friends." She felt Kerry stiffen in surprise next to her, heard the faint hiss of indrawn breath.

Charlie turned red, and directed his eyes to the deck of the boat. 'Damn," he muttered softly. "I know you ain't understanding that at all, huh?"

Dar felt very little satisfaction in her guess being on the mark.

She finished her program and compiled it, finding it very soothing
to her jangled nerves to be doing something at which she was
comfortably competent. She had a brief, incongruous memory of
her mother retreating to her easel after a stressful bout, losing
herself in the canvas where she alone had control of what
happened, and felt an odd sense of comprehension about that,
finally.

"Understanding?" Kerry spoke up. "So, you know those
pirates?"

Charlie didn't answer for a bit. He flexed his hands, then rested
them on his knees. "It's not what you think," he started off. "Things
are tough down here."

Kerry tore her eyes off the coding Dar was doing and
concentrated on their guest. "And?" she prompted. "That makes
what they're doing okay?"

Charlie shrugged. "Survival is what counts," he said. "Bunch of
folks got together and kind of worked out a deal: if you had a little
extra, you'd toss it in the kitty; and if you needed a little, you'd
take." He shifted, still gazing at the floor. "Worked out okay."

"Okay?" Kerry could hardly believe what she was hearing.
"That's not what those pirates do. I know. I saw them," she said.
"They weren't Robin Hood and his merry men."

He gave her a guilty look. "Didn't start out that way. It was
just... One day this guy who was in with us, his cousin came in
from the States. Slick guy."

"Bet we know who that is," Dar muttered, her eyes fastened on
the screen.

Kerry grunted agreement.

"They'd just been doing little stuff—salvage, selling bits of
wood and stuff to the shops, that kinda thing," Charlie explained.
"A little smuggling, just bullshit stuff. But this guy talked them into
a deal where he could get them big money, he said, if they could get
him abandoned boats."

"Abandoned?" Kerry said. "You're not seriously saying anyone
believed that those boats were abandoned, are you?"

Another shrug preceded Charlie's continuing. "Anyway, they
got him one, nothing big, just a little skiff, and he sold it off for
them. Worked out pretty good. Made it nice. Helped out a lot of
folks." Charlie still couldn't meet Kerry's eyes. "Nobody got hurt."

"Except the guy who lost his boat," Kerry said.

"They got their money back," Charlie argued. "Them insurance
companies pay off but good. Probably went out and got him a brand
new one, like the rest of them did," he said. "He gets a new boat; we
get what we need. Who gets hurt?"

"The insurance company," Dar said.

"They can afford it," Charlie said, his voice going harder. "All these folks out here—not the big shots who stay in them hotels, but the rest of us, just trying to scrape out a living—can't." He finally lifted his head. "They never went after little people, just the big rollers with more money than sense. The fat cats."

Dar looked up at him. "People like me." She glanced at Kerry. "Like us."

Charlie took a breath. "No, that ain't true."

Dar cocked her head. "Of course it's true." She lifted a hand and gestured around. "I've got a five million dollar condo to go with this, and four times that in the bank, Charlie," she told him. "I run one of the biggest computer companies in the damn world. Hell, they came after me the other day."

Charlie sighed. "Jackasses," he muttered. "Bud told 'em to steer clear of you."

"Gee, thanks," Kerry murmured.

"You don't understand," Charlie told her.

"You're right. I don't," Kerry readily agreed. "So let me ask you this—if these guys are so wonderful, how come you had to get a loan from the greasy bastard we paid off this morning?"

Dar's eyebrow inched up at Kerry's tone. She set the laptop down on the table, all its programs busily running, and leaned back. "Good question."

Charlie sucked his lower lip for a moment, then shrugged again. "Same old story," he said quietly. "After they started this all up, they'd put up with us taking a few bananas. But when it came to hard cash, it was 'just say no to the dirty fags.'" His eyes held theirs steadily. "They tolerate us now. Took a while. Bud just refused to ask 'em to pay down the loan, though."

Dar just shook her head.

"Like I said, you don't understand," Charlie said. "You got it all." He got up and walked to the door, going out onto the back deck and closing the portal after him.

"Whoo," Kerry murmured. "This is getting really icky."

Dar found herself relaxing, despite the truth of that statement. She took Kerry's hand in hers and clasped it, then brought it up to her lips. "He's right, though."

Kerry's blonde eyebrows hiked up almost to her hairline. "Huh?"

"I do have it all." Dar looked steadily into Kerry's eyes, watching the expression on her face soften as warmth crept into the green orbs. "I don't agree with what they did, but I understand what drove it," she added. "It's been tough for them out here, and I think they were looking for a way to survive more than anything else."

Kerry nodded briefly. "I know. It's not like they got rich off it," she admitted. "But I can't go along with the fact they think no one gets hurt. Someone does, Dar. People could get hurt; they could even get hurt themselves."

"Like they almost did the other day." Dar sighed. "Let's save that problem for after we solve this one, huh? I'm about out of crusader coupons at the moment."

Dar had a point. "Okay," she concurred. "Let me go talk to him. I know he's under a lot of stress. I can imagine how I'd be acting if I were in his place." She got up, leaned over and brushed Dar's lips with her own, then eased past her partner's outstretched legs and headed for the door.

Dar exhaled heavily, the air puffing her dark locks up off her forehead as she slumped back into the couch and regarded her laptop. She still felt like an idiot for getting into the situation, but her more practical side had taken over and put itself in charge—at least for the moment. Logic made a lot better platform for problem solving than hysteria.

Dar let her head drop back against the couch, easing a hand behind her neck and rubbing the tense muscles just at the base of her skull. "What next?" she asked the ceiling. Her instincts were urging her to action, but aside from the digital searching her programs were doing on her behalf, she wasn't sure if there was anything else she could do until DeSalliers called again.

Calling the police captain crossed her mind, but Dar rejected that idea out of hand. Even if she thought he might be on the up and up, and would keep the contact under wraps, she had no such confidence in anyone he worked with. Besides, she wasn't sure he was honest, and she wasn't about to risk Bud's life on it. After all, the people there had no reason to trust or help her any more than they did DeSalliers. *We're both just rich Americans, aren't we?* Dar's face scrunched into a frown as she applied that label to herself and didn't like the sound of it.

Charlie was right, she realized, but not for the reason he thought. She really didn't understand condoning piracy, but it had nothing to do with not knowing what scraping by was. She'd spent her whole childhood knowing that intimately. Maybe she'd just never bought into the whole Robin Hood thing.

That brought up the question of whether DeSalliers would make good on his threat. He'd avoided using brutal force in their first encounters, but as things had progressed, she'd gotten a sense that he was getting closer to crossing the line.

Okay, Dar, she lectured herself, *let's think of this in more familiar terms.* She got up and picked up her milk glass, carrying it back to the galley. "DeSalliers has a contract he's got to execute. He makes good on it, and he wins—he stays in business, he's got the money to keep going, life is good." She poured another glass and stood there sipping from it. "He probably figured this to be a no-brainer. He's got power, he's got people, just head down here and rope off the wreck, dive it, destroy it, bring back proof, and he's home free."

She poked in the basket and retrieved one of the cookies Kerry had made earlier, dunking it in her milk and taking a bite of it.

"Think of it from his perspective, Dar. You think you're frustrated? Picture how he has to feel — he's got Bob to deal with, then he runs into you and you wreck his boat, then you keep him from Bob again, then your friends enlist with Bob to mess him up, then you call his contract holder and tell them he's a loser." Dar finished the cookie and fished around for another one. "Bet he's got a stuffed Rottweiler with my name pinned to it that he's using for target practice."

The thought put her in a slightly better mood. "Okay — so now I've got to convince him I've really got something he's looking for, long enough to trade it for Bud or at least find out where he's got him." She licked her lips. "Just like bluffing out a competitor, Dar. You can do that."

What was DeSalliers expecting? He was expecting her to run scared, back off, wait for him to make all the moves. *All right.* Dar took the basket back to the couch, then sat down cross-legged and retrieved the laptop. She opened her mail and started typing.

KERRY EASED OUT of the cabin and spotted Charlie sitting on the stern bench they used for gearing up. She walked over and took a seat next to him, resting her arm on the back of the boat and gazing out across the marina.

"Y'know," Charlie spoke first, "that's why Bud never could stand Andy, I'm guessing."

"What do you mean?" Kerry asked.

"He had everything. Everybody liked him; he was real good at what he done; he had a good marriage, had a kid he was proud of... He made it seem like everybody should be just like him." He glanced at the door. "She's just like him."

Kerry thought about that. "I wish more people were like him," she remarked. "I wish my father had been."

Charlie shifted and looked at her.

"When I first met Dar and we were getting to know each other, every time she talked about her father, deep down in my heart, I found it hard to believe what she was saying." Kerry spoke softly. "Because my own experience had been so different."

"Dar got off lucky," Charlie said. "Most of us don't."

"True," Kerry agreed. "But then I met Andy." She turned her head and met Charlie's eyes. "He gave me something my family never had, and I cherish that, and him, more than I can tell you."

The ex-sailor leaned back and rested his arm on the stern

railing. "I'm not gonna apologize for us doing what we had to do to keep our heads up," he said. "I got a kid to take care of."

Kerry regarded him. "I'm not into judging people. I've been on the receiving end of that too many times myself," she said. "I think the important thing right now is just to get Bud out of that nutball's clutches and resolve this."

One of Charlie's eyebrows twitched. "Thought you weren't inta judging," he drawled. "Calling that sonofabitch a nutball like that."

Kerry produced a faint grin.

"Anyhoo..." Charlie shook his head. "Dar's just like Andy, got that same attitude. Reminded me of him real strong there for a minute. I know she's right, a little, but sometimes you just ain't got no choices in life except the bad ones."

Kerry tipped her head back and looked up at the sky. "I know," she said. "I've made some of them."

Charlie studied her. "You ain't old enough to make that case, lady," he told her bluntly. "Come back here in twenty years and we'll talk."

Kerry merely smiled. "Dar has a very strong sense of right and wrong, and you're right— she got that from her father." She propped her foot up against the railing. "I, on the other hand, only got a sense of wrong from mine. But no matter who was needing what, those guys were pointing guns at us, and let me tell you something, they're lucky I wasn't pointing one back."

Charlie sat up. "Huh?'

"Mm." Kerry looked steadily at him. "I would have shot them."

"They never hurt no one," the ex-sailor said. "No one. Them guns were just for show."

"I don't care." Sea green eyes took on a cool tint. "They were threatening the only thing in the world that matters to me." She leaned forward and rested her elbows on her knees. "So that's the way that is."

Charlie scratched his jaw thoughtfully. He studied Kerry's profile for a few minutes in silence as the boat rocked gently under both of them, the rigging clanking softly in the warm air. Finally, he half smiled. "Feisty thang, huh?"

Kerry glanced up at him with a wry grin, acknowledging the unlikeliness of it all. "Don't look it, huh?"

Charlie managed a chuckle. "Get your point, Kerry," he added, suddenly turning serious. "Think those guys maybe got into something we don't know about. Wasn't that serious before."

Kerry pondered that. Could it possibly tie in to what was going on with them? Was it coincidence the pirates had come after them right after they'd gotten away from DeSalliers? "Could be."

Hearing footsteps approaching down the dock, Kerry cocked

her head. She got up and leaned over the side of the stern, spotting a familiar figure moving toward them. "Ah." She exhaled. "Bob."

Charlie got up and joined her. "That little asshole."

"Mm." Kerry climbed up onto the side deck and jumped to the dock just as Bob trotted up to the boat. "Hi."

"Oh! Hey!" Bob seemed a little out of breath. "Glad I found you. Listen, the cops are after me. Can I hide out in there for a while?" He glanced behind Kerry and spotted Charlie's glare. "Oh. Ah...okay, maybe not."

Kerry sighed. "C'mon. We need all the help we can get." She paused. "Even yours."

"Huh?"

Kerry took hold of his shirt and pulled him after her as she jumped back onto the boat. Left with a choice of following or losing his clothing, Bob joined her. "Our friend DeSalliers has been busier than you think," Kerry told him.

Bob hid behind Kerry as they moved onto the stern. "Listen, Kerry did explain to you what happened the other night, didn't she?" he asked Charlie hopefully.

"I know what happened the other night, you pissant," Charlie told him. "You ran out and left us. C'mon over here and let me pop your damn little..." Charlie limped toward them.

"Uh... uh..." Bob started moving backward.

"Hold it!" Kerry stepped between the two of them and held up her hand. "C'mon, guys, we don't have time for this." She raised her voice when Charlie kept coming. "Stop it!"

One, two, three, four... Kerry counted silently, feeling the boat shift a little under her as something started moving.

The door to the cabin slammed open and Dar bounded out onto the deck, her eyes immediately taking in the situation. She pounced on Charlie, grabbed his shirt, and unceremoniously hauled him backward. "Hey!" she barked. "Cool it!"

"Let go of me!" Charlie yanked against her grip. "I owe that bastard a big right one."

Dar got in front of him and blocked his way. "I said, cool it." She bristled. "We don't have time for this crap. Like you said at the hospital—you made the choice to trust him. No one forced you."

Charlie tried to brush by her. "Dar, get out of my way."

"No." Dar didn't budge. "Don't even think about trying to move me."

He stopped and stared at her. "You think you're Andrew? Get your ass out of my way, girl." He put his hand against Dar's shoulder and pushed.

Dar didn't budge. She lifted her hand and closed her fingers around Charlie's wrist, tightening her grip with sudden explosiveness. "Charlie," she gazed steadily at him, "this is my boat, and you're on it," she said. "Stop it." Their eyes locked. "I'm *not* my father," Dar warned him softly.

Charlie examined the glittering blue eyes, cold as ice, that were fastened on him, then he stepped back. Dar released his arm and he resumed his seat on the stern bench. "When we get off this boat," he told Dar, "you ain't stopping me."

Satisfied with the answer, Dar turned. "All right." She looked at Bob. "This has gotten a lot more serious. You can stick around, but keep your mouth shut, and if we need you to do something, don't make me have to explain it in words of less than one syllable."

Bob took a step backward. "Maybe I should just go hang out somewhere else."

Kerry turned. "DeSalliers kidnapped our friend Bud and he's threatening to kill him," she said. "Sure you want to go out wandering around?"

Bob looked honestly shocked. "No kidding? I didn't think he... I mean, yeah, he's famous for all this salvage crap, but I never thought he'd get as serious as that."

"Let's go inside." Dar opened the door. "Hopefully, he'll call soon and we'll know where we stand."

Kerry led Bob inside, taking a moment to give Dar a wry look and a pat on the side as she passed her. "Would you like some coffee?"

Dar gave a tiny moan in response. She turned and waited for Charlie to get up and limp over, standing back to let him enter. He paused as he came even with her and their eyes met again. After a minute, Charlie shook his head and walked past.

Dar turned and briefly surveyed their surroundings. She scanned the nearby boats, assessing their occupants. Nothing jumped out at her, and of course, DeSalliers' yacht was nowhere to be seen. Her eyes spotted two policemen, however. One was standing near the beginning of the wooden dock, and the other was walking up and down near the beach.

She heard the sound of engines behind her, and she walked to the other side of the boat and looked out over the water. A racing boat was idling into the marina, big, throaty engines rumbling as it moved past them. There was a man behind the controls, with what Dar could only describe to herself as a babe next to him.

The man looked around and caught Dar's eye, producing a smile and a wave in her direction. "Nice boat!" he yelled.

"Same to you," Dar responded with wry civility. She watched the boat move past, making note of the name and the Miami Beach home port under it. The racer pulled into a slip two past theirs and disgorged its occupants onto the dock. The man gave the woman a slap on the butt and pointed up to a nearby restaurant. He turned and walked the other way, toward Dar's boat.

"Figures." Dar stuck her head inside the door. "Got company. Ker, watch my phone, will ya?"

Kerry had artfully positioned Bob and Charlie as far away from each other as she could in the living area and was preparing coffee behind the galley. "Aye aye, Cap'n Dar."

Dar shut the door and walked to the side of the boat to meet their visitor.

"ANYWAY, SINCE YOU'RE a neighbor, I thought I'd pass the word," the man said with a wry grin. "It was a hell of a weather system, and since it's headed this way, you might want to check your float plan."

Dar exhaled. "We had a bad storm here the other day," she said. "I thought we'd finished with the tropical weather this year."

The other boater shook his head. He was a relatively good-looking man, of medium height and the type of build that indicated he guilted himself into a gym a few times a week. "Yeah. And you know, I just heard we're up for an El Nino again this year. Weather's been real weird."

Dar glanced up. "Well, if what they say about global warming is true, better enjoy the islands now," she said. "We'll be diving them as reefs some day." Her hand extended over the water. "Thanks for the warning, Roger. I appreciate it."

"No problem." The man clasped her hand. "Hey, you said your name is Roberts?"

Uh oh. Dar nodded warily. "Yeah."

His head tilted and he looked at her. "You're not any relation to Andrew and Cecilia Roberts, are you? They're my slip neighbors over at the South Beach Marina."

Oh. Dar managed a relieved smile. "Yeah. They're my parents."

"Had a feeling." Roger pointed at her. "You look like Andy. He's a trip. Well, good to meet you, Dar. Have a safe trip back, and watch out for that storm." He lifted a hand and started back down the docks.

"Small world," Dar murmured in bemusement. "Small, small world."

"SO THAT'S WHAT happened." Kerry put the Thermos of coffee on the tray and added some cream and sugar. She picked it up and brought it over to the table. "Whatever it is you're looking for, Bob — it must really be there."

Bob exhaled. "Yeah, that's what I thought too, when the cops came after me. No smoke without cigarettes, right?"

Kerry looked up with a dubious expression. "Right." She set down the tray, and then jumped as Dar's cell phone rang. With a quick glance toward the laptop, she picked it up and opened it. "Hello?"

"Roberts?"

Kerry considered lying, but discarded the idea. "No," she answered.

"Put the bitch on the phone right now."

The door opened and Dar entered. Kerry held up the phone and then directed a rude gesture toward it. Dar's eyes narrowed as she crossed the deck and took the instrument. "Yeah?"

Kerry dropped to the couch and pulled the laptop over, clicking on the window Dar had running for the cell phone. The program had activated. She noticed Charlie had moved to the edge of his chair, listening intently to Dar's conversation.

"Write this down, Roberts. If you fuck it up, your little buddy's toast."

Dar took a deep breath, willing herself to patience. "Go ahead."

"I'll give you two coordinates. You be there at midnight tonight. Bring what you've got, plus twenty-five thousand dollars," DeSalliers said. "That's to cover the cost of fixing my boat."

Considering his demands, Dar pulled her new pocket watch from her shorts pocket and opened it. "Forget it," she told DeSalliers crisply. "Try again."

There was a momentary silence. "You're not really understanding the situation, are you? You don't tell me what to do, Roberts; you do what I tell you to do."

"Listen, moron, the bank's closed," Dar said. "If you want to recoup the cost of repairs to your hull breach, gimme the bill or rethink your plan."

"That's not my problem, Roberts. It's yours. Bring the cash and the relic, or I'll chop this piece of shit up and use him for bait."

The phone went dead; Dar closed it. "Shit."

Kerry studied the screen. "Looks like he's out on the water, Dar," she said. "Nearest coordinates are just west of St. Johns." She tapped a few more keys. "Jesus, you captured the digitized output?"

"I never do things halfway." Dar sat down. "We've got a problem. He wants twenty-five grand." She studied the phone. "So now, in addition to a relic I don't have, I also have to turn over a suitcase of cash I don't have. This is getting better and better every damn minute." Her disgust was evident in her expression. "And to top it all off, a damn tropical weather system's headed this way and it might be developing circulation."

Kerry frowned. "At this time of year? Dar, it's December!"

"No kidding." Dar rubbed her eyes. "All right, let's see where these coordinates are."

Charlie got up and walked over, leaning on the couch arm to see what Dar was doing. "Weather means trouble," he commented. "But not 'til after this damn thing's over."

Dar typed in the two coordinates DeSalliers had given her and waited for the program to plot them on a map. The grid drew in, then a sketchy outline of the islands, then a blinking crosshair. It was set in the middle of the water, as she'd expected it to be, in a lonely stretch of water south of the islands.

"No-man's-land." Charlie grunted. "'Bout two hours run out there. Not much but a hole in the ocean."

"So he has to get from here..." Kerry put her fingertip on the place where the cell signal had been tracked from, "...to here. And we have to get from here..." she pointed to where they were in St. Thomas, "...to here. Much shorter."

"We could get there first," Bob commented. "You think they'll have your friend in the boat with them? I guess they'd have to, huh?"

Dar studied the screen. "If they actually intend on making the swap, yeah." She heard Charlie suck in a breath. "I figure I need to make him show me he's got Bud before I agree to anything."

"You think he'd double-cross... Oh, what a stupid question." Kerry rubbed her face with one hand. "Dar, if we don't really have anything to give him, what are we going to do?" she asked. "You can only bluff him so far."

Dar folded her hands together and rested her chin against them. "I know that." Her pale eyes became hooded, the lids becoming mere slits over icy eyes. "If it takes us two hours to get out there, we've got until around nine thirty before we have to leave the dock. We've got until then to get something to turn over to him that'll seem real enough to pass."

"What about the money?" Charlie asked. "Got some people I can call."

"Not that creep from this morning!" Kerry blurted out. "Christ, I'd rather hock the boat than see his face again." She reached forward and pulled over the coffee tray, setting up two cups and starting to prepare them.

"No." Charlie cleared his throat gently. "Somebody else." He stood up and took out the cell phone. "Damn bill's gonna cost me an arm this month." He limped toward the door and went outside, closing it behind him.

Kerry and Dar exchanged glances. Dar pulled the laptop over and opened another program. "I'll get a wire transfer through, but it won't clear until tomorrow. Maybe if he can get something temporary until then..."

"Expensive vacation." Kerry leaned against her lover's

shoulder. "Next time, how about we just go do something traditional, like visit Niagara Falls?"

"It'd probably stop while we were there and we'd have to fix that, too." Dar finished her request and hit enter with an annoyed click. "Okay." She examined her other running programs. "Nothing else yet."

"You think there will be?" Kerry asked.

Dar shrugged and shook her head. "I don't know. And you know something? I'm getting pretty tired of saying that I don't know." She rested her head against her hands again, banging her forehead against her fists lightly as she rocked back and forth.

Kerry put an arm around Dar, rubbing her back with light fingertips. "Okay, Bob, what specifically did you think you'd find here? Really, I mean."

Bob had been staring at Dar in fascination. Now he looked at Kerry with startled eyes. "Um...I dunno, really. I kinda expected...um...well, Tanya thought the old man would maybe work a deal with us if he knew we were trying to rake something up."

"No, huh?" Kerry's brow creased. "Somehow, a guy who would steal from his own mother doesn't seem to me to be the type to deal." She gently moved the laptop away from Dar and cracked her knuckles before opening a database request and starting to type. "Now, if we assume Grandpa Wharton wasn't nuts, then he was here for a reason, right?"

"Mm," Dar grunted.

"Okay. I'm going to search the exports from here during that time period and see what I can find. If he was here, it must have been for something worth his while. Since he was a fisherman, I doubt it was timber." Kerry typed quickly and accurately. When she felt warmth on her shoulder, she looked up to find Dar's chin resting on it. Her hand stopped moving for an instant, then started up again. She was very aware of Bob's watching eyes, but the comfort of Dar's cheek pressed against her jaw trumped the mild embarrassment at the intimacy, and she leaned her head against Dar's.

"Hey," Dar breathed into her ear, "while you're there, do a search in the public archives for smuggling busts during that time period."

Kerry turned her head slightly and looked into Dar's eyes at very, very close range. "Smuggling?"

"Smuggling?" Bob asked.

"And do a public records search on him in Maine," Dar said. "We're assuming he was here for a reason. Nothing says it had to be a legal one."

"Hey!" Bob protested. "He was a good guy."

Kerry nodded slightly as she typed.

Charlie came back in, his face visibly red. He limped over and sat down, juggling the cell phone as though he wanted to chuck it against the cabin wall. "Waste of a phone call."

Dar looked up from a conversation on her own cell and shook her head.

Kerry motioned him over to the galley where she was standing. "Want a beer?" she offered sympathetically.

Charlie sat down on the stool bolted to the deck and rested his arms on the galley counter. He played with the phone, still visibly upset. "All we done for them, and they tell me to get lost." He rested his fist against his jaw. "Thought after all this time, things'd changed. Guess I was wrong. Wait 'til the next time those bastards show up with a busted head, wanting Bud..." He stopped suddenly and his eyes blinked a few times. "Damn, I hope he's all right."

Kerry set an opened bottle of beer in front of him and leaned on the counter. "I'm sure he will be, Charlie. We'll do our best to make sure of that," she assured him in a gentle tone.

Charlie looked at her. "I feel like a first-rate fool. Thinking them people'd gotten to be our friends."

Dar walked over and leaned next to him. "All right. I arranged for a draft for tomorrow. When I talk to DeSalliers tonight, I'll have to work a deal with him. I can't get it any sooner. There isn't a big enough supply of cash on the damn island. The nearest place I could get it from was one of the cruise ships, and the closest one isn't due in until tomorrow night."

Charlie looked at her. "DeSalliers ain't gonna buy that. He wants to get the hell out of here."

"I know," Dar agreed. "So I have to make what I'm gonna give him good enough for him to forget about the cash."

Kerry tapped her on the arm. "Dar, we don't have anything."

"He doesn't know that."

"You can't risk it," Kerry protested quietly.

"Kerry, what choice do we have?" Dar asked, just as quietly. "The searches came up with zilch. We've got no clue as to why Wharton was here. We have no proof he was nuts, no proof he wasn't. What we have is a damn wooden cigar box and my ability to lie through my teeth."

Kerry closed her eyes. "Christ." She exhaled, staring at the counter. Then she looked up. "DeSalliers is probably going to head around St. Thomas and then around the east part of the island to the meet point, right?"

"Probably. Why?"

"Why don't we go dive the site? What do we have to lose? Maybe we can find something," Kerry said. "We've got a couple of hours."

"Hey, that's a great idea!" Bob had joined them. "He won't

even be paying attention to the site now." He sounded excited for the first time since he'd joined them. "Let's do it!"

Dar calculated the times, then turned and headed for the door without a word. Maybe they would find something, maybe they wouldn't, but it was something physical she could do and that sure as hell beat the crap out of sitting around the boat for four hours pulling her hair out. And sometimes, she acknowledged, she got lucky. Dar hoped this was one of those times.

Chapter
Twenty-three

IT WAS VERY quiet at the wreck site. The sun was gliding seaward, and there was just a very light chop on the water. The air was cool and dry, and Kerry tipped her head back to see a cloudless sky above her. "Nice." She was dressed in her shortie wetsuit for the evening dive, the neoprene compressing her body with a slightly annoying snugness that would relax once she was underwater.

Dar, also in her wetsuit, was standing by their gear. She put a bootied foot up on the bench and strapped a dive knife to her leg, then turned and sat down, getting into her BC and strapping it across her chest.

"Are you sure I can't go down too?" Bob asked for the fourth time. "Honest, I think I'd have a better idea of what to look for."

"No." Dar stood up and cinched her straps tighter. She tied an extra dive light to her belt. "You said you didn't have any clue what you were looking for; don't change your story now." She motioned Kerry over to get her tank. "We don't have that much time."

Kerry didn't deny the feeling of half-excitement, half-nervousness that tickled her guts. She walked over and sat down, put her arms through her BC, and stood up. The tank felt heavy, and she had to take a breath before she shrugged it into place and fastened the inner belly strap. She wasn't really used to wearing the wetsuit and she flexed her arms, then ran a finger inside the sleeve constricting her biceps. It seemed snugger than she remembered, but then, the last time she'd worn it had been the previous year, and all those curls at the gym probably had something to do with that.

Dar stepped over to her and tightened the front clasp, then patted her on the side. "Ready?"

"Ready." Kerry checked the fastenings holding her various hoses and tapped the inflation valve on her BC. She picked up her mask and followed Dar to the stern gate, already pulled back to give them access to the sea.

"Charlie, if anything's going on up here, use this." Dar handed him a ball peen hammer. "Smack it on the ladder, not the hull, huh?"

The ex-sailor took the hammer and nodded tensely. "If that phone rings, I'll answer it," he said. "See if I can get that asshole to let me talk to Bud."

Dar patted him on the shoulder.

"Good luck." Bob stuck his hands in his pockets, looking spectacularly useless. "Anything I can do while you're down there?"

Dar paused, adjusting her mask. "You any good at heating up soup? There's some in the cabinet. Give us forty-five minutes and we'll be back up here, whether we find something or not."

"Okay, sure," Bob agreed readily. "It's kinda chilly up here. Good idea."

"Thank you, honey," Kerry murmured under her breath.

Dar smiled, then stepped off the stern and dropped into the water with a light splash, disappearing under the surface almost immediately.

Kerry made a last minute adjustment to her dive knife and then followed, committing herself to the sea.

THIS DIVE WAS different. Kerry felt it as soon as she entered the water and traded the warm sunset for the dim cool of the water. She could see Dar waiting for her, one hand resting lightly on the anchor line, and she headed toward her as her body adjusted to the change in temperature. The wetsuit really did help ward off the chill. It was only a shortie, but it kept the core part of her body a lot warmer than it would have been in just a swimsuit, and once the neoprene got wet and loosened up, it became fairly comfortable.

She caught up to Dar, and they started downward at a rate faster than they usually went. Kerry had to equalize the pressure in her ears a few times as it built up during her descent. She could dimly see the wreck below, Dar having anchored the boat a lot closer this time than on their previous dive. The sunlight above was already fading, and as they got closer to the wreck, Dar turned on her dive light. Kerry did likewise.

On the bottom, they paused to regroup. Dar clipped her light to her vest, and then spread her hands out to encompass the wreck. She then indicated a point halfway, and swept her hand out again and pointed at Kerry.

Kerry nodded, understanding that they would split up and each take half of the wreck. Dar then pointed to the interior of the ship and closed her fist, shaking it. She pointed at herself, then at Kerry, and then clasped her hands together before pointing at the interior again.

With another nod, Kerry agreed that she didn't want to explore inside the vessel without Dar there. Dar held up a thumb and forefinger in an okay sign.

They separated and swam off in opposite directions. Kerry took a moment to do a complete 360-degree turn, just to place herself inside the ocean. She fixed the location of the anchor rope in her mind, just in case, then went to the very front of the wreck debris and started looking around.

The wreck wasn't really all in one piece. Dribbles of it were spread out a little, pieces of wood and iron half buried in the soft, white sand. Kerry slowly swam over them, letting the tips of her gloved hands lightly brush their encrusted surface. There was nothing out of the ordinary that she could see. The pieces of metal were cleats and other marine hardware she readily recognized.

Kerry drifted a few feet further and then she stopped and turned, looking back at the debris. *Wait a minute.* Her brow creased. *I do recognize all of it.* She scanned the wreckage again, and then looked closer. Anchor chains, railings, braces — it was all there.

What was bothering her was what *wasn't* there. She'd never been on a fishing vessel, and that was the point. Even after all this time, there should have been a lot of junk lying around in pieces that she had no clue about — things like nets, and winches, and whatever the heck fishermen used when they did it on a commercial basis. Kerry paused and thought about what she'd seen inside the hold of the vessel: crates, boxes, bunks.

She flipped over onto her back and studied the wreck as a whole, spotting Dar's light down around the stern area. The sunlight was all but gone, and the boat was settling into a morose gloom, blending in with the reef surrounding it.

With a soft grunt, Kerry went vertical again and continued her search. She spotted a tumbled piece of wreckage off to one side and swam over to it, settling to the sand on her knees as she let the buoyancy out of her BC. She carefully eased the old wood aside, then lifted the piece and examined it. The wood was covered in sea growth, which she gently eased off of one part of it. She could see darker markings underneath, and she worked at it until she'd cleared a small area of the wood. Her light revealed a partial word, or something that might be a word. It didn't mean anything to her, however. She put the piece of wood into her catch bag and continued exploring.

DAR FOUND HERSELF at the back end of the boat, seeing nothing remarkable in the debris trail leading out from it. She drifted down to the bottom and looked at the half-buried stern, where there were still faint traces of the name of the boat on the encrusted metal. She ran her hands along the slanted deck, jerking back when an eel squiggled out of what had once been the engine exhaust.

Diesel inboards, Dar noted, not that different from what powered her own craft now eighty feet above her head. She eased up over the stern and onto the deck, startling a grouper. A small school of gorgeous blue and yellow angels swarmed around her as she slowly swam along, looking for any signs of something she knew she wouldn't know even if she spotted it.

A cleat on the deck drew her interest and she descended, touching the round, heavy iron circle with her hand. Meant to hold down a vertical piece of equipment, she found the center of it — coral-encrusted wood, indicating it hadn't been in use when the vessel went down. Her eyes tracked to a second cleat, and then a third, much larger one. Dar frowned, thinking about the fishing vessels she'd seen in the marina. The net winches would have been bolted down here, she realized, along with the heavy motors to draw in the thick nets so their contents could be dumped into the open hold.

The hold doors were there, cracked open and granting the access to the ship's interior that she and Kerry had used the last time, but as she circled around the deck, she realized that nothing else was there — no cranes, no winches, no mechanism the fishermen would use to retrieve their catch.

She felt something approaching and her head jerked up, only to find Kerry soaring up over the wheelhouse, moving toward her. Her partner slowed to a halt, then pulled out her small slate and a grease pencil and started to scribble. Dar left her to write, as she drifted off into the wheelhouse.

It was fairly dark inside. She directed her flash around and examined the dim, silent place where the captain had likely spent his last moments. For a second, her skin prickled and she looked around, sternly telling her imagination to pick a better time to become active. The inside of the structure was covered in coral, and she had to move cautiously so as not to get her gear tangled or snagged.

The chair bolted to the floor had come loose. Dar ducked around it, and examined the console that held the ship's wheel. The old-fashioned, nubbed wood was surprisingly intact, and she curled her hand around one of the spokes. The wheel had a brass inset, and she leaned closer, shining her light on it. The sea had corroded it badly, but she could see the plate was loose, and she pulled out her dive knife and gently pried at it. It came loose and floated down. Dar ducked around the wheel after it and snagged it in one hand near the decking of the wheelhouse. She was just turning to come back up when she spotted an odd profile under the front console.

Curious, she flipped over onto her back and wriggled underneath the metal shelf, shining her light on her find. It was covered in growth, but Dar could just make out something clamped there, and she cleared away some of the coral to get a better look. The outline was sinister. Dar felt a chill down her spine and she glanced behind her in pure reflex. Shaking her head in annoyance, she moved in closer and worked carefully at the clamp, trying to pry it free.

A hand grabbed her ankle. With a surprised burst of bubbles, Dar lurched upward, slamming her head against the console and knocking herself silly. Disoriented, she lashed out with an arm, then felt a familiar grip on her and realized it was Kerry. She went limp with relief, and rubbed her head where it had impacted the metal. Kerry pulled her closer and removed her regulator to kiss the spot.

Dar rolled onto her back and gazed up at her partner reproachfully. Kerry gave her an apologetic look, but handed her the slate to read. Dar scanned the message and nodded vigorously, giving Kerry a thumbs-up. Then she pointed under the console to her prize.

Kerry floated over her, going belly to belly with her in the small space. She directed her light on the item, then jerked back in surprise, looking at Dar in a questioning manner.

Trapped comfortably under Kerry's body, Dar spread both hands in an attitude of questioning also. Kerry pointed at the item and then made a tugging motion. Dar nodded agreement, and gave her a gentle poke in the side.

Kerry pushed back out of the way, allowing Dar to roll over and take hold of the encrusted relic. She braced herself, then pulled. The item didn't budge. With a scowl, Dar got a better grip, pressed her fins against the console, and hauled backwards with all the strength of her powerful shoulders and thighs. There was a sound they could hear even underwater as the metal ripped loose abruptly, sending Dar shooting backwards into Kerry, and both of them into the wheel in a clash of bodies, tanks, and dislodged coral.

Kerry rolled out of the way, but her hose caught on one of the wheel spokes and yanked her around. She twisted in surprise, and with a pop, the hose ruptured and pulled loose from her second stage. Air stopped. Kerry's eyes snapped open wide and she reached back, her other hand grabbing for Dar's arm nearby. She spat out her regulator and stuck it into her pocket, reaching down for her secondary. The broken line was spewing bubbles, however, and she realized it was her life running out and gathering up along the ceiling.

Dar whirled at the sound of air releasing, spotting the problem immediately. She dropped her hard-won relic and pounced on Kerry, pulling her around to get at her second stage. In an instant, she grabbed Kerry's hand, pulled out her own reserve regulator, and handed it to Kerry.

Kerry grabbed her residual air computer and showed it to Dar. Dar just pushed the regulator at her as she turned the valve on the top of Kerry's tank to shut her air down. Kerry took the regulator and exchanged it, now breathing off the same tank as Dar. She picked up Dar's computer and looked at it, clutching Dar's arm in alarm.

Dar patted her cheek comfortingly and kept working. It was getting dark. Dar propped up her light and grabbed Kerry's broken hose, examining the end of it. Discarding the hose a moment later, she pulled a small packet out of her BC and unwrapped it, disclosing a multipurpose tool and some small, shiny things that looked like foreshortened bullets.

Kerry waited tensely, unable to see what Dar was doing and very conscious of the air they were both expending. On Dar's tank, they would not have enough for both of them to get to the surface with a safety stop, which would expose them to the danger of the bends. Kerry tried to remain calm, breathing slowly and evenly. The water closed in around her, now dense and dark, flickers of unknown life visible at the perimeter of her vision.

Dar closed the end of her pliers on the bit of hose stuck in the second stage, twisting it hard and unscrewing the end of the broken part. It jammed a little, but she finally coaxed it out and let it drop to the ground. From the selection of small bullets, she picked up one and inserted it into the hole, gently working it in and screwing the threaded plug into place. She tightened it down, and then slowly opened the valve again, watching carefully for any bubbles. There were none.

She tapped Kerry on the shoulder and motioned for her to exchange regulators again. Her lover did so immediately, sucking in air from her own reserve with a look of utter relief. Dar put her tools away, and then checked her watch. They had been down too long, she realized, and from the look in Kerry's eyes, Kerry knew it too. Dar pointed toward the wheelhouse entrance, knowing they didn't have time to even glance into the ship's hold. But there wasn't anything she could do about that. All she could do was grab up the relic she'd found and head for the surface.

She followed Kerry out into the dark ocean. Almost no light was coming down now, and the wreck was receding into a mysterious shadow. Dar hefted her bit of metal in one hand and got her bearings, moving slowly away from the boat toward their anchor line.

Kerry checked her compass, shining her light ahead of her until it reflected off the silvery chain reaching up toward the surface. She took hold of the anchor line, grateful for its security as they began to inch their way upward. It was the first time she'd ever had an equipment failure, and she had to admit it had rattled her badly. She knew that if she hadn't had Dar with her and Dar hadn't been prepared as she always was, she'd have been facing an emergency ascent and the very real possibility of a diver's nightmare. The bends meant the trapping of nitrogen bubbles inside her bloodstream, bubbles that would grow bigger as she shot to the surface and potentially cut off her circulation. A normal rate of ascent gave the gas plenty of time to be gradually reabsorbed, but doing anything else opened you up to the risk of a heart attack, a stroke, paralysis, or death. Kerry wasn't ready to die yet, and just the thought of a stroke like her father had suffered made her blood run ice cold.

But she had been lucky; Dar had been there. Kerry felt a lump in her throat as they paused for a safety stop. Watching her from behind her mask, Dar circled her leg with an arm and squeezed it. With the dark water around them, it was an oddly intimate moment. Kerry leaned forward and pressed her mask against Dar's, just looking into her eyes. She forgot about their mission. She forgot where they were, and for just that moment, Kerry was simply glad to be alive.

Dar brushed her fingertips against Kerry's jaw. Her eyes smiled. Kerry caught her hand and clasped it. She could feel the powerful emotion running between them so strongly; words would just have been window dressing. Above them, their conjoined bubbles twirled lazily for the surface.

Breaking the surface first, Dar pulled off her mask and shook the hair out of her eyes. She spotted the boat, Charlie and Bob waiting anxiously on its deck, and moved toward it.

Kerry emerged just behind her, surprised at the chop that the water had developed. Glad their dive was over, she kept her regulator in her mouth as she followed Dar through the waves. She hung onto the ladder while her partner hauled herself up on board, Dar's catch bag heavy with the relic she'd recovered as it banged against her knee.

As Dar cleared the ladder, Kerry tossed her fins on board, then grabbed the metal rungs and, with a surge of energy, pulled herself and her gear up out of the water. She was already stepping onto the deck by the time Dar turned, and she gave her lover a tiny wave as she made her way over to the bench and sat down on it. *So, Kerry,* her mind gently mocked, *wanted to look macha in front of the boys, hm?* She hooked her tanks up on the holder and unfastened her BC, sitting back and relaxing as the weight came off her shoulders.

"Find anything?" Bob asked. "Looks like you did!"

Dar shed her catch bag, which clattered onto the deck. "Found a couple things," she said. "How are we doing on time?"

"All right," Charlie told her. "Wind's come up."

"So I noticed." Dar shucked her gear and stood up straight, pulling her hair back and wringing the water from it. "We found some things I can't really explain, but I'll tell you what we didn't find." She put her hands on neoprene-covered hips. "We didn't find fishing gear."

Charlie and Bob looked at each other. "Huh?" Bob said. "What d'you mean? It was a fishing boat."

"Yeah." Kerry stood and went to the cabinet, where she pulled out two towels. The night air was cool, and she was starting to chill. "But Dar's right. There wasn't any fishing gear on it. No nets, no whatever-those-things-are they use to pull the nets up, nothing." She tossed Dar one of the towels. "I found a part of a crate I brought up." She wrapped the other towel around her, closing her jaw to prevent her teeth from chattering. "I need to go put on something dry."

"Go." Dar pushed her gently towards the cabin. "Where's that soup?" she asked Bob, giving him a direct stare.

"Oh. Um...inside." Bob pointed. "I'll go get it." He opened the door and let Kerry enter ahead of him, then closed it behind them both.

Dar went to her catch bag and opened it.

"If he wasn't fishing, what was he doing here?" Charlie asked curiously.

"Good question." Dar lifted the salvage she'd retrieved and handed it over to him. "Found that clamped under the bridge console."

Charlie's eyes opened wide as he handled the big, coral-encrusted item. "Sonofabitch, Dar. That's an M-16!"

"Mm." Dar fished in the bag and pulled out the brass plate. "I need to clean this off." She sighed. "So we know he wasn't fishing, but we're not any closer to figuring out what he was doing."

"Chances are, it wasn't somethin' legit," Charlie said. "Not with this on board. You think he was running dope?"

Dar shrugged. "Beats the hell out of me." She toweled her hair a little drier and exhaled. "Not a fun dive. Kerry severed one of her hoses in the wreck." She walked over and examined the tank. "Thank God my father pounded into me about carrying a quick kit all those years back."

Charlie was at her shoulder, looking at the hose. "Sonofabitch." He touched the plug. "Damn straight that's lucky." He put a hand on Dar's shoulder. "Tell you what, Dar. Why don't you go on inside and get some java in you. I'll start the crate up and head us over down south."

Dar blew out a breath. "All right." She gave him a grateful grin. "Careful going up that ladder."

Charlie snorted. "Swab." He gave her a gentle push toward the door, much as Dar had given Kerry earlier. "G'wan. Put those brain cells to figuring out what to tell that whack job when we get there."

Dar picked up the brass plate and collected Kerry's bag, then headed for the door. Something hot to drink and dry clothes sounded like a great idea. Off in the distance, she heard the faintest hint of a rumble, and reminded herself to turn on the marine radio. With their luck, the damn storm was coming, and she had, at best, five hours to figure out what the hell she was going to use to bait DeSalliers. Dar shook her head as she entered the cabin, glad to be out of the cool breeze and inside the well-lit space. Bob was in the galley stirring something in a pot, and Kerry was presumably in their bedroom getting changed.

Dar gave Bob a brief smile and walked right past him toward the closed door beyond. She dropped the bag on the deck near the bathroom and continued on, knocking lightly on the bedroom door before she opened it.

Kerry was reclined on the bed, completely naked, her head propped up on one fist. She lifted her other hand and motioned Dar forward.

Who the hell, Dar wondered suddenly, *needs any damn soup to get warm?* She quickly went inside and closed the door behind her. "Hi."

"I need your help," Kerry drawled softly. "But first take off your wetsuit. I don't want you to drip all over the bed."

Caught just a trifle off guard, Dar felt her eyes widen as she looked at her lover. "Um...okay." She reached behind herself and caught the zipper strap, tugging it down and releasing the wetsuit. She peeled it off her arms and then stripped out of it, leaving her in her swimsuit. "Something wrong?"

Kerry cocked her head to one side. "Not with you," she said. "C'mon, c'mon."

Dar got out of her suit and toweled herself off, then sat down on the bed next to Kerry. "You know we've got guests outside," she reminded her lover wryly.

"Yes, I know." Kerry sighed and rolled over, laying her head on Dar's thigh. "But when I fell over in the ship, I got something stuck in the back of my neck. It's sharp, and I can't reach it, and it's driving me crazy."

Dar blinked. "Oh." She stifled a tiny laugh. "Hang on." She gently probed the soft skin on Kerry's back, seeing a red spot near the base of her skull.

"Mm." Kerry exhaled. "You're nice and warm, Dar. How did you do that so fast?"

"Sweetheart," Dar murmured, her eyes on her task, "you're lying here in front of me naked. If I was even slightly chilly, we'd have a problem." Kerry's low, rich laugh surprised both of them.

"Ah. Got it." Dar gently grasped the metal splinter and eased it out of Kerry's skin. A tiny bead of blood followed, and she pressed the spot carefully, squeezing out a little more to make sure she'd gotten everything out. "Bad boat. Sticking my Kerry." She felt Kerry exhale, a flutter of warm breath along her thigh. "Better?"

"Much. Thanks," Kerry said as she rolled over onto her back. She rubbed her hand along Dar's leg and gazed up at her with deep affection. "And thank you for being there, and for knowing what to do today."

Dar disposed of the sliver and eased down next to Kerry. "Thank Dad. He beat dive safety into me within an inch of my life." She put her hand on Kerry's knee. "Are you okay? I know that was scary."

Kerry nodded. "I'm okay," she said. "I was kind of nervous when it was happening, because going to the surface fast wasn't something I really wanted to do, to risk."

"No," Dar murmured. "Lousy place to risk a case of the bends," she admitted. "I had a mild hit once, and it's not something I ever want to repeat." She flexed her hand in front of her face. "Lost feeling in my arm for a week."

Kerry eased over and curled up against Dar. "I thought about my father," she said softly. "About what that must have felt like." She drew a deep breath. "Yeah, I was scared."

Dar put her arms around Kerry's body. "I wouldn't let anything like that happen to you," she assured her. "Believe that, Ker. It's my job to keep you safe down there."

Kerry felt herself cradled in Dar's embrace, her body now warmed through and through as the lingering fears evaporated. "I believe it," she whispered. "I know I'm safe with you."

They rocked together in silence for a few minutes, listening to the engines rumble to life and the anchor retract.

"Do we have anything to give DeSalliers, Dar?"

"A little."

"Enough?"

"I don't know," Dar said. "I just don't know."

Chapter
Twenty-four

THE WEATHER WAS getting worse. Kerry held on to the edge of the door as she waited for the boat to steady, then continued toward the couch. Dar was already sitting on it, her laptop in front of her and a stack of disorderly papers scattered over the table. Bob held several, his brow creased as he looked at them. "Anything?" Kerry asked, taking the spot right next to Dar on the couch.

"A lot of crap." Dar sighed. She nudged the bit of wood Kerry had brought up with her knee. They had scraped off enough sea life to reveal three letters of a name, but the possible permutations of "RTE" in the middle of a word were... "This list is endless," she handed it to Kerry, "even parsing it down to marine related companies and terms."

Kerry took the page. "It could even be an abbreviation for route," she agreed mournfully. "This is worse than looking for a needle in a haystack."

Dar sat back and let her hands fall to her thighs. "We've got pieces, but we've got no idea what the puzzle looks like," she grumbled. "We know one thing for sure — he wasn't here fishing."

"Okay, and if he had an assault rifle on board, he probably wasn't running a sightseeing charter," Kerry added. "He had supplies on board for a long trip, which makes sense, since he was pretty far from home port."

"Right." Dar got up and paced, her body automatically compensating for the roll of the boat. Suddenly she stopped. "Ker, did you take any pictures inside the hold when we were down the first time?"

Kerry's brow creased in thought. "It was pretty dim in there. I don't think I would have," she told her partner apologetically. "Besides, we were too busy trying to get underneath those...those... What were those metal things we found the eel behind anyway, Dar?"

Upside down and tilted sideways, the wreckage hadn't been that intelligible to Dar either. Her mind drew a picture of the huge pile of twisted metal that she'd edged behind. She remembered reaching out to try and move it, and her hands had closed around something roundish, and relatively smooth... "Cages." The word came out of Dar's mouth unexpectedly. "They were cages, with bars."

Bob and Kerry both stared at her. "Cages?" Kerry repeated thoughtfully. "Wait... Yeah, they were. One of the doors was open and I was lying on top of it." She nodded. "The hinge was poking me in the ribs." Her voice rose in excitement. "You're right, Dar!"

"Cages?" Bob looked extremely puzzled. "For what? People?"

Dar slowly shook her head. "No. Too small." Her brow contracted. "Must have been for animals. They were spread out all over the hold, just in pieces everywhere."

Now Kerry looked slightly confused. "I don't get it. Why would he be trying to get animals into the islands? Or..." Her eyes widened. "No, he was trying to take them from here, wasn't he!"

Dar nodded slowly, feeling a mixed sense of elation and disgust. "They're a commodity," she told Kerry bluntly. "In some places, the black market for them is huge."

"Like for zoos?" Bob asked. "I thought they could pretty much breed their own."

"No." The tall, dark-haired woman exhaled. "Well, yes, there are some places that'll pay for exhibit animals, sure, but mostly the market is for...ah..."

"Parts," Kerry murmured. "Skin, fur..."

"Even more for traditional folk medicine," Dar confirmed quietly. "It's big money. Alastair did an analysis of emerging markets two years ago, and I think even he was shocked. One of our far eastern offices was contacted to provide database services and processing for a company that acts as a clearing house for the legal stuff."

Kerry stared at Dar.

"He rejected the contract." Dar gave a slight shrug of her shoulders. "He told me his mother would spank him raw if she ever heard he'd helped poachers." She pulled the wood over and studied it. "Okay, now we've got something to go on. Ker, do a search on these letters, only hit veterinary databases instead of marine."

"Right you are, boss." Kerry assumed the laptop and commenced typing. "They're gonna faint at the cell bill this month," she commented. "You'll get another set of tickets to the Super Bowl from Bell South. Maybe this year we can go."

Dar turned the wood over in her fingers, examining it carefully. It seemed likely it was from a supply crate. She could see the faint indentations where metal strapping might have held it in place.

"So I guess he wasn't really nuts, huh?" Bob said suddenly.

"Crazy like a fox," Dar murmured, tipping the wood to the light.

"Holy Jesus. That means we've won. I've gotta call Tanya." He stood up and ran a hand through his hair. "We really did it."

"We?" Kerry said under her breath. "Not so fast. We haven't proven anything. All we've got is a reasonable theory," she added in a more audible tone. "Oh. Dar, look." Kerry pointed at the screen, which showed a list of responses to her request.

"Carter International." Dar exhaled. "Zoological supplies. What's the odds?" She tapped the wood on her knee. "All right. It's a theory. We've got the M16, this bit of wood, our memories of the hold full of cages, and a fishing boat without any fishing gear on it."

"And the cigar box," Kerry reminded her. "Not that it's relevant, or even able to be opened." She pushed the laptop aside and got up, heading for the gear room. The boat rolled and she put her hand on the wall for balance, then continued.

Charlie's voice crackled through the radio. "Hey, Dar?"

Dar set the wood down and headed over to the console. She keyed the mic and answered. "Yeah? What's up? I think we've got something here, Charlie."

"Waal, I think we've got something here. You might want to come up a minute," Charlie said. "We might have company."

Crap. Dar leaned her head against the doorjamb. "Okay. I'll be right up," she answered, tossing the mic down in a mild fit of frustration. "Damn it! Can't anything ever go like it's supposed to?"

"What's that?" Kerry returned, carrying her box. "What's going on?"

Dar turned and faced her. "Charlie thinks someone's following us. I'm gonna go check it out." She waited while Kerry continued walking towards her, tilting her head as her partner ended up at her side. "Maybe it's just someone out late doing some night fishing."

"Maybe cats put on jackets and do the tango." Kerry set the box down on the console and dusted off her hands. "I'll go with you."

"Me too," Bob agreed.

Dar sighed. She picked up the box and examined it. "This'll take time to pry open, Ker. It's completely encrusted." She glanced at Bob, who was peering curiously over her shoulder.

"It's just an old cigar box," he said, sounding disappointed.

Dar put the box down. "Yeah." She opened the door, jerking a little as a gust of fitful wind puffed against her and blew her hair back off her forehead. "Time for that later." She edged outside, shading her eyes against the boat's running lights and spotting the whitecaps riffling around them. "Damn."

"Got nasty fast," Kerry observed. "Is it that storm system?"

Dar pulled herself along the cabinet over to the ladder. "I don't

think it was moving that fast. Maybe this is just a thunderstorm."
She reached up and caught an upper rung, and started her upward
climb. The pitching of the boat threw her slightly from side to side,
but she got to the top and caught her balance. "Charlie."

The big ex-sailor turned from his seat at the controls.
"Weather's up," he said. "Looks like a squall."

"No kidding." Dar grabbed the edge of the bridge railing and
got behind the wheel. She felt Kerry thump against the back of her
seat, and then the pressure of a hand on the back of her neck.
"Where's the signal?"

"Here." Charlie pointed to the radar. Amid the clutter of the
storm, a small, pulsing green blip emerged some distance away
from them. "Could just be a false. Not getting much closer in the
last bit."

"Not with our luck." Dar studied the dot. It didn't seem to be
moving quickly, just meandering after them, keeping about an even
distance from the *Dixie*. "You think it's DeSalliers?"

Charlie shook his head. "Too little."

"Pirates?" Kerry suggested

"Not in this weather. They ain't that stupid."

Kerry leaned in next to Dar. "Maybe they changed their minds
about helping you out."

Charlie snorted. "Anyhoo, we got three more hours of this
before we get to the meet point. Weather's getting worse. You want
to pull in somewhere 'til it clears a little?"

Dar lifted her eyes and peered off into the darkness. The wind
whipped her hair back, and a crack of far off lightning illuminated a
bank of heavy clouds ahead of them. "You think it'll clear?"

The big man shrugged. "Depends. Might just be a squall," he
said.

"Or an outer band," Dar replied dryly. "How far are we from
the spot?"

"Hour," Charlie said. "Got a small atoll five, ten minutes from
here we could anchor by. Give our snoopy friend a chance to get out
of our hair."

"All right," Dar said. "Once we're anchored, you can go take a
look at what we found out. See if it makes any sense to you."

Charlie nodded and turned the boat into the wind, nudging the
throttles forward as the waves rocked them from side to side.

KERRY WASN'T A happy person. She leaned her elbows on the
counter and studied her hands, regarding the tiny lines on the back
of her thumbs as she tried not to chuck up her guts. *It isn't fair*, she
moaned silently. *What is it about the Caribbean that brings on
seasickness in me?* She'd sailed in the Great Lakes in waves higher

than these and it hadn't bothered her a bit.

"You okay?"

Kerry turned her head to find Dar standing next to her. "Um." She held her breath as the boat rolled in the surf. "Sorta."

"Sweetheart," Dar affectionately ran her fingers through Kerry's hair, "you're greener than your eyes. Want something for that?"

"Do you have something?" Kerry asked hopefully. "It wasn't so bad when we were moving." They'd been at anchor for twenty minutes. Charlie was studying the clues they'd found, and Bob had retreated to the chair near the door.

"No, it wouldn't be." Dar fished up in the cabinet over the refrigerator. She retrieved a small box, then leaned against the wall for balance as she ripped it open. "It's the wallowing."

Kerry closed her eyes. "Don't say that word again."

Dar popped open the foil on two of the tablets and set the box down, turning to retrieve a cup and fill it with water. "Here." She handed Kerry the pills. "Dramamine."

Kerry took the pills and the water and made quick work of swallowing them. She set down the cup and sighed. "Got anything else? Any old folk remedies you want to try?"

Dar cocked her head to one side, then with a tiny smirk, she leaned over and captured Kerry's earlobe between her teeth and nibbled at it gently.

"Orf...bu...Dar!" Kerry squeaked very softly, her eyes widening as she lurched up toward their guests. The attention was causing tiny, interesting jolts to travel down her body, however, warring effectively against the panic.

"Yeees?" Dar murmured.

Kerry wondered if it was the Dramamine working that fast. Her nausea eased and she felt her shoulders relax, despite the continued roll of the boat. "Wow. That works," she whispered.

"Mmhm," Dar agreed. "A little tough to do to yourself, though." She put her arms around Kerry and pulled her back against her body. Kerry clasped her hands around Dar's and exhaled, seemingly very content.

As the meeting time got closer, Dar was getting more and more worried about it. The knowledge that Bud's safety was resting on her shoulders weighed on her, and she knew they only had the slimmest number of facts on their side.

"Dar?"

Dar rested her chin against Kerry's hair. "Hm?"

"I'm going in there with you, to meet with DeSalliers," Kerry stated. "Just in case you were thinking about asking me not to."

Was I thinking that? Dar could feel Kerry's breathing under her hands, a slow and steady motion. "To be honest, I hadn't really thought about it, Ker. Does it make sense to risk both of us, though?"

Kerry didn't answer for a few minutes. Her hands stroked Dar's, a gently comforting sensation. "I just want to be with you," she finally said. "I want to be there."

It seemed right, somehow, if not logical. "Okay," Dar said. "I'm gonna need all the help I can get, and you're the best help I could hope for." She couldn't see the grin on Kerry's face, but she knew it was there from the change in her voice.

"Thanks." Kerry rested her head against Dar's collarbone. "So, what's the plan?"

Very good question. "I figure we'll meet with him," Dar said. "Try to set some ground rules. I want to get the money straight first, because if he doesn't go for that, we've got a real problem." She kept her voice down, out of Charlie's hearing range.

"Mm."

"Get him to show us Bud, to make sure he's on the boat," Dar went on. "Then, I guess we let out what we know a bit at a time, see what happens."

"We don't know much."

"I know," Dar said. "Hey, let's see if we can get that box open."

They walked across to the console and leaned over the box as Bob watched them curiously. Dar picked up a pocketknife and opened it, starting to pry gently at the barnacles covering the box as Kerry held it.

"You think anything's in there?" Bob asked.

"Probably not," Kerry admitted. "I think Dar and I are just antsy and bored, and we want the time to pass faster."

Dar glanced at her, a trifle startled at having her inner thoughts expressed with such clarity. "Hey," she pried off a bit of sea life, "that's pretty good, Madame Fifi."

Kerry smiled and fiddled with a clump of the discarded shells.

"How's your stomach?" Dar asked.

"Fine," Kerry answered absently. "See if you can get that part off, Dar."

Bob got up and wandered over to them, peering over their shoulders. Charlie remained poring over the pages of data on the table.

Dar paused to listen to the radio as a weather bulletin crackled to life.

"This is the National Weather Service special advisory number six, for the Eastern Caribbean islands and surrounding waters. A tropical depression has formed just south of the island of St. Croix. Minimum central pressure has been detected at 1008 millibars, and there is some indication of a developing circulation."

"Son of a bitch," Dar cursed with feeling.

"*Marine interests in the area are advised to take precautions. Highest detected winds are 30 knots, with gusts to 35 knots. The storm is moving west northwest at approximately ten knots.*"

Charlie got up and limped over to them, his brow creasing with concern as he heard the radio. "Damn." He looked worried. "We left everything open at home."

"Tell you what, we'll get Bud and just head over there," Dar told him with quiet confidence. "You'll both be home tonight to take care of things."

Charlie gave her a speculative look and sighed.

A soft crack made them all jump, then everyone looked at Dar. She blinked at her hands, which had of their own volition continued to work on opening the box. The coral around the lid had broken off under her knife and fallen to the counter. She put down the knife and fit her fingers around the edge of the box, lifting it up and easing it past the last obstructing coral. Everyone clustered around and peered inside.

Bob craned his head to see. "What is it?"

Dar tilted the box to the light. A slim metal case was nestled tightly inside, its surface corroded by contact with the sea. She put her penknife to good use again — inserted the tip between the edge of the box and the case, and pried up. It resisted briefly, then popped free.

As Dar levered the edge up, Kerry reached inside and grasped the case, lifting it free of its wooden case and setting it on the cabinet top. "There's a catch." She touched the front side. "Like an old fashioned compact or something."

Bob leaned closer. "Are those initials in the top?" He reached over timidly and scraped a bit of debris off the container. "I think they are!"

"Wharton's?" Kerry picked up a rag from underneath the shelf and rubbed the top of the case. Faint indications of a monogram appeared, thinly traced lines that were difficult to interpret. "Could be."

Dar gently picked at the rust around the catch. Having removed the bulk of it, she set down the knife and curled her fingertips around the front of the case, pushing down firmly on it. It didn't budge, and she felt the metal digging into her skin. She flexed her hand to put more pressure on the catch, forcing it in with a soft, sodden crack. As she set the case down, water spilled from the edges, along with grains of fine sand from the bottom. Dar lifted the top and laid it fully open on the cabinet, exposing its contents.

Not unexpectedly, the inside was full of sea bottom. A layer of sand covered whatever was tucked inside. Kerry brushed away the sand with her fingertips and removed the contents, which felt hard and slick to the touch.

"What is it?" Bob asked eagerly.

Kerry pulled it free and unfolded it. "Something plastic." She opened it fully and laid it on the shelf. It was a notebook-sized sheet, encased in a stiff laminate, heavily creased where it had obviously been folded many times.

The writing on it was tiny. Even Kerry, whose vision was darn near perfect, had to squint at it. Dar didn't even try. Instead she angled the light closer and turned, heading back toward the living area. "I'll get a magnifying glass."

"It's been reduced," Kerry said. "It's a bunch of pages, laid out."

The trembling in his hand indicating his excitement, Bob pointed. "Is that a will? That cover page looks like the one that got tossed out!"

Charlie grunted. "That's a fisherman," he said. "Knew what he was about in keeping that stuff. Bud 'n I have our important stuff done the same way, 'cept we got it full sized."

Dar returned with a small, handheld magnifier. She handed it to Kerry, who focused it on the first square of miniscule lettering. Everyone waited while the blonde woman read.

"It's a trust," Kerry murmured. "This part, and yeah — that section's a will." She pointed at a third set of pages. "Those are the documents of ownership for the boat. It's all legal papers." She looked up at Dar. "And this section at the bottom looks like his float plan for the Caribbean."

Dar exhaled. "Proof he wasn't nuts," she said, "and that he was here for a reason."

"Yes! Yes!" Bob yelled in elation. "There it is! We got him! We got the damn bastard!"

Dar held the slim, metal case in one hand and stared at it, her head shaking in patent disbelief. "I can't believe we've had this damn thing the whole freaking time," she cursed, lifting the top of the case and shutting it.

"Damn." Looking profoundly relieved, Charlie exhaled. "Damn, damn,damn!"

"I'm damn glad to see this." Dar sighed. "At least we've got something to work with now."

"What?" Bob said. "Give it to me. That's Tanya's!"

"Hey!" Kerry covered the sheet with both hands to block his hasty grab.

Dar clamped her fingers down on his wrist. "Leave it. That's our only real bargaining chip."

"You can't give that to him! No!" Bob wrenched his arm free from Dar's grip and lunged for the packet. Avoiding Charlie's outstretched fingers, he yanked at Kerry's shoulder.

Dar reacted instinctively. Her left hand whipped up, tangling with Bob's arm as she shifted and threw her weight against him. "Get away from her," Dar warned, aware suddenly of Kerry's gently bemused look.

Charlie stepped between them and forced Bob back, shoving him against the wall. "Don't give me no excuses, you gutless git," he told Bob. "I don't give a damn about no money or what you're gonna get out of this. That there's the key to me getting my partner back."

"You can't take it," Bob panted. "You don't understand what's at stake here."

Kerry slipped around them and carried the sheet with her over to the couch. "No," she advised Bob. "*You* don't understand what's at stake here. Or what's worse, you don't care. Someone's life is in danger; how can you even think about keeping this?" With a disgusted shake of her head, Kerry used a cloth to pat the sheet dry. "Dar, I can't even scan this. It won't pick up these letters, even as a hi- res graphic."

"I won't let you turn that over to him," Bob warned. "I won't. I won't; I...urp." His eyes bugged out as Charlie got a big hand around his throat and started to squeeze.

The ex-sailor had lost his patience. "Shut the hell up 'fore I toss you overboard."

Bob glared at all of them, but subsided. Charlie released his throat, staying close by just in case. "You can't," Bob muttered. "You can't."

"We will," Kerry replied steadily. 'And if you try to interfere, you're going to get hurt."

"Damn straight," Charlie agreed.

Chapter
Twenty-five

"DAR?" KERRY TIED the laces on her sneaker. "I have a question." They were in the bedroom changing, by only the dim light of the bedside lamp. It was quiet and cool, and presented a last moment of peace before they went to do battle with the weather and DeSalliers.

Dar was fastening the top button on her jeans. "Mm?"

"How are we going to get to DeSalliers' boat?"

Dar's hands paused and she looked up. "He's got a skiff, I think. I saw it hanging off a winch when we were onboard."

Kerry at her gazed seriously. "What if we need to get back in a hurry? I hate to be at his mercy like that."

The boat pitched, making them both grab for balance. After it steadied, Dar put her hands on her hips and frowned thoughtfully. "We could swim, I suppose," she said. "But in this weather, damn, I hope we don't have to."

Kerry stepped closer and slid her fingertips inside Dar's waistband. "You think we should dress accordingly, just in case? Not that I don't love you in jeans, sweetie, because I do, but they're a bitch to swim in." She gave the waistband a tug. "Even if they are loose like these."

"You've got a point," Dar acknowledged, studying Kerry's own outfit of a T-shirt tucked into shorts. "I could just go in my bathing suit with a pair of gym shorts over it," she said. "You have a suit on under that?"

"Yes, I do, so that would be perfect," Kerry agreed. She watched quietly as her partner changed, sliding out of the jeans and folding them neatly before she donned her bathing suit. "Dar?" In the relatively dim light, she could still see the reflections off Dar's eyes. "Are you scared?"

Dar adjusted the shoulder strap on her solid black suit. "Of doing this?"

Kerry nodded.

"A little." The dark-haired woman sighed. "Scared something else will happen and someone, us maybe, or Bud, will get hurt. Sure

I'm scared."

"I feel a lot better now that we have this." Kerry touched the plastic coated sheet on the dresser. "It's not just a bluff anymore."

Dar nodded.

"Shame he gets to win, though," Kerry observed. "Kind of frustrating, really. We get the answers at last, and now it's for nothing. Patrick Wharton wins anyway."

"I've got a theory about that." Dar pulled a light, cotton short-sleeved shirt on over her suit, leaving it unbuttoned. "What goes around, comes around. He'll get his one day." She carefully stored her precious pocket watch in a drawer, tucking it into a fold of one of her spare shirts.

"Like my father did?" Kerry asked quietly.

Dar paused and looked at her thoughtfully. "You could say that," she agreed slowly. "It catches up to you." Her eyes dropped. "Like it did to me."

Kerry moved closer and her voice rose with her indignation. "You're not seriously comparing yourself to either Wharton or my father, are you?"

"No, not exactly."

"Good." Kerry bumped against her. "Then what are you talking about?"

Dar circled Kerry's neck with her arms and rested her forehead against her partner's. "I'm not really sure. Ask me again later," she said.

The boat swayed and they both swayed with it. Kerry took hold of Dar's waist and leaned in to kiss her. "Time to get going," she said. "I'll be glad when this is over."

Dar rubbed noses with her. "Me, too," she admitted. "Because when it is, I'm gonna kick everyone off this damn boat and put a do not disturb sign on the railing."

"Right there with you," Kerry said.

Dar tucked the plastic sheet into her back pocket and zipped it, then put her arm around Kerry's shoulders and steered her toward the bedroom door. "Know what I was just thinking? The old man was a bastard. Maybe it's poetic justice the kid took everything."

Kerry sighed. "That thought had occurred to me. Though I'm not sure that the wife should be punished for the sins of the husband."

They opened the door and walked out into the boat's living area. "I'm going to go start up the engines," Dar told Charlie, who was keeping a dour eye on the still-glowering Bob. She grabbed her rain slicker off the counter and slipped into it, fastening the catches. "Might as well get moving."

"I'll go on up there with you." Charlie got up carefully, getting his balance over his artificial leg.

'*Thanks a lot, guys,*' Kerry telepathically sent to them, as they hastened to leave her with the furious Bob. "I'm going to heat up the soup, Dar. We missed dinner."

Soup. Dar's stomach suddenly rumbled loudly. "Great idea." She gave her partner an appreciative look. "Thanks."

"Mm." Kerry let her eyes rest on Bob, then met Dar's. One pale eyebrow quirked.

Dar returned a mildly sheepish look and a shrug. "Call me when it's ready. I'll come get you," she said. "I mean, get it."

'I liked the first one better,' Kerry mouthed, before she turned and made her way into the galley.

Up on the bridge, Dar navigated carefully through the storm, edging closer and closer to the meeting point. It was so dark she could barely see past the bow, and she was relying only on her radar and her depth finder to keep her out of trouble. The rain lashed hard against them, moving almost sideways in its intensity. Charlie was huddled in the seat next to her, also staring out into the darkness. "Nasty," Dar murmured.

"Yeah," the ex-sailor replied softly. "Listen, Dar—I'm sorry about that mix up before."

Dar glanced at him. "It's all right. It's too much stress for all of us right now. I know you're worried about Bud. So am I." She watched the radar, then pointed at the screen. "Looks like our friend abandoned us. One less complication."

Charlie nodded. "Saw that," he said. "I feel a damn sight better about the whole thing now that you found that paperwork," he added. "Ain't that I didn't trust you to do the right thing, Dar, but—"

"But it's a hell of a lot easier when you've got something to bargain with," Dar finished for him. "I wasn't feeling any too comfortable, either. There's just so much bullshit I can dish out before I run out of cards." She made a slight adjustment to their course. "I'll be glad to give him that damn paper, get Bud, and get the hell out of this God damned storm."

"Doesn't bother you that the bad guys win?" Charlie asked, watching her face.

"Bad guy's a relative term in this viper's nest," Dar muttered, turning as she heard someone coming up the ladder. "Ah." A smile crossed her face as she recognized the sturdy form in its rain slicker. Kerry, a Thermos jug hanging around her neck by a lanyard, was using both hands to pull herself up the ladder. "Told you I'd come and get you!" Dar called out.

Kerry steadied her balance and made her way across the pitching bridge. "Let's just say there's only so much petulant whininess I can take in one sitting, okay?" She thumped down into the third seat, on the other side of Dar. "Stupid little wuss bag. I almost put him through a porthole." Her voice sounded exasperated. "We almost there?"

Dar nodded. "Almost."

A crack of thunder made them jump and the entire sky lit with lightning, brushing the heaving waves with silver incandescence for a brief instant.

"Wow." Kerry exhaled. "This is getting pretty bad. What if he doesn't show?"

No one answered or looked at one another.

"He'd better," Dar finally said. "If he doesn't, we'll go find him."

Lightning flashed again and Kerry started, grabbing Dar's arm. "Dar!" She pointed off the bow. "There's something out there!" she shouted. "Someone! I saw a person!"

"What?" Dar barked, incredulous. Immediately, she cut the throttles and slowed the big boat into a wallowing idle. "Where?"

Charlie half stood and peered. "Can't be, Kerry. Not in these waters."

Kerry strained her eyes. "There was," she said with utter certainty. "I swear it."

Dar checked the time, then looked at Kerry's face. "Get the spotlight," she said. "I'll circle."

Kerry jumped up and started for the ladder, then froze as a light from the darkness of the waves seemed to ignite, pinning them with its brilliance. "Oh!"

Dar felt the world going out of balance. "What the hell? Now what?"

"Dar." Charlie's face had a strange expression. "That there's a Navy underwater lamp."

Naval light? A suddenly realized possibility made Dar's heart jump. As she idled the engines, she heard the faint echo of a much smaller craft nearby. "Kerry, stay up here." She held on to the railing as she edged around her partner. "I think we're okay."

Kerry held onto the rail for dear life as she watched Dar scamper down the ladder to the lower deck. "I hope she's right." Her only answer was thunder rolling ominously overhead.

So close to the water, Dar could see the outline against the waves. It was a low riding boat with a single occupant. The light swept across her and blinded her for a moment, then went out. She opened her eyes and blinked. "Dad!"

"Hey there, Dardar," Andrew Robert's voice boomed back. "Toss me one of them lines."

With a feeling of relief so profound it almost made her dizzy, Dar lifted one of their dock lines and tossed it over, aiming accurately at the shadowy figure. She felt it go taut. "Keep it steady, Ker!" she yelled up to her partner. "It's Dad!"

"Yes!" Kerry hopped up and down a few times. "Something goes right at last!"

Dar smiled as she caught the words. She leaned over the railing and watched as her father lashed the black rubber boat to the rope. "Want me to let the ladder down?"

"Yes, ma'am, I would like that," Andrew shouted back, tying off a second line to his waist, then making a neat dive over the side of the craft into the water.

Dar scrambled across the deck and got to the back ladder, hanging on as the boat pitched wildly in the worsening seas. She unlatched the diving hatch and booted it open, then unhooked the diving ladder and let it down into the sea.

It was only there, it seemed, for a brief moment before its sheen was engulfed by a large, dark figure that rose dripping up out of the water and invaded the deck. Despite the boat's rocking, Andrew easily held his balance as he removed his neoprene headgear. "'Lo, there."

"Hi, Daddy." Dar felt the words emerge before she could censor them. Andrew's grizzled eyebrows lifted in mild surprise, but he acknowledged them by stepping forward and clasping Dar in a brief hug. "What's a nice guy like you doing out in a storm like this?"

Andrew chuckled. "Don't you go there, Paladar," he warned, releasing her just in time to be assaulted by a smaller figure bolting across the rolling deck. "You prob'ly don't know it, but a storm like this here one's the reason you're standing out in it."

Without a moment's hesitation, Kerry threw her arms around her father-in-law. "Whoo!" she gurgled. "Hi, Dad!"

Andy's voice gentled perceptibly. "Hey there, Kerry," he said. "Ah do thank you for keeping them letters coming."

Dar's ears pricked. "Letters?"

Kerry peeked at her. "After that initial outline we sent when he called on your birthday, I've been emailing him about all the stuff that's been happening," she told her lover with a touch of apology in her tone.

"You knew he was coming out here?" Dar asked.

"Naw." Andrew put a big arm around his daughter. "Just decided that this here morning. Let's go topside and have us a chat, and get out of these here damn swells." He looked up. "That Charlie up there?"

"Yeah," Dar said.

"Got us a regular boatload of trouble, don't we?" Andy commented.

"Where's Mom?" Kerry asked as they started towards the ladder.

"Painting that there dog of yours," Andrew replied, pausing as the cabin door opened and Bob looked out at him. "This here that feller that ran out on Bud and Chuck?"

Bob's eyes widened at the growl, and he hastily closed the door again.

"Yes," Kerry answered, distracted. "Dad, she's painting a *picture* of Chino, right?"

Andrew peered at her, then chuckled. "Yeap."

"Phew. Just checking." Kerry started up the ladder first. "I like her current cream color."

That even got Dar to smile. Andrew turned to her as they waited for Kerry to ascend. "Your momma knows them people up in Boston," he said in a serious tone. "And Ah will tell you, she does not have good words to tell about the lot of 'em."

"Gee, what a surprise." Dar gestured upward. "G'wan. I just want to get this damn thing over with."

As Andrew started up the ladder, the door to the cabin opened and Bob peeked out again. "Who is that?" he hissed at Dar. "Where did he come from?" he added. "What's he doing here?"

Dar rested her elbow on the step. "That's my father. Do yourself a favor and just stay in there and out of our way."

A flash of anger crossed Bob's face, but he retreated and closed the door. Dar let her hands rest on the ladder for a moment, then started her climb to the top.

Andrew emerged onto the flying deck, which now seemed very cramped. He greeted the deck's other occupant casually as he followed Kerry over to the controls. "'Lo, Charles."

"Hey, Andy," Charlie murmured. "Nice surprise." His eyes stayed on the console, unaware of Kerry's attention on him. "Glad they got the paperwork wrong on you."

"Yeap," Andrew replied easily, settling into one of the seats. "All right now, you got us a plan, kumquat?"

"Dar does." Kerry waited as her partner joined them. Dar took the center seat and revved up the engines, starting them forward. The boat's motion slowly counteracted the swells, and Kerry relaxed as her stomach settled down somewhat. It was hardly the time to ask Dar for another dose of her ear medicine. "I didn't get a chance to tell you, Dad, we found something concrete, finally."

"Did you now?" Andrew studied the controls.

"Yes." Kerry fished inside Dar's back pocket and removed the folded sheet, leaning past Dar's shoulder to hand it to him. "It's all kinds of legal stuff."

Andrew studied it, cocking his grizzled head to one side. "Well, lookit that," he murmured. "You fixing to give this up as part of your trade off?"

"For Bud," Charlie blurted suddenly. "Yeah."

Andrew rested his jaw on his fist. "Mah wife says that feller

Wharton is one right scumboat," he said. "He's using all them dollars to fix up folks the same kind as your papa was, Kerry."

Kerry stiffened, then frowned. "He's a conservative, you mean," she said. "There's no law against that, is there?" Her hands were resting on Dar's shoulders for balance, and she leaned in a little against her.

"No, ma'am, there surely is not," Andy agreed. "But seems they've taken a right dislike to folks who ain't just like them." He hesitated uncharacteristically.

Dar spoke up finally. "You mean he's funding hate groups?" she asked. "I know there's a couple up there that think people like Kerry and me..." her eyes went to Charlie, "and Bud and Charlie should be euthanized," she added bluntly. "Is that what you mean, Dad?"

Andrew released a breath. "Your momma does think that, Dar," he acknowledged quietly. "And Ah do believe she's right."

"Son of a bitch," Charlie whispered.

They all looked at the sheet resting in Andrew's big hand. The rain drove harder against the console Plexiglas, making a sound like rapid gunfire.

The situation had changed, Kerry realized. Andrew's arrival and the information he brought threw a whole new facet into the mix, and now there was a question of what they should do, and she wasn't sure who exactly was going to make that decision. Dar had once told her there could only be one captain of the boat.

"Well," Dar broke the silence after a long period, "regardless, we have to get Bud out of there." She focused on the problem at hand. "There's always going to be assholes out there who want to take over the world. We have to deal with the critical issue first, and that issue's a friend in trouble."

It was a quietly strange moment, and Kerry felt the oddness. Dar had, she realized, simply moved forward and taken on the leadership of the situation, making the decision and accepting its consequences in a completely natural way. Both Andrew and Charlie were watching her intently, and Kerry held her breath as she waited to see what their reactions would be.

"So, we're going to continue with our plan the way it is," Dar went on. "If something develops that lets us come back around and nail Wharton or DeSalliers, or both of them, great. But we get Bud out first." Her voice was quiet and steady.

Andrew nodded in acceptance. "Right. Ah figured Ah could get up there on that boat and see if Ah could rock it while you had them there people distracted."

Dar thought about it. "I'm sure they have him below decks," she said. "I'm going to try and force them to bring him up before I start dealing, but I don't know how far I can push." She edged the throttles forward a bit. "It would make me feel a lot better to know you were there. Just in case."

A tiny smile appeared on her father's face. "Ah jest bet it would," he drawled. "Though it seems like you done got most of your bases covered already." His eyes watched his daughter with silent pride.

Dar accepted the compliment with a slight nod. "We tried. But I like having a card up my sleeve. Makes the game a lot easier."

"You can say that again." Kerry held on as the boat cut through what appeared to her to be twenty-foot waves. "Now let's just hope they show." She felt the muscles in Dar's neck relax under her hands and felt her own follow suit, glad that her partner was comfortable in taking the lead and that the two ex-sailors were willing to accept that.

It had been a tough moment for Dar, she knew. Her lover was a natural born leader, but just as naturally, she loved and worshipped her father who was also, Kerry knew, a natural born leader. Dar could have deferred to Andrew, and yet she'd chosen to trust her instincts, and do otherwise. Time would have to prove whether or not those instincts were true.

THEY FOUND THEIR spot in the ocean. The wind had risen, driving the waves against the boat, but Dar had anchored them into it, and the bow rose and fell with steady regularity instead of rocking side to side. Andrew had tethered his boat to the back of the *Dixie*, and now they were simply waiting.

"Kerry was worried about trusting DeSalliers to carry us over there. I think she's right," Dar commented to her father. "Better if you drop us off." They were standing side by side in the stern, protected from most of the wind by the craft's cabin.

"Hell, yes," Andrew agreed. "Ah'll park that thing 'tween us, then go off. Won't even realize it."

Dar eyed him curiously. "It's a pretty high bow," she said. "You planning on roping up it?"

Andrew gave her a mildly smug look and fished in one of the belt packs he was wearing over his black neoprene dive suit. "Nope." He held out something that had a cup-like surface of what seemed to be soft rubber, and a sturdy hard rubber handle of some kind. "Put that there up on that fiberglass and twist this piece. Makes you a handle."

Dar took it and fit her hand in it, then activated the suction. "Hmph," she murmured. "Pretty cool."

"Dar!" Kerry called down from the bridge. "Radar just picked up something."

Dar handed her father back his toy. "About damned time." She felt tension grip her guts, and she wanted the confrontation to be long over and done with.

"Heck of a vacation there, Dardar," her father commented wryly. "Maybe next time ya'll should go find you some little farm somewhere and just do you a picnic or something."

Dar shook her head. "I should have guessed. Even when we spent a couple days up at the lake, Kerry's horse got bee stung, she fell off, we almost capsized, and we managed to out ourselves on a family hay wagon ride."

Andrew ruffled her hair. "You always did get into the damndest things. You remember that time we done went up to that ranch and you rode up on that bull?"

Dar covered her eyes. "Don't mention that to Kerry, please?"

"Mention what to me?" Kerry materialized at her elbow, peering out through the rain. When it appeared that neither of the Roberts was going to answer, she asked, "Any sign of them yet? Charlie's going to stay up at the controls. It's tough for him to get up and down the ladder." And it gave him something very useful to do, Kerry reasoned, since no one was willing to trust Bob with the boat.

"Couldn't hardly see nothing yet in this spit," Andy said. "You two ready?"

Kerry patted her rain slicker. "About as ready as I'm going to get. Dar?"

Dar had her hood down, and the wind was whipping her dark hair relentlessly. "I'm ready." She lifted her chin. "Lights."

They looked in the direction she indicated, and sure enough, a moving speck could be seen very faintly through the storm. Kerry flexed her hands nervously, her heart rate picking up speed now that things were happening. She wasn't stupid enough to ignore the fact that she was scared; any reasonable person would be in her place.

She trusted Dar, and she certainly trusted Andy. However, she didn't trust DeSalliers, and part of her worried that logic didn't have a lot to do with his planned actions. She worried about Bud, trapped in the man's hands, and she worried about what they would find over on the other boat.

The cabin door opened and Bob stuck his head out. "I think he's on the radio," he said, just as Charlie called down from the bridge with the same news.

Dar squared her shoulders and walked over to the door. Bob backed out of her way as she went for the radio console inside, Kerry and Andy at her back.

DeSalliers' voice cut through the static. "Roberts? One more chance at answering, then I slit this piece of shit's throat."

Andy's eyes narrowed. "Ah already do not like this man."

Dar picked up the mic. "I'm here," she answered shortly. "About time you showed up."

"You have what I asked for?"

"I have what you need," Dar replied. "So let's get this over with."

DeSalliers laughed. "You don't like not being in control, do you, Roberts? Well, that's too bad. You just sit there. I'll tell you when I'm ready."

The transmission was terminated and Dar dropped the mic on the console as though it were a dead rat. "I've encountered more appealing things than that six days dead on the roadside up to Marathon," she commented. "What an asshole."

"Yeah, well, he's going to get what he wants, isn't he?" Bob asked bitterly. "To hell with the rest of us." He stomped over to the chair and flung himself down in it. "Fuck you all."

Andrew folded his arms over his broad chest. "This here situation's just chock full of jackasses, ain't it?"

"Yeah, isn't it?" Bob shot back at him.

"You know something?" Kerry addressed Bob before either Dar or Andrew could answer. "I'm really starting to regret risking my life for you, and I hate that. So cut it out and grow up before I have to do something about it."

Bob subsided into a sullen silence, his eyes fixed firmly on the floor.

Kerry expelled a breath in disgust and gave herself a tiny shake. She pushed her hood back, revealing damp and tangled blonde hair that she ran her hands through in agitation. "Jesus."

Dar put an arm around her and pulled her close. She hit the intercom. "Hold steady here, Charlie. Let's wait to see what this bastard has in mind."

"Ain't no good, whatever," Charlie replied glumly. "Sons of bitches."

"Mah gosh, listen to this here language," Andrew drawled. "Ah ought to spank the lot of you."

The comment eased some of the tension and drew a smile from both Dar and Kerry. "I hate waiting," Dar admitted. "And he's right. I hate not being in control." She released Kerry and turned, choosing a path and pacing it across the living area.

Kerry leaned against the radio console and watched her, resigning herself to the knowledge that all they could really do is wait.

As Dar paced, Andrew merely leaned back against the door frame and relaxed.

At last, DeSalliers' boat approached them, circling their position twice before they were contacted again. Dar's nerves had tightened almost to the breaking point. She'd stopped pacing and ended up back out on the stern in the rain, counting to several thousand under her breath in a vain attempt to relax.

Kerry stuck her head out of the cabin. "Dar. He's on."

Dar stalked to the door and ducked inside. She could feel her breathing coming quickly, and she took a second to inhale, hold it, then exhale before she picked up the mic. "Yeah?" She unkeyed and waited. The sudden warmth of Kerry's hand on her side almost made her jump, but after a second she relaxed a little, calming as Kerry's thumb idly rubbed her skin.

"I see you've got a canoe back there," DeSalliers said. "Get in it and get over here. No bullshit, no smart talk, or I'll gun the engines and run your sorry ass over."

"Make sure you hit me the first time," Dar growled back. "Or you'll end up upside down talking to crabs." She keyed off and dropped the mic, then headed for the door. "C'mon."

Andrew held the door and waited for them to go ahead of him. As they passed him, he turned to face Bob. "You mess with anything while them girls are over there, Ah will kill you."

Bob stared at him.

"That is not a bluff, it's a promise," Andrew said quietly. He turned and closed the door after him.

Dar made her way down the ladder and into the solid black watercraft in which her father had arrived. It was a familiar sight: two incredibly tough rubber pontoons and a flexible but stiff inner structure, and engines that could probably propel a jet. It had hooks and catches everywhere that were intended for military use, not surprising since its primary purpose was to carry Navy SEALS into battle. She didn't ask how Andrew had gotten it.

Dar turned and took hold of Kerry as she climbed down, keeping her steady as she joined her in the bottom of the craft. They were both in dark rain slickers, and Andrew was almost invisible as he made his way into the boat, causing it to rock under his weight. He was dressed in full-length black neoprene, with a canvas vest buckled over it that held all sorts of things, including one waterproof case Dar knew usually housed a sidearm. The thought put a sudden prickle down her back, and she tried not to think about how dangerous the situation was.

DeSalliers sounded like he was capable of anything. Dar let out a slow breath, acknowledging the fear she was now feeling in her guts. But the fact was, her father was also capable of anything, and having him there shifted the odds, if not in their favor, at least more toward equality.

Andrew took a seat at the controls and started the powerful engines. "Want to let us loose, Dardar?"

"Sure." Dar untied the craft and tossed the end of the rope up onto the *Dixie.* The waves were pitching up and down severely, but apparently she'd gotten used to them because they didn't disturb her much. Kerry, however, sat down on one of the hard seats and wrapped her arms and legs around the stanchions.

Andrew aimed the boat toward DeSalliers' craft, visible as a brightly lit outline against the rain. "Here we go."

Dar held on with one hand and put her free hand on Kerry's shoulder. She leaned close to her ear. "Scared?" Kerry turned, and Dar knew she was looking up at her even though the darkness made her features invisible.

"Yes."

"Me too," Dar replied. "My knees are shaking so badly I don't want to sit down in case I can't get up again."

Kerry laughed faintly. "Are you trying to make me feel better?" She squeezed Dar's hand. "If you are, it's working."

Dar pressed her cheek against Kerry's. "I love you."

Kerry smiled, a motion Dar could feel against her skin. "That works even better," she admitted. "I love you too."

"We're gonna be fine," Dar went on. "But if you want to stay in the boat with Dad, it's okay, Ker. I'm not joking. I know this is scary as hell, and it's no reflection on you if you want to stay here."

It was so tempting. The thought of staying at Andrew's very, very safe side was so enticing, Kerry could almost feel the agreement tickling the back of her throat. However, the image of her waiting in the darkness while Dar went into danger alone was far more horrific. "Thanks for the offer," she turned her head and kissed Dar, "but where you go, I go. I'd croak from anxiety if you left me here."

Dar nodded, as though she had fully expected Kerry's answer. "Okay." They watched the boat grow larger and larger in front of them. "I need to play tough with him, because of the twenty five thousand."

Kerry nodded. "I know."

"So, if I sound like I don't give a damn about Bud, it's for a reason."

Kerry patted her hand. "Honey, I know that. If you didn't give a crap about Bud, you wouldn't be here," she said. "I'll back you up, whatever you do or say. I trust you."

"Even if I walk out?"

Kerry drew in a breath. "I'm with you, no matter what."

As the motor slowed its rhythm, Dar straightened up. DeSalliers' boat swam in her vision, armed men visible on the stern deck.

"Paladar, those fellers have rifles," Andrew said suddenly.

"I know, Dad," Dar acknowledged. "We'll be careful."

"Ah do not like this," Andrew objected. "Ah do not like this one bit."

Dar clenched her hands on the grips that lined the edge of the boat. "Neither do I, Dad, but I can't leave Bud there. What else can we do?"

Andrew frowned at the approaching vessel. "You listen here," he said, suddenly. "I signal you duck, you do it, hear?" He took hold of Dar's arm. "Ah am not fooling, Dar."

Dar could see the utter seriousness in his eyes. "I hear," she repeated. "Be careful."

The big ex-SEAL snorted. "You all be careful or else ah'm going to be spanking the both of you for a long time."

"We'll be okay." Kerry stood up as they neared the back of the boat, which was pitching up and down nauseatingly. "We'll keep their attention, Dad. See if you can cause them some trouble while we do, okay?"

"Ah will give them trouble," Andrew muttered, pulling the boat even with the deck and holding his position. "Ah will blow that god damned thing up and out of this here ocean if that feller so much as tweaks any of your toenails."

Dar took a deep breath. 'Here we go."

"Paladar Katherine, you be careful," her father said suddenly. "Please."

Dar felt a little warmth spread in her guts. "I will, Dad." She reached for the ladder hanging down from the stern of the huge boat, ignoring the armed men watching her from above. Now that it was happening, she felt some of her nervousness drop away as it was replaced by adrenaline. Her nerves steadied, and she felt her heart rate slow as she climbed up to the pitching deck.

She put her hands on the top railing and pressed her body over in a swift, easy motion, forcing the guards to move back or else be slammed into. Dar took a step forward, her body blocking access to the ladder in order to give Kerry time to climb on board.

"Only one of you," the man nearest her said suddenly. "Tell the other one to get lost."

Dar turned as Kerry's head emerged over the top of the ladder. Ignoring the guard completely, she offered Kerry a hand over,.

"I said—"

"Shut up." Dar pinned him with a hard stare. "Either we both come, or we both leave. You choose." She watched him hesitate. "Pick!" she added in a loud bark.

He backed up a step and Kerry climbed down and joined Dar on the deck, brushing off her rain slicker. Dar took a breath. "All right." She caught her balance on the heaving stern. "Let's go."

The guards looked over the side as the engines on the watercraft gunned and it backed away from the yacht. The guard captain regained his attitude. "Who is that?"

"My canoe paddler," Dar told him. "Now, are we going inside, or should I just call him back?"

The guard gazed at her. "I didn't forget you from last time, bitch. You'll pay for that before you leave." He gestured with the gun barrel toward the door to the yacht's cabin. "*If* you leave."

Dar and Kerry walked past him. Three guards fell in behind them, guns held at the ready. It was too late to turn back.

ANDREW RAN THE watercraft back to the *Dixie*, and fastened it to the line he'd left in the water for that purpose. He slipped his slimline tank on, adjusted his mask, and entered the water in barely the time it took to think about it.

Under the surface, the conditions were a lot easier. He could feel the pull of the waves above him, but they didn't impede his progress, and he finned quickly toward the other boat. The sound of the hull breeching the water guided him, his light left unlit on his belt. No sense in advertising.

He could sense the boat near him and he went vertical, pulling out his new gadgets and fitting them to his hands. Carefully, he approached the hull of the boat and extended one arm, feeling the jolt as it contacted the fiberglass. "Gotcha."

He triggered the lock and hung on as the boat nearly heaved him out of the water. "Hell." Andrew got his other hand up quickly and latched on, hanging from both hands as the boat rolled. He waited for the hull to dip back down into the water, then released his first hand and stretched higher, moving up the surface like an extremely large spider.

Inside the door to the cabin, Dar paused, ignoring the prodding from the guard behind her. She checked out the room, then walked inside, keeping a light hand on Kerry's back. DeSalliers was standing near the bar, and three men holding guns were stationed around the room.

Dar's lips twitched into a feral smile. "Six guys with rifles?" She glanced between herself and Kerry. "I'm flattered."

"I feel so dangerous," Kerry added, folding her arms over her chest. "And I'm not even wearing my brown belt."

"Shut up." DeSalliers waved three of the guards out. "You're empty handed, Roberts. I thought you were smarter than that, but on second thought, I should have realized you aren't."

Dar deliberately turned her back on him, strolling across the cabin's interior to study one of the maps on the wall. "I'm not empty handed; you're empty headed." She looked over her shoulder at him. "Here's my deal: you show me Bud."

"This is not your deal," DeSalliers interrupted. "Now you just shut up and listen to me."

"No!" Dar turned and walked right past the gun barrel of one of the guards. "You listen to me, you scumbag." She felt her temper rise, and a rush of energy filled her body. "You want the information I have? Do you? Otherwise, I'll just walk out of here and sell it to the highest bidder."

"You don't have shit."

"Don't I?" Dar smiled. " You're wrong about that. I know about the poaching." She ticked off one of her fingers. "I know Wharton cut a deal with the locals." She paused and waited. DeSalliers now watched her with lethal, bitter silence. "I know about the will. So, you jackass — if you want what I've got, then you do what I say and it's yours."

DeSalliers' entire face twitched.

"You've only got two days before your loans default," Kerry broke in. "If I were you, I'd just salvage what I could out of this."

The man stared at her. "You don't know shit."

"Sure I do." Kerry kept an even, almost kind tone. "It's all in a database somewhere. You realized that, didn't you? Public debt filings."

DeSalliers snorted softly. "Yeah. That's how you ruined your old man, isn't it? Killed him, didn't it?"

It was like taking a spear in the gut. Kerry only just clamped down on her emotions and somehow managed to keep her expression unchanged. "Yes, it is," she answered. "I'd gladly do the same to you."

Dar dealt with the realization that if she'd had a gun in her hand at that moment, she would have shot DeSalliers without a moment's regret. "So, here's the deal," she repeated. "You show me Bud. You give me a transfer account, and I'll transfer your skunk money. Then I give you your smoking gun, and you let Bud go."

DeSalliers watched her from narrowed eyes. He remained silent for a minute, then very, very slowly, he nodded in agreement. "How do I know you've got a smoking gun?"

"Because I say I do," Dar told him. "You're not worth lying to, and Wharton's not worth lying for."

The tall man's head cocked slightly to one side. "Fucking amazing. We finally agree on something." He walked over to the window, keeping them guessing as to what his answer would be. "Tell me something first." He turned. "What is your real percentage in this, Roberts?"

Leaning against a bulkhead, Dar ears picked up a soft clanking somewhere nearby. "I've already told you," she said. "You just don't believe me."

"That you stumbled on this by accident?" DeSalliers laughed bitterly. " You're right. I don't. He pointed at one of the guards. "Bring the piece of scum up here."

Kerry released the breath she was holding and wished for a

glass of water. Her insides were churning so badly, she felt like a washing machine. She forced herself to move slowly and casually, wandering back across the cabin to end up next to Dar again. Her eyes met her partner's, and for a brief moment Dar's mask dropped and Kerry saw sympathy and regret in the pale blue eyes watching her.

Kerry tensed her lips in acceptance and patted Dar's hip as she came to a halt beside her. *So far*, she decided, *the plan seems to be working.* She prayed to God it stayed that way.

ANDREW SLOWLY LIFTED his head above the edge of the hull and peered across it. It was empty. The guards had clustered on the stern, out of the storm, exactly what he'd been hoping for. With a light sniff, he released one of his grips and removed it, sticking it in its pouch and transferring his hand to the railing. He repeated the motion with the other one, then pulled himself up and over onto the deck.

He lay there a moment, listening and catching his breath. "Ah'm too damn old to be doing this," he muttered to himself. The deck remained silent, so he lifted himself up and snaked across the top of it to the two prominent hatches set in its center. Then he lay back down and examined the hatches.

With a soft grunt, he fished in a vest pocket and drew out a slim tool. He slipped the edge of it under the hatch and pried gently upward near the hinge, working the fiberglass cover back and forth. With a soft crack, the hinge broke. Andy left it as it was and eased to the other side of the hatch, working on the next hinge point.

A soft creak sounded a warning, and he pressed his body against the hull and listened. Someone was coming along the railing toward the bow. Andrew cursed silently but remained very still, tensing his muscles as he watched the space between the cabin and the railing. A man wandered through it and leaned on the rail, watching the waves. Even after a few minutes, he didn't seem inclined to move on. Andrew put his hands on the surface of the hull and pushed himself upward, getting silently to his feet and rising to his full height behind the man. He paced forward even with the roll of the boat until he was just behind his target.

The man had a rifle slung over his shoulder. Andrew studied him for a brief moment, then balled his hand into a fist and slugged the man in the back of the neck. With a soft choking sound, the guard's knees buckled. Andrew stripped away the rifle and dropped it into the water, then debated throwing the man in after it. Wouldn't have been the first time, by any means.

With a faint sigh, he dragged the man over to the edge of the bow instead, and laid him down on the curve. Then he went back to the hatch and dropped down next to it, easing the edge up and peering underneath.

THE GUARDS DRAGGED Bud up to the edge of the steps that led to the cabins of the boat and held him in Dar's view. Bud's eyes were swollen shut and his face was covered in bruises. He didn't appear to be conscious of what was going on around him.

"You're a nice host." Kerry kept her voice even.

DeSalliers laughed. "He probably enjoyed it. He's the type." He motioned to the guard. "Put him back until I call you again." He seemed to be in a slightly better humor now. "Here's the numbers." He handed Dar a slip of paper.

Dar was still gazing at the doorway, seeing the beaten form in her mind's eye. She took the paper and stared at it. "Blood money." She took out her cell phone and accessed its web features.

DeSalliers watched her. "Must be killing you," he taunted. "Loser."

Pale blue eyes fastened on him. Dar handed the paper back. "It's done. It'll process when the banks open tomorrow."

"You expect me to believe you?"

Dar shrugged. "DeSalliers, it's pocket change," she said. "It just means a bit more of your crap I have to clean off my shoes."

"Pocket change?"

"Actually," Kerry spoke up, having to say something to keep from throwing up, "it's the budget for table mints for Dar's outer office." She paused thoughtfully. "For six months."

DeSalliers looked at her, then looked back at the paper with a shake of his head.

The guard returned and leaned against the door, watching Dar and Kerry with scornful eyes.

DeSalliers crumpled up the paper and tossed it. "Enough bullshit. Hand it over." He held out a hand towards Dar. "You're polluting my boat and I want you off it, along with your disgusting faggot friend."

Dar reached behind her and unzipped her pocket. She withdrew the folded piece of plastic and tossed it at DeSalliers almost casually, zinging it across the cabin and hitting him in the chest with it. "There," she said. "Now get Bud up here, and we'll be more than glad to vacate this shit hole."

DeSalliers unfolded the plastic and leaned over to read it, bringing it to the light. "You can't think I'd go for th..." He stopped speaking for a moment. Then he slowly looked up at Dar. "Well." He seemed a bit incredulous. "Imagine that. You told the truth."

Dar felt extremely tired, and she wanted nothing more than to get Kerry, herself, Bud, and presumably her father off the damn boat and out of that patch of water. "Yeah. So give me what I want and you can go crack a bottle of bad champagne over it."

Their host folded the paper and put it into his pocket, patting it with one hand. Then he removed his cell and dialed a number. "When I'm ready." He smirked at Dar as he waited for the call to process. "I want a chance to savor having beaten you."

Kerry let her hand rest against Dar's back. It was almost over. The tension had given her a migraine to compete with her already upset stomach, and she felt like walking over and kicking DeSalliers right in the shins.

"Wharton? DeSalliers here." The man spoke briskly into the phone. "I've got your proof, right in my hand." His eyes lifted and regarded Dar. "No, I got it out of her. No problem."

Dar felt a burn start at the back of her neck.

"What?" DeSalliers said. "That wasn't part of the deal." He listened again. "Now, look —" He was cut off, and they could hear an angry voice, though not the distinct words. The sound ended abruptly, and he was left looking at the phone with an expressionless face. After a moment, he lifted his eyes and stared at them coldly. "Well, it wasn't something I really didn't want to do anyway," he said.

"He double-cross you?" Dar asked, as a sudden dread filled her gut.

"No. *You*," DeSalliers said remotely. "Gregos?" He turned to look at the guard near the door. "Kill them." He stepped back through a small doorway nearby. "I guess the pirates will get blamed for something else."

"Yes, sir." The guard lifted his gun and pointed it. "My pleasure."

Chapter
Twenty-six

AFTER A BRIEF instant of utter shock, Dar reacted. The muzzle of the rifle had just pointed its deadly bore at her when she moved, grabbing Kerry out of pure instinct and throwing her down to safety. The sound of the shot deafened Dar. She felt a hot scorching across her cheek, then she was diving for the deck herself as she scrambled for something, anything, to put between her and the gun.

Her hands hit the legs of a chair and she rolled over, pulling the chair up and over her head. Another explosion nearly ripped it out of her hands, and splinters of wood flew everywhere. She felt a sting along her neck and she turned, then arced her body up and whipped the remainder of the chair in the direction of the gunfire.

She heard the sound of it hit, then another shot blew through the roof of the cabin. Dar took the chance and got up, focusing her vision on the rest of the room. She spotted the guard brushing the chair fragments off his arms and searching for her, and knew she only had seconds to take advantage of his momentary distraction.

Dar leaped forward and jumped onto the table that was between them, launching herself off it as the guard yanked his gun around in her direction. As his finger curled around the trigger, she let out a yell and he jumped slightly, just enough to give her time to crash full into him.

When Dar had thrown her to the floor, Kerry hit the carpet and rolled, the breath knocked out of her. She heard the gun go off and her guts clenched, until she caught a flash of motion coming from where she'd last seen Dar. Kerry had fallen close to the side door and her eyes suddenly settled on DeSalliers' face as he watched in puerile fascination, one hand on the door and the other readying his escape.

Anger erupted inside her. She scrambled up and headed for the doorway. He spotted her and turned to escape, but Kerry leaped at him and caught his leg as he almost vanished out the door. Despite his struggling, she got a grip on his calf and whipped her body around, getting her feet against the doorway and pulling him back with all her strength. "Get back here, you bastard!"

He screamed something at her and kicked hard, but Kerry had her arm wrapped around his leg and she reached up with her other hand and grabbed his belt. She braced her legs and yanked, using her thigh muscles to push with.

With a curse, he stumbled over her and crashed back into the cabin. Kerry rolled over and pounced on him, her temper getting the better of her as she went wild, hitting at whatever bit of flesh she could get a fist on. All the anger that had been building up the last few days poured out, and she ignored his attempts at grabbing her as she struck at him again and again with both fists.

THE GUARD WAS a big man. Dar had her arms around his throat, and she hooked a leg around the arm with which Gregos was holding the gun. Arching her back, she pulled the gun around and released one hand to grab it, twisting sideways as he screamed and cursed at her. Panic drove her. She ripped the gun from his hand and slammed the butt of it against his head, evading the grip he was trying to get on her. He hit her hard in the stomach and she doubled over, but the gun came with her and she slammed it into his legs.

They were too close, and it was too chaotic to even consider using the weapon for its actual purpose. Dar staggered back and caught her balance, then saw Gregos coming at her, and pure instinct gave her the means to keep him away. She lashed out in a roundhouse kick and boxed him right on the side of the head. The jolt traveled all the way down her leg, but her momentum let her drive through the kick. He rocked and staggered back, and then he shoved off the wall and came back at her. Already balanced, Dar drew her knee up, then slammed her leg out straight, and got him in the nose with her full weight behind the kick.

Blood spattered everywhere. His hands clutching his face, Gregos went down. Dar whirled and her eyes frantically scanned the cabin, her ears already picking up more guards headed their way. She heard a commotion near the door and bolted for it, rounding the edge of the couch to find an enraged Kerry sitting on DeSalliers' chest and beating him to within an inch of his life.

Kerry's shirt was half ripped off, exposing most of her chest. She was pinning DeSalliers down with her weight, her knees resting on his biceps as she slugged at him with both fists. After a second of frozen shock, Dar yelled at the top of her lungs, "Kerry!"

"Bastard!" Kerry smacked the man across the chops with her conjoined hands. "You're an asshole!"

Dar got behind Kerry and slipped her hands under her lover's arms, physically lifting her up off DeSalliers. "C'mon! Let's get the hell out of here!"

Kerry was breathing hard, her green eyes almost gray with anger. DeSalliers frantically rolled away from her and started crawling toward the center of the room, and Kerry's entire body twitched as though she wanted to go after him. A growl erupted from her throat, surprising them both.

"C'mon," Dar urged. "I hope to hell Dad's gotten to Bud. We can't stay here; hear them coming?" She dragged Kerry toward the small door DeSalliers had been attempting to use. A gunshot echoed through the boat again, and Dar could hear screaming. Her jaw tensed, knowing at a gut level it wasn't her father doing the screaming but he might be causing it.

"Ker?" she murmured in a gentle tone. "C'mon, sweetheart. Come back to me here," she urged the still angry woman, whose hands were clenched in balled fists. "It's over."

Kerry's furious eyes tracked to Dar and their gazes locked. "Oh." Kerry drew in a shaky breath and found herself abruptly, her entire body shaking in reaction. She clutched Dar's arms and shivered, her heart beating so fast in her chest she couldn't count the flutters. "D..." She had to stop and pant. "Shit."

Dar half led, half carried her to the door and shouldered it open. The boat pitched wildly, and she paused as she figured out what to do next. She felt Kerry slump against her, and she rubbed her lover's back. "You okay?"

Kerry sucked in a deep breath, and expelled it. "Yeah," she whispered. "He just really pissed me off, I guess." She took a moment to collect herself, then peered anxiously past Dar. "Where's Dad?"

"There." Dar edged out the door and held on to the railing as the rain pelted them. She spotted her father on the bow with Bud slung across his shoulders. "Dad!" she yelled, hoping he'd hear her above the storm.

His head turned her way and she saw the relief in his eyes. "Go!" she hollered at him. "Get the hell out of here!"

Two guards were headed toward the bow, struggling against the rain just as they were. Andrew took a step toward them, then shook his head and ran for the edge of the bow, gathering himself and leaping over the railing to plunge feet first into the water. He immediately disappeared beneath the surging waves.

Dar spotted the men dashing for her and Kerry. "Can you swim?" she yelled. "Kerry!"

Kerry hesitated, judging the shakiness of her muscles. Her body seemed to have recovered during the brief rest and she took a cautious breath. "Yes," she answered, knowing she had little choice at any rate. She grabbed the railing and held on, judging the distance to the water as the boat rolled. "I'm okay!"

Dar held onto her. "Go on. I'll jump after you when you're clear." She grabbed the back of Kerry's shirt to keep her steady as the boat dipped toward the water, then gently shoved her just as she leaped, pushing her well clear of the boat. Anxiously, she watched the waves, her heart in her throat until she saw a faint, pale blur break the surface.

Just as she readied herself to follow, a hand grabbed her roughly from behind. Dar whirled and found a pistol barrel in her face. Her reflexes saved her life as she twisted and her hand snapped up, smacking the gun to the side just as it went off. The space was too close for fighting, but Dar managed to draw back her arm and punch the guard in the face, somehow evading his grasping hands. It didn't really stun him, but he blinked and paused long enough for Dar to push free and slam the cabin door in his face.

She grabbed a fending pole clamped next to the door and jammed it sideways, blocking the door shut as the guard inside threw his body against it, trying to get out. Shaken, Dar glanced at the water, the ocean's savage waves looking more and more friendly to her every single second.

Faintly, over the thunder and slap of the waves, she heard the sound of Andrew's watercraft engine roar to life. A sweet sound. She grabbed the railing and prepared to leap overboard, when motion on the bow caught her eye. Two guards were there, one shining a blazing, handheld spotlight into the water. The light pinned Andy's small boat, and the second guard raised his rifle and aimed.

Dar heard the *Dixie*'s horn sound a warning. She released the rail and bolted forward toward the bow instead, heading straight for the two guards. With a growl, she dove headlong at the first, hitting him at the knees and taking him down. Together, they crashed into the second and he stumbled backward, falling down and rolling across the pitch of the deck. He slid under the railing and hung there, his light falling down into the water with an unheard splash. Dar found the rifle clattering by her and she kicked it, sending it spinning over the side.

The guard who had held it jumped on top of her, pinning her to the deck and slapping her hard across the side of the head. "You're dead, bitch."

Dar felt the truth of that. She gathered her flagging strength and fought him, ripping one hand loose from his grip. Her fingers brushed against something hard and she clutched at it, pulling hard when she recognized the outline of a diver's knife strapped to his thigh. As he lifted a fist and aimed for her head, Dar pulled the knife free and drew her arm out sideways. Swinging it inward a hair's breadth before his fist arced for her face, she buried the blade

in his side, feeling the harsh, ethereal sensation as the knife
penetrated his clothing and entered flesh. His scream was a
testament to her accuracy.

Dar arched her body, rolling to one side with all the effort she
could muster. She managed to throw him off, and as he rolled one
way, she rolled the other. The boat pitched as she was trying to
squirm under the rail, she felt him grab her by the back of her
jacket, and the next thing she felt was a sudden shock that rattled
her whole body. Then it all went dark.

KERRY WATCHED ANXIOUSLY, her eyes widening. "Dad!"
She pointed to where she could see Dar struggling with the thug.
"Oh...oh, my God!" she screamed, seeing her partner go down as
the man hit her in the back of the head. "Dar!"

Without the slightest hesitation, Andrew dove overboard,
regulator already in his mouth, and mask already settled on his
face. He paused to yell back at Kerry, "Take hold of that damn
rudder!" before he ducked under the waves and disappeared.

Kerry scrambled back and did as he had ordered, hauling the
boat around and heading it back toward DeSalliers' yacht. "Son of a
bitch. Son of a bitch. Son of a *bitch*!"

Behind her, the *Dixie's* horn went off again, three short blasts
that sounded urgent. Kerry kept her eyes glued on the yacht in
front of her, her heart almost stopped as she heard the yacht's
engines fire. "No!" But as she watched, the big boat turned and
started moving, heading away from them. Kerry felt like she was
going insane. She gunned the engine of her watercraft, then
abruptly slowed as she saw a head poke from the surface. "*Dad!*"

Andrew waved her on toward him, signaling urgently. "C'mon,
girl. Move it!"

Her instincts in conflict, her hand shaking, Kerry directed the
boat toward him, panic starting to overtake her. She slowed the
raft, and Andrew reached for one of the grips and pulled himself
over the gunwales and aboard with seemingly little effort.

He rolled over and came up next to Kerry, taking the tiller from
her. "Bastards." He watched the boat draw away from them. "Ain't
catching them in this thing," he said, whipping the watercraft
around in a tight, vicious circle that nearly swamped the boat in the
following waves.

"Dad, they've got Dar!" Kerry gasped out. "We've got to get
her!"

"Ah know that." Andrew said, setting a course back to the
Dixie. "Ah know that." He looked behind him, tension written
clearly etched across his scarred features. "Mah God."

Kerry could only sit there, clenching and unclenching her

hands, her heart beating so quickly she could barely breathe. Every instinct was pushing her toward simply jumping overboard and swimming after DeSalliers' yacht; only the fragile remnants of her sanity kept her where she was.

Dar was gone. Helplessly, she started crying, one hand holding on to the boat and the other gripping her hair, wanting nothing else but to scream, and scream, and just keep on screaming.

"GO! MOVE! HURRY!"

Dar heard the noises and felt the motion, alarm sending a shock wave through her as she realized what had happened. She was lying on a hard surface inside the cabin of the boat, and she could feel rug under her fingertips as she started to move.

"Fucking bitch!"

Instinct made Dar roll out of the way, just as something whisked by her head and crunched into the fiberglass wall. She got to her hands and knees, trying to keep her balance as the boat pitched in the waves.

"Ow!" Gregos, who'd missed her and kicked the wall instead, hopped backwards and fell down, unused to the motion of the boat. "Fucking bitch! Fucking bitch! Bitch!"

Dar shook her head to clear it and looked dazedly around at the cabin. DeSalliers appeared from the steps, staggering up them with an ice pack held to his face. He spotted Dar and stared at her. She stared back.

He dropped the ice and reached for a pool cue, the fury in his eyes showing he was beyond reason. Spittle flying from his bruised mouth, he went after Dar with the stick, swinging it at her head.

Dar really didn't process what happened next. She knew she was being attacked and her body reacted, ducking under the pool cue and spinning around to land a kick on DeSalliers' side.

"Bitch!"

"Let me do that, boss." Gregos, face swollen from her earlier kick to his head, got up and grabbed for Dar. "I'll break her fucking neck." The boat lurched and he fell again. "Fuck!"

Dar got to the side of the room and collected herself, a pounding headache causing flashes of light to obscure her vision. She put her back to the wall and raised her hands in a defensive posture, as DeSalliers held on to a chair while the boat pitched wildly.

"They're comin' after us!" a voice crackled from the radio. "Holy shit!'

Unable to move, DeSalliers stared across the room at Dar. "I'm going to kill you," he managed to get out. "I don't care what it takes, if I hafta gut you with a fucking harpoon."

Dar somehow managed to gather her wits. "What does that get you?" she asked, wincing at the rasp in her throat.

"Satisfaction," he spat.

"A prison sentence," Dar corrected. "Because they all know I'm here."

DeSalliers looked through the window. "We'll lose 'em. Then I'll dump your stinking body overboard. They'll never find it."

Dar straightened a little. "You'll never lose them."

DeSalliers laughed and spat out a mouthful of blood. "Your fucking girlfriend? Bet she's crying her eyes out."

Did she have a chance to talk her way out of this? Dar swallowed. Well, at least she was alive, and she had to do everything she could to stay that way. "What is it you want, money?"

"No." The man stared at her in utter hatred. "There ain't enough to keep me from killing you. I'd even take a rap for it."

Oh crap. Dar started looking for a way out of the cabin. The boat was traveling at high speed, and jumping off would probably kill her, but— Above the sound of the storm, she suddenly heard a booming roar.

"Boss!" the radio screamed. "They're fucking shooting at us!"

DeSalliers grabbed the radio. "What? Get away from them, jackass!"

"I can't! One of the god damned engines is blown!"

Another booming roar and suddenly the window beside DeSalliers dissolved into a thousand shards of glass, which went flying across the cabin. Dar pressed her body against the wall and threw her arm up to protect her face.

"Shit!" DeSalliers shoved off from the bar and bounced into Gregos, grabbing the gun from his henchman's belt and heading in Dar's direction.

SOMEWHERE BETWEEN GETTING on the *Dixie* and finding a way not to collapse, Kerry managed to get herself under control and put a screeching halt to her runaway panic. She staggered across the pitching back deck as Andrew threw himself at the ladder, yelling to a very scared-looking Charlie up top.

Bud was lying on the deck, still out cold. Bob was clinging to the railing, his eyes as huge as baseballs. "Oh my God," he was saying, over and over again. "Oh my God. Oh my God. Oh my God."

"Please shut up." Kerry went past him and into the cabin, her knees barely holding her as she made it to the bench seats and yanked them up. She grabbed the shotgun case and pulled it out, her hands shaking. *Can I even load it?* With impatient fingers, Kerry shoved shells into place and worked the pump action. Then she stood up and headed for the door, grabbing the frame as the *Dixie* heeled over and picked up speed. She went outside, stopping short as she almost plowed into Andrew.

He looked at her, his eyes flicking to the shotgun. "Ya'll wanna give me that there thing?"

"No," Kerry answered hoarsely. "I know how to shoot it."

The boat bounced over the waves, the spray drenching both of them. "Figured you did," Andrew replied. "But Ah figure Ah got more practice at it." He held out a hand. "And Ah know what part of that boat to hit."

Kerry handed the rifle over without another word. She followed him as he went to the side rail and got up onto the edging, then moved around to the bow of the boat. The storm almost obscured the DeSalliers' boat, but Kerry could see it crashing through the waves ahead of them, and she hung on to the side cleats with both hands as she squinted into the rain.

Andrew went to the front rail and knelt on the deck, curling one arm around the metal and propping up the shotgun with his other.

DeSalliers' boat was much faster than theirs, Kerry suddenly remembered. "Dad! They can outrun us!" she yelled as loud as she could.

"Naw," Andrew yelled back. "Ripped the fuel line out of one of them engines." He glanced behind him with a tense, rakish expression. "Jest in case."

Kerry crawled up behind him and held on to the rail, willing the *Dixie* to go faster. Her insides were tied in knots, and she realized then, just kneeling there, that she had no idea if Dar was even alive. A soft sound emerged from her throat and she gripped the rails with both hands. "Oh, God...please, please," she begged in a whisper. "Please don't take her from me."

She wasn't sure if Andrew heard her, but when she looked up again, he was looking back at her, those quiet, gentle blue eyes so very much like Dar's visible in the light from the *Dixie*'s windows.

"S'gonna be all right, Kerry," Andrew told her. "We're gonna get them."

Kerry felt tears welling up again. "I don't want to lose her," she managed to get out. "I can't."

The big man gazed back at her with compassion and understanding. "Me neither, sweetheart. Only kid Ah got." He turned back around and threw the gun to his shoulder, sighting down the barrel and squeezing the trigger in a move just that fast. The gun discharged, hitting DeSalliers' yacht just above the waterline. It swerved, and in the light from the cabin he saw a silhouette, one he recognized. He pumped a shell into the chamber and shot again, blowing out the window. "Step closer, you piece of meat," he muttered under his breath. "Hope them fish are hungry."

DAR WATCHED THE muzzle of the gun as DeSalliers pointed it directly at her. She was out of room to run, and the door was on the other side of the cabin. *Trapped. Fuck.*

"Take this." DeSalliers threw the radio mic at her. "Tell them to fucking back off, or I'm going to blow your fucking head off."

Dar caught the mic by reflex and held it, her finger brushing the button.

"Tell them!" DeSalliers screamed. He pointed the gun at her head, balancing himself against the wall with his other hand as the boat pitched in the waves. "Now!"

In that moment, Dar understood that she was likely to die. She didn't believe for one second that DeSalliers would hesitate to shoot her if she called off the *Dixie*, and frankly, she didn't believe for one second her father and her partner would stop, even if she asked them to. *So.* Dar wondered what it would feel like, and hoped it would be fast. Then she reserved the pain in her heart for missing Kerry, and how sorry she'd be to leave her. God, how much that hurt.

"Tell them!"

The pain echoed through her. Dar whipped the mic back at him. "Fuck you," she yelled back. "I ain't telling them shit! I hope they run right over this piece of crap, with you in it!"

DeSalliers ducked the mic and thrust the gun toward her, squeezing the trigger with a ghastly grimace.

Dar flinched reflexively, and brought her hand up in a futile attempt to protect her face, closing her eyes as she waited for the pistol to fire.

Click.

Dar stared past her hand at DeSalliers. He squeezed the trigger again.

Click.

Dar jumped forward and grabbed the gun, wrestling it from his grasp. "Stupid asshole." She threw the gun from her with as much force as she could. "I'm gonna kick your stinking ass."

He stumbled backwards but she was on him now, pouncing like a cat and grabbing him by the lapels. Kerry had done damage to his face, but Dar wasn't interested in disfiguring him. She went for his throat, her hands closing on it as she let out a roar of anger and dug for his windpipe.

"Aough!" DeSalliers grabbed at her hands, kicking her in the knees as he tried to get away. "Help!"

Dar kept her grip as the boat pitched wildly and they fell

against the wall, her shoulder smashing against the window painfully. She saw Gregos trying to get to his feet, but she kept on squeezing DeSalliers, hearing the gagging noises her adversary was making.

"Hang on, boss!" The bodyguard grabbed a chair and threw it at Dar.

As she sensed the motion, Dar turned them both and the chair slammed into DeSalliers' back. He screamed, best he could with his throat being compressed, and fell heavily against Dar.

She twisted and tried to keep her feet, but just then the boat leaned over radically, and she found herself, DeSalliers, and the guard all falling through the air and smashing against the huge window on the far side of the cabin. When it shattered, Dar felt the surface drop out from under them and then she smelled the sea and diesel, and thought she heard screaming.

Maybe it was her.

"THEY'RE SLOWING DOWN!" Charlie yelled from the bridge. "Taking on water!"

"Bet your ass," Andy yelled back. "Get this damn thing nose up to the back of that damn thing!" He put down the shotgun and pulled a large automatic from the pack at his belt, standing up and holding the railing as they closed in. "Teach them bastards to mess with mah kid."

Kerry could see men running around over on the yacht, and two came up on deck, yelling in alarm as they spotted the *Dixie*. She strained her eyes, searching for Dar's figure among all the shadows and willing it to appear. Praying for it. Begging a God she'd lately wondered about for this one small favor. This one little thing, in the cosmic sense. This one life. "Please."

The bow swung closer and Andrew got ready to jump from one ship to the other, his body coiled in waiting, the gun held in ready position as he prepared to attack.

As the two vessels converged, the bigger one suddenly heeled over, listing toward them as a muffled explosion sounded deep within. Just as Andrew was about to leap, the windows in the cabin shattered from the inside and bodies came flying out, hitting the water as the boat listed onto its side and came perilously close to capsizing.

Kerry bolted forward, and without thinking, leaped into the water from the bow, her eyes finding the outline she'd been searching for.

"Son of a..." Andrew scrambled to put the gun away and go after her. "Son of a... Ya damn kids!"

"Andy!" Charlie yelled. "What's goin on! That damn boat's sinkin'!"

"Damned if I know!" Andy jumped overboard into the water.

Kerry found herself being swamped by the waves. She realized that without any gear, she was at the mercy of the sea, and she struggled, taking half a breath before a wave crashed over her head. Then she started swimming toward where she'd seen the bodies enter the water, taking gasps of air whenever she could. The water was dark around her, and she could hear men screaming as DeSalliers' boat slowly capsized, low booms still coming from the interior.

She heard a splash behind her, and then the surface of the water lit up as the *Dixie*'s searchlight came on. She coughed up a mouthful of water and kept swimming, searching the surface desperately as no sign of the fallen figures showed itself to her. A shudder ran through the water, and Kerry heard a cracking noise nearby. Part of the boat was breaking off, and furnishings were falling out through the broken window. She ducked as a chair plunged into the water next to her.

It was raining hard, and Kerry could feel her arms and legs growing heavy as they churned the water, moving her forward a little at a time as her eyes roved over the surface. The waves swamped over her and her head went under, making her swallow a mouthful of seawater. She broke the surface again, coughing. Another wave swelled, but she ducked under it before it could knock her down. When her eyes opened, the dark roil of the sea was punctured briefly by the *Dixie*'s light, and she saw a figure beneath her, hanging limp in the water.

Kerry's heart stopped. Then a hand gripped her ankle and she surged upward in shock, her head breaking the surface as her lungs inflated and a scream emerged.

Dar broke the surface next to her and grabbed hold of her arm. "Ker!" She held her other hand up to block the light from the boat. "Let's get outta here!"

Kerry reached out and touched Dar's face, ignoring everything else.

Dar gave a faint smile. "C'mon." She started for the *Dixie*, fighting through the waves and rain, keeping hold of Kerry with one hand.

Buoyed by Dar's presence, Kerry felt as if the waves now gently cradled her, ushering her toward safety in a world turned right way up and blessed, and full — for her — of God's grace. Even the thunder sounded like laughter in her ears.

"CAREFUL." ANDREW MANAGED to get a hand on the dive ladder as the *Dixie* wallowed in the waves. He got a foot on the bottom rung just as the stern of the boat lifted up out of the water, taking him with it and nearly sending him flying off into the engine wash. "Jesus."

Bud was on the other end of the wall, battered face swollen and still bleeding. He leaned over and extended a hand. "Grab on!"

Andy did so without hesitation, being pulled from the water and rolling up onto the deck as Bud hauled backwards, only to come back up onto his knees and immediately head back to the ladder. "Dar!"

"Holy shit." Bud had tied a rope off to the deck railing and now he tossed it into the water, where two heads could be seen appearing and disappearing in the waves. "I left the Navy 'cause I didn't want to do this shit no more."

Andrew muffled a snort of laughter. "Tell me 'bout it." He held on to the side of the boat and anxiously watched his daughters catch hold of the rescue rope. "Spent more tahm with mah ass in alligators after Ah signed them discharge papers than before."

"Bud!" Charlie yelled down from the bridge. "We got waves coming in; we're gonna swamp!" He gave the diesels a little gas, sliding the stern sideways.

"Get them engines in idle!" Andy roared back. "Hold it! They ain't got no tow!"

Dar now had both hands on the rope, and Kerry had both arms around Dar, relying on the taller woman's strength to pull them toward the boat.

"Help me pull 'em in." Bud started hauling in the line. "C'mere, useless! Get your hands on the rope!" he yelled at Bob, who had, to his credit, been anxiously hovering, unsure of what to do.

"I got it!" Bob took hold of the rope and pulled, almost losing his balance as the waves rolled the boat in a half circle. "Shit!"

The stern of the boat rose and fell, slamming the dive ladder into the water, nearly hitting Dar in the head. Stopping her forward progress just in time to miss being struck, she released the rope at the last second, then grabbed the ladder.

"Oh, she ain't never gonna be able to... Jesus!" Andy scrambled for the ladder, lunging half off the back deck as the stern came up again, pulling both women with it. He grabbed for Dar's shirt. "Le—"

"I got it!" Dar yelled back, her biceps curled into stark muscularity as she held both of them up against the pressure. "Get out of the way!" she gasped, scrambling to get a foot on the lower rung as the bow rose and the stern plunged back down into the water.

Kerry just hung on as tightly as she could. She considered releasing her grip to grab the ladder, but the thought of falling backwards into the sea alone just... She couldn't.

Dar got both feet on the ladder and waited, feeling the rear start to rise again. "Get ready, we're coming in!" she screamed, lunging forward as the ladder lifted under them and pitched them almost right into the back of the boat.

Hands grabbed them and held them as Andy slammed back the hatch and hauled on the line. "Go! Go! Go!" he hollered. "Git, Charlie!"

The engines roared to full power in an instant, and the boat went from a wallowing helplessness into an almost painful arc. "Hang on!" Charlie bellowed. "Going head in!"

Ahead of the boat, a monster wave rose, higher than the bridge as they plowed into it. Andy and Bud both dove for the deck, covering Dar and Kerry with their bodies and wrapping hands, arms, and legs around anything that might possibly hold.

"Holy Mother," Bud grunted, as the wave crashed over the boat, drenching them in a freight-train carload of cold seawater. He looked up to see the cabin door slamming behind Bob's retreating form. "Piss head."

The back drains swirled, and then they were out of it, and the *Dixie* was plunging into the next wave, engines howling.

Kerry could feel the motion, but with Dar wrapped around her and the two ex-sailors covering them, she couldn't see anything. Maybe that was for the best. She pressed her cheek against Dar's shoulder, breathing air full of salt and tasting it on the back of her tongue. Every inch of her hurt on the outside, but on the inside, all she felt was gratitude and a sense of relief as profound as death would have been. Another wave of seawater drenched her and she held her breath as it swirled around her body and Dar's, before it drained out the back openings.

"Ker?"

Her throat hurt too much to talk, so she gave Dar a kiss on the neck to show she was listening.

"You okay?"

Kerry nodded, knowing Dar could feel the motion.

"Uuuggghhhhh!" Dar exhaled raggedly.

Kerry felt the boat shifting again, and she hugged Dar all the more tightly as cold water blasted over them and they pitched up so high in the front she felt herself being pressed against the rear wall of the deck.

"Shit!" Bud rasped, loudly enough for them to hear over the storm. "We're goin' over!"

Oh God. Kerry started to panic, trapped as she was under all of them and thinking of the tons of water about to roll over her as well as the huge yacht.

"No, we ain't!" Andrew hollered back. "Git your hand back down on there and watch your mouth!"

"Dar!" Kerry rasped, trying to squirm around and get a better grip on the boat's hardware.

"Shh." Dar got an arm around her just as the ship heeled over to the left and they all almost went flying to the other side of the deck. "Just hang on."

The *Dixie*'s horn sounded, loud and brassy to counter the howl of the wind, and they felt the engines go to full power, the boat bucking the waves as it headed into the wind. Dar lifted her head and shook the hair from her eyes, squinting into the driving rain as lightning cracked overhead and etched a picture of what was happening deep into her awareness: high seas; the *Dixie* crawling up the front side of a wave easily fifty feet high; screams; DeSalliers' boat cracking in half as the sea twisted it; darkness.

"Hang on!" Her father grabbed her by the back of the shirt and wrapped the fabric into his fist, tightening it across her chest. "Jesus!"

Dar locked her legs around one of the deck supports and grabbed a cleat with one hand, wrapping her other arm around Kerry. The *Dixie* almost went to vertical, and she knew a stark moment of terror as she thought the boat was going to flip and bury them under it. They seemed to hang in the air for an eternity, before the bow turned slightly to one side and the engines gunned, and then they were cresting the wave instead, topping it and plummeting down the other side at a frightening speed.

"Son of a *bitch*," Dar managed to croak.

Kerry spat a mouthful of water out and coughed. "Tell ya what," she gasped right into Dar's ear. "Next time, we go to PetsMart for our vacation."

They rose up on another wave but it wasn't as high, and the *Dixie* now was making reasonable headway against the seas. Still, water kept surging over the bow and sides, shoving them painfully against the fiberglass.

"Dad!" Dar turned her head. "We're getting pounded!"

The weight lifted up off her and Dar was able to half sit up and look around. The roar of the engines was overtopping the sound of the storm, and she could see the angry white froth behind them as the boat rocked side to side in the wind. She looked over the stern, back the way they'd come, and saw nothing but churning sea, the darkness limiting her view.   There was no sign of DeSalliers' boat or any of its occupants. Her conscience poked her. Should they go back and look?

Kerry hauled herself up next to Dar and shoved her hair back off her forehead, her face tense. She licked her lips and grimaced, and then rested her head against one faintly shaking hand. "Wow."

Dar transferred her attention instantly, unapologetically. "You okay?" She shifted around and got behind Kerry, giving her something to lean against. "Ker?" She felt chilled and knew Kerry must be as well, since she could feel her shivering.

Kerry swallowed, glad enough to lean back against Dar's body. "I'd be a lying idiot if I said yes," she replied. "Who in the hell could be okay after that?" She looked over at Andrew, who was now crouching nearby, both arms spread out across the back railing to keep steady. "Thanks, Dad."

Andrew gave her a half grin, his gaze shifting as Bud rolled over and grabbed the back rail near him. "We ain't done yet."

"No shit," Bud rasped, splaying his legs out over the deck. "I'm gonna move back to fucking Arizona. I goddamn swear it."

Andy frowned at him. "Would you watch yer mouth?"

"Dad," Dar interjected. "We both know what fucking is."

Andrew turned and shot her a look. Bud snorted softly, but managed a lopsided grin anyway.

"Honest," Dar assured him, as the boat rose up on another wave and crashed down, dousing them all again. She waited for the deck to steady, then turned to Kerry. "Let's get inside."

Amazing idea. Kerry felt motion around her, and hoped she had the strength to actually get up and walk. She reluctantly released Dar and they staggered to their feet, hanging on to the railing as Andy got the door to the cabin open.

"I'm going up with Charlie," Bud yelled, grabbing the ladder.

"Be up in a minute," Andy replied, grabbing Dar as she got across the back deck and steering her inside. "Let's move it!"

"I'm moving." Dar blinked against the light in the cabin, its glare painful. Things were tossed around, but the couch was there, and she fell onto it, Kerry collapsing next to her with their legs in a tangle.

Across the deck, in one of the bucket chairs, Bob was huddled, watching them nervously. His face was definitely green, and there was a plastic bag clutched in one hand. "I...is it over?" he croaked.

Dar glared at him "No."

The boat pitched again. Bob clamped his jaw shut rather than continuing the discussion. After a brief moment, he got up and scrambled for the steps, crashing into the wall on his way to the head.

"Jerk." Dar glanced up as the door opened and her father entered, his figure outlined in lightning from behind.

Andy knelt down next to the couch. "You kids all right?" he asked gently. "All that piss ass aside."

"Ugh." Kerry rubbed her eyes, stinging with salt water.

Dar looked at him. "Glad I went into computers, after all," she said with a faint, wry quirk of her lips. "Thanks for coming after us."

Her father put a hand on her knee and patted it. Then he got up, fishing in one of his pouches with his other hand. "Ah'm glad, too, Dar, but you all did a fine job over in that there boat" He removed something and reached down, casually pinning it to Dar's shirt. "You all sit tight. We got some rolling to do 'fore we get through this." He ruffled Dar's hair, then turned and made his way out the door and back into the chaos outside.

The door slammed behind him and latched, and above the storm, Dar could hear the sound of her father climbing up the ladder to the bridge. But inside, it was almost peaceful, and she blinked a little at the water dripping off her legs onto the teak floor and the creaking of the fiberglass hull around them.

She turned to look at Kerry, who was looking back at her with wide, utterly stunned eyes. A piece of seaweed was draped over her nose, and almost hypnotically, Dar reached over and removed it, her hand shaking so badly the bit of weed almost smacked Kerry in the face again. "Boy," she whispered, "what a fucking night."

Kerry blinked, nodding a little. "But we made it," she rasped. "For a while there I didn't..." Her eyes filled and she stopped speaking, a blink sending a scattering of tears to mingle with the seawater still dampening her skin. "We made it," she sniffled.

Dar exhaled slowly and let her head drop back against the cushion, exhaustion overtaking her. "We did," she uttered in wonder, seeing again DeSalliers' face as they hit the water. "Damn right we did." She pulled Kerry closer and hugged her. "Damn right." As an afterthought, she looked down at her shirt to where a glitter attracted her eye. She stared at the gold in numb bewilderment. Pinned to the sodden fabric was her father's SEAL insignia, winking calmly back at her in the cabin's light.

Why? Dar found herself too tired to think about it. She put her hand over the pin, draped her other arm around Kerry's shoulders, and just went blank for a while, hoping the sea woudn't toss her any more surprises before they got to safety.

Kerry closed her eyes and let her head rest against Dar's shoulder. It was enough for her, right now, to simply live the moment and forget about everything else, even the storm outside. God had given her this much; it was enough.

DAR DIDN'T KNOW how long they sat there, feeling the boat surge and twist under them and the storm outside thunder against the hull. She just knew it was long enough for all her joints to stiffen up, and for the sore throat she'd barely felt as she came out of the water to turn into a fire that made even swallowing difficult. She needed a drink. Dar glanced at Kerry, who was slumped against her with almost closed, bloodshot eyes, and grimaced. "Ker?"

"Uhng?"

"I gotta go get something to drink."

Kerry produced a sound somewhere between a whine and a groan.

"You too?"

Kerry lifted her head and observed the pitching deck. She nodded, and eased back so Dar could get up from the couch, waiting until her partner had pulled herself up before she attempted to follow.

"No, stay here. I'll bring you one," Dar objected.

"Unh uh." Kerry determinedly crawled after her. "Y' need both hands." She held on to the couch and pulled herself along, following Dar into the galley.

It was easier there, because there was so little room they could wedge themselves between the wall and the counter. Dar raked her fingers through her hair and opened the small refrigerator, grabbing hold of the counter as the boat pitched sideways. "Damn it."

Kerry bumped her impatiently. "Moo."

Dar handed over the milk jug and took a bottle of Yoohoo for herself. She closed the door and braced her foot up against the counter, freeing both hands to open the can and hold it.

Kerry did the same, and they drank in silence together for several moments. Then Kerry wiped the back of her hand across her lips and cleared her throat. "Paladar?"

Dar was caught in mid-gulp. "Mmph?"

"Next time, we call the police."

"Mm?"

"Or the Coast Guard, or the Army, or the Navy, or the Secret Service, or whoever, whatever it takes," Kerry rasped. "Because we're not going to do that ever again."

Dar put her Yoohoo down in the sink and leaned over, kissing Kerry on the lips for a long, sweet moment. Then she backed off a few inches and looked Kerry in the eye. "Deal."

Kerry licked her lips. Then for good measure, she licked Dar's, but her face grew serious. "I thought I'd lost you," she whispered. "I was going insane."

From somewhere inside her, some echo, some inner core rarely tapped, Dar smiled. "Take more than that asshole and his entire crew put together to make me leave you," she replied, resting her head against Kerry's, the image of the gun, and the click, and the horror already fading. "Way more."

Kerry studied Dar's face. "Were you scared?' she asked. "I was."

Was I? "I think I was too freaked out to be scared," Dar admitted, then fell silent, her brow creasing.

Kerry took another swallow of milk, washing the taste of salt from her mouth with a sense of relief. "We should get dry," she said. "I feel like warmed over puppy poo." She held on as the boat rolled again. "But hey...you know we did it."

"We did it," Dar confirmed softly. "Bud's okay. We're all okay." Slowly, she slid one arm around Kerry and hugged her carefully.

Kerry put down the milk jug and returned the hug, pressing her body up against Dar's despite their mutual dampness. Then she pulled back a little and looked at Dar's chest. "Oh."

Dar looked down, at the pin. "Yeah. Don't know why he did that."

The blonde woman looked at it for a long moment, then tipped her head up to look at Dar. "Honey, you saved his life," she said with a little frown. "Don't you remember?" From the expression on Dar's face, Kerry knew she didn't. "You did. When we were in the little boat before you...before that bastard hit you."

The pale blue eyes shifted and lost focus, then Dar gave her head a little shake. "I don't remember. I remember getting out of the cabin...those guys were running around..."

"Dad was in the boat. They focused a light on us," Kerry told her. "The guy on the yacht had a gun and he was going to shoot Dad. You tackled him."

"I did?" Dar vaguely remembered being angry, and a lot of yelling, and... "Oh. Yeah." The smell of hot blood came back to her. "Now I remember," she murmured. "Wow."

Kerry put her arms around her partner and hugged her again, tightly.

"Let's go change." Dar rocked her back and forth. "Then see if they need any help up there."

Kerry felt a faint laugh shake her body. "With three sailors driving?"

"Yeah." Dar started to move toward the bedroom with Kerry stuck to her like a barnacle. "It's my name on the captain's license."

"Little late to be worried about that."

"Mm."

Chapter
Twenty-seven

THE MARINA AT St. Thomas was in total chaos. Boats from all over were coming in to shelter there from the storm, and the tossing whitecaps made the possibility of collision a very real danger.

Dar put on her rain slicker and climbed up to the flying bridge to join Andrew as they rumbled at just over idling speed in a holding pattern. "What a mess," she murmured to her father.

"Yeap," Andrew agreed. "Told them dockmasters we had us a problem. They're getting us a slip," he informed her. "How's Kerry doing?"

"She's all right," Dar said.

Andrew studied her. "You doing all right?"

Dar nodded. "I feel like I was hit by a bus, but other than that, Mr. Lincoln, I enjoyed the play." She sat down in one of the seats at the console and rested her hands on it.

Her father chuckled. "Tough day."

"Hell yes." Dar tried to remember the start of it and found she simply couldn't. "Crazy." She glanced down the pin on her shirt, then looked over at her father. "I... um..." She touched the pin and shrugged one shoulder.

Andrew leaned on the console next to her. "Tell you something," he said in a mild tone. "Ain't never been nothing you ever done Ah wasn't proud of."

Dar interrupted him with quiet finality. "You don't know everything I've done."

Her father gazed at her. "That's all right, Dardar. You ain't heard everything Ah done, neither."

Their eyes met in a moment of uncommon understanding. Dar nodded slightly and looked away, folding her hands together in an oddly pensive gesture. "Gotcha."

"Anyhow," Andy said, "one thing you can't teach nobody is guts and when to use 'em." He studied Dar's profile. "Ah'm a damn lucky feller you got 'em and you know."

Dar stared at a droplet of rain trickling down the gas gauge. "I didn't even think about it," she admitted. "I just..."

"Yeap." Andrew patted her on the back.

Unwilling to think about the logical extension of their talk and what she'd ended up doing, she went for a subject change. "I owe you a big one, Dad." Dar leaned her elbows on the console. "I was pretty much out of my depth here."

Andrew shrugged a little. "Happens."

Dar looked out over the harbor chaos. "Yeah," she murmured. "But where do we go from here?" She glanced sideways. "Who do we tell about this? The cops? The Coast Guard?"

Her father tapped his thumbs together, giving her a surprisingly furtive look. "Let's see what's left coming back of those fellers," he said. "Ain't no point in telling more than you hafta."

Dar's head dropped forward a little. "Are you saying we should cover this up?" she asked in an incredulous tone. "Dad, they kidnapped Bud, they almost killed us! What the hell!"

Andrew stared evenly at her. "Chances are, they already done paid for that," he stated. "Paladar."

Dar stared back. "You think they sank," she said. "And—"

"Ah do," her father agreed. "And Ah do not feel sorry for that, and you shouldn't neither."

Dar sat back in her chair, her heart thumping erratically in her chest. "Could we have—"

"No, ma'am." Andrew shook his head firmly. "We got lucky to get out of that storm our own selves, and you know that."

She knew. "I called the Coast Guard for them," she admitted.

Andrew's face wrinkled into a frown. "You done a step more than Ah woulda," he said. "So...wall, let's see what comes of that then. Ain't likely they found nothing, neither."

Dar stared at her hands, clenched on the console. "You taught me—"

'Yeah, Ah know." Her father laid a hand on her shoulder. "But that was a long time back, Dar. Learned me about some rules between then and now."

The rain cleared a little in front of them, and Dar could now see some order in the boats being shifted. "Like the difference between what's right, and what's legal?" she asked, watching his profile.

He gave a half shrug. "Somethin' like that."

Well. Dar wasn't sure if she should be relieved, nervous, or disappointed. Maybe she was just too tired to really care all that much about moral issues she couldn't do anything about at the moment. "Okay." She nodded. "Let's see what happens, I guess. Sorry we had to end up in such a damn mess."

He relaxed, giving her shoulder a pat. "Seems to me like you done all right," Andy replied. "I figured you two had things covered 'til Kerry done sent that last note, about Bud and all." He shook his head. "Took me one of them there seaplanes over." He paused. "Ah do not like them things."

Dar had to smile. "Me neither." She watched through the rain as the lights seemed to diminish ahead of them. The radio crackled.

"*Dixieland Yankee*, dockmaster. Come on in."

Dar picked up the mic. "Dockmaster, this is *Dixieland*. We copy." She set the device down and straightened. "Want me to take her in?"

Andrew eyed her. "You speculating on mah driving, young lady?" he asked. "Ah am not the one who—"

"I've gotten better since then," Dar interrupted.

"So Kerry was saying." Andy slid over and offered her the pilot's seat. "G'wan."

Dar took the controls and settled into the chair, still warm from her father's body. She curled her fingers around the throttles and adjusted them, focusing her attention on the dark sea before her. On ether side of them, the channel markers bobbled wildly, barely visible in the high surf. Slowly the engines overcame the chop and they were moving forward through the cluster of boats on either side. "Kerry's got coffee downstairs if you're interested," Dar remarked, keeping her eyes flicking over the patch of water just in front of them.

Andrew grunted. "Ah'd rather not," he answered. "This here 'pears to be more fun watching."

It wasn't fun doing. Dar concentrated on navigating the obstacles, guiding the big craft through the channel littered with smaller boats. Some were trying to get out of their way or stay out of their way, but others were being tossed by the weather to the point where their pilots had little control.

Dar half stood, her weight coming up onto her thighs as she gave the engines a little more diesel. "Damn." The rain came down harder, almost obscuring her view and making the surface near indistinguishable. She could feel the wind rising at her back, and a gust fluttered her slicker hard against her body. And yet, she felt no fear. "You ever been scared out in weather like this, Dad?" Dar asked in sudden curiosity.

"Naw," Andrew replied absently. "Part of bein' a seaman is knowin' you're a part of all that," he said. "Can't control it; no sense in being scared of it."

Mm. Dar felt the rhythm of the sea under her and understood what he meant. She followed the riffle of the waves, carving a careful path through them.

A sailboat heeled with sickening suddenness. It arced into their path, not a length in front of the bow. Dar reacted, swinging to her right and gunning the engines. The wind shoved the sailboat just shy of their hull, the spar scraping lightly against them before falling free. In the rain, she could just barely see its crew frantically working to regain control of their sheets, and was more than glad to have the secure power of her engines under her. The seawall loomed ahead, and Dar was glad to see most of the boats keeping well clear of it.

"Careful there, Dar," Andrew murmured. "Got a strong riptide coming in."

"I feel it," Dar answered, and did, through her legs. "Hold on." She turned the boat into the wind and increased the power to the engines, now able to hear their rumble above the weather. The boat surged against the waves, cresting them and fighting against the strong current. She gave the engines full power and they surged past the jetty, heading full on into the cluster of boats beyond it. Dar heard her father inhale, and she grinned privately as she cut the throttles and swung the bow around. The current picked them up and turned them very neatly into the center of the marina channel. Dar edged the throttles forward again slightly and headed for the concrete docks.

"Son of a biscuit." Andrew chuckled. "Damned if you can't drive this here bus."

Dar approached the docks and swung around to the larger ones. She could see a cluster of people waiting at the empty slip they'd been assigned, and she thought she saw medical personnel. The waves were rushing up against the docks, breaking over them and dousing the watchers. Ordinarily, she would have let the boat drift gently in, but the tide was running the wrong way. Dar swung the boat into line, then set the engines into reverse, allowing the water to pull them very grudgingly into the slip. The dockmasters had already thrown bumpers over the side, and she skillfully maneuvered into place until her hull just touched them.

Two of the men on the dock hopped on board and grabbed their lines. Dar cut the engines and sat back, cocking her head and giving her father a questioning look. "Better than when I was ten?"

Andy ruffled her damp hair affectionately. "Good job," he complimented seriously. "You'da made a damn good sailor, Dar."

Dar crossed her arms and smiled. "Thanks." She glanced behind her. "Guess we'd better get moving. Kerry and I have a room up at one of the hotels, if it's still open in this mess. We can probably get you in there." She stood up and eased around the console chair.

"Ah do think Ah can scrabble up my own bunk," Andrew remarked. "Let's get Bud and Charlie settled down first off, and git that cowardly pissant off'n this boat, then find us some shelter."

That sounded very good to Dar. Some place dry, and quiet, and ideally supplied with lots of ice cream.

KERRY HAD FINALLY dozed off, nestled into the bed in their bedroom on the *Dixie*. She hadn't thought she'd be able to sleep, owing to the boat's motion and the stress of the day, but her body had simply taken over and demanded she close her eyes and shut out the world for a while.

Her dreams were formless. She kept seeing fireworks, as though replaying the Fourth of July in her mind, over and over again. Finally, the last cracker went off and the faceless crowd around her faded away, their clamor slowly morphing to a sound of clinking that beckoned her toward consciousness.

She opened her eyes, gazing at her surroundings in momentary confusion before memory kicked in. "Urmf." Kerry rubbed her face and rolled over, missing Dar's presence. She spent a moment wondering where her partner was, then realized the boat was relatively still and the engines were off.

"Jesus. We must be in dock." Kerry rolled out of the bed and straightened, holding on to the chest of drawers for balance as the *Dixie* rolled with the waves. "Why the hell didn't she come get me?" She flipped on the lamp and stretched, feeling aches along the entire length of her body. Her arms hurt. Kerry leaned against the drawers and flexed her hands. They were stiff and felt slightly swollen, and there were bruises across the heels and knuckles of both. For a brief moment, her stomach churned at the thought of how she had pounded DeSalliers against the floor of the cabin, and then she had a flash of how Dar's hands had looked after Dar had saved her from a pack of scrungy carjackers — painfully bruised, but in a good cause.

Kerry lifted her head and gazed into the dimness of the stateroom. "You know what, Stuart?" she addressed herself. "You don't have a damn thing to be sorry about. That guy was a scum-sucking, whore pig, and he deserved to have his clock cleaned."

As the echo of the words died away, she felt a little better. She twitched her shirt straight and ran her fingers through her hair, then slipped into the head. It was quiet on the boat. As she splashed water on her face, she listened for sounds of Dar's presence. Hearing the cabin door open, she stuck her head out, a smile appearing as she spotted her lover entering. "Hey."

Dar pushed back the hood of her slicker and walked over to Kerry. "Hey."

"What did I sleep through?"

"Some brilliant maneuvering on my part," Dar said. "How are you feeling? I didn't want to wake you up."

"Better," Kerry announced briskly. "What's our plan now? Stay here?"

"We can't. That damn storm's due here in two hours and they're evacuating the marina. Winds are up to seventy miles per hour, and I'm damn glad we're tied up." Dar rubbed Kerry's back. "Dad went up to the hotel with Charlie and Bud."

"Oh."

"I kicked Bob off the boat."

"Ah." Kerry nodded slowly. "You think the cops are still looking for him?"

Dar fiddled with the edge of her shirt, refusing to meet Kerry's eyes in the mirror. "I'm not really interested in finding out."

"Mm." Kerry drew in a breath and released it. "So, are we going up to the hotel, too?"

"Would you like that?" Dar asked. "Is that what you want to do?"

It seemed to Kerry that was a strange question. She finished brushing her teeth and rinsed out her mouth, then turned and faced her partner. "You know what I want to do?"she asked Dar, who had been standing and patiently waiting for her.

"What?"

"Be with you," Kerry replied simply.

Dar smiled and nodded. "Right back at you."

"You look really tired." The blonde woman brushed a bit of Dar's hair out of her bloodshot eyes. "Let's go find us a nice bed on dry land."

"I am really tired," Dar admitted. "And, um..." she shifted slightly, "sore. I think I twisted a couple of things in the fight."

Kerry could see the drawn lines in her lover's face. "You sure you don't want to get yourself checked out up at the hospital?" she asked, already knowing the answer.

"Nah." Dar dismissed the idea. "They'll have more real injuries to deal with than they can handle right now. I just need some rest, and maybe some aspirin," she said. "And you."

"And that Jacuzzi," Kerry reminded her. "C'mon. Let's go."

Dar put her arm around Kerry's shoulders, and they headed out into the storm.

As they entered the hotel lobby, they were greeted with the sight of a mass of humanity, jostling for space. "Jesus, I hope they kept our room," Kerry whispered.

Dar shouldered their overnight bag. "Me, too." She nudged Kerry toward the stairs. "Let's go find out. If they did, I have a feeling Dad might be sleeping on the couch in there."

Kerry followed Dar as they climbed the stairs and made the turn toward their room. The upstairs hallway was busy also, and they had to edge past several groups of arguing people to get to the end of it. Dar removed the key from her jeans pocket and tried it, opening the door cautiously and sticking her head inside. She was met with silence.

Dar flipped on the light and entered, waiting for Kerry to

follow her before she closed the door after them and leaned against it. "This room isn't moving, is it?"

Kerry explored the room briefly, then returned to take the bag from Dar's hands. "Thank God, no." She unbuckled her rain jacket and removed it. "Those windows look kind of scar...oh." She'd drawn aside the drapes to reveal wood planking protecting the plate glass. "Nifty. They work fast."

"You get used to it after a while," Dar remarked, removing her rain gear and trudging over to the bed. She collapsed onto it and lay there looking up at the ceiling. "Getting ready for storms, I mean. Especially out here."

"Yeah, I guess you would." Kerry let the drapes close. "Will the boat be all right out in the marina?"

Dar's eyes were closed. "As much as it would be anywhere," she said. "They've got it tied down and bolstered pretty good. I feel bad for those little guys they don't have space for."

Kerry set the bag down, opened it, and pulled out their pajamas. She set them on the table and walked over to the bed, sat down and picked up one of Dar's feet. "What will they do?" She rested the foot on her knee and started to unlace the sneaker.

"You don't want to do that. They're wet," Dar warned her.

Kerry shot her an amused look. "And?"

"You know what wet sneakers and socks smell like."

"Like our dog when she gets wet. Yes, honey, I do." Kerry pulled off the sneaker and then the damp sock under it. "What's your point?" She tickled the bottom of Dar's foot and felt the leg under her hands twitch.

Dar just smiled.

"I don't think we're going to be able to get room service right now," Kerry went on, putting Dar's foot down and picking up the other one. "I'm going to see what they left us here in our palatial abode besides rum."

"That works too," Dar murmured. "But it's better over ice cream."

Kerry rubbed Dar's ankle, feeling the joint flex under her touch. "Isn't everything?" She tossed the footgear toward the door, and kicked off her own. Then she eased down onto her side next to Dar and started working on the top button of her lover's jeans. "You know, something really profound just occurred to me."

Dar rolled her head to one side and opened an eye. "What's that?"

"Button fly jeans are much sexier than zippered ones," Kerry told her seriously.

A tired snicker shook Dar's belly.

"No, really." As she undid the second button, Kerry examined Dar's waist. "Think about it. With zippers, you undo one, then boop! It's done. This way, you have to take your time."

"Kerry, I think you're overtired," Dar advised.

"Hey, I got a nap. You didn't." Kerry smiled and continued her task. "It's like gloves."

"Gloves?"

"Yeah. Back in the days when women wore gloves, like the ones that went all the way up your arm." Kerry glanced over, seeing an obviously puzzled expression on Dar's face. "C'mon, Dar, you watch the History Channel. Don't give me that what-the-heck-is-the-WASP-talking-about-now look."

Dar's brow scrunched. "Oh." She rubbed her temple. "You mean the evening dress things."

"Right," Kerry agreed. "They had buttons all the way up, and they even had little hook things they used to button them. It was considered very sexy back then to watch a woman take off a kid leather glove. Some of them had a hundred buttons."

There was a stretch of silence as Dar contemplated that. "Really?"

"Uh huh." Kerry undid the last button and plucked at the waistband of Dar's underwear. "You know something else?"

"You're glad you were born in the latter half of the twentieth century after gloves went out of style?" Dar suggested. "Because if I had to wait for you to unbutton a hundred buttons, I'd come after you with a pair of leather cutters."

Kerry chortled and leaned her head against Dar's hip.

"Well, I would,"Dar insisted.

"I bet you never sucked your Tootsie Pop down to the chocolate center, did you?" Kerry continued the playfulness. "You chewed it."

"No," Dar replied with a dignified sniff. "I just bought Tootsie Rolls to begin with."

Kerry squirmed up a little and started working on Dar's shirt. "I knew that." She watched the gentle rise and fall of Dar's chest under her hand. The wind outside rattled the wooden shutters against the building, and they could hear a rumble through the walls. "Are we safe here?"

Dar glanced around the room. "This place has been here for a hundred years," she stated. "I think we're fine."

"Okay." Kerry laid Dar's shirt open and put gentle fingers on the bruises mottling her chest. "Are you hurting, sweetheart?" Her tone went from playful to serious. "You're kinda scraped up here."

"I'm too tired to hurt right now," Dar admitted. "Maybe later I will be." She sat up slowly and stripped off her shirt, then stood up to remove her jeans. "You joining me in this strip show, or are you snoozing in your clothes?"

"You think we're going to get a chance to sleep?" Kerry

remained where she was, watching Dar cross the room in her underwear to put her now-folded clothing near their bag. The soft lamplight erased the marks of the fight from her body and rendered it in golden shadows for Kerry's appreciative eyes. She loved the strength of her, the grace and solid power evident in every move. Nothing about Dar was for show. It was all real, and all functional. And all hers.

Kerry smiled to herself at the thought. She spared a moment to revel in the knowledge of what it felt like to love someone like this and to be loved to the very core. It was a true gift and she knew it, and in that one moment, it humbled her.

"God, I hope so," Dar sighed as she pulled on her pajamas. She turned and looked at Kerry, sprawled on the bed in casual disarray. "I've had enough adventures for today." She peered closer at the woman watching her. "Ker?"

It was like wading through the mists of time. Kerry suddenly sensed the depth of what was between them, sensed the ancientness of it and heard the faint echoes from lives beyond their own. It was weird, and scary, and her eyes widened as she stared into Dar's.

Curious, Dar came over to her and sat on the bed. "Ker?" she repeated, her brow furrowing with concern. "You okay?"

Kerry took a breath. "Yeah," she murmured. "Just had some weird déjà vu thing happen," she said. "I think it's been too long a day for both of us."

Dar patted her cheek. "Get undressed, and let's hope the storm doesn't..."she paused as the lights flickered, then went out "...knock the power out," she finished. Dar sighed as she turned and peered around the pitch black room. "Shoulda gotten out candles. What a bonehead move that was."

"I've got a flashlight in the bag." Kerry chuckled wearily, rolling off the bed and getting to her feet. She felt her way over to the table, fished it out and turned it on. "Are there candles in the room somewhere?"

Dar joined her, took the light, and made her way over to the cabinet that held the television. She poked inside and discovered a few hurricane candles, some that had apparently been previously put into use. "Here."

Kerry took the candles, lit them, and placed them around the room in strategic places. By candlelight, the interior took on a new look, the tiny flickering flames bouncing shadows off the ceiling and lending a quaintness to the old-fashioned bed. Kerry found the courtesy bar by accident, and raided it after she changed into her pajamas.

Dar listened to Kerry rummaging for a moment, then brought a last candle over to the bed and set it on the bedside table. She pulled down the top sheet and got into bed, fluffing up the pillows and settling back against them.

Kerry appeared from the shadows shortly thereafter, her pale hair now dry and collecting glints of the candlelight as she joined her partner. She handed Dar a mug and set a basket of goodies between them. Then she crawled into bed and relaxed, letting out a heartfelt sigh.

Outside, the storm continued to rage. They could hear things slamming against the windows, and far off, the sound of sirens. "Dar?" Kerry asked suddenly. "What do you think happened to DeSalliers?"

Dar sipped from her mug, finding an agreeable mixture of rum and pineapple juice. "You mean out there?"

Kerry broke a cookie in half and put a portion into Dar's mouth. "Yeah."

It would be easy to say she didn't know. Anyone would believe her, given the chaos they'd been through. She could just shrug. She could give a non-answer. She could even say she didn't care. However... Dar chewed her cookie and swallowed before she answered. "I think he drowned," she said in a quiet tone. "We went off the ship together just before it capsized." She licked her lips and looked up into the candlelit shadows around them. "I was doing my best to choke him at the time."

Kerry hitched herself up on her elbow and peered down at her partner. "Why?" she asked. "What was he doing to you?

"Wanted to kill me," Dar said. "He had a gun..." The sublime irony hit her. "But it wasn't loaded. The poor bastard couldn't even get that right."

"So you got mad."

Dar nodded. "I saw red," she admitted. "Or blue, or whatever it is you're supposed to see when you're so mad that you lose your mind."

Kerry laid back down. "So we have something in common." She lifted one hand and examined the knuckles, the bruises vivid against her skin. "Does that feel ugly to you, Dar?"

Dar looked into the eyes of her soul and smiled. "No."

Kerry nibbled on her cookie thoughtfully. "Really?"

Dar considered pretending otherwise. She decided she was just too damn tired. "Really," she repeated. "I guess it should, but he was a bastard and he was trying to kill me." She put her hands behind her head and winced as her shoulder popped into place. "I guess it's that old 'fight or flight' thing."

Kerry studied the ceiling. "Have you ever run from anything in your life, Dar?"

Her partner remained silent for a very long moment. "No," she finally said, a note of surprise in her voice. "I almost ran from love once." Her eyes shifted to Kerry's profile. "But you tripped me up in time."

"Did I?" In her exhaustion, Kerry felt a willingness to take the conversation to something more comfortable.

"Yeah." Dar seemed equally willing. "I remember sitting at home one night and thinking to myself how much better it would be for both of us if I...if *we* kept our relationship just business."

Kerry rolled over onto her side and looked at her partner.

"And..." Dar paused. "And I could almost... I could feel, sort of, how that would make you feel if I did that, if I told you to forget it."

"My God." Kerry rested her head against the cover. "That would have killed me."

Dar was silent again, for a few breaths. "Yeah. I think it would have killed me too," she replied. "Anyway, I couldn't. I was in too deep and I knew it." She reached over and put her hand on Kerry's, folding her fingers over her partner's smaller ones and gently squeezing them. "But I was scared."

"I wasn't," Kerry admitted with a wry note in her voice. "It was like a dream I never knew I had coming true." She lifted Dar's hand to her lips and kissed it. "I never looked back."

"I know." Dar felt a huge wave of exhaustion beginning to settle over her. "Lucky me."

"Mm." The blonde leaned her head against Dar's shoulder. "I think you're right about DeSalliers," she said, gently changing the subject back. "I know it's late, but I have to tell you this; I have to."

Dar looked at her.

"I saw...someone. Down there. Under where you were," Kerry expanded hesitantly. "I was terrified for a minute, and then you grabbed me."

"Ah."

They lay there together for a few minutes, deep in thought. Kerry drew in a deeper breath at last and looked at Dar. "No one deserves to die," she murmured. "But I can't feel bad about it."

"Except that he did get what he wanted," Dar reminded her wryly.

"No, he didn't." Kerry reached over to her bedside table, picked something up and tossed it onto Dar's chest. "Damned if I was going to let him get away with this." She eased up onto her elbow and reached for her mug.

Dar stared at the laminated sheet laying on the center of her chest. "Son of a bitch."

"Daughter of a bastard, actually," Kerry corrected. "One of the things you and I don't have in common." She took a sip of her rum and swallowed it, then leaned against Dar. "So."

"So," Dar repeated, turning the sheet over in her fingers.

"Death is a high price to pay for stupidity," Kerry said. "And

I...hate to have that on my conscience. Is there any way we can help them...the rest of them, I mean?" she asked in a serious tone.

Dar's lips twitched. "I called the Coast Guard for them on the way in," she admitted. "So yeah, I don't give a damn that they sank, but I wasn't about to disregard a maritime law I had drummed into me from the age of four."

Kerry pulled herself up and gave Dar a kiss. She licked her lips as they parted and gazed into her lover's eyes. "I feel...really strange about what we did tonight, Dar," she said. "Part of me is freaking out, but part of me —"

"Liked fighting for the greater good?" Dar replied in a casual tone.

A little silence fell. Kerry dropped back against the pillows without taking her eyes off Dar. She inhaled sharply. "Greater good." The words felt interesting in her mouth and she played with them a little, tasting their meaning. "Is that what we did?"

Dar shrugged. "I don't know. It's something my father used to talk about all the time — doing things for other people, or acting when it's not in your best interests just because it's the right thing to do." She reached over and combed through Kerry's disheveled hair with her fingers. "It's what the folks in the military do, if you think about it."

"Depending on who's defining 'right' this year," Kerry replied with a touch of wry skepticism. "But I know what you mean." She put her arms around Dar. "Did you like doing that?"

Dar returned the embrace as they listened to the wind howl. "I'm not very good at it," she said. "I'd much rather take care of my own best interests than anyone else's."

Both eyebrows raised, Kerry leaned up on her elbow and looked at her partner. "Dar, that is such a lie," she stated flatly. "You put yourself on the line for me after we'd barely even met."

Dar put a fingertip on Kerry's nose. "That's because you *are* my best interest."

Wasn't really much she could say to that. Kerry curled up next to Dar and shook her head. The wind was getting stronger outside, and she heard a loud bang as something hit the building. She put thoughts of the greater good out of her mind for the moment. "Are you scared?"

"Of the storm?"

Kerry shook her head. "Of what might happen. I mean...we were involved in a lot of not so legal things last night."

"No," Dar replied. "I'm not afraid."

"Really?"

"Really." Dar closed her eyes. "I'm too tired to be afraid."

Kerry took the hint and pulled the covers up over Dar's long frame, tucking them in around the two of them. She put her arms around Dar and laid her head on her partner's shoulder, feeling Dar's muscles relax almost immediately despite the raging noise outside. The heartbeat under her ear evened out and slowed, and she concentrated on counting its rhythm.

They would weather the storm; they always had, a muzzy internal voice reminded her. Kerry thought about that, losing herself in the flicker of the nearby candle as the winds blew around them.

THE HOTEL WAS warm and clammy inside as Kerry ventured into the lobby. The power was still out, but the staff had risen to the challenge and put out a table full of relatively tasty-looking foods for the guests to pick through. Her eyes roamed the room, and stopped as she spotted Andrew seated on the porch, his hand curled around a cup. "Ah." Kerry grabbed a muffin and walked out to join him. "Hi, Dad."

Andrew looked up at her. "Morning, there, kumquat," he greeted, as his eyes drifted past her shoulder. "Where's mah kid?"

"Sleeping." Kerry sat down and nibbled her muffin. "She was so tired last night, I thought it would be better if I let her get some rest while I scrounged breakfast for us."

Andy nodded in agreement. "She done things to be tired from," he said. "She okay?"

"I think so."

"Took them fellers up to the hospital. Looks like them bastards put a few cracks in Bud's head, but the docs took a few x-rays and let them go on after that.   Then Ah came back down here and bunked out with some of the marina folk," Andrew volunteered.

"You could have come up to our room," Kerry scolded. "We had plenty of space up there."

"Nah." Andrew took a swallow of whatever was in his mug. "You two young ladies deserve your privacy."

Kerry propped her chin up on her fist. "Dad, we were just sleeping." She grinned at him. "I'm glad Bud's going to be okay."

"Yeap, me too."

"Does he know it was you who pulled him out of the boat?"

"Yeap."

Kerry studied his profile. "Not really happy about that, was he?"

"No, ma'am, he was not." Andrew turned and looked at her. "But how would you be knowing that all?" He set his cup down and studied his tablemate. "They say something to you?"

Kerry nodded. "Yes, and Dar told me a little," she said. "I almost kicked Bud in the nuts a few times until he finally calmed down and stopped saying mean things." Her fingers played with the edge of the table. "What was up with that?"

A server came up to them with a pitcher and offered them a drink. Andrew held out his mug and they refilled it, then the server handed Kerry a cup as well.

"Thanks." Kerry took a cautious sip, relieved to find somewhat tepid fruit juice. She sensed Andrew wasn't comfortable discussing Bud with her, and decided not to push the subject. "I thought I saw cereal in there. Did you eat yet?"

"Ah did," he told her. "Went down and checked out the boat. Hull got banged up a bit, but nothing big. Should be fine to head back with."

"Thank you," Kerry said. "Did anyone say if DeSalliers' boat was brought in?"

"No, ma'am."

Kerry gazed quietly at him. After a moment, Andrew met her eyes. "Sorry if I butted in where I didn't belong," she told him.

Andrew's expression softened and he blinked a few times. "Wasn't that, Kerry," he answered. "Just somethin' that burns my shorts, and Ah don't like chatting about it."

"Okay." Kerry nodded. "Are you flying back home?"

"Yeap," Andy said. "Ah figure you two got things all squared away now. Got a flight back out tonight. They ain't reopened the airport yet," he informed her. "Still cleaning up. Storm wracked up some fuss, but not a whole lot outside the marina."

Kerry studied the horizon, which was clear and cloud free. "It's funny. I almost feel like last night was a dream," she mused. "But I know it wasn't."

Andrew cocked his head in a listening attitude.

"I'm glad you came out here after us," Kerry said. "Thanks."

A smile tugged at the scarred face across from her. "S'what a father's for, ain't it?"

Kerry stared off past him, her eyes distant. "Only if you're very lucky." She exhaled, dusting the muffin crumbs off her fingers. "I'm going to grab something for me and Dar." Pushing against the table, she stood up, suddenly wanting to be out of the sun and back with her partner. "Maybe we can find you for lunch?"

Andy got up and patted her on the shoulder. "Lemme give you a hand with your grub, kumquat," he said. "We maybe need a chit chat, and Ah want to see mah kid."

Kerry smiled, feeling the tension between them ease a little. "Okay, Dad. It's a deal."

They went inside to the table, which didn't have much in the way of plates. Andrew improvised by appropriating a basket of flowers, dumping the flowers, and standing helpfully behind Kerry as she filled it. They were halfway down the table when Kerry's path was intercepted, and she looked up to see the police captain politely blocking her. "Oh. Good morning," she greeted with wary cordiality. "Guess you had a busy night."

"Most certainly, yes, Ms. Stuart. That we did," he replied with courtesy. "I am glad to see that you are safe. Is Ms. Roberts safe, as well?"

"Very much so, yes," Kerry told him, noticing his eyes flicking over her shoulder. "Oh, I'm sorry. This is my father-in-law, Andrew Roberts. Dad, this is Captain Alalau, of the St. Thomas police."

Andrew issued a moderately cordial greeting. "'Lo."

Alalau gave him a brief nod. "Sir." He turned his attention back to Kerry. "Might I ask, Ms. Stuart, if you and your friend Ms. Roberts could find a moment to chat with me later on today? Perhaps over lunch?"

Uh oh. Kerry didn't think they were in trouble. She figured criminals weren't invited to lunch, even in the Virgin Islands but given all that had happened so far, one never knew. "Um...sure," she agreed cautiously. "I'm sure that would be no problem at all."

"Excellent." The captain smiled and bobbed his head at her. "Please, enjoy your breakfast. Unfortunately, the power will most likely be out for the rest of the day, but we are working on restoring it."

"Thanks." Kerry watched him walk off. "Hm."

"Nice feller," Andrew drawled.

"Very nice." Kerry sighed, dumping a last few items into their basket and snagging a Thermos of juice. "C'mon. Let's go wake Dar up and tell her the social agenda's changed."

They left the increasingly crowded lobby behind them.

THE CELL PHONE buzzed near her head and Dar jerked out of a deep sleep, reaching for it blindly in the darkened room. "Buh." She captured the instrument and opened it, her head pounding as her body tried to wake itself. "Yeah?"

"Dar!"

Alastair's voice was so normal, it almost hurt. "Morning, Alastair."

"Are you okay?"

Dar opened an eye and rolled it around, taking in her surroundings. "Yeah, I'm fine. It was just a damn storm."

"Storm? What the hell are you talking about? I got a call last night saying you got held up or something," Alastair said, his voice audibly upset. "What the hell is going on out there, Dar?"

Where do I start? Dar cleared her throat. "Hang on and let my brain boot," she told him. "I was sleeping."

A momentary silence preceded his exclamation of surprise. "At ten a.m.? Good heavens. Let me get my diary."

"I am supposed to be on vacation," Dar said in a peeved tone. "In case that slipped your mind." She rubbed her eyes and tried to shake some sense into herself. "First off, I didn't get held up."

"Well, that's sounds like a good thing."

"My hotel room got broken into."

"That's terrible!"

"But they didn't take anything, so the inn just moved us to a bigger room."

"Well, that's not so bad," Alastair said. "Jesus, Dar, you had me worried. I've got a lot of company resources sitting out there in the islands at the moment." He cleared his throat. "I didn't mean that the way it sounded... Well, hell's bells, I don't know what it sounded like."

Should I tell him about the rest? "We ran into a couple of snags out here, matter of fact." Dar admitted. "There was some trouble out on the water."

"Uh oh," her boss said. "Maybe that's what he was talking about. Your man Mark sounded half nuts."

"Mark? What the hell is he calling you for? Does he think he's my mother all of a sudden?" Dar snapped.

"No, she called me last time," Alastair answered benignly. "Apparently Mark picked up something on a police record, and wasn't happy about it."

"So he called you??"

"Well," Alastair cleared his throat, "he's a direct report to Kerry. Who is a direct report to you. And you're a direct report to me. Who else would he have gone to?"

Bah. Mother hens. Dar scowled as she gazed up at the ceiling. "Well, we ran into a couple of my father's old buddies and had to help them out of a jam. That, and the storm is currently making my life miserable," she said. "Everything okay there?"

"Here?" Alastair's voice dripped with surprised innocence. "Oh, sure. Right as rain, Dar. No problems here."

Uh huh. Can't wait to see my inbox. Dar stared at her phone, then sighed. "Great. Guess I'll talk to you next week when I get back in the office then, huh?"

"Sure, sure. You two having a good time otherwise?" Alastair asked. "Getting some rest and relaxation?"

"Well," Dar's ears picked up the sound of footsteps approaching, "right now I'm flat on my back, and you woke me at ten. What does that tell you?"

"Good to hear, Dar. Good to hear. You take it easy, and try to keep out of trouble for the rest of your trip, hmm?"

"I'll try," Dar said. "Talk to you later." She folded the phone and set it aside as the door opened, admitting Kerry and the unmistakable bulk of her father. She felt mildly embarrassed at being caught in bed. "Ah...hi."

"Morning, sleepyhead," Kerry teased as she closed the door, then set down the basket. "I figured you might be up by now."

"Only by the grace of Alastair," Dar admitted. "Mark told him we were having problems."

Kerry stopped and stared at her. "What?"

"Yeah. Hundred bazillion dollar corporation being run by two nanny worrywarts." Dar laid her arm across her eyes, wincing at the dull headache. "Hi, Dad."

"Hey there, Dardar." Andrew crouched down by the bed and patted her arm. "You doin' all right?"

"Mmpfh," Dar grunted. "Any chance of getting some fresh air in here?"

Kerry walked to the windows and opened the blinds. A portion of the wooden covering had been apparently been removed by the groundskeepers earlier that morning, and light flooded in. She unlatched the windows and pulled them open, rewarded when a gust of air puffed back her hair. "How's that?"

"Better." Dar still had her eyes closed. "What's going on outside?"

"No power, grumpy tourists, muggy weather, and the police want to have lunch with us."

Dar's eyes popped open and she hitched herself up onto her elbows. "Us?"

"Us," Kerry confirmed.

"Bck." Dar laid down and pulled the covers up over her head.

"Yeah," Kerry agreed ruefully. "That about covers it."

Chapter
Twenty-eight

THE BOAT ROCKED gently under Kerry as she jumped on board the *Dixie*. Dar was still on the dock, examining the mild damage the hull had taken, and Kerry dropped into one of the chairs on the stern to wait for her. The sun was out and the air was clearing of its moisture, the light breeze idly lifting strands of her hair. She leaned back and looked around the marina, wincing at the small boats tossed up onto the seawall and the debris floating in the water.

The marina itself had taken little damage; its concrete docks had weathered the storm quite nicely, and provided protection to most of the boats sheltered inside it. Many of the boat owners were there checking out their crafts, and around the shore, crews were removing downed limbs and other debris.

Kerry felt oddly itchy. She'd realized on the walk down to the boat that she wanted, more than anything, to be gone from the island and away from the chaos their vacation had become.

"Um, hello?"

Kerry looked up, to find Bob's unwelcome form standing on the dock. "Oh. Hello, there."

Bob stuck his hands in his pockets. "I...um..." He cleared his throat. "Can we talk?"

"Do we have to?" Kerry refused to budge from her deck chair, forcing him to crane his neck to address her. "I think you said pretty much everything you needed to last night."

He edged around closer to her. "Listen, I was just way out of my league, you know?"

"We weren't?" Kerry rolled her head around to look at him. "Getting involved with you almost got us and our friends killed."

Bob shrugged uncomfortably. "I didn't think it was that serious. I didn't think he'd go...nuts like that." He leaned on a pylon. "I'm sorry."

Kerry got up and went to the side rail, facing him. "What really sucked was you wanting that paper back...before we got Bud."

Bob looked down at the dock. "You don't understand," he

muttered. "It's like a hatchet he holds over all of them...especially Tanya. I was only thinking about her."

"A hatchet?"

"The money." Bob looked up. "But like I said," he gestured at the *Dixie*, "you don't get it. "

Kerry leaned on the railing, studying him with an enigmatic expression. "I understand that better than you'd ever imagine," she replied. "But people are more important than money, no matter how much of it you have...or don't have."

Bob shook his head. "Easy for you to say," he said. "Tanya's coming down here. Now that we know for sure the old man wasn't nuts, we'll find a way to get what we want. Without anyone else's help." He turned and walked away quickly, almost colliding with one of the other boat owners. The man shoved him off, and cursed, shaking his head as Bob just kept on going.

Kerry sighed. "What a jerk."

Just then, Dar appeared on the dock and circled the stern, hopped on board and stepped down onto the deck. "Yep. That he is," she agreed, joining Kerry on the side. "Hope we don't need him as a witness."

"Witness?" Kerry turned to her. "You think we will?"

Dar shrugged.

Kerry exhaled. "Any damage?" she asked, glancing over the side of the boat. "Didn't look like much."

"Not too bad," Dar confirmed. "Just a few scrapes."

"Good. Do we have a plan?" Kerry held out a hand.

Dar stepped closer and took it, walking around behind Kerry's the chair and letting her other hand rest on Kerry's shoulder. "A plan." Dar yawned, her jaw cracking softly. "I'm still too wiped to have a plan." She eased into the chair next to Kerry's and slung one long leg over its arm. "I guess we'll go talk to the cops first." She rested her head on one hand. "What do you want to do after that?"

Leave. Kerry bit back the answer, knowing her sense of responsibility would berate her for it. "Well, if that all turns out okay..."

"You think it won't?" Dar interrupted softly. "He asked us to lunch, not down to the station." She studied her knuckles. "Wonder how much we should tell him." Her eyes lifted and gazed across the water. "We could be in trouble, Ker."

"I know," Kerry agreed. "So I'd rather not take anything for granted. Now, if that turns out okay, we could go see Bud and make sure he and Charlie are okay."

"Mm, yeah," Dar grunted.

"We could take Dad out for dinner before his flight."

That got a much more interested response. "Okay, that sounds good," Dar agreed. "Where did he run off to, anyway?"

Kerry shook her head. "He didn't say. Just that he'd be back." She glanced at the deck pensively. "I think I pissed him off earlier."

The chair creaked as Dar leaned toward her. "You?" Her voice expressed disbelief. "How?"

"I asked him about him and Bud and Charlie," Kerry admitted. "I don't think he likes people knowing about all that. I guess it's embarrassing for him." She paused thoughtfully. "Or something." She turned her head and gazed at Dar. "I'm sorry I mentioned anything."

Dar reached over and gave Kerry a scratch on the back of the neck. "Sweetheart, it's not what you think," she said. "Yeah, the whole damn thing embarrasses the hell out of him, that's true."

"Having them think he was gay, you mean?" Kerry asked. "In that world, it's kinda understandable."

Dar chuckled. "No. He didn't really care about that. But let me start at the beginning." She cleared her throat. "It was really all my fault."

"Your fault?" Kerry asked in much the same tone Dar had used moments earlier. "How?"

"I'd just come out to him and Mom," Dar related. "It was tough for my folks, being part of the military world, and seeing as I was such a pain in the ass child anyway..."

Kerry smiled but kept quiet.

"So, my dad went out and read a whole boatload of stuff about homosexuality at the library," Dar went on. "He even checked out a few books, and apparently took one of them with him on a maneuver with a couple of squads off the base."

"Uh oh."

"Yeah." Dar nodded. "So then he got assigned to sea duty for four months. The captain of the boat he was on was a real tight assed conservative, and one day he went off about gays in front of the guys." She paused to reflect, then sighed. "My dad, being my dad, took him into a torpedo room and nearly removed a couple of teeth from his mouth."

"Yikes."

"Word got around about it, and everyone put two and two together and got six." The dark-haired woman stretched out her legs. "After that, Charlie figured Dad was fair game."

"Oh." Kerry frowned. "But... I mean, Dar, he was married and had a child. Didn't they get a clue?"

Dar looked at her, one eyebrow lifting in wry sarcasm.

"Yes, I know that's not necessarily an indication of heterosexuality, but Jesus! Your father drips it," Kerry protested.

"True. But that's not really what he's pissed off about," Dar explained. "It wasn't that they thought he was gay. Since I am, that wasn't something he found offensive."

Kerry cocked her head. "O...kay..." Her brows contracted. "But..."

"He was furious that they thought he was the kind of man who would cheat on his wife," Dar said simply. "He never forgave them for that." She pushed herself out of the chair. "Want a drink?"

"Sure." Kerry quietly absorbed the information. "Wow. That makes sense." She shook her head. "It was hard for me to think Dad would have been that embarrassed about someone thinking he was what we are," she admitted. "But I can understand now."

"Mm," Dar agreed. "He told me about it when he came back that time. He said he couldn't tell Mom, but he wanted to share it with me so I knew what really happened, in case I heard anything on the base."

"Did you?" Kerry asked in a soft voice. "Hear anything?"

A half smile twitched at Dar's lips. "Not directly," she said. "By that time, I...um...had quite the reputation for a temper, and most of the other kids on the base knew if they ribbed me about my father, it meant a fight."

Kerry tipped her head back and regarded Dar with a slight grin. "Two of a kind." She reached up and touched the insignia now threaded through the silver chain around Dar's neck. It nestled against Dar's joining ring and collected just the faintest hint of reflection off its dully burnished surface.

Dar stuck her hands into her pockets and looked down at the item, unable to hide the unabashedly proud grin. "Yeah." Her eyes twinkled. "That we are." Her attention returned to Kerry's face. "Don't worry, Ker. Dad would never be mad at anyone just for asking a question. Especially you." She stroked Kerry's hair. "He loves you."

The green eyes looking up at Dar filled with unshed tears. Kerry remained silent, just watching Dar's expression.

"We've got a while before lunch," Dar said in a gentle tone. "Let's go inside and relax. Okay?" She held out a hand. When it was taken, she guided both of them through the cabin door and out of the sun.

Inside, Kerry tugged her to a halt. She moved close and put her arms around Dar and hugged her fiercely.

Dar returned the hug, rubbing Kerry's back as she did so.

"Urgh," Kerry exhaled. "Can we just go out and get lost somewhere tomorrow, Dar?" she asked. "Find another of those blue holes and just leave our minds out to dry?"

"Hmm. That's an appealing thought." Dar inclined her head and nipped Kerry on the jawbone. "As a matter of fact, I could see spending a couple days lost somewhere with you." She felt Kerry's body press against hers. "I think I know some nice, deserted islands out there where it'll just be you, me, and if they're very lucky, a couple of dancing lobsters."

"Dancing into my nice big pot?" Kerry burrowed into Dar's chest, greedily breathing in her scent. "I have a bottle of champagne in here that would love to meet them."

"Oh yeah," Dar assured her. "We'll spend the whole day just being sea bums." She squeezed her partner, feeling her shoulders shift and relax. "Hey, I've got an idea."

"M'sure it's a good one," Kerry mumbled into the skin of her neck.

"I know we were going to go up to the condo for New Year's. How about we spend it down at the cabin?"

"Mmm."

"Kind of get a couple of days of vacation back?"

"Kerry made a low, pleased humming noise. "Even if we don't have furniture, I think I'd really, really like that."

Dar rested her cheek against Kerry's hair, pleased with the reaction to her plan. While she knew the interruptions had really been neither of their faults, she still felt bad about the net effect of it robbing them of their needed time off.

It was funny, but despite the fantastic nature of the events of the preceding day, she already found them fading into memory. She'd always had a philosophy of setting things aside once they were over and done with, but she found it strange that she could look back on what she'd done the night before and not have it seem terrifying to her. It had been a bad situation; she had dealt with it as best as she'd been able to; and in the end, things had turned out all right. What more, really, could she have asked?

It was over. Most often when traumatic things happened, she examined them for lessons to hopefully avoid the problem the next time around, but usually that was in a business context. Dar sincerely hoped she would not have to put her experience in escaping wacko salvagers or pirates to use any time soon in the ILS boardroom. Her blue eyes twinkled suddenly. *Well...*

"What are you doing?" Kerry asked.

"Just thinking," Dar replied. "Why?"

"I can feel you smiling."

Dar chuckled. "I was just imagining Alastair dressed as Captain Blood."

Kerry's body convulsed in abrupt laughter. "I can barely imagine Alastair dressed as Captain Kangaroo."

"Heh."

The blonde woman sighed and circled Dar's neck with her arms, swaying against her as the boat rocked. "Well, there's one thing to be said for all the stuff that's happened."

"Hm?"

"Made me totally forget my family," Kerry murmured.

Dar lifted her head and looked down at Kerry's profile. "Is that a good thing?"

Kerry nodded. "Maybe it helped some to see other people with crummier relatives than me," she stated. "I was thinking about that this morning after I talked to Dad down in the hotel lobby. My parents were pedantic and clueless, Dar, but you know something?"

"Mm?"

"I think you were right. I think at some level, somewhere they both did love all of us." Kerry blinked. "Even my father. Even me. Because as bad as he was, somewhere in all that twistedness he thought he was doing the right thing."

Dar blinked, surprised at the speech.

"I think I've seen enough true hatred the past few days to tell the difference."

"Ah."

"He hated what I was doing. He hated us. He hated my being gay, he hated me squealing on him," Kerry went on. "But I don't think he ever hated me."

Dar nodded silently.

"I can live with that," the blonde woman said. "Because it gives us something in common, because I never hated him either. Even after everything he did."

And then, Dar considered, *I've always lived by the theory that things happen for a reason.* She cupped Kerry's face in her hands and smiled at her. Their eyes met, and she could see a note of tired peace in Kerry's expression for the first time since they'd gotten back from Michigan. She leaned forward and rubbed noses with her.

Kerry pulled Dar towards her and traded a nose rub for a kiss. Then they hugged each other again. "Okay." Kerry released a long, heartfelt sigh. "Let's get back to the serious business of having fun."

Dar kissed the back of Kerry's neck, moving the pale hair aside as she was rewarded with a sudden intake of breath at the action. "I've had about enough..." she growled into Kerry's ear, "of real life intruding on my hedonistic vacation. How about you?"

"You bet." Kerry felt a nudge. "Hey!"

Dar nudged her again.

"I think I'm being bumped."

"You are." She followed the admission with another gentle shove.

"Looks like it's toward the bedroom."

"Good sense of direction," Dar said.

"Heh."

KERRY LAY ON her back, her body half tangled in sheets and Dar's head pillowed on her stomach. With one hand, she idly stroked the dark hair fanned across her belly, twirling a few strands of it around her fingers. After a moment, she lifted her arm and examined her palm, flexing it a little and turning it into the light. The bruises were already fading. It felt a little stiff, both her hands did, but more like she'd had a tough workout on the bag at the gym than anything else.

With a pensive sigh, she went back to playing with Dar's hair, her eyes tracing her lover's face and watching the faint twitches of a dream flicker under the closed eyelids. Dar had gotten a little bruised herself, Kerry noticed, as she smoothed a fingertip over a discolored patch of tan skin across one high cheekbone. She leaned closer. More of a burn, really, than a bruise. Kerry frowned, thinking back over the fight and wondering where it could have come from. She remembered hearing Dar curse as she'd been tossed head over tail to safety, and then the sound of a gun going off and... Kerry's eyes widened. *Had it come that close?* Horrified, she stared at the mark, imagining if it had been just a fraction of a hair different in its path.

It had come that close. She had come that close to losing Dar.

Kerry tipped her head back and looked up at the ceiling. Her eyes closed and she whispered a few words of heartfelt thanks to the God that surely, surely had been watching over both of them. She had no doubt now that she was blessed, that Dar was blessed, and that the love between them was as sanctified as any that had ever been. It would have been so easy to punish her, otherwise. Kerry looked back down at Dar's face. Just a fraction of an inch and like a wisp of smoke, it all would have been gone.

She felt Dar's breath warm the skin on her bare belly. She'd still been tired, even after their night's rest, and lying there sleeping she looked as peaceful as a child. Kerry absorbed the sight of her, newly aware of just how fragile, how precious life was.

With a soft murmur, Dar stirred, stretching out her body and curling it up again. Her eyes drifted open and she regarded Kerry with sleepy affection. "Mm... W'time is it?"

Kerry stroked her cheek. "Nearly one," she said.

Dar sighed, a reluctant expression appearing on her face. "I guess we should go find out what our lunch date's all about, hm?" she drawled. "Didn't mean to fall asleep on you."

"Literally." Kerry smiled. "You were tired."

Dar nodded. "I tossed around a while last night. Too much noise, I think."

"Too much excitement," Kerry suggested. Her index finger traced the mark on Dar's face. "I didn't notice this until now."

"Hm?" Dar's brow contracted in puzzlement. "Didn't notice what?"

"The burn on your face."

"Burn?" Dar lifted a hand and touched the spot, then her expression cleared. "Oh." She nodded. "Yeah, stupid bastard nearly blew my damn head off."

Kerry rubbed the spot with a trembling hand. "Yeah, so I see."

Dar's expression gentled. "No chance I was going to let him get away with that, though." She settled back down atop Kerry. "I'm not nearly done living this life with you yet." Her fingers clasped Kerry's and she pulled her hand close and kissed it, nibbling the skin with frank sensuality.

Kerry could only smile at that. "Dar, did you ever get the weird feeling that the place we knew each other from before we met during the buy-out wasn't in this particular lifetime?"

Both of Dar's dark, finely shaped brows hiked upward. She gazed at Kerry in silence for a few moments, muscles in her face moving slightly as she thought. "I never really considered the question," she finally answered, with a barely visible shrug.

"Hm." Kerry felt slightly silly for mentioning it. "Well, never mind. Just something that crossed my mind, I guess."

"Interesting idea," Dar mused. "I think I'd accept the notion of reincarnation if I knew it'd be with you." Her face creased into a pleased grin. "That'd be very cool."

Kerry grinned back. "Yes, it would, wouldn't it?" She released her residual morbid thoughts and gave Dar a light scratch on her bare back, rubbing in little circles with her fingertips. Dar responded by purring, and arching her body at the touch. "You're very playful today."

Dar rolled over and changed position, sliding her arms and legs over Kerry's and blowing a gentle puff of air into her ear. "Just glad it's today and not yesterday." She rested her chin on Kerry's shoulder and gazed at her. "C'mon. The sooner we get all this over with, the sooner I can steal you and take you off to my deserted island."

"Ooh." Kerry found it very hard to resist the mischievous grin being directed at her. She tilted her head and kissed Dar gently. Then they both rolled out of bed, still tangled together, giggling as they attempted to prevent themselves from crashing headlong into the bulkhead.

They separated and Kerry handed Dar her clothing, which was draped haphazardly across the dresser. She watched Dar slide into her swimsuit, then reached out and touched the soft, silken fabric. "I like this."

"It's like wearing tissue paper," Dar remarked dryly. "Or nothing."

"Mmhm. That's why I like it," Kerry agreed with an impish grin. "It only leaves a tiny bit to the imagination."

Dar looked down at herself then up at Kerry, as a faint chuckle of surprise escaped her. She reached out and tickled Kerry's still bare navel. "I think you're outgrowing your upbringing."

Kerry chuckled a little herself and donned her underwear. She looked up to find Dar holding her bra, and obligingly put her arms through and turned to allow her partner to fasten it. She felt Dar's knuckles warm against the skin of her back, then a much more intense warmth sent goosebumps over her as Dar nibbled at her neck. "Mm."

Dar released her and picked up Kerry's cotton shirt, holding it for her to don. She adjusted the collar and returned to her nibbling as Kerry attempted to button it, then reached around to help her when the holes seemed to elude her fingers.

"Dar?"

"Mm?"

"If you keep that up, this is a pointless exercise."

"What's pointless?"

"Dressing."

Dar relented and just finished her buttoning, giving Kerry a pat on the behind as she released her again. She put on her shorts and buckled the belt, then pulled a polo shirt over her head and tucked it in.

Kerry regarded her, then plucked at the rich, royal blue polo. "Black and blue. Are you sending a message, honey?"

Dar ran her fingers through her hair and settled her wraparound sunglasses on her nose. "Do I look mysterious and intimidating?"

"Until I look down at your Dilbert socks, sure," Kerry snickered. "Nerd."

Dar stuck out her tongue and went in search of her sneakers. Kerry finished buttoning her denim shorts and followed, shaking her head.

THEY FOUND THE captain waiting for them at the front entrance to the hotel. As he spotted them, he smiled and inclined his head, then indicated the outside garden area. "Our power is still off, and the inside is quite stuffy."

"I can imagine." Kerry glanced up at the sun, out in its full glory. Despite the breeze, she could feel a little sweat gathering under her clothing, and she was unapologetically looking forward to taking them off again. She followed the captain into the garden, and they took a seat at one of the only two open tables, the wooden chairs warm from the sun.

Dar settled next to her, watching the captain warily from behind her sunglasses. "So," she said, "what can we do for you?"

The policeman motioned over a harried looking waiter. "Some iced tea, if you please."

The man gave him an apologetic look. "We have no ice, sir."

"How about some lukewarm tea?" Kerry suggested. "And a couple of whatever sandwiches you probably have available."

The waiter glanced at the policeman.

"As the lady says." The captain smiled. "Since we have little choice, I gather."

"Yes, sir." The waiter scribbled, then ducked away.

The captain sat back and clasped his hands around one khaki-covered knee. He regarded them both in silence for a moment, then spoke. "Many things have occurred over the past several days."

Now, that was a true mouthful. Kerry propped her chin up on her fist. "Sure have."

"We were not able to locate the intruder into your rooms," he stated. "And it appears as if the reputed employer of that person has also left the islands." His eyes studied them intently. "We found that quite curious, since the marina tells us he had prepaid his engagement for some time"

"Really?" Kerry murmured. "Hm."

"We heard that he left the marina last night and was going to meet someone. Would you know anything about that?" The policeman's sharp eyes watched them intently. "He seemed so very interested in you."

"Ah."

"And then, I also hear that his boat was having some trouble in our storm last night," the captain went on. "Not so surprising, yes? It was a terrible storm."

Dar studied him, aware of Kerry's now tense form next to her. "It was pretty bad," she agreed. "We got caught out in it too."

"So I understand," the policeman said. "Do you, perhaps, have any information on any...mishap that may have befallen this gentleman? Out on the sea?"

Dar evaluated her options. She pulled down her glasses and met his eyes squarely. "If we knew why he wasn't here, would you want us to tell you?" She heard Kerry's indrawn breath, and considered the possibility that she'd just gone too far. "Captain?"

The captain's face twitched a bit and his head cocked to one side. "I have heard some interesting things about this man, and about yourself, Ms. Roberts," he commented. "If I investigate your statement, perhaps I will learn more interesting things."

"You might," Dar agreed.

"However, I might also learn some things that would require me to work very, very hard." The captain gave her a charming smile. "And it is too beautiful a day to be working so hard. So, Ms. Roberts, I will regretfully decline your so generous offer of information."

Dar gave him a mental point and removed a moral one. "Good choice," she said. "Because, frankly, Captain, nice as your island is, we're looking forward to seeing it behind us."

"That is excellent to hear, Ms. Roberts." The man turned as the waiter put down a plate of sandwiches and a flask of tea. "May I assume, then, that you have no interest in pursuing your complaint concerning the break-in here in the hotel?" he asked. "Or the disagreeable encounter you had at sea?"

Dar leaned forward. "I've settled with DeSalliers, and no, your friends the pirates are safe." She enunciated the words carefully, but lowered her voice. "I've had enough trouble the last few days to last me the entire next year, thanks."

"My friends?" the policeman replied. "Ah, but you have such friends as well, do you not?"

Dar inclined her head in affirmation. She picked up a half sandwich and inspected it, then grinned. "Oh, I bet this is popular with the rest of the tourists." She showed Kerry the contents. "Peanut butter."

"It does not spoil so quickly." The policeman graciously accepted the change of subject and selected his own square of white bread. "Other than these unfortunate incidents, you have enjoyed our hospitality, I hope?"

Kerry paused in the act of pouring some tea. "The islands are beautiful," she said. "I can guarantee we won't forget our visit any time soon."

The captain took a bite of his peanut butter sandwich, set the remainder back on the table, and smiled. "Excellent." He got up, giving them a sketchy salute with his free hand. "Do have a good day, won't you?"

They watched him leave, his slim, uniformed figure gliding through the crowd with ease. Kerry waited until he disappeared, then she sighed and leaned back. "Wow."

"Mm." Dar took a sip of her lukewarm tea. "So, that's that, I guess."

Kerry nudged her sandwich with one finger. "Does that mean...he's just going to ignore the fact that a whole boat and its crew has disappeared?"

Dar bit the edge of the glass as she looked at Kerry through it. "I guess he figures it's just one more boat gone missing in a long list of them," she said. "I don't know."

"Wow. So much for the law." Kerry frowned.

Dar folded her hands around one knee. "Yeah," she said. "Well, maybe it's for the best."

"What?" Kerry said. "After what happened to Bud? And the map? And DeSalliers' goons and his gun and —"

Dar looked at her. "And me choking him as we went overboard?" she interrupted in a low tone. "And what happened with that guy spotting the raft with the searchlight, and Dad shooting holes in the boat?" She leaned over nearer to Kerry.

"They were trying to kill us!" Kerry hissed, in a mere whisper. "What were we supposed to do, let them? Call the police?" she added with a touch of sarcasm. "Call CNN?"

Dar touched her fingertips to Kerry's lips. "All I'm saying is, it's over."

Kerry stared at her for a long moment, then she let out a breath. "What about the pirates?" She took another tack. "We can't just leave that alone. Even if Bud and Charlie are involved, damn it, Dar."

"No," Dar conceded. "But we're not going to get any help from the cops here." She glanced around, but the tables near them were quite empty. "On the other hand, nothing's stopping us from contacting those insurance companies when we get back to Miami.

Kerry relaxed a little. "That's true," she agreed. "If we take away their gains, maybe it'll stop."

"Exactly."

"Think they'll believe us?" the blonde woman asked wryly. "It all sounds so melodramatic." She rubbed her temples. "How do we get ourselves into this stuff, anyway?"

"Natural talent." Dar stood and offered Kerry a hand up. "Let's go. I think we've overstayed our welcome."

Kerry joined her, and they started off back toward the *Dixie*. "This place's overstayed my need to be here," she muttered, dodging a flock of pigeons. "Next time, we hike Yosemite."

"We'll end up being chased by a bear."

"That's Yellowstone."

"Whatever."

"ARE YOU SURE this is a good idea?" Kerry whispered, as they relieved the grateful grocers of some of their perishables. "I don't think those guys get along, Dar."

Dar reviewed the choices in the rapidly melting ice. "They'll be fine." She pointed at a fish. "Get that one. Dad likes them."

Kerry motioned to the man behind the counter. A call to the hospital had revealed that Bud was refusing to remain in its care, and he and Charlie were more than ready to leave the place behind. Dar had immediately offered them a ride back to their island, and casually invited them to join her, Kerry, and Andrew for dinner on board their boat.

There was, everyone had realized, no real way for them to refuse, given the circumstances, and now Kerry was gathering enough food to feed them, while hoping the evening didn't turn out to be a disaster. "I don't know, sweetie," she sighed. "I hope you know what you're doing."

Dar added several loaves of local bread to Kerry's basket, and sent the grocer into raptures by taking some endangered ice cream off his hands. "Dad agreed to it, so don't worry." She tossed in a jar of hot fudge. "Time to put all that crap behind them. Besides, whatever you make's gonna be a lot better than anything we'd find out here tonight."

Kerry accepted the compliment with a grin. "Only because we've got power," she reminded Dar. "We're going to have to run the engines to charge the batteries if you want anything more than half cooked."

"No problem," Dar murmured. "They've got hand pressured pumps. I was able to get them to fill the tanks this morning." She eyed the rather pitiful looking vegetables. "Those look nasty."

Kerry snorted. "Dar, if they were perfect examples of their species, presented in the best refrigerated case Publix could offer, you'd still think they were nasty."

"Mm."

"However, I'll need some of them, so close your eyes or go look at the cupcakes."

Dar chuckled. "I'll go get something for us to drink," she said. "Meet you at the register."

KERRY WAS JUST finishing the folds on the aluminum foil she'd wrapped around the filets when she felt the boat rock and looked up to see Andrew poking his head inside the cabin. "Hi, Dad."

"'Lo there, kumquat." Andrew entered and wandered over to where she was working, observing her creation curiously. "Making us some fancy dinner?"

"It's not fancy." Kerry dusted the fish with some finely chopped herbs, then poured a capful of cider over it before she sealed the packets. "It just a different way of cooking it."

Andy leaned on the counter. "Seems a lot of trouble for a bunch of old sea dogs."

Kerry turned her head and smiled at him. "Nah." She put the packet with the others on top of the steamer grill insert in the big pot on the stove, and then set a layer of vegetables on top of it. Another pot held water for pasta, and she put a lid on it before she wiped her hands on a towel and leaned back. "Okay, we're ready," she said. "Coffee just finished. Want some?"

"Surely," Andrew replied, taking hold of her sleeve. "Go sit yourself down and relax. Ah'll grab it." He tugged. "G'wan."

Kerry decided to humor him. She eased out from the galley and walked over to one of the chairs, dropping into it and leaning back. She watched her father-in-law setting the cups on the counter and fixing the coffee, his motions measured and precise as always. She saw Dar in that. Her partner had the same unconsciously methodical way of doing things. "Hey, Dad?"

Andrew glanced at her and raised one grizzled eyebrow.

"Are you okay with our dinner plans, or are you just humoring your daughter?"

A twinkle appeared in his blue eyes. "Waal..." He picked up the coffee cups and walked over, setting Kerry's down and folding his big hands around his own as he took a seat next to her. "One thing Ah done learned about my kid—she does something, it's got a reason," he said. "She ain't the frivolous type."

That forced a chuckle out of Kerry. "Uh, no. That's very true."

"So, if she wants us to mix up, Ah figure we'll all survive it," Andrew said. "Don't you worry, Kerry. Ah know you had a tough time the past few days. Nobody's gonna make this a bad night for you if Ah can help it."

"Thanks." Kerry smiled at him with quiet affection. "But I think it's been tough for all of us. Bud didn't have any picnic out there."

"No," Andrew said. "That's true enough. He done all right though. Coulda been a lot worse. Them fellas on that there boat were mean folks."

Kerry sipped her coffee. "Mean people really suck."

"Yeap." Andrew put his cup on the small table and leaned forward, letting his elbows rest on his knees. "Hell of a thing to go on during your R and R," he said. "You two should go find some quiet spot for a bit now."

"We are," Kerry said. "We're going to spend a few days at the cabin. We figure we can't get into too much trouble there."

Andy snorted softly.

"Yeah, I know. I suggested Niagara Falls, and Dar said it'd probably stop flowing while we were there and we'd get blamed." Kerry sighed. "I think we're fated for that sort of thing."

"Waal," he reached out and patted her knee, "least you know if you get into trouble, you got family to call on to help you out."

Kerry blinked at him, then exhaled. "That's true." She nodded. "That's kind of new for me."

Andrew nodded back, his expression serious. "Ah know that, Kerry, 'cause it's the same thing Ah had with my own folks," he said. "When Ceci and Ah ran off, they scratched me off the front page of the Bible, so Ah know what it feels like to have your own kin turn their backs on you."

"It sucks."

"Yeap," Andy agreed. "It does that. Took me a long time to get past it."

"But you did."

"Yeap," he said again. "Ah come to realize you can't figure nobody else's attitudes. All you got control over is your own, so Ah got mine and just put them all out there." His eyes met hers. "Ah ain't talked to my folks in thirty-some years."

Kerry leaned forward until they were almost knee-to-knee. "Do you ever feel guilty about that?"

"Some," Andy admitted. "Ah was close with my ma," he said. "But Ah knew the hating wasn't on my side, and living mah life with Ceci made it worth all the trouble."

Kerry took his hand and squeezed it. "Thanks." He winked at her. She grinned, then found herself pulled to her feet as Andrew stood and offered her a hug, which she accepted willingly. "You rock."

"You're not so bad yourself, kumquat." Andy patted her on the back and released her. "Don't you worry about me and the boys. 'Bout time we flushed that old mess down the bilge anyhow."

"Okay." Kerry smiled. "Now all I have to worry about is whether or not everyone likes fish."

"Kerry," Andrew put a hand on her shoulder, "you spend the time putting what we did down the hatch, you like damn near anything that ain't crawling or made of sandpaper."

"Ew."

"Wanna hear about what live crickets taste like?"

"No."

"How 'bout worms?"

"No!"

DAR WALKED TOWARD the docks, having settled their bill with the hotel and picked up a few last minute things for their outbound trip. The hotel, she was sure, was more than glad to be rid of them, especially since they'd comped their room and only charged them for a few incidentals. Dar found herself just as glad to be vacating it, and had graciously left a decent tip in the room.

As she turned the corner that led to the waterfront, the sound of loud engines made her pause, and she stopped as she saw the big red and white Coast Guard cutter idling into a slip. Dar leaned a hand on the wall and looked at it thoughtfully. She could just walk on past it and get on the *Dixie*, but her sense of curiosity was getting the better of her and instead she angled her steps toward the boarding ramp the crew was muscling into place.

A tall, blonde officer trotted down the ramp, his steps slowing as he got to the bottom and spotted Dar coming straight for him, making eye contact just to remove any doubt that he was the object of her interest. He stopped at the base of the ramp and waited, twitching his shoulders straighter as Dar closed in. "Ma'am?"

"Captain." Dar inclined her head. "Mind if I ask you a question?"

"No, ma'am, go ahead," the officer responded. "What can I do for you?"

Dar collected her thoughts a moment. "We were out in the storm last night," she began.

"And it was a rough one," the captain commented. "We were out there ourselves. I trust you got in safely?"

Dar nodded. "Yes. But we radioed in a distress call for a boat we saw out there. I was wondering if you were the ones we talked to, and what happened."

The man cocked his head to one side. "We had quite a few calls," he said with an apologetic grin. "What time was it?"

"Late. Eleven, maybe. Out to the southeast of here." Dar's eyes flicked to the man's nametag, then back to his face.

"Ah," the captain murmured. "Yes, I remember the call. Tell you what, let's go check the logs." He turned and led the way back up the ramp with Dar at his heels. "I don't want to give you the wrong information."

As she followed the captain on board, Dar gave a friendly nod to the scattering of Coasties busily working. They entered the bridge, and the captain ducked inside the communications room and picked up a book. He brought it out and thumbed through it as she stood there watching.

"Ah." He leaned on the book. "Yeah, here it is. 11:32 local. Are you the *Dixieland Yankee*?"

Dar chucked. "Well, I own her," she drawled. "She's a little bigger than I am."

The captain glanced at her and grinned. "Sorry." He glanced back down. "SOS reported in with latitude and longitude. We went to those coordinates, Ms...?"

"Roberts."

"Roberts. But unfortunately, I have to tell you we didn't find any boat there to rescue," Captain Culver told her with an apologetic look.

Dar was momentarily stunned. "Ah," she murmured. "You didn't find anything?"

"Well," the captain lifted his hand, "to be honest with you, we didn't spend a lot of time looking. The storm was about on us and we were pitching like nobody's business. We didn't see any boat and our spotlight didn't pick up any debris, if that's what you mean."

"Mm." Dar inhaled. "Well, I understand, since we were being

tossed around last night, too. We were glad to see the marina."

"Good job to get in safely," the captain complimented. "Were they friends of yours?"

Dar shook her head. "No. Just a fellow boater in trouble."

"After we finish here, we'll take a run out there and see if we see anything," the Coast Guardsman told her. "And if you're in the area I'll...ah..."

Dar glanced at him as he hesitated. "Yes?"

He blinked. "Oh, sorry." He rubbed the back of his crewcut in mild embarrassment. "Your necklace caught my eye. I've never seen a woman with one of those before."

With what? Dar's brow contracted, then she looked down at herself. "Oh," she murmured. "It's my father's," she told him with a faint smile. "No, they haven't let women into the program."

The captain grinned. "Gotcha. We'll let you know if we find anything. Will you be in port for long?" He closed the book and folded his arms across his chest, watching her.

"We're leaving tonight," Dar replied. "But we'll be around. Give us a holler."

"Absolutely." Captain Culver held out a hand. "Nice to meet you, Ms. Roberts. Have a safe trip."

Dar clasped his hand, then allowed him to guide her out of the bridge and down the ramp. She left the cutter behind and walked on down the dockside, deep in thought. Had they all drowned? She was hard pressed to admit anything but relief if that's what had happened. It put a closure on the incident, didn't it?

Or did it? Wouldn't DeSalliers' friends, his family, want to know what happened? Wouldn't they come searching, trying to find out? Wouldn't there always be questions, following them?

Dar sighed as she paused to watch the waters of the marina ripple past. Then she shrugged, and started walking again. If questions came, then they did. She had questions of her own, and after all—they'd been in the right through the whole mess, hadn't they? So, if someone wanted to investigate, well... she'd cross that bridge when she came to it. Right now, she had other things to do and places to be, and that was that.

"HEY, KERRY?" CHARLIE spoke up as Kerry was pouring another round of wine. "You interested in changing professions? I got a job for you if you are. This is some first rate chow."

Kerry seated herself, giving Charlie a smile as she acknowledged the compliment. "Thanks, but no. I'm happy with the job I have."

"You sure? Hospitality business's got great benefits," Charlie persisted.

Kerry sucked on her fork. "Well." She pretended to mull the idea over. "Let's see: in my current position, I can walk into my boss's office, shut the door, and get a kiss that sends my stockings flying out the window. Can you beat that?" she enquired with a completely serious expression.

A tiny squawking noise from her right made her look in time to see Dar caught in mid-chew, her blue eyes widening in startlement as everyone turned to stare at her. "Ooh," Kerry murmured. "I've never seen you blush like *that* before."

Dar swallowed and shook her spoon at her partner. "I'm gonna make you blush in a minute, Kerrison," she warned. "I'll tell them what you like to do with i..fmpf."

"Dar!" Kerry covered her partner's mouth. "Bad girl! Not in front of your father!"

Andrew started laughing, his low rumbling breaking the moment.

Dar nipped Kerry's fingers, making her yelp and remove her hand.

"Lord." Andrew chuckled. "If you two ain't something."

"Yeah?" Dar turned her head. "Remind me to tell you sometime about Kerry's views on parental sex."

Kerry covered her eyes. "Jesus, Dar, I'm going to kill you," she uttered in a hoarse squeak.

Bud, who had been silently eating his dinner since his arrival, chortled softly at that. He was still obviously stiff and sore, but he'd remained peaceable during the meal, his usual acerbic comments absent

Cautiously, Kerry peeked out from behind her hand, trying to ignore the twin pair of twinkling blue eyes. Dar poked the very tip of her tongue out at her, and Kerry made a grab for it, snatching her partner's nose instead and tweaking it. "Troublemaker."

Dar pointed at herself in feigned innocence, then at Kerry. "You started it."

"Kerry, I gotta admit it I can't beat that benny pack." Charlie shook his head, his bearded face crinkling into a grin. "And I wouldn't wanna try."

Kerry leaned her flushed cheek against her fist. "I know. I asked for that." She poked Dar's shoulder. "But thanks for the compliment. I've always enjoyed cooking, and I especially like doing it for people who appreciate the results."

"Hey, I appreciate it," Dar interjected.

Kerry smiled. "I know, honey. That's why I always do it for you."

Everyone chuckled and Kerry relaxed, relieved that the evening hadn't been nearly as uncomfortable as she'd imagined it would be. They were all clustered around the small table, enjoying her fish and vegetables as the boat rocked gently, the windows open to catch the cool evening breeze. She'd lit candles to save the drain on the *Dixie*'s batteries, and in the background Dar had a light, peaceful, New Age CD playing.

She smiled to herself as she thought of the surprise she had for Dar, something she'd held in the back of the small freezer and earlier had put in the refrigerator to thaw. "Ready for dessert?" Kerry inquired.

"Does it involve chocolate?" Dar asked immediately.

"Heh." Kerry got up and went into the galley. She put an already brewed pot of coffee on the counter, along with cream and sugar.

"So, Andy, Dar said you're living out on a boat now?" Charlie asked, breaking the brief silence.

"Yeap," Andrew agreed solemnly. "'Bout pulled my shorts out when Ceci up and figgered she wanted to live on one, after all them years kicking me to get off 'em."

"Hard to believe," Bud contributed in a low mutter.

"She still doing her painting?" Charlie said.

"Definitely," Dar answered. "She's got a workshop set up in the living space, right around there." She indicated the similar area in their boat. "Only it's bigger."

Charlie put his fork down. " You got one of these things?" he asked Andrew in surprise. "What the hell'd they pension you off with, excess Sandinista funds?"

Andy chuckled, refusing to take offense. "Naw." He reached over and tugged a lock of Dar's hair. "Mah kid took care of it."

Charlie and Bud both looked at Dar, and she shrugged modestly. "Not really. My Aunt May left me a trust fund when she died; I signed it over to them." She glanced at her father. "It was their choice how to use it," she said. "I never felt like anything was owed me anyway, especially after she left me the condo and this thing. "

Charlie whistled under his breath. He looked at Andrew. "Bet you're glad she didn't end up a swabbie, ain't you?"

Andy snorted. "Hell, Ah'da been happy in a Quonset hut." He leaned back. "But that there boat's a hoot and a half, no question. Ceci's having her a good old time with it."

Bud eyed him. "You guys lucked out," he remarked, but his tone was mild, not grudging.

"Hell yes." Andy hitched a knee up and circled it with both big hands. "Spent all them years in hell, now we got some good times. Life's evened out for a change." He glanced at both men. "Ah done paid my dues."

"That's for sure," Charlie murmured. "Glad things came out all right for you, Andy."

"Mm," Bud grunted in accord.

A short silence fell over the group. Kerry picked up the tray and returned, setting it on the table. "This is a favorite of Dar's," she explained, pointing to the round, fudgy looking creation in the center. "So if you don't like chocolate, blame her."

Dar exhaled as the tension around her dissipated. She cast an appreciative glance at the tray, recognizing the chocolate on chocolate on chocolate mousse cake Kerry had created for her for her last birthday. "Mm...where did that come from?" she asked. "Don't tell me you made it while I was out this afternoon."

Kerry passed around fresh plates for the dessert and collected the used ones. Surprisingly, Bud got up and took the dinner plates from her, carrying them to the galley and setting them in the sink. "Not quite. I made it before we left home. It's been in the freezer."

Dar observed the carving of her portion with a jealous eye. "You didn't tell me that."

"Because I wanted it to last the trip," her partner dryly commented. "And I wanted to get at least a small piece."

"Wow." Charlie had tasted the cake. "Mind if I get this recipe from you, Kerry? I'd sell a million pieces of this in the shop."

Kerry sat down and picked up her fork. "Not at all." She rested her free hand on her knee and found it immediately captured and squeezed under the table. "I'm just really glad everything turned out okay."

Everyone murmured agreement. Bud cleared his throat and reluctantly met Andrew's eyes. "Thanks," he muttered.

"Welcome," Andy replied.

"Any word on the jerk and his crew?" Charlie asked suddenly.

There was another awkward silence. "The Coast Guard didn't find them," Dar stated matter-of-factly. "There wasn't anything at the coordinates we gave."

Andrew snorted. "Serves them bastards' right if they sank."

"Damned if we don't finally agree on something," Bud said. "Assholes."

Charlie nodded. "Yep. Hope the fish had a damn good dinner."

"Hey." Bud spoke up. "You and Ceci ever ride out this way?"

Andrew finished his cake. "Thinking about it," he replied. "Ceci's done into painting them ocean things again. Looking for new stuff."

"Stop by and have dinner."

Even Charlie looked surprised.

"Surely," Andy drawled. "Thanks for the invite."

Bud grunted and went back to eating, apparently having exhausted his sociability for the moment.

Dar and Kerry exchanged looks. Kerry felt the clasp on her hand tighten and she squared her shoulders, digging her fork into her dessert and taking a bite with determined enjoyment. After all, they'd done what they could, more than most would have, given the circumstances.

Dar was right, Kerry thought. At some point you had to accept responsibility for the things you did. She had, and whatever fate DeSalliers had come to, he would have to do the same. What you cast out onto the waters came back to you in the end. Sometimes it took a while, and sometimes you had to go through hell before it did, like for Andrew. Sometimes you got off scott free for a lifetime and had it all your way, like her father had. But eventually the circle would close.

Kerry smiled, and looked up to find Dar smiling back at her. Sometimes, you didn't even have to wait a lifetime.

Epilogue

KERRY SWUNG GENTLY in the hammock, doing nothing more strenuous than watching the seagulls. She lifted a hand and took a swig from a longneck bottle of beer, finding an interesting patch of clouds wandering its way across the clear blue sky. "Hey, Dar?"

The other occupant on the hammock grunted in her ear incoherently.

"Y'think I should check my blood pressure right now?"

"Does that mean I gotta get up?" Dar mumbled. "I think your pressure's fine. I can hear your heartbeat. It's whistling *Dixie*."

"Mmm," Kerry agreed. "I feel very, very relaxed." She lifted her other hand, linked with Dar's, and kissed her partner's fingers. "Coming back here was a really good idea."

"Uh huh."

"I could stay here for weeks."

"Uh huh."

"There's a rabbit on your hip."

"Cool."

Kerry turned her head and indulgently watched Dar's mostly asleep profile. There was a dusting of beach sand on her cheek, and the dark hair, slightly overgrown, was hiding almost all of one eye. "Would you like to take the bike out and ride naked down US 1 with me?"

"Sure."

"I think that idea sounds better than it really is." Kerry blew a lock of Dar's hair back. "It's gnat season."

One blue eye opened. "Ew."

"Mm." Kerry pushed against the porch railing, swinging them both gently. "I was joking about the nude riding, but we could go down the road a bit and watch fireworks tonight."

"We could do that," Dar agreed sleepily. "How about we bring that bottle of champagne with us and toast the New Year out on the beach?"

"Ooh." Kerry rubbed the side of her nose, which itched. "You missing not going to the company party?"

Dar just snorted. "Only thing I'm gonna miss is not getting to

dance with you in front of all of them," she grumbled. "And we can
do that here without having to suffer through high heels."

"Okay." Kerry rolled onto her side and sprawled over Dar,
drawing in a breath full of cocoa butter and apricot body scrub. "I'll
bring my MP3 player with us on the bike."

"Does it have speakers?'

"I intend for us to share the ear buds."

"That means Who Let the Dogs Out isn't on the playlist, right?"

Kerry chuckled happily. "Ah, now *this* is a vacation, Dar." She
nuzzled her partner's ear. "Just you and me. No pirates, no land
sharks, no snooty but curiously ineffective private eyes."

"Uh huh. A vacation from our vacation," Dar said. "From now
on, we'll just take 'em two weeks at a time: one week to get into
trouble, one week to recover from it." She turned her head slightly
and kissed the lips that had been nibbling her ear. "Mm. You taste
like hot peppers."

Kerry licked her lips. "Those were very tasty mud bugs." She
held up her beer. "I've been trying to cool down my mouth since we
had lunch."

Dar tasted her lips again. "There's a little redneck steak joint
about three miles south of here. Wanna join me there for a very low
class New Year's Eve dinner?"

"Is this the kind of place where you get a side order of butter
with your deep fried garlic bread?"

"Uh huh."

"And they serve brown gravy with the fries?"

"That and cheese sauce."

"I'm there." Kerry glanced over her shoulder at the sun. "Let's
go grab a shower and dress down," she suggested. "We can laugh
about poor Mark in his tuxedo."

Dar took her time getting up, wrapping her hand around the
back of Kerry's neck and giving her a thorough, passionate kissing
first. Then they eased out of the hammock and went inside, still
attached to each other.

SHOWERED AND DRESSED, Kerry perched on the wicker
stool next to the kitchen counter and studied the envelope in front
of her. She picked up her black, permanent marker and wrote on the
manila face, carefully penning a name and address.

When she was finished, she picked up the battered, much
folded piece of laminated plastic and spread it flat, pressing it
between two pieces of cardboard. She taped it in place, then slid the
entire thing into the envelope.

"Bob, I'd like to believe you're on the up and up, but you know,
you're pretty skunky," Kerry said as she sealed the envelope. "And

as much as you praised your friend Tanya, I gotta wonder about
anyone who would either hang out with you, or hire you to do
something."

She picked up the stamps she'd gotten at the local post office
and affixed the proper number of them to the packet. "So, I figure
the one person who actually should get this will probably know
what the best thing to do with it is."

Dar came out of the bedroom, tucking a pristine white
heavyweight T-shirt into her worn jeans. "Ready?"

"Yep." Kerry held up the envelope. "I need to call Richard and
thank him for agreeing to deliver this to the nursing home for me."

"He's a good guy," Dar agreed, picking up her leather jacket
and slinging it over her shoulder. "He's also agreed to help her out
if she needs it. He's got a criminal guy he works with, if it turns out
that way." She gestured to the door. "There's a mailbox in town.
We can drop it there."

Kerry picked up her own jacket and followed Dar out the door.
The bike was already waiting for them, and she shrugged into her
jacket as they walked over to it "Hey. I wanna drive."

Dar paused and eyed her.

"C'mon, c'mon." Kerry handed her the envelope. "It's just a
few miles, remember?"

"Uh huh." Dar held the bike steady while Kerry climbed on,
then she settled herself behind her partner, her longer legs able to
hold the machine up despite her perch. "Y'know, Ker..."

"I know. I know." Kerry hopped up onto the seat. "Humor me."

Dar chuckled.

"Watch it, Dixiecup," Kerry warned. "Or I'll have them put
tiny tires on this so I can reach."

Dar kissed the back of Kerry's neck. "You're so cute." She
handed her partner her helmet. "Here."

Kerry started the engine and waited for Dar to wind a long arm
around her middle before she started off, heading for the road and
turning onto it carefully. "Where's the post box?" she asked,
getting used to the difference in balance with both of them on the
bike.

Dar's hand pointed, and she directed the bike toward it,
pausing there long enough for her partner to drop in the envelope.
"That's that," Kerry called behind her. "Let's go have some fun!"
She felt Dar's other arm wrap firmly around her, and she gunned
the throttle. "How fast does this go, anyway?"

"I don't remember," Dar answered. "Why?"

"Let's find out!" Kerry opened the bike up. With a roar and a
back blast of sand, they headed off toward the sunset.

FORTHCOMING TITLES

published by
Yellow Rose Books

Dark Dreamer
(Heartstopper Series)

by Jennifer Fulton

"Jennifer Fulton has rescued the romance from formulaic complacency by asking universal questions about friendship and love, intimacy and lust."
The Lesbian Review of Books

Best-selling horror author, Rowe Devlin has had two flops in a row and keeps falling in love with straight women. Seeking inspiration and a fresh start, she abandons life in Manhattan for an old Victorian house in Maine. But Dark Harbor Cottage is a far cry from the tranquil writing environment she envisioned. For a start, the place is haunted and the ghost is none too friendly. To make life even more difficult, her neighbors are a huge distraction. The Temple twins, Phoebe and Cara, are identical and profoundly alluring, and Rowe is soon under their spell, unable to decide which of the two she is more in love with. Just when it seems things can't get any worse, she finds herself embroiled in a mystery more bizarre and frightening than anything she's ever written.

Intrigue, passion and suspense combine in this taut paranormal thriller/romance, the first in Jennifer Fulton's new *Heartstoppers* series.

OTHER MELISSA GOOD TITLES

published by
Yellow Rose Books

Eye of the Storm - Just when it looks like Dar Roberts and Kerry Stuart are settling into their lives together they discover that life is never simple — especially around them. Surrounded by endless corporate and political intrigue, Dar experiences personal discoveries that force her to deal with issues she had buried long ago and Kerry finally faces the consequences of her own actions.

Red Sky At Morning - This fourth chronicle in the Dar and Kerry series continues where *Eye of the Storm* ended. The lives of Dar Roberts and Kerry Stuart seem to get more complex rather than moving toward the simpler lifestyle they both dream of.

Thicker Than Water - The fifth entry in the continuing saga of Dar Roberts and Kerry Stuart finds Kerry forced to acknowledge her feelings toward and experience with her folks and Dar determined to support Kerry in the face of grief and hatred. They must face down Kerry's extended family with a little help from their own.

OTHER YELLOW ROSE TITLES

You may also enjoy:

INFINITE LOOP
by Meghan O'Brien

When shy software developer, Regan O'Riley is dragged into a straight bar by her workmates, the last person she expects to meet is the woman of her dreams. Off-duty cop, Mel Raines is tall, dark and gorgeous but has no plans to enter a committed relationship any time soon. Despite their differing agendas, Mel and Regan can't deny an instant, overwhelming attraction. Both their lives are about to change drastically, when a tragedy forces Mel to rethink her emotional isolation and face inner demons rooted in her past. She cannot make this journey alone, and Regan's decision to share it with her has consequences neither woman expects. More than an erotic road novel, *Infinite Loop* explores the choices we make, the families we build, and the power of love to transform lives.

GALVESTON 1900; SWEPT AWAY
by Linda Crist

Forced to flee from her family at a young age, Rachel Travis finds a home and livelihood on the island of Galveston. Independent, friendly, and yet often lonely, only one other person knows the dark secret that haunts her. That is until she meets Madeline "Mattie" Crockett, a woman trapped in a loveless marriage, convinced that her fate is sealed. She never dares to dream of true happiness, until Rachel Travis comes walking into her life. As emotions come to light, the storm of Mattie's marriage converges with the very real hurricane of September 7-8, 1900, the storm that destroyed Galveston. Can they survive, and build the life they both dream of?

Other YELLOW ROSE Publications

Georgia Beers	Turning The Page	1-930928-51-3	$ 16.99
Georgia Beers	Thy Neighbor's Wife	1-932300-15-5	$ 13.95
Carrie Brennan	Curve	1-932300-41-4	$ 16.95
Carrie Carr	Destiny's Bridge	1-932300-11-2	$ 13.95
Carrie Carr	Faith's Crossing	1-932300-12-0	$ 13.95
Carrie Carr	Hope's Path	1-932300-40-6	$ 17.95
Carrie Carr	Love's Journey	1-930928-67-X	$ 18.99
Carrie Carr	Strength of the Heart	1-930928-75-0	$17.95
Jessica Casavant	Twist of Fate	1-932300-07-4	$ 12.95
Jessica Casavant	Walking Wounded	1-932300-20-1	$ 13.95
Jessica Casavant	Imperfect Past	1-932300-34-1	$ 16.95
Jennifer Fulton	Passion Bay	1-932300-25-2	$ 14.95
Jennifer Fulton	Saving Grace	1-932300-26-0	$ 15.95
Jennifer Fulton	The Sacred Shore	1-932300-35-X	$ 15.95
Jennifer Fulton	A Guarded Heart	1-932300-37-6	$ 16.95
Anna Furtado	The Heart's Desire	1-932300-32-5	$ 15.95
Gabrielle Goldsby	The Caretaker's Daughter	1-932300-18-X	$ 15.95
Maya Indigal	Until Soon	1-932300-31-7	$ 19.95
Lori L. Lake	Different Dress	1-932300-08-2	$ 19.95
Lori L. Lake	Ricochet In Time	1-932300-17-1	$ 18.95
Meghan O'Brien	Infinite Loop	1-932300-42-2	$ 18.95
Sharon Smith	Into The Dark	1-932300-38-4	$ 17.95
Cate Swannell	Heart's Passage	1-932300-09-0	$ 17.95
Cate Swannell	No Ocean Deep	1-932300-36-8	$ 18.95
L. A. Tucker	The Light Fantastic	1-932300-14-7	$ 24.95

Printed in the United States
122979LV00002B/93/A